THE SURVIVORS BOOK III: WINTER

V. L. DREYER

Paperback ISBN (Legrand Cover): 978-0-473-29176-1
Paperback ISBN (Frank Cover): 978-0-473-41357-6
Kindle ISBN: 978-0-473-29179-2
ePub ISBN: 978-0-473-29178-5

Written by V. L. Dreyer
Published by Cheeky Kea Printworks
Cover art by Rebecca Frank Design
Edited by Holly Simmons

The following is a work of fiction. Any resemblance to persons living or dead is purely coincidental, or used in the form of parody.

Second Edition.

To my grandparents, Lesley & Clarence Merrick. So many of my happiest childhood memories feature one or both of you, and I love you both beyond measure.

Sorry about the swearing, Granddad!

TABLE OF CONTENTS

The Journey So Far…

Ten years ago, I lost my family and all of my friends to the devastating plague that came to be known as Ebola X. I've spent the last decade running for my life, always alone, constantly afraid, with nobody that I could trust.

This summer, everything changed. I met a group of good people. For the first time in my adult life, I've started to feel like I belong again. Like I'm worth something. I've found my long-lost sister, alive and well after all this time. I've found friendship, with Ryan Knowles, Doctor Stuart Cross, and even little Madeline. I've even found love, with a man named Michael.

A little over a week ago, we responded to a call for help from the Arapuni power station, where we met Jim and Rebecca Merrit. They needed help, and we gave it — but when we returned to Ohaupo we found our home in chaos.

A misunderstanding has left our home engulfed in flames. Even more terrifying, we've discovered that the deadly mutants from Hamilton have followed us home...

www.vldreyer.com

1
Auckland
2
Hamilton
Ohaupo
Arapuni
Tokoroa

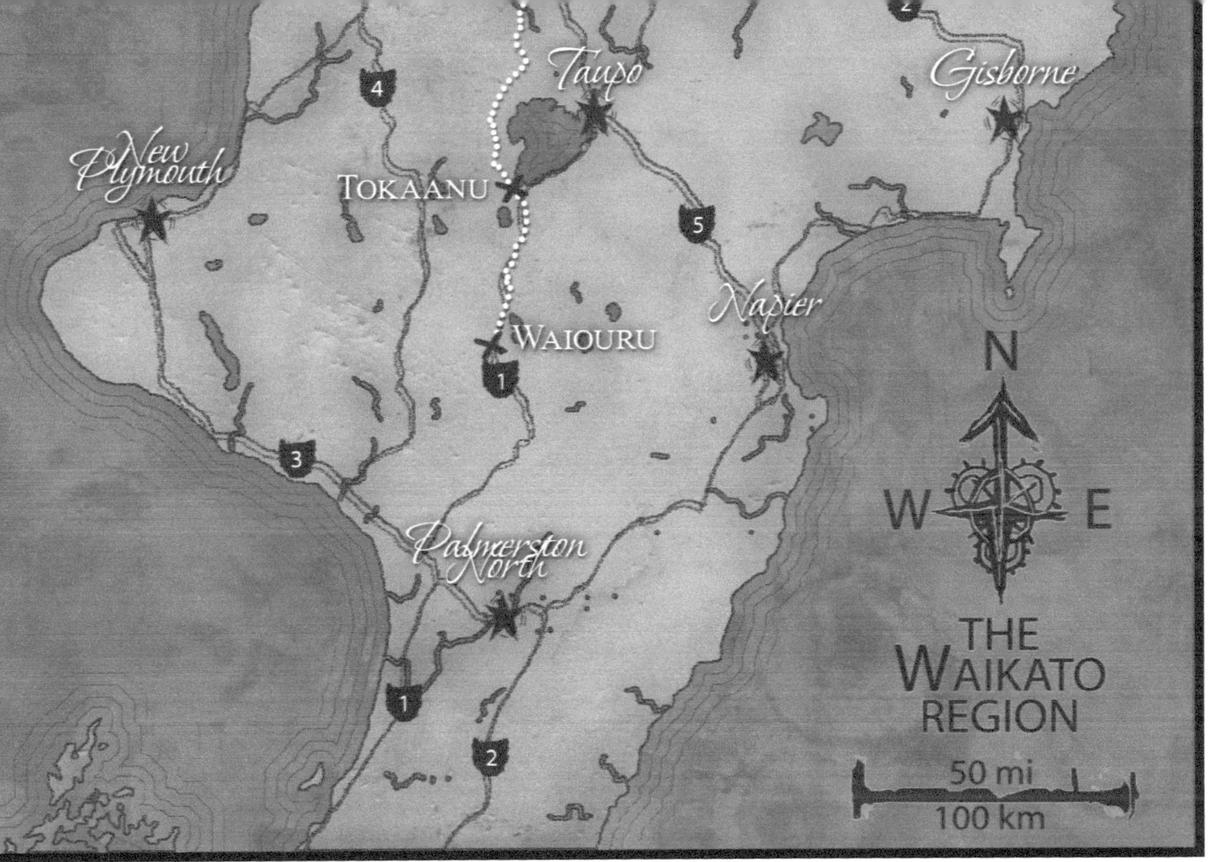
THE WAIKATO REGION
50 mi
100 km
New Plymouth
Taupo
Gisborne
Tokaanu
Waiouru
Napier
Palmerston North
N
W
E

CHAPTER ONE

"On the count of three. One, two, three – Lift!" I shouted. Right on command, we strained with every ounce of strength that we had, and the girder moved. First one inch, then another, then suddenly it came free completely. We shuffled the beam awkwardly out of the ruins of our motel, into the street beyond, and dumped it unceremoniously on the asphalt. Ash billowed up when it struck the ground, enveloping my filthy group in yet more dirt. It was starting to feel like I would never be clean again.

I ran my hand over my blackened brow and shot a glance towards the Hilux to check on the children. They were sleeping now, cuddled together like five exhausted puppies in the back seat of the truck. In the front seats, two of the adults from my original group sat recovering from their night's ordeal, given an exemption from the physical labour due to their injuries.

The doctor was fast asleep, but Skylar was not. She was wide awake, watching anxiously as we struggled to save as much as we could from the remains of our former home. When I looked her way, she caught my eye and waved tentatively. I smiled and waved back, then turned my attention back to the task at hand.

Despite everyone's best efforts, the western half of the motel had been reduced to blackened rubble by the fire that had raged through the night. We'd managed to save the rest of our home, though, including the storage rooms where we kept the majority of our supplies. The burned-out areas were still too hot to get inside safely, so we were on a retrieval mission while we waited for them to cool down. Everyone desperately needed food.

Although we were really too busy to get to know one another, I had learned the names of our newest members: Zain and Elira Yousefi. The names of their children were still a mystery to me, but there was too much work that needed to be done for me to worry about that right away. I brushed my hands off on my filthy cargo pants, and beckoned for Elira to follow me over to the truck.

By the time we arrived, Skye's door was open and she was halfway out. She didn't get far, though — a second after she stood up, she put a hand up to her head and plopped right back down in her seat again.

"I told you to stay put," I scolded her gently, though there was no anger behind my words. Skylar was my sister, my one living relative, and I loved her so much it hurt.

"I'm just a little concussed, I'm fine," she protested, trying to stand again. This time I caught her and sat her back down myself.

"Don't worry, you can help in a minute. This is Elira," I said, gesturing to the woman behind me, "Elira, this is my sister, Skylar."

"Please, call me Elly." Elira bobbed her head in a half-bow. Despite the fact that her family were responsible for accidentally starting the fire, I had come to like her in the few hours I'd known her. She was a soft-spoken, no-nonsense woman in her mid-thirties, with wild brown hair and a faint Middle Eastern accent. "My husband and I came to this country with the intention of becoming Kiwis. I prefer to use a Kiwi name. I am very sorry about what my foolish husband and son did to you, Skylar. They panicked."

"Yeah... I'm sorry we had to meet like that, too," Skye replied, absently rubbing the bruise on her forehead.

"You'll make it worse if you rub it too much," I scolded her softly, reaching up to capture her wrist and pull her hand away from the bruise. Skye gave me a long-suffering look, but I just smiled back at her. On a sudden, spontaneous impulse, I pulled her into a hug. "Sis, I need you to help Elly get some food into these kids, please – it looks like they haven't eaten in days. There's a camp stove in one of the bags in the back. Can you two get it started? I'll bring you some food as soon as we find something that looks edible."

"Okay," Skye agreed readily. We looked at Elly, who also nodded her agreement.

"I cannot thank you enough for accepting us after what we put you through," Elly added, reaching out to take my hand. I glanced at her and found her studying me with eyes that shone with gratitude. "I thought there was no kindness left in this old world."

"Just remember what I said," I told her softly, giving her hand a gentle squeeze.

"Yes. For the children, we must work together." She cast a glance at her sleeping progeny, and then she looked back at me and sighed heavily. "I would do anything to give them a chance at a better life."

"And we will," I assured her. "Just remember that, so we can keep up the strength and determination to protect them – through the good times and the bad."

I'd never been much of a public speaker, but over the last week or so I had found myself with the right words to say in the most unexpected moments. I guessed that my new-found eloquence was a side-effect of finding a goal that I really cared about: the idea of building a city, and bringing together the last survivors of the plague to try and craft a better future for all of us.

As I left Elly and Skylar and returned to the burned shell of our former home, I found myself wondering at the changes I'd begun to notice in my own personality. I glanced around at the others, all working hard to salvage what they could from the ruins, and suddenly realised that they were all following my commands. It was bewildering to think that after ten years living as a recluse, I was becoming a leader.

Someone had to, though. Michael had been the leader of the small group of survivors I joined over the summer, but he readily admitted that he hated being in command. He led because he had to, but he was happy to let that responsibility go to someone else, someone he trusted implicitly. I still wasn't sure how I felt about the way I'd just sort of fallen into the role, but at least I knew I could rely on myself to do the right thing for everyone.

Michael stood watch half-way between the building and the truck, looking tense and anxious. I knew that he longed to be helping more directly, but I needed him to stand guard in case the mutants returned while we were unaware. I went over to check on him on my way back. He glanced at me when he heard my footfalls, and gave me a faint smile. "No sign of trouble."

"That's strange. I didn't think they were intelligent enough to pick their battles," I replied. I leaned up to kiss my fiancé softly, trailing my fingers across his cheek. We were both equally filthy, but even through the layer of ash I could taste the sweetness of his kiss. It reassured me and bolstered me up, even in the face of exhaustion.

"I'm a bit worried about Anahera's tribe," he admitted. I shot him a curious look, before suddenly understanding dawned.

"Oh, my God – you're right!" I gasped. A sudden stab of panic struck me right in the chest, and stole away my breath. "I didn't even think about them. They're alone and defenceless. They don't even have any weapons. What if the mutants circled around and went to their camp instead?"

Michael shot me a worried look. "We should check in, and warn them."

"I agree." I pulled my walkie-talkie off my belt, switched it on, and quickly tuned the radio to the frequency that we had established for communicating with our neighbours. As soon as the radio was in band, we heard a voice screaming.

"Hello? Hello? Is anyone out there? Christ, we need help! Where is everyone?"

The voice was female, and although it was a struggle to make out her words, I could hear panic in her voice. Behind her, we heard the crash of flesh on wood, and the screams and groans of people in pain. Then, a shriek. A deathly, blood-curdling shriek that sent a shiver down my spine like a bolt of ice. I shot a wide-eyed look at Michael. Bile rose in the back of my throat, but I fought it back down and took a deep breath to try and calm myself. I had to keep a clear head if we were going to help our friends at all.

"Michael, I need you to go get the guns," I said quietly, pointing him towards the old video store that adjoined the motel. "When Maddy started having nightmares, I got Skye to move all the weapons into the downstairs office. It should be locked up. I want you to get them, and make sure everyone that's strong enough to use one is armed and trained to use at least one of those guns."

"I thought we were going to hide them?" he asked, staring at me uncertainly. I just shook my head.

"We've got a simple choice here. Either we take the risk that one of them might turn against us later, or we watch our friends die now. I know which one I pick." I fished a bunch of keys out of my pocket and offered them to him. He nodded once, took the keys, and hurried off. While he was gone, I turned my attention to the radio. "Anahera, it's Sandy — can you hear me?"

"Sandy! Oh, Sandy, thank God, I was starting to lose hope." Anahera's voice was shaking; I couldn't tell if it was from fear, adrenaline, or both. "We need help, desperately. Creatures attacked us a few hours ago and they've got us trapped. They killed two of my boys; there's only four of us left and one is seriously wounded. Can you help us?"

"We're on our way," I replied, trying my best to keep my voice calm and reassuring. "How many creatures have you seen?"

"I saw four but I think there's more," she answered breathlessly. "I can't be certain."

"Just hang on, and stay put. Do not open that door until you hear my voice. We're coming to get you," I told her resolutely. "Do you understand? We're coming to get you, Ana."

"I understand. Please... please, hurry."

"We will," I answered. "We'll be there soon. Stay safe."

I clicked the radio off and put it back on my belt, then I looked at the people milling around. Several of them were looking at me. They weren't stupid, they knew something was up. Although it went against every one of my instincts, I had to get their attention all at once. I drew a long, deep breath, and pushed my instincts aside.

"Everyone, urgent meeting," I shouted at the top of my lungs. "Drop whatever you're doing and assemble in front of the truck!"

I repeated myself a couple more times, then I raced over to the truck as well. There, I found Skylar and Elly watching me with trepidation. I forestalled their questions with a gesture, and vaulted up to stand on the bonnet of the car so that I could be clearly seen by everyone in the group.

Within a few minutes, all the adults had gathered around and stood looking up at me, waiting to hear what I had to say. I looked down at them, feeling a strange mix of pride and fear, but I did what I had to do without hesitation.

"As of right now, everyone is being issued with a gun," I told them, loudly enough that no one could pretend they hadn't heard later on. "I expect you to learn to use it, but to only use it in self-defence. These guns officially belong to me, and if anyone is caught using their weapon against another member of this group, or even threatening someone with it, they will lose the privilege indefinitely.

"There is a lethal enemy in the area, and I need all of you to help me protect our innocents. Can I rely on you?" I looked down at Zain and Elly. They both nodded, though Zain's expression was harder to read than his wife's. "Good, because there is a complication."

This time I looked at Hemi, who stood with his brethren gathered around him. "As we speak, your home is under siege. I'm sorry to be the one to tell you that two of your friends are dead. I have a plan to save the rest of them, but I'm going to need everyone's help."

"Just tell us what we have to do, and we'll do it," Zain said suddenly, his voice clear as a bell in the silence that followed my announcement. I glanced at him, and saw the same unreadable expression on his face as before, but there was something in his eyes that I understood. I nodded to him, and then I looked at Hemi and his friends, who stood in mute shock.

"Hemi, Tane, and Iorangi." I looked at each of them as I named them. "We're going to go rescue everyone that's still alive. Time is of the essence, so we'll take your quad bikes. Michael will issue each of you with an assault rifle and teach you how to use it. Make sure you all have a water bottle. We're not going to have time to eat, so we'll just have to go hungry until we get back. Go meet Michael in the video store; I'll join you once I'm done here."

Hemi stared at me for a second, and then grabbed his friends and rushed off. Once they were gone, I looked down at the people that remained.

"Each of you will be given a small handgun, something light and easy to use," I explained. "We'll work on getting you cleared to use the bigger guns later. Skye and Doc, you're in charge of protecting the children. I want you to feed them and move them into my loft as soon as possible. It'll be a tight fit, but at least we can defend it easily until we decide what we're going to do next.

"Everyone else, I want you on salvage duty. Gather everything you can out of the ruins and move it into the bottom level of the video store — Skye will show you where. If you finish before we get back, just get inside and stay there. We don't know what these creatures will do next. If you must go outside, then take someone with you. No one goes out alone.

"I'm leaving Alfred here, and he knows what those things smell like. If he starts to growl, listen to him." I paused and glanced around again. "Does everyone understand?"

Grunts and soft-spoken words of agreement met my orders. I nodded once more and hopped down off the bonnet of the truck. As I started towards the video store, Skylar fell into step beside me. Once we were out of earshot of the others, she turned a pleading look on me. "Can't you stay here? I'm scared. I don't want you to go."

It was a tone I'd never heard from my strong-willed baby sister. I glanced at her, and found her watching me with eyes that seemed way too big for her face.

Assuming she was afraid of our newcomers, I reached out and slid a reassuring arm around her shoulders. "It's okay, they won't hurt you. They didn't mean to hurt you last time. You'll have Doc right here, plus Ropata and Richard as well – you know you're safe with them."

"What?" She blinked at me owlishly. "No, I mean, I'm scared for *you*. You're going into battle. You might get hurt – or worse. I don't want you to end up like Sophie and Dog."

"Oh." I blinked right back at her, processing her words. "I have to go, Skye. Anahera's in danger, and she's my friend. If I can do anything to help her, then I'm obligated to do it. I wouldn't be able to live with myself if I just left her to die."

"I know," Skylar lamented, scuffing her toe on the dirty asphalt. "But I still don't want you to go."

"Are you just being a big baby?" I teased, trying to use humour to lighten her mood. "And after all the effort you've put into trying to convince me that you're a grown up now."

My reward was a cheeky smile and a nudge in the side. "I am grown up. All grown-ups worry about their big sisters. You're the only family I've got now."

"Well, if I have any say in the matter, then that's going to change." I wrapped my arms around her and drew her into a tight hug. "These people are going to be our family now. All of them. I need you to be a big sister to those little kids, and I need you to be strong for me. I trust you to keep things organised while I'm gone."

"I will." Skylar hugged me back and then released me. "Just... stay safe, okay?"

I sketched a playful salute, then I pulled away from her and hurried the last few steps to the entrance of the video store. The stench of smoke was thick on the air, but aside from a layer of soot on the front door and the window sills, the building had survived unscathed. I shoved aside a few broken movie cases and made my way behind the counter, where I found Michael instructing the chosen few on the use of automatic weaponry.

He glanced up when I entered and smiled at me; even in the tension of the moment, his smile made my heart race. The others looked at me, and each of them gave me a nod. Hemi's face was a grim mask, and his friends looked no better.

I joined their ranks and gave Hemi's shoulder a reassuring squeeze. "We'll get to her in time. I promise."

"No matter how fast we get there, it'll be too late for the guys that are already dead." Hemi looked miserable, and his shoulders sagged beneath my touch.

"Then we'll just have to make sure no one else joins them, right?" I gave him a gentle shake, and looked at the ring of faces around me. One by one, they nodded. Sensing that morale was at an all-time low, I looked each of them in the eye to try and assess their state of mind.

Michael looked as determined as I felt. He met my eye squarely, his jaw set in the look I'd come to know so well. His smile was reassuring. The others were not so confident. Tane's face mirrored Hemi's; they looked sad and completely bereft of hope, and neither of them would meet my eye.

Iorangi was another story altogether. When our eyes met, I saw hot rage surging behind his impassive mask. He was angry, really, really angry. I drew a deep breath to steady myself, and then set about the difficult task of rallying my troops.

"Guys, I need you to be here with me," I said softly, sympathetically, reaching out to my friends to try and give them hope. "Anahera is relying on us. We can still save her and the others, but we need to work as a team. It's the only way we'll have a chance. Can I rely on you?"

Unsurprisingly, Michael was the most vocal of the group and supported me without hesitation. Iorangi joined in a moment later, though I could see on his face he was motivated more by revenge for his fallen friends than any real hope of success. His older brother glanced up at me when I spoke, his gaze lingering thoughtfully on my face, but something about my words did seem to stir him. A few seconds after the others, his voice joined in, leaving only Hemi quiet and withdrawn.

"Hey." I shifted my attention to the young man, and put my hands on his shoulders. "I need you, too, man. Your mum needs you."

"Damn, Sandy. I don't know if I can do this." Hemi's voice was laced with despair. "I'm no fighter, man. I'll just get in the way, and then Mum will die."

"Don't talk like that," I protested. "Your friends believe in you – I believe in you. I know you can do this." I was studying him closely enough that I could see he wasn't entirely convinced, so I decided to switch tack. "Do you remember when we first met?"

"Yeah, of course," he said, nodding. "That pig, man. How could I forget?"

"Right, the pig. And do you remember what you said to us afterwards?" I didn't wait for him to respond, but supplied him with the answer. "You said that you didn't know what you would have done if we hadn't arrived when we did. You called us heroes. Do you remember that?"

"Well, not the exact words, but yeah, I remember." He was staring at me now, trying to figure out where I was going. I didn't keep him waiting long.

"This is your chance to learn what it takes to be a hero," I elaborated. "None of us are soldiers. We fight because we have to, to preserve what's ours. That's how heroes are born. We're going to teach you, and we're going to save your mum at the same time." I tugged him into a quick hug, then pushed him back and looked at him again. "Can you do this for us? For her?"

This time, there was fire burning in his eyes. "Yeah, okay. Yeah. I can do this." He looked around at the others and saw conviction written across every face. That seemed to bolster him up even more. At last, he puffed up his chest and looked me right in the eye. "Hell, yeah. I can do this. Let's go!"

"Good lad." I grinned at him and gave his shoulders a squeeze, then I released him and looked at the others. My little pocket-sized, rag-tag army. There were only five of us, but we had determination and courage on our side.

It would be enough. It had to be enough.

Chapter Two

The quad bike's engine thrummed beneath me as we bounced along the overgrown path towards Lake Ruatuna. Even though it was the first time that Michael or I had driven one of the little bikes, we were rattling along at breakneck pace, exercising just enough caution to keep ourselves from getting killed.

I spent half the time standing up in the saddle, bracing myself with my knees as we passed over uneven ground. Through the bike's suspension, I could feel the change in texture as we moved from the bush into the emerald tunnel lined with old railway sleepers. We were getting closer. A branch reached out and tried to grab my hair, but I ducked beneath it at the very last moment. I gained a few scratches on my cheeks from accidents early on, but I was a quick study — the vengeful trees with their grabbing claws wouldn't get me again. They were certainly trying, though.

It was the height of midday, yet the world we were travelling through was all shadows, ferns, and dappled light. We were jumpy and on high-alert, fully expecting one of the creatures to leap out at us at any moment, but nothing had so far. If they were in the area, then their attention was elsewhere.

I held up one hand to signal the others to halt, and then eased off the throttle and let my bike cruise to a stop. Ahead of us, the side passage that led towards the village opened up, dark, ominous, and too narrow to ride through safely.

"We'll leave the bikes here and go the rest of the way on foot," I said, looking back at the others. "I want to be able to make a quick getaway if we have to."

A chorus of determined noises answered me. No one questioned my orders; they just accepted them. It was a feeling that left me both proud and confused. Even Michael deferred to my judgement; he seemed relieved that someone else had taken on the burden of leadership. Our footsteps rustled in the grass as we dismounted and wheeled our bikes around so that they were facing the right direction for when the time came to flee.

While the others were preparing for combat, I pulled out my walkie-talkie. I quickly checked in with Skylar to let her know that we'd arrived safely, and then I switched the band over to Anahera's channel.

"Anahera, are you still there? Come in, Anahera."

It was the longest twenty seconds of my life before someone picked up on the other end — but the person who answered wasn't Anahera.

"Sandy?" The voice was male, and it sounded terrified. It took me a second to recognise him.

"Wiremu? Is that you?" I asked, keeping my voice as calm as possible in hopes that it would rub off on the others. Behind me, I could feel the men gathering to listen. "Is everyone all right?"

"No." The man was struggling to keep his fear under control, but I could tell his heart was racing a mile a minute from the way he was panting into the radio. "Anahera fainted. From blood loss, I think. I don't know what to do. The things are still out there. I can hear them growling."

I swore under my breath.

"She said someone was injured – she didn't say that it was her." I looked back at the boys behind me, my face a grim mask. I clicked the send button down and spoke into the radio again. "We're not far away now, and we're coming to get you. Where are you?"

"W-we're in the pantry." The man laughed, but there was a hysterical edge to it. Behind him, I heard the faint sound of a thud and an inhuman scream. His laugh turned into a gasp. "Aw, Christ. They won't give up. Sweet mother, we're going to--"

"Stop." It was not a request, it was an order. "You're not going to die. We're coming to get you right now, and we'll be there in a few minutes. I need you to be ready to move the moment we get there. If I remember correctly, you guys have a couple of old knapsacks in there, don't you?"

There was a pause, and in the background I heard Wiremu shifting around. "Yeah, there's some here. You want me to fill them up with food?"

"Yes," I answered simply. "You probably aren't going to be able to come back again, so grab everything you can carry that won't weigh you down too much. Fill the knapsacks up, put them on, and be ready to run the second that you hear my voice. Okay?"

"O-okay." He stumbled over the word, sounding so frantic and terrified it made my heart lurch. "Please, please hurry; I'm not sure how much longer the door will hold."

"We're coming right now." I tried to be firm and reassuring to hide the shaking in my own voice. "Just hold on a few more minutes."

There was a wordless grunt of agreement from the man on the other end. With no more time to waste on talking, I clicked the radio off and tucked it onto my belt. I looked back, and found myself ringed by four very determined faces, each clutching his weapon as though his life depended on it.

I nodded to them and unslung the shotgun off my back. In a swift, well-practiced motion, I slipped off the safety and loaded a shell into the chamber. A chorus of soft metallic clicks told me that the others were ready as well, so I didn't delay any further. I spun around and charged down the narrow green corridor at a run.

My heart hammered in my chest, but there was something cathartic about finally being in action instead of just worrying about it. I'd always been the kind of person that chose diplomacy over brute force unless I had no other choice, but now I felt surprisingly calm and rational. I was ready for this. We were ready for this. We could do it. I thought the pep talk had been to rally the troops, but apparently it had worked just as well on me.

My feet crunched over the leaf litter as we charged through the passageway, then out into the fields beyond. What greeted me was a scene of carnage. The last time I'd visited that little fortress, it had been a pleasant, picturesque sight, surrounded by fields full of animals grazing peacefully. Now, every single one of those poor farm animals lay dead and dismembered, torn to pieces. I snatched a deep breath to calm myself and ran on, trying to ignore the smell of death hanging on the air.

I leapt over a mound of entrails that I chose not to try and identify, and powered my way up the hill towards the fortress itself. The doors hung open, still damaged from the recent fire; just inside the entrance, we found the first human corpse. There wasn't much left, just a tattered heap of skin and bones with half a face attached. The organs were all gone and the puddle of blood spread in all directions; there was no way the man could have survived.

Another body lay not far beyond the first, and it was in an equal state of disarray. His face was completely gone, but I recognised him from the tattered remains of his favourite old plaid shirt.

Honi. His name had been Honi. I'd known him. I'd counted him as a friend.

I swallowed and tried not to look at Honi's corpse, but it was hard. Every death was a step closer to the permanent annihilation of our species. A death was no longer just a sad event worthy of mourning – it was an absolute tragedy for all of humankind. What was even harder was the knowledge that yet another one of my friends was dead and gone. I had so few left that each of them was precious to me.

If we didn't hurry, then more friends would end up like that. We could not allow that to happen. I shot a quick look around us, then sprinted across the clearing towards the nearest wall. The compound our Maori friends had built over the years was a maze, but it wasn't a big one. I knew the layout well enough.

The pa had been built up around an old yacht club, which was one of the few buildings that had survived the fire relatively unscathed. It was scorched with soot even weeks later, but it was still intact. The door hung ajar and I could see into the hallway beyond. Without hesitation, I threw myself down that narrow passageway, half-expecting to get attacked at any moment. Nothing sprang at me, but the moment I was inside I could hear the low, guttural growls and thuds of a creature on the offensive.

A creature. Just one. That was worrying. Anahera said they'd been attacked by at least four – where were the others?

I could feel Michael's protective bulk at my back as I crept forward, keeping myself low to the ground to present as small a target as possible. My ears were alert for every sound, but the only thing I could hear above the sound of our breathing was the uneven thump of flesh on wood.

Suddenly, the creature howled in rage and there was a louder thump than before, followed by an ominous cracking sound. I heard guttural human cries behind it, muffled but terrified. The thing had almost finished breaking through the door.

My shoes crunched across the debris that littered the floor as I followed the noise towards the kitchen. It took all of my willpower to move slowly and cautiously, and not give in to the urge to run. We passed a doorway. I swung my weapon around to scan the empty room, found nothing, and moved on.

The kitchen was the next door on the left. I took a long, deep breath to steady my racing heart, and then silently gestured Hemi and the brothers to watch the halls around us for trouble. Michael was a step behind me as I slipped around the corner and into the kitchen, my protective knight that refused to let me out of his sight.

The creature had its back to us, and was distracted by its desire to break through the door and get at the helpless prey within. It yowled in rage and reached up high, its fingers leaving bloody trails on the warped door. Michael lifted his gun and prepared to fire, but I held up my hand to forestall him. It took a second before understanding dawned on his face: the door wasn't all that thick. If we fired at the creature from behind, then chances were good that we'd also hit the people huddled inside the pantry.

He nodded and looked to me for guidance. I took a moment to consider my options, then decided that the one I least wanted to do was unfortunately the best. With a gesture to Michael to keep him from following me, I stepped forward to do the unthinkable. I walked towards the howling undead.

It didn't seem to notice me. At least, not at first. I managed to get within three feet of it without being seen, and then I circled around it to the left and carefully lined up my shot. Just as I was preparing to fire, it finally realised I was there and turned to stare at me with wild, bloodshot eyes. A horrifying shriek escaped from its bloody jaws.

That blood probably belonged to one of my friends, I realised with a detached certainty. But in that moment of danger, something happened that I still wasn't used to. Clarity. I didn't even flinch at the sound. I just pulled the trigger, and a blast of buckshot delivered at point blank range reduced the creature's head to a pulverised mass of flesh. I fired again, and a second shell sent the writhing mass tumbling away. It wasn't dead, and it wouldn't be unless we set it on fire, but that didn't matter. It couldn't do us any substantial harm without a head.

Cold, calm, and collected, I fired one last time, reducing the creature's legs to splinters of bone and flesh. "And stay down."

When I glanced back, I caught Michael staring at me with surprise on his face, but I didn't have time to ask what was wrong. I could hear the sound of human voices shouting from the other side of the door, begging for help, even praying. They were the most important thing, and everything else could come later.

"It's us," I called through the door, tapping on it with my knuckles. "Open up; we need to get out of here before those things come back."

"Praise the Lord!" someone cried. I wasn't sure which one it was, but it didn't really matter. It was a sentiment shared by everyone. I heard the sound of heavy objects being moved, and then the door was flung open from within. The group looked wrung out and exhausted from their ordeal, but they were ready to move in a few seconds. Anahera was still unconscious, so two of the men lifted her between them and carried her towards the door.

"You have no idea how glad we are to see you," Wiremu said, sounding terrified and exhausted.

"Oh, I have some idea," I answered dryly, then I glanced back at Michael and the others. "We need to get out of here, and I don't think we're going to be able to come back. If you have room in your gear, grab any spare food you can carry and let's get out of here."

He nodded and hastily grabbed whatever extra supplies he could out of the pantry. I quickly shoved a few things into my empty backpack, but not enough to hinder my ability to flee. Within less than a minute, we were all ready to go.

A blood-curdling screech and a human shout from the doorway warned me that we'd finished just in time. A few seconds later, I heard the sound of high-powered bullets being fired in an enclosed space. By the time I reached the door, the creature was down and twitching.

"Just one?" I shot Hemi a worried look. He nodded and lowered his rifle. "There should be at least two more. Where are the rest of them?"

"Somewhere else," Michael replied. "Would you rather they were here?"

"Definitely – then we could take care of them and not have to worry anymore," I answered dryly, shaking my head. "It doesn't matter. Let's just get out of here before the damn things find us again. Tane, Iorangi, cover the rear. Hemi, you stay in the middle with your friends. Make sure nothing gets near them, and no one falls behind. Michael, you're with me."

A chorus of grunts acknowledged my orders. As I moved off in the lead, I heard my friends falling into formation behind me. We had to move at a slightly more sedate pace than before, but we still made good time. Nothing jumped us along the way; while I should have been glad for that fact, under the circumstances, it just made me even more nervous.

"Everyone, keep your eyes peeled," I shouted over the sound of our running feet and harsh breathing. "I smell a trap, and it stinks worse than week-dead fish."

More grunts. No one seemed to have the willpower to answer me at that moment, but it wasn't necessary. They heard me, and that was all that mattered. A few seconds later, we burst out into the courtyard, and raced past the bodies of the fallen on our way out the door. Someone cried out again at the sight of the dead men, but I couldn't tell who it was.

No matter how much we might have wanted to stay and bury the dead, there was simply no time. We passed them and hurried down the ramp outside the complex, heading for the forest. A moment later, I was running through cool shadow, but this time it wasn't a relief. This time, it definitely felt like the darkness only concealed death.

Nothing happened, though, and that was the worst part. We made it to the far side safely, and tumbled out into the clearing where the bikes waited, but there was no sign of where the mutant undead had gone. The tension was just about killing me, but an old saying kept ringing in my mind: 'Don't look a gift horse in the mouth.'

"Michael, I want you up front with Anahera," I instructed, pointing him towards one of the big quad bikes. "Take the lead, and don't stop for anything. Your task is to get her home safely so Doc can fix her up. Got it?"

"Got it," Michael agreed, hurrying over to his bike. The others helped him to load the unconscious woman in front of him, and then he was off.

"Everyone else, double up. I'll cover the rear and make sure nothing follows us." I made a quick gesture for them to fall in, and they jumped to obey. In less than a minute, they were ready to go. I shooed them off, then hopped on my own little bike and headed after them, keeping an eye peeled for trouble.

The scenery flashed past on either side of me in a river of verdant green, but the ground beneath me was rough. I stood up in the seat and braced myself against the uneven trail, my bike bouncing and juddering over railway sleepers hidden under the thick grass. Within a few minutes, we'd successfully traversed the long tunnel of the old train line, and I saw my companions up ahead turning off to make their way into the brush beyond. I glanced back over my shoulder to check the trees behind us, but I saw nothing.

Unfortunately, that also meant that I didn't see whatever was hidden under the grass in front of me. I faintly heard a thud, and then I found myself flying head-over-heels. I had enough presence of mind to try to tuck and roll, but it wasn't enough. I landed messily. My forehead struck something hard, and I blacked out.

Chapter Three

When I came to, the only sounds I could hear were the peaceful tones of nature: the trill of birds in the trees, the wind in the leaves, and the faint, low growl of a predator stalking nearby.

Wait. A predator?

My eyes snapped open to a sight that I had never wanted to see. Squatting beside me was one of the mutants, blood still dripping from its jowls. It was just sitting there, watching me, covetously stroking my belly with its horrid fingers. For reasons that only it knew, it hadn't attacked me yet.

My gut twisted in disgust. Even though my body ached from the fall, every one of my instincts screamed at me in unison to get away from that horrible dead thing before it changed its mind and decided to hurt instead of pet. I rolled away and came up to my feet in a fighter's crouch, fully expecting the thing to attack me at any second.

It didn't, though. It just sat there, staring at me, looking almost... contented.

And then realisation struck me. It was drenched in blood; it had killed recently, and already eaten its fill. It was playing with me, like a cat plays with a mouse even though it's not hungry. It would kill me for fun if it decided that I no longer amused it.

"Screw you, buddy," I told it quietly, side-stepping around the languid undead in search of a weapon. Where was my shotgun? It wasn't on my back, so it must have fallen off when I'd taken my tumble. The grass was so long that I wouldn't see it until I stepped on the damn thing. With no other choice, I snatched up an old branch that lay on the ground at my feet, and armed myself with that while I hunted for my gun.

The mutant didn't seem to care much. It was perfectly content to sit there, watching me, as if amused by my fighting spirit. I can't say that I felt the same way, but at least that gave me time. A little bit of time. How much time? A few seconds, a few minutes?

I spotted my little dirt bike sprawled in the long grass and circled around towards it, careful not to turn my back on the mutant. One glance was enough to tell me that it had been damaged beyond repair by the crash; the entire front half was all bent out of shape. A glint of steel beneath it gave me hope, though. I shoved the bike aside, to find my shotgun beneath it.

Not a moment too soon, either. Just as I dropped the branch and darted down to grab the gun, I heard a low, deep growl in the bushes behind me. Instinct kicked in; I flicked off the safety, spun, and fired from the hip. Shrapnel tore through the creature that had been creeping up behind me and sent it tumbling off into the grass. I swung back to finish off the lazy mutant that had been watching me, only to find that it had vanished while I was distracted.

I swore beneath my breath, but there was no time to stop and look for it now. None of us had any idea how many of the things existed, or if the mutated plague was spreading. There could have been dozens, even hundreds. They could be anywhere. I was not about to stick around and find out. I spun on a heel and raced off into the brush as fast as my legs could take me.

My feet crunched over the leaf litter as I dove into the shadows amongst the trees, and ran for home. So long as I didn't lose my way, I could be there in a couple of hours. It wasn't far, as the crow flies. I wasn't a crow so I couldn't go in a straight line, but I was well-adept at racing through the wild, overgrown world that New Zealand had become in the decade since her population had vanished.

There was a problem, though. My head throbbed in time with the pounding of my feet. I'd spent enough time alone to have a good sense of my own body, its limitations, and its needs. Right now, it wasn't happy with me. I estimated that I'd probably sustained a mild concussion, and running was the last thing I should be doing.

Although I'm no doctor, I spent a lot of time reading and I was aware enough to recognise the symptoms. My limbs weren't responding quite the way they should, and my vision was a little blurred around the edges. I was alert, though, and fully awake, which were both good signs so soon after being knocked unconscious. Judging by the angle of the light filtering through the trees, I'd been unconscious no more than half an hour; it was still early afternoon, and the sunbeams came almost straight down from above.

"Just keep running," I told myself softly, using the sound of my own voice to keep me going. "It's not far. Just a little bit more. Michael will be worried about you. Just keep running, okay? Okay. Good girl."

The undergrowth was old and thick, but I knew the pathways, and I knew all of Mother Nature's tricks. I knew which trees would have tangling roots that would try to grab my feet. I knew which bushes hid thorns, and which ones were safe to cut through. They were lessons I'd learned the hard way, but they were ones that I would never forget.

Eventually, I reached the edge of the trees, where I slowed to a jog. The sun seemed entirely too bright as I stepped out of the comfortable shade and into the fields beyond. Waist-length grass swayed placidly in the breeze, but it felt like every movement was hiding an enemy. I didn't like that feeling, not one bit. I felt exposed, and a little befuddled. The light stung my eyes and made my head hurt.

"Just... keep going. Walk for a bit, but keep going," I said softly, trying to keep my spirits up. "It's not far. Where are our tracks? I should be able to find them, then I can follow them home." I nodded to myself and set off with renewed determination, using my instincts like a homing pigeon to guide my way back to where my family was waiting for me.

I made it a few hundred paces before my vision began to blur again, and my balance faltered. Whether I liked it or not, I was going down for a bit, so I chose to sit rather than fall. I plopped down on my backside in the grass, and dug my water bottle out of my backpack. The water helped; it cooled my throat as it flowed down, and left me feeling refreshed.

"Okay... okay. You need to keep moving," I ordered myself softly. "Up we get. Come on, Sandy."

Getting up again was harder than sitting down, but I made it. I tried to run, but all I managed was an unsteady trot. That was an unsustainable method of travel, so I settled for walking. I knew better than most that a person could walk further than she could run, particularly when that person was dumb enough to go getting herself a concussion.

"Shut up, Self Doubt," I scolded my inner demon irritably, and squeezed my eyes closed for a second to try and steady myself. When I opened them, the world was spinning. "Whoa. Okay, that's not a good sign. I'm also talking to myself. Some people say that's not healthy, but you know what?" I paused again, and took a sip of my water, then continued where I left off. "Most of those people are dead. So, stuff it. Just keep going, Sandy. You can do it."

Normally, I wasn't one to hold conversations with myself. Ten years of hiding from danger had driven that trait right out of me. However, there were some times when you needed to. I remembered that you were supposed to talk to people with concussions, to keep them awake. There was no one to talk to me now, except for myself. I was used to being self-reliant, so that was nothing unusual to me.

I plodded along carefully, paying close attention to every twinge and complaint that my body had to offer so that I could keep track of how functional I was. It was getting harder to move, to the point where I was putting one foot carefully in front of another to keep my balance steady. It wasn't the easiest task in the world when my body was in such a disagreeable mood, but it seemed to work.

As I walked, I sipped my water to keep myself refreshed. If I estimated my timing right, Michael and the others should reach home very soon, and when they did they were bound to notice that I was missing. A few minutes later, the radio on my belt crackled to life.

"Sandy?" Michael's voice was crackly and distant, but clear enough that I could make him out. "Sandy, where the hell are you? Please respond."

I picked the radio up, and answered him. "I'm here. I had an accident, but I'm okay. Mostly okay. I'll be home in a couple of hours."

"Jesus, you just about gave me a heart attack," he answered; his relief was so audible that I could detect it in his voice even through the walkie-talkie. "Wait — what do you mean by 'mostly okay'?"

"I took a bit of a tumble," I admitted, absently rubbing my eyes. When had the sun gotten so bright? It hurt just to look around. "I've got a mild concussion, but I should be fine. Add it to the list, right? Seems like you're the only one that doesn't have a head injury right now."

"Head injuries are no laughing matter," he scolded me, concern thick in his voice. "You stay right where you are; I'm coming to get you."

"No, don't waste the fuel," I protested. "I'll be fine. Just focus on getting the others comfortable. I should be home before suns—"

A blood-curdling screech cut me off mid-sentence, and my words died in my throat. The sound was less than a kilometre away.

"Yeah, I heard that," Michael's voice crackled from the radio in my hand. "I'm coming to get you, and that's final."

"Yeah," I agreed, nervously scanning the treeline far behind me. "Yeah. Yeah, okay. Um. I'm going to try the running thing again now. Wish me luck."

He didn't bother to respond. There was no need, and no time. I shoved the radio back onto my belt, and took off at a sloppy, wobbling trot. My body didn't want to respond the way it should, but a spurt of adrenaline kept me going.

Behind me, I heard a handful of inquisitive growls, carried on the soft breeze. I couldn't tell which direction they were travelling in, and the long grass made it impossible to spot them unless they stood up straight. The mutated undead were an unknown element, though. I didn't have enough information to try and predict what they'd do. My only choice was to keep going, and hope that Michael arrived before they caught up with me.

The grass rustled and swayed; the movement made my head swim. At least I was travelling mostly eastwards, so the sun was at my back; the intensity of the sunlight hurt, but at least it wasn't constantly in my eyes, blinding me. That was a small blessing, but a blessing nevertheless.

The sound of my own breath in my ears felt deafening, like it would lead the undead right to me. I tried to breathe quietly, but that just made me even dizzier. My footsteps sounded like an elephant crashing through the brush.

The fact that I could hear anything at all over my own noises was a miracle, but I did. I heard the growls closing in on me. Every so often one of them would start to get further away, then another one would shriek and draw it back into the hunt. There was definitely more than one, and I had no doubt that they were following me. Stalking me. I was wounded prey, and they were after me.

"I'm not prey," I told myself softly, shifting my shotgun around into a defensive position. There was a soft click as I eased the safety off again. I had a handful of spare shells in my pocket for easy access, so I pulled them out and carefully reloaded them by touch as I jogged eastwards.

The combat shotgun held eight shells, which was usually more than enough. Would it be enough now? How many were after me?

"There's at least two," I murmured. There was no point in trying to be stealthy when I couldn't move quietly. If talking to myself helped me stay grounded, then so be it. "At least two, maybe more. I think there's more. I gotta conserve my ammunition. I think I should hit the road soon. That's good. Clear line of sight. Yeah. I am not prey."

I took a deep breath and spurred myself on, forcing myself to pick up the pace even though all my body wanted to do was lie down and go to sleep. I couldn't do that. Sleeping meant death. I was too damn stubborn to die. My family needed me. Michael needed me. The future of my species needed me.

For some reason I couldn't define, that thought steadied me and helped me to keep going well beyond the point of collapse. Adrenaline and determination meshed together into some kind of bizarre hybrid emotion that erected itself like a wall between my conscious thoughts and the desperate, panicked animal instincts that pressured me to just drop everything and run for my life.

"I'm running, but I'm not running away," I told myself firmly. "I'm running, but I'll fight you. I'll fight you all, if I have to. I am no one's prey!"

As if understanding my words, a blood-curdling screech behind me drew my attention. I spun and dropped into a crouch, aiming my shotgun from the shoulder so that I could sight along the barrel. Every shot had to count now. There would be no firing until I had a clear target. I drew a deep breath and held it, so that I could hear the sounds all around me as clearly as possible.

There, to the right!

A twig broke beneath a humanoid foot. I swivelled around and stared into the long grass, watching, waiting. They were like a school of piranhas, circling me before they closed in for the kill. As frustrating as it was, I knew that following them into the grass would be suicide; eventually, when they were ready, they'd come for me. They had no brains, so surely they had no patience either. But, as the seconds stretched out into minutes, I started to wonder. They were there, but they weren't showing themselves. Were they waiting for me to pass out? Or were they just waiting for my guard to drop a little?

Whatever they were doing, I wasn't about to sit there and wait until they decided to kill me. I did have a brain, and it told me that every second I was away from the safety of cover as one that I'd end up regretting – if I lived to regret it at all. I took a deep breath, then I launched myself back to my feet and raced off towards the east again.

In the process, I almost bowled over the creature that had been working its way around to take me from behind. I screamed in surprise, swung my shotgun around, and frantically fired at it before it had a chance to recover from my unexpected movement. I would love to say that my success was based on skill and awareness, but in this case it was just pure luck. If I'd waited a few seconds longer, then the thing would have had me.

My heart hammered in my throat as I leapt over the buckshot-riddled pseudo-corpse and ran for my life, and this time it was fear that kept my head steady. Pure, animal terror. The creature had been so close that I could still smell its stink, still feel the unnatural chill that radiated from its body.

"Oh, Lord. Screw this. Screw this!" I gasped as I fled, using the words as a mantra to keep me going. "Screw this shit right out of the goddamn water!"

Behind me, the creatures lost their pretence of stealth and began shrieking in what sounded so very much like rage – but it couldn't be, they didn't have emotions. They didn't have thoughts or feelings or anything that made us human. They were hollow shells that did nothing but kill, kill, kill. And if I stopped, they'd kill me, too.

I found the old roadway quite by accident. As Anahera had warned me weeks earlier, it was in terrible condition, a shattered grey ribbon broken into uneven strips, with grass sticking up through the cracks. Still, it was relatively flat and straight, and that would give me a chance. I dashed out onto the tar seal and pulled my radio off my belt as I sprinted along as fast as I could go.

"Michael?" I called into the receiver. "Michael, I'm following the old east-west road. They've found me. Please, please hurry." I risked a quick glance over my shoulder, and saw half-a-dozen dark shapes emerging from the long grass behind me. "Oh, God! There's so many of them. I see... at least six—no, seven. Please, please hurry!"

There was no answer, but I didn't expect there to be one. He was too busy driving to answer. I could only hope that he'd at least heard. With no other choice but to rely on myself for now, I shoved my radio back onto my belt and ran as hard and as fast as I could.

Every so often, I glanced back and saw the creatures chasing after me, but they didn't seem to be gaining any ground. The problem was, I couldn't keep that pace up forever, not with my head the way it was. Right at that moment, I was fuelled by nothing but panic, and as powerful as that was it wouldn't keep me upright forever. Stars began to dance around the edge of my vision, warning me that a faint was incoming sometime soon if I didn't stop for a rest.

But the moment I stopped, they'd be on me.

Even with my particularly good sense of direction, I had lost track of how far it was to home. It could be a kilometre, or it could be ten. I couldn't outrun them, so I'd just have to outsmart them.

"Okay," I panted. "Okay, think smart. What can you do that they can't? Um... aside from thinking. Love? No, that's useless. Christ, come on, Sandy." I paused to jump over a particularly wide crack in the road, then lifted my head and scanned the horizon for any signs of Michael. Nothing.

"Wait, no. Not nothing," I exclaimed. "Yes! Inspiration!" With an unladylike whoop, I channelled what little reserves of strength I had left into one last burst of speed, and raced towards the buildings in the distance. Even with my vision wobbling and my head throbbing in time with my racing feet, I could see that one of those buildings was a barn, with a pair of doors up high that indicated there was a hayloft above it.

The kind of hayloft that would have a ladder. A ladder that would require human coordination to climb. If my undead friends couldn't operate a door handle, then it seemed unlikely that they'd be able to climb.

Seconds later, I raced across the overgrown courtyard in front of the barn, and plunged into the pleasant darkness within. I felt instant relief, after being out in the sun's glare, like plunging into a cool swimming pool on a hot summer's day. My pupils must have already been dilated from the concussion, because it only took a second for my vision to adjust to the gloom; the first thing I spotted was a ladder leading up towards the loft, and safety.

I shoved my shotgun back on its shoulder strap and darted forward, dodging around a few rusted farming implements and pieces of equipment. Right behind me, I could hear the creatures screaming. Their prey was out of sight, but they were closing on me fast.

I threw myself at the ladder and raced up as fast as I could go, but not quite fast enough. I was one rung away from safety when I felt an icy-cold grip close around my ankle. I kicked out and felt my foot connect with something solid, but I couldn't see what I'd hit. It didn't matter; it was enough for me to pull free. A few seconds later, I was at the top of the ladder, and safely out of reach.

"Thank God," I gasped breathlessly as I threw myself onto the dusty platform of the hayloft. If there had been any hay up there before, it had long ago turned to mulch, then to dirt, and eventually to dust without enough access to sunlight and rain for the grass seeds lying dormant within it to grow. Frankly, I didn't care how dirty it was. I didn't care if there were slaters, spiders, or even wetas making their home up there. Anything was better than the mutants.

As if reading my mind, one of the creatures below me let out a blood-curdling screech, which was quickly answered by a second and a third. Enough light filtered in through the open doors for me to see them circling around beneath me, like sharks waiting for their prey to come back within reach.

A sudden flash of anger clouded my judgement. Before I realised what I was doing, I had my shotgun back in my hand, and trained on one of those circling creatures. The shot rang out in the silence like a clarion call, and sent birds shrieking up into the clear blue sky from their nests nearby. One of the undead collapsed in a mound of blackened blood, its limbs writhing and flailing grotesquely around its shredded torso.

"I am *not* prey," I growled, taking aim again. Before I could fire, it retreated out of my line of sight and left me seething in impotent rage. I lowered my gun and gritted my teeth, then took a deep breath to calm my tension.

"I've been prey before, but I won't be prey again," I said softly to myself once the blind anger started to drain away. "Never again. Not for you. Not for him. Not for anyone. I am no one's prey."

***

I sat for a while in that dirty hayloft to catch my breath, and let my spinning head recover. Just as I'd predicted, the creatures didn't seem to be able to climb up after me, nor could they jump high enough to put me at risk. I could still hear them growling and circling around below me, but it was a frustrated sort of noise that told me that they couldn't get at me.

Once I had my breath back, I inched back over to the edge to see if I could remove the ladder and haul it up after me. Unfortunately, it was firmly bolted to the deck, so it wasn't going anywhere.

"Well, shit – there goes that idea," I muttered to myself, then paused. "Sorry, Mum. I'm sure you'd understand. There has to be something else, though. Something I can use."

I drew a deep breath to steady myself, and hauled myself back to my feet. Now that I was relatively safe, the adrenaline was starting to drain away, and with it went the frantic burst of energy that had kept me going through the pain and the dizziness. I quickly searched through the equipment that had been stored in the loft, but came away with nothing more useful than an old shovel. Still, if I ran out of ammunition, I might need it.

I could feel my strength beginning to wane by the second, so I went over to the loft doors and tried to open them while I still could. They squealed in protest on ancient, rusted hinges, but with enough brute force I managed to let in the afternoon sun.

"Christ, that's bright," I mumbled, easing myself down to sit on the edge of the loft with my legs hanging over the edge. I wasn't a fan of heights, but I was too dazed to care. When I went to pluck my radio off my belt again, I found my fingers trembling uncontrollably. It took three tries before I managed to successfully line my fingers up with the receiver and press the button. "Michael? Michael, if you can hear me, please stop for a second. I need to talk to you. Please?"

The wait was only a few seconds in reality, but it felt like it took forever. Eventually, the radio crackled in my hand, and then I heard his deep, reassuring voice in my ear.

"I'm here, sweetheart. Are you okay?"

"I'm... I'm not doing so hot, to be honest," I admitted. "But I am kind of safe for now. I found the road, and I managed to get to a barn. I'm up in a hayloft, out of their reach. Apparently they can't climb, so that's pretty awesome. Downside is that I'm trapped up here. I have some food, but my water's almost gone. I managed to shoot one, but there are six more down there. I don't think they can get up here, but... I don't know."

"I'm almost there. You just need to keep it together a little bit longer, okay? Now, tell me exactly where you are."

"Yeah... yeah, okay. Yeah." I paused and blinked up at the sun, trying to get my bearings. "I'm a little bit north of the road that runs westward out of Ohaupo. There's a house. It used to be painted blue, but it's faded now. So, you know, faded blue. It has a collapsed roof in the front. There's a barn about a hundred meters further back. That's where I am. There are mutants in the barn, though. Be careful. I don't think I... I—" Tears welled up in my eyes. I knew I was rambling, but that was the concussion kicking in. "I don't think I could handle it if anything happened to you. I love you. I love you so much."

"Nothing's going to happen to me," he told me in that deep, husky voice that sent shivers down my spine every time. "I am coming for you, do you hear me? Just stay strong a little bit longer. I love you, too, and I won't let anything happen to you. Not again. Okay?"

"Okay," I agreed softly; the weakness I could hear in my own voice was alarming, but I was too exhausted to care. I switched the radio off and clipped it back onto my belt, then lay my head against the old wood and settled in to wait.

***

I had no real sense of time passing as I waited, drifting in and out of consciousness. Every so often, one of the mutants below me would snarl or yowl and bring me awake again, but I couldn't see what they were doing. I could hear them circling below me, like a school of piranhas, just waiting for me to come down so that they could devour me.

"Leave me alone," I mumbled sleepily, closing my eyes. Maybe if I wished hard enough, they'd go away, and I could just go home. That'd be nice. I missed home. I missed Michael.

"Sandy? Are you still with me?"

"What?" I blinked owlishly, startled by the unexpected voice. It took a few seconds for my addled brain to comprehend that it was actually coming from my radio. I picked the radio up and pressed the receiver. "Hey, I'm here. Please tell me you're nearby."

"I am. I see you. Look towards the road."

I lifted my head and stared into the distance. My eyes didn't want to focus properly, but I could just make out the figure on the big quad bike, waving at me. Relief rushed through me as I raised my hand and waved back.

"Thank God. I don't feel good, and the barn is full of mutants. What do I do?"

"I'm going to give them something else to worry about," he answered, his voice deep and commanding even through the radio. With a direct line of sight to him, the connection was as clear as a bell. I could almost feel his arms around me... right up until he threw a spanner in the works. "You just get ready to jump."

"Wait, what? Jump?" I shot a glance down at the ground below me. "Are you crazy? That's gotta be like three, maybe four meters."

"Don't jump now, silly," he answered dryly. "Just get ready. I'll tell you when to jump."

"I'm not sure I like this plan, but... okay," I agreed grudgingly. "Be careful."

While he was doing whatever he had to do, I quickly unloaded my shotgun and shoved the spare rounds back into my pocket, then strapped the gun to my back. If I was going to have to fall that far, then having the gun loaded was a terrible idea, even with the mutants swarming below. Besides, Michael said that he had a plan.

Once I was ready, I inched close to the edge of the platform and watched him getting ready. I couldn't see the details, but I could see him doing something with an object in his lap. Suddenly, he looked up and waved at me, then I faintly heard the sound of his bike revving up.

A few seconds later, he turned the bike around and tore across the overgrown fields that separated the barn from the road. As he drew closer, I realised that I could see his M-16 resting across his lap, ready for action at a moment's notice — and there was something else, something that I couldn't quite make out.

He came on hard and fast, at an angle that kept him out of the direct line of sight of the things inside the barn. At the very last moment, he took a hard turn to the left and came to a halt directly below me. Shrieks of what sounded like either hunger or rage filled the air. Michael didn't even hesitate. He threw the thing he'd been holding into the dark recess of the barn, and then lifted his gun and opened fire.

The sound of bullets filled the air with their terrible tattoo, and I smelt the stink of gunpowder on the air. Then, I realised that I could smell something else, something familiar. It took a second for me to realise that it was gasoline. Just as that realisation struck me, an explosion ripped through the back end of the barn below me, and the smell of gasoline was replaced by one of burning.

Michael shoved his gun back on its shoulder strap, and looked right at me. "Jump!"

"But--" I started to protest, but the rapidly spreading fire drowned out my words.

"Just do it!" he shouted over the noise. "You trust me, don't you?"

A second explosion shook the barn, and very nearly made me lose my seating on the edge of the hayloft. There was no choice. I had to do it. I had to trust him. I took a deep breath to steady myself, then shoved myself off the ledge. For a second, I felt the sickening sensation of falling, but it barely lasted long enough for me to start panicking. A moment later, I felt strong arms catch me and suddenly I was enveloped in warmth.

"You're okay, I've got you," Michael whispered in my ear as he sat me down on the seat in front of him. I started to say something, but a third explosion left my head ringing and my mind unable to focus; whatever I had been intending to say vanished like water through a sieve.

It didn't matter, though. Michael had me. He helped me get comfortable on the seat in front of him, and reached around me to grab the handlebars. I heard the bike rev up, and then we were off at high speed, heading for home. The motion made my stomach reel in protest, but I couldn't bring myself to care. Relief was a tangible force inside me, so overwhelming that all I wanted to do was wrap my arms around Michael's waist and bury my face in his chest.

So, I did. There comes a time in every person's life when they need someone else's help to survive. This moment was mine.

That's what having a family is for, isn't it? The bike was too loud for me to bounce my thoughts off Michael, so I didn't even try to speak. It had taken some time for me to acknowledge it, but they were there for me in my darkest moments, to help, protect, save, and love me. How had I survived for so long without that safety net of social acceptance?

Hard questions. Shut up and rest, brain, I scolded myself, then I closed my eyes and let myself relax.

Chapter Four

At some point during the trip back home, I fainted. Even if I'd been aware of it happening, I probably wouldn't have been able to do anything about it. As far as my body was concerned, enough was enough; it was time to rest.

When I started to come to again, I could no longer hear the sound of the bike, just someone moving around nearby. I opened my eyes slowly, then immediately regretted it. The world around me spun like an out-of-control roller coaster. Someone must have heard my groan, because I felt a hand alight softly on my shoulder.

"Don't try to sit up," Doctor Cross said quietly. Curiosity overwhelmed my urge to avoid the dizzying sensation, so I opened my eyes again and carefully looked around.

I was lying in my own bed, in the loft above the DVD store, but the place looked like it had been converted into a triage unit. Supplies, primarily medical in nature, were stacked up along the walls, and beside me lay Anahera's still form. She was still unconscious.

"Is everyone all right?" I asked, my voice coming out far huskier than I intended. The doctor nodded, and put a glass of water against my lips. I drank gratefully, then lay my head back on the pillow and looked up at him.

"More or less, yes," he elaborated. "I haven't seen this many concussions in one room since the time my son dragged me off to watch a roller derby match. Everyone is alive, though."

"And they'll be all right?" I repeated, glancing towards the enigmatic woman that lay beside me. "What about Anahera? Is it serious?"

"She's the only one I'm concerned about at the moment," Doc admitted. "Everyone else is going to be fine. Only time will tell for her, though. The human head is a delicate object, and she sustained quite a severe injury."

"I need to get up, doc," I told him, shooting him a look. "How long do I have to wait until it's safe to do so?"

"Until you feel better," he gave me a stern frown in return. "Your sister has everything under control. Stop worrying and rest."

"Ugh. Don't wanna." I sighed heavily and closed my eyes. "You know, I'm actually kind of surprised that Maddy didn't warn me that this was going to happen. She was pretty spot-on about the fire."

My answer was silence. After a few seconds, I opened my eyes and looked up at him. Eventually, he glanced at me and shrugged. "I don't know what to make of Madeline's... premonitions, to be frank. I am a man of science. I believe what I can see, touch, and feel."

"I know exactly what you mean," I replied. "If you'd suggested I'd be taking guidance from a psychic kid six months ago, I would have laughed at you. Well, there isn't much we can do about it now, is there? Tell me what happened while I was away, Doc."

"That much I can do." The portly gentleman hiked his scratched glasses a little higher up his nose, and sat down on the bed beside me. "Things went as well as can be expected in your absence. The Yousefis have done nothing to violate our trust, and have been working hard to make up for what they did."

"Good." I nodded, gesturing for him to continue. "How are we for supplies?"

"Better than we initially thought." He gave me a rare smile. "I might even venture to say that we have been very, very lucky, considering the circumstances. The fire started in the kitchen, and consumed most of Skylar's room. We've been able to clear enough debris to get inside, but it's still fairly hot. The storage rooms have survived mostly intact. With the exception of what was in the refrigerator, our food supplies should be fine – though, everything may taste like barbeque for the next few weeks."

"We're going to need to find a new food supply before then." I paused and did a quick head-count, then grimaced. "We've got twenty mouths to feed, including Anahera's men. There isn't enough here to last more than a fortnight, and that's if we ration it to the mouthful."

"You plan to keep them, then?" Doc stared at me, his expression thoughtful. "Somehow, I'm not surprised."

"What's that supposed to mean?" I asked, giving him a quizzical look.

"Well, you and the boy do have a habit of picking up strays." Suddenly, the old man chuckled and shook his head. "Just where are you planning to put them all, Ms McDermott? We didn't have enough room for them before the fire. It'll be near-impossible to house them all now."

"I don't know," I admitted. "I just know that we need to find somewhere safe and secure. I want to build a city, Doc. These people are the future of humankind; we need to find somewhere safe enough to put down roots, and plan for the next generation."

"Bold, idealistic, and slightly naïve," he summarized dryly. "Sounds like just what we need."

"Hey, if you have a better plan to save us from extinction, I'm all ears." I stuck out my tongue and blew a raspberry at him. Despite the childish gesture, he actually paused to think about it for a second.

"I don't," he replied thoughtfully. "Frankly, it's a valiant plan. I have no idea if we can achieve it, but we do need to try." His affirmation surprised me. I shot him a startled look, and caught him smiling. Before I could say anything else, he put his hand on my shoulder. "Go to sleep, Sandy — or is it Sandrine now? You'll need your strength if you're going to lead us to this idealistic new world of yours."

"But I don't wanna sleep," I protested without really meaning it. "You're so mean. Hate you, Doc."

"No, you don't." He chuckled softly as he turned away, and walked back towards the door. "If you hated me, then you would have left me to die in that inferno instead of risking your life to rescue me."

I had nothing to say to that.

***

I slept for another few hours, until my head finally started to feel right again. Although my body ached from the tumble I'd taken, I had been through worse and was more than capable of dealing with a little bit of pain.

When I woke again, the room was murky with the shadows of twilight. There were no windows in my little bedroom, but I had come to know it well over the time I'd lived there. Darkness was falling, but it hadn't fallen yet.

I sat up slowly, careful not to set my head spinning again, but the rest had done its job. I felt much better.

Even when I switched on the light, my body didn't protest too much. Thinking about my own condition made me worry about my friends, though; I glanced back at Anahera, and heaved a deep sigh.

"Get better, mate. I need you," I told her. She didn't reply, of course. Still, she was alive. That was more than I could say for a lot of my other friends – and hers, too. I blew out a soft breath, and murmured thoughtfully, "There are going to be a lot of people grieving tonight. I should get out there."

I turned away from her, and eased myself out of bed. I'd been stripped down to my underwear, but my filthy clothing and shoes weren't far away. A few months before, I would have freaked out over that, but now I didn't even bat an eyelash. I grabbed a clean t-shirt and a pair of jeans out of my dresser and pulled them on, then made my way out into the living room.

The sight that greeted me was unexpectedly heart-warming. The five children in our group – Maddy, Priya, and the three younger Yousefi boys – sat in a circle on the living room floor with Tigger, the kitten that had adopted me earlier that summer.

"Mama!" Priya squealed in delight when she saw me. A second later, she was latched around my waist, hugging me fiercely.

"Mama?" I peered down at her, curious. "When did that happen?"

"I decided," she answered firmly, and gave me one of her radiant smiles. "My old mama is gone, so you're my new mama now." Suddenly, a look of anxiety crossed her face. "Is okay, yes? You mama, Michael baba?"

That look melted any protests I might have had about my new status. I just smiled, and hugged her back.

"Sure, Priya. I'll be your mama," I agreed, then looked up at the other children. "What are you guys doing?"

"Babysitting!" Priya said proudly, pointing at the little group. "The pretty lady said I'm old enough to look after the little ones."

"Well, you seem to be doing a good job of it," I praised her gently, and looked up at the circle of little faces again. The three boys were shy and wary, but it was Madeline's expression that took me by surprise. She looked sullen, her attention intensely focused on the kitten. "Maddy? Are you okay?"

The little girl just shrugged and said nothing. She didn't even look at me. I looked at Priya for answers instead, since she seemed to be the only one interested in talking to me.

"Maddy is sad-sads, because of the fire," Priya explained in a dramatic stage whisper. "I think she be okay, but is sads now and does not want to talk."

"Ah. A bit of shock, then." I nodded thoughtfully, and looked back at the little girl. "Maddy, I wanted to thank you for telling us about your dreams. I don't know how you did it, but you may have saved everyone's lives. You're a good girl, and you've done well."

A flicker of something that I couldn't identify passed through her eyes. She nodded and gave me a faint smile. "Thank you for believing me, Miss Sandy."

"I always believe you, Maddy," I said softly, prying myself out of Priyanka's grip so that I could go over and kneel down beside her. "You're special, Maddy. I don't know how it happened, or what kind of special you are, but you're definitely special. I remember how you helped me when I first met your family, and now this? You're one of the most special people I've ever met."

"I—" She hesitated, staring up at me with huge brown eyes. Suddenly, they filled with tears. "I'm sorry, Miss Sandy. I didn't mean to make the fire happen."

"What?" I blinked, startled. "You didn't start the fire, honey. Zain did, by accident. You weren't even there."

"But I started it by dreaming about it," she said. Suddenly, she burst into tears. "I'm sorry! I didn't mean to. Please don't be angry with me."

"Whoa!" Flabbergasted by the sudden outburst, I grabbed the little girl and pulled her into a hug. "Shh, honey, it's okay. You didn't make the fire happen. It's not your fault. I promise."

"B-but I dreamed it before it happened," the little girl blubbered, clinging to me as though her life depended on it. "If I hadn't dreamed it then it wouldn't have happened."

"Okay, I'm no expert on these things, but I know that it's not your fault." I gently held her back away from me, and wiped the tears off her cheeks. "Sweetie, you did not cause the fire. The fire was going to happen anyway. You just... sensed that the fire was going to happen, and you warned us. You saved lives by giving us the advanced warning to prepare. You did not cause the fire."

"I didn't?" She sniffled loudly and looked up at me, her little face stained with tears.

"No, you didn't," I told her firmly, and gave her a smile. "You saw what was going to happen and told us about it. The fire was caused by a gas stove falling over. You weren't even in the room when that happened, so it couldn't be your fault. Could it?"

"Well... no, I guess not," she agreed, then took a deep breath and rubbed her hands across her cheeks to wipe the tears away. "I was so scared, Miss Sandy. I thought Granddaddy was doing to die."

"Nobody's going to die on my watch," I reassured her, and gave her another quick hug. "Everyone's okay because of you, Maddy. You saved them. Look, even Tigger knows that you're a hero."

Maddy looked down at the purring bundle of fluff in her lap, and shot a dubious look at me.

"No, really," I said, grinning at her. "She won't even let me pat her, but she's letting you hold her. That's special right there, isn't it?"

Maddy looked down at the kitten, then picked her up and gave her a cuddle. Tigger barely even stirred, but the sight made me smile. It might take some time to get over the shock, but I decided that she was going to be fine.

"Okay, kids," I announced, easing myself back to my feet. "I need to go see what the others are up to. You be good for Priya and stay inside where it's safe."

"Okies!" Priya agreed cheerfully. I waved and headed out of the apartment. As I made my way down the stairs, I heard voices speaking on the other side of the door. I tried the handle and found the inner door locked, so I knocked instead.

The voices on the other side stopped for a moment, then I heard my sister. "Priya, is that you again? I told you to stay upstairs."

"It's me, sis," I called back. "Let me out."

"Oh, hey! Just a second." I heard the sound of a key turning in the lock and the door opened. Skye yanked me into a quick hug, then pulled me into the office where she and Elly had been speaking. "Man, am I ever glad to see you up and about again. I've been so worried."

"Sorry about that," I answered sheepishly. "I'm feeling a bit better now. How's your head doing?"

"Better. Doc says that it wasn't too bad, all things considered." Skye chuckled and shook her head. "Look at us. We're like concussion twins or something."

"I'm pretty sure that's not actually a thing, but I know what you mean." I grinned at her, then looked back and forth between the two women. "So, how are we situated? It's about to get dark, and those things could get here any moment if they decide to come back this way."

"There's no sign of them at the moment, but we've got Michael and his boys on guard duty anyway," Skye explained, then she grabbed my hand and led me out of the office. When she opened the door, I was surprised to see that the lower level of the old store had been cleaned up, and all the old trash removed. In its place, supplies had been stored in neat piles.

"Wow, you guys have been hard at work," I commented, impressed. "This has to be just about everything we had in the motel. Good job."

"Almost," she agreed, nodding. "We still have a bit more to retrieve, but we should be finished tomorrow morning. We've also sent Zain and Ropata out in the Hilux to look for cars and trailers that we can salvage. If we're going to be leaving, then we'll need transport."

"Do they know what they're looking for?" I asked, shooting a glance at Elly. To my surprise, she laughed.

"I would hope so," she said dryly. "I do not know about the other man, but my husband was an automotive engineer for twelve years before the plague, if you include his apprenticeship. We were only travelling on foot because we ran out of petrol, and couldn't find any more. Skylar says that you have fuel, so there is no problem."

"You mean we actually have someone who knows what they're doing now?" I stared at them wide-eyed for a second, then let out a whoop of delight. "Finally! I don't know how to tell you guys this, but I've just been faking it the whole time."

"Faking it, huh?" Skylar gave me a long, sideways look, followed up by a wicked smile. "That's the only thing you've been faking though, right?"

"Eh?" I stared at her, my joviality replaced by confusion. "What do you mean by that?"

"I mean, you're not faking it for Michael, are you?" she answered in a gleeful, sing-song voice, then danced over and threaded her arm through mine. "So, when were you planning to tell me, huh? I'm your sister; it's not nice to keep secrets from your sister."

"Whoa, suddenly this conversation has gone into uncomfortable places!" I exclaimed, holding up my free hand in self-defence. "What the hell are you talking about, Skye? You already know about me and Michael."

"Yeah, but you didn't tell me about... this!" She snatched the chain that held my engagement ring out from beneath my shirt before I could hope to stop her. "We had to undress you while you were unconscious. Did you think you could keep that hidden forever?"

"Oh, that." Embarrassed, I tugged the ring back out of her grip and shoved it back under my shirt. "I was going to tell you eventually, but we've been a little busy, you know? It only happened a week ago, while we were away, and it's not a full-on engagement. Just sort of a... promise.

Michael gave it to me so I'd have something to show for our relationship if anything ever happened to him."

"Awww, how sweet," Skye crooned. Behind her, Elly giggled girlishly, a sound that seemed far too young to be coming from a face that looked twice my age. The years had not been kind to her, but her eyes were alert and intelligent despite her weather-worn skin. I gave her a faint smile, and pointedly changed the subject.

"So, you guys already figured out that we're going to be leaving," I said, glancing back and forth between them. "That's good. It's going to be dangerous, but it'll be safer if we stick together."

"I don't think we have much of a choice, to be honest," Skye answered, her demeanour changing from playful to serious. "Those things have already killed six people, and from Michael's stoic silence I gather that they almost got a seventh today. You've mentioned gangs in the south, but we can deal with those. These things are just... monsters."

"I'm concerned that the mutated virus may be spreading," I admitted, shooting a glance back over my shoulder towards the heavily-barricaded front door. "There were so many of them out there. At least nine, by my count."

"Yeah," Skye agreed, nodding thoughtfully. "I doubt you're the only one thinking that, either. Speaking of which, we better get everyone inside. It's starting to get dark. Elly, can you grab the bullhorn?"

"Bullhorn? We have a bullhorn?" I asked curiously, but Skye just gave me a grin and said nothing.

Instead, she reached into her pocket and pulled out one of our walkie-talkies, and spoke into it. "Home-time, guys. Everyone start heading back to base."

A chorus of agreement came back to her from the holders of the other radios. When Elly returned with the bullhorn, she stuck her head out the door and repeated the message loudly enough for anyone without a radio to hear. Within a few minutes, the other survivors began to return.

The first to return were the men who had been involved in the salvage operation at the old motel, covered in soot and looking exhausted. I was a little surprised to see Anahera's men among them at first glance, but after a moment of thought I realised that it made perfect sense. One of the many things that had changed since the fall of the human empire was the average person's attitude towards group effort.

Back when we could rely on a steady food source and a roof over our heads, it was okay to be fully focused on your individual wants and needs, or those of your direct family. Now, it had become second nature to do your part for everyone in the group, regardless of how you were feeling. Helping the group was helping yourself. If you didn't work, you didn't eat. They'd been through a lot of trauma and were grieving for their lost friends, but they were still willing to work for their supper. I understood that, and I respected it.

As they filtered through the door, I took a moment to greet them. I could see the deep sadness in their eyes, but also relief and gratitude. All of them had a smile for me, even if it was a little weak. One by one, we sent them upstairs to the loft.

"It's going to get pretty crowded up there tonight," I commented. Just at that moment, Doc arrived with a huge armful of sooty blankets and pillows. The three of us rushed over to help him.

"Yeah," Skye agreed as we unfolded the blankets, and shook them out the door to get the worst of the soot off them. "We've retrieved as much bedding as we can, but it's still going to be a bit uncomfortable for everyone. Better safe than sorry, though."

"Well, we're going to need to have some people on night watch, anyway," I answered, glancing around the little building for inspiration. "I'm thinking two watching upstairs, two downstairs. We don't want those things sneaking up on us while we're sleeping."

"Now, that is an awful thought," Elly commented quietly; I glanced at her just in time to see her shudder. "It frightens me to think how close they came to taking my children from me."

"I won't let them," I said firmly. "I'll protect your kids to the death, if I have to. I'll protect all of the kids, one way or another."

"Well, aren't you Little Miss Determined now?" Skye teased impishly, and gave me a nudge in the side. I stuck my tongue out at her and gave her a shove back.

"Someone's got to be." I folded the blanket I'd been shaking over my arm, and turned to look her in the eye. "We may be all that's left of humanity in this country right now. Even if we aren't, we have a duty to try to protect ourselves, and to grow this group so that the next generation can have a decent chance. We owe them that much, don't we?"

"True." Skye sighed heavily, the humour draining out of her face. "I barely remember what it was like before the plague came. I just remember everything being... so clean. And smiling people everywhere. It would be nice to have that again." Suddenly, she glanced up and gave me a cheeky wink. "I also miss chocolate. Chocolate was awesome."

All of us laughed at that.

Chapter Five

By the time full darkness fell, everyone had returned safely from whatever mission they'd been about. The last people to return were Michael and his crew, who had taken responsibility for keeping the rest of us safe. Not really a huge surprise. I won't lie and pretend that I was all dignified or coy about seeing him again. The second he came through the door, I threw myself into his arms and smothered him in kisses, much to the amusement of everyone around us. And you know what? I didn't care. I didn't care at all. After the kind of day that we'd had, we had both earned a moment of weakness.

Once we had finished reuniting, we closed, locked, and barricaded the front door with the heaviest things we could find, then we filtered upstairs into the crowded loft.

"Elly and I will take care of dinner," Skye volunteered, heading off to the kitchen. That left the rest of us standing awkwardly in a small living room, crammed with way more people than it was ever meant to hold.

"You know, I really hope the floor doesn't collapse or something," I joked lightly, nudging Michael in the side.

He smiled faintly in response to my joke, but his expression stayed serious. "We should probably do something about getting people bathed, though. It smells like a frat house in here."

"Good point." I nodded and cleared my throat loudly, putting an end to the quiet conversations taking place around the room. One by one, they all turned and looked at me expectantly. "All right, everyone. Michael says you stink. Bathroom's through that door there, on the left. I'd like the kids to go first, since they have to go to bed earlier than the rest of us – Doc, Zain, can you please take care that?" I glanced at them. They both nodded, and stood to round up their respective progeny. "Thanks, guys. As for the rest of us... well, there isn't going to be enough hot water for everyone to have a warm shower. Sorry. No fist-fights, okay?"

There were some groans from the younger men, but there was really nothing that any of us could do to alleviate the situation so there were few real complaints. A cold shower was better than no shower, and most of us were used to going without modern conveniences when we had to. The conversations resumed, but with so many people crammed into a single room it was hard to follow any of them. Michael was clearly in one of his dark moods, and that always bothered me.

Ever since the death of his niece, there were times when he went into a strange, black place that was so out of keeping with his personality that it made me worry. I hated to watch him brood, so I gently reached out and touched his arm. When he looked at me quizzically, I tilted my head towards the door, silently telling him I wanted to talk to him without alerting the others that anything was amiss.

He followed me out onto the landing without a word, and closed the door softly behind him. Before I could say anything, he grabbed me and drew me into a fierce hug. The gesture was unexpected and took me by surprise, but not for long. Michael was not one to stay silent; he was a deeply expressive man, who tended to take things to extremes. Whether he was laughing or crying, he never hid himself from me.

"Hey, it's okay," I whispered, wrapping my arms around his broad shoulders. "I'm fine. Everything is fine. You made it in time."

Michael drew back and looked down at me, then let out a low, deep sigh. "I know – but I almost didn't. I've been kicking myself that I didn't notice when you fell behind. I could have lost you, and never known what happened."

"Better to never know than watch me get torn apart, right?" I answered with my usual dry sarcasm, but the look that he gave me immediately made me regret my choice of words. It was a look of total horror. It took a moment for me to put together what I'd said with what he had seen when Sophie died. "Oh my God, I didn't mean it like that! I'm sorry, honey. I-I didn't mean--"

"It's okay," he answered, cutting me off mid-stammer. "I know, it was supposed to be a joke. I'm just... having trouble with this whole situation. I feel so helpless."

"You saved my life once again," I reassured him, gently reaching up to grab his shoulders. "Again and again, you're there for me. Honey, you're the strongest man I know. Please don't doubt yourself like this, because I don't. I have absolute confidence in you. I trust you. You know better than anyone how hard it is for me to say that."

He nodded, his expression softening. "Yeah, I do. It means so much to me to hear you say that. But, still... it's hard to feel in control when you have no idea where the enemy is going to strike from next."

"I know what you mean." I sighed heavily, turning away to stare out the little window at the dark sky, and the ashen ruins of our former home. "I haven't felt like I'm truly in control of my own destiny in a long time. Hopefully, this voyage south will change that. No more waiting."

"It's going to be a hard trip," he said quietly. I felt his warm body come up behind me, and his arms slid around my waist. "For everyone, but especially for the little ones. Do we even know where we're going?"

"No, not really." I shrugged and leaned back against him, drawing comfort from his strength. "I figure that we head for Wellington, and see where the winds take us. We'll stop by that corn field along the way and stock up on food. That'll keep us going for a while."

"I've never been to Wellington," he said, resting his chin comfortably on my shoulder. I shot him a glance, and saw his dark eyes were distant, focused on nothing.

"I have – well, I've been in the area." I nuzzled his cheek and then closed my eyes to think. "It's been a long time. If we stick to the areas that used to be farmland, then we should have an easier time foraging along the road."

"We could find boats. Take the river south," he suggested.

I opened my eyes and gave him a curious look, then shrugged. "Maybe. They can't follow our tracks if we're on the river, but the river would only take us part of the way and then we'd be stuck scavenging for trucks in an unfamiliar location. We're heading through Arapuni, so we can check while we're there. I don't want to leave without offering Rebecca and Jim the chance to join us."

"It can't hurt to ask." Michael smiled at me, and gave me a gentle hug. "You know, I can hardly believe how much you've changed since we met."

"For the better, I hope?" I laughed and nudged him in the side.

He chuckled back and nodded. "Of course. I fell in love with you just the way you were, but this person that you're becoming... I love her, too. You're metamorphosing before my very eyes, from someone that was impressive to begin with, into someone truly amazing. Words can't express how glad I am that we met."

"And to think, if it hadn't been for these undead, then we'd never have found each other." I grinned at him, turning within the circle of his arms so that I could drape my own across his shoulders again. "Think we should thank them?"

"Hm, let me think about that." He tilted his head, pretending to think about it, then grinned at me. "Nah, I think we should just keep shooting them."

"Good plan," I agreed, leaning up to plant a kiss on his lips. When we parted, I glanced over his shoulder at the room beyond. "We should probably assign people to the night watch. I was saying to Skye that I think we should have two groups of two, one downstairs watching the door, one upstairs keeping an eye on the sleepers, just in case."

"Sounds good," he agreed amiably. "First shift from bedtime until just after midnight, then second shift from then until sunrise?"

"Yeah." I nodded my agreement. "I think we should try and divide it up between the newcomers and the old — both so they can get to know one another, and so we can keep an eye on them."

"I'll take care of it." Michael smiled down at me, then leaned down and planted a kiss against my forehead. "You worry about organising the journey."

"I don't mind taking a watch," I started to protest, but he just shook his head.

"You're one of the walking wounded today, sweetheart," he rumbled in that soft, deep voice of his. "I want you to rest. I'll be watching over you, so you know you'll be safe."

"Sometimes I think you're way too nice to me." I sighed, lifting a hand to trace the contours of his cheek.

"Do you want me to stop being nice to you?" he asked, raising one eyebrow inquisitively.

"Nah." I laughed, then leaned up and planted another quick kiss against his lips. "To be honest, I've almost forgotten what my life was like before I had you in it. Which is a good thing, because my life was pretty awful before I met you."

"I understand." He drew me back in and wrapped his arms around me. "Everything happened so quickly, but it feels so right. I've never felt as sure about anything as I feel certain that you and I are meant to be together. I only wish that you'd had a chance to meet Sophie."

"Me too," I murmured, snuggling in against his warmth. "You're just the kind of guy to take home to meet the parents, if you remember that old saying. I think my folks would have loved having you for a son-in-law."

"My dad would have liked you, but I have this sneaking suspicion that you and my mother would have fought like cats." He pulled back and looked down at me, a playful twinkle in his eyes. "I suppose that would have been funny to watch, though. From very, very far away."

"Hey!" I laughed and gave him a playful shove. "You never know, we might have gotten on so well that we'd spend all our time plotting ways to make your life miserable."

Michael groaned. "Don't even joke about that. That's so not funny."

"Yes, it is." I gave him an impish grin, and wriggled my way free of his grip. "Anyway, we should get back to work. You take care of the defences for the night, and I'll sort out our travel plans."

"Yes, ma'am!" He gave me a mock salute, then moved past me and headed back into the living room where the others were waiting.

I followed a few paces behind him, but while he started talking to the group, I headed into the kitchen. There, I found Skye and Elly hard at work, preparing something that remotely resembled food. Most of our fresh food had been destroyed by the fire, but the years had taught all of us how to be resourceful.

"Hey," Skye greeted when she noticed me. "Dinner's still a wee while away yet. We'll let you know when it's ready."

"Oh, I'm not here about that." I moved the rest of the way inside, and closed the sliding door that separated the kitchen and living room, to cut off the noise the men were making. "I needed to talk to you, actually. Both of you."

"Oh?" Skye shot me a look, her brows raised curiously. "What's up, sis?"

"A couple of things, actually. One at a time, though." I paused for a moment to gather my thoughts, glancing at the stack of supplies wedged into the corner of the room. "You know we're going south as soon as possible. I want you guys to take care of provisioning. You have my permission to rope in anyone else you need, but I need someone who's in charge to keep things from getting messy. If you're cool with it, I'd like to put you in charge, and have Elly serve as your second-in-command."

"Yeah, sounds fine," Skye agreed, waving a wooden spoon at me. "We're already doing that anyway, so make it official. What else?"

"I need to know if you managed to salvage the radio," I asked bluntly; there was no point beating around the bush where my sister was concerned.

To my surprise, she hesitated. "Um... sort of."

"Sort of?" I raised a brow.

"Well, it's a little melted," she admitted, sounding sheepish. "I can't make it work, but you might be able to. I think it's just the shell that's melted, but something inside must have come loose from the heat. I mean, it's not totally melted."

I muffled a chuckle behind a cough. "Ah, right. Radio's melted. Got it."

"Just a little melted!" she protested. "It's probably still good. I mean, I hope so. It's in with the supplies downstairs."

"I'll take a look at it tomorrow," I answered dryly. "How much bedding did you manage to collect?"

"Not enough for everyone," she said with a shrug. "Some people are going to have to share. I guess we'll just have to get used to getting a little cuddly if we're going to stay together."

"Not for long." I gave her a smile and a wink. "We'll look for some more as we head south. I'm sure we'll find more than we need."

"True." Skye heaved a sigh and stretched. "Is that all? I'm knackered; I just want to get dinner done and curl up to sleep."

"Yeah. Thanks, sis." I waved to her and ducked out of the kitchen again, then went off to begin the arduous task of assigning bedding. I found a mound of it downstairs, and dragged it all up to hand it out. Sure enough, there wasn't enough to go around, but the group was pretty relaxed about being paired off with cuddle-buddies for the night. By the time dinner was served, half the men were laughing and teasing one another, and then they were distracted by food.

I deemed that a good thing, considering that so many of them had lost close friends that day. The longer I could keep them distracted and smiling, the better it would be for everyone. When dinner was served, I sat down quietly on the floor between Skylar and Michael, and ate my serving without a word, lost in my own thoughts.

It was going to be a long night, and an even longer few months as we headed south, but it had to be done. We couldn't just stay here and wait to see what the mutants decided to do next. As hard as it was to accept that it was better to flee than to stand and fight, I knew in my gut that I'd made the right choice for everyone. It wasn't the easy choice, but it was the right choice.

Chapter Six

It took us three days to prepare to leave Ohaupo – three very tense days, and very long nights. Every night, the guards reported hearing strange sounds outside our building, but by dawn there was no sign of anything there. It was unnerving, to say the least. We were all tense and on edge, and it was beginning to grate on everyone's nerves. People were snappish, and more than once I found myself having to step in to diffuse a potential explosion.

On the fourth morning, I woke early with my head nestled on Michael's belly, to the familiar sound of Priya's soft snores beside me. My concussion had healed fine, as had Skylar's, but Anahera was still unconscious.

I lifted my head, careful to avoid disturbing the people around me, and discovered that I was the first one awake in the pre-dawn gloom. It took me exactly three seconds to decide that made it the perfect time to get up and have a quick shower, before we had twenty people all clamouring for the bathroom at once.

As gently as I could, I extracted myself from my cuddle-pile and snuck towards the bathroom, tiptoeing around the sleeping forms of my friends. It was a nerve-wracking trip, but somehow I made it without waking anyone – or so I thought. When I glanced back over my shoulder at the last moment, I realised that Michael had somehow snuck up behind me. He gave me a playful grin and held a finger up to his lips, then grabbed my hand and dragged me into the bathroom.

There were very few moments of privacy with that many people living in such close proximity. Since the bathroom door had a lock, and the shower was one of our favourite spots anyway, it seemed logical. We were quick and stealthy, but it was enough. A brief moment of stolen passion was enough to leave me feeling happy and revitalized.

By the time we were finished, bathed, and dressed, the others were starting to wake up around us. Michael and I went into the kitchen to get breakfast started; one by one, the others dragged themselves out of bed and toddled off to the bathroom to relieve themselves, yawning broadly.

By the time a bleary-eyed Skylar wandered into the kitchen, breakfast was almost ready.

"What's going on?" she asked sleepily. "I thought you guys hated cooking?"

"Well, we need an early start this morning if we want to make it to a secure spot by sunset, so we figured we should get breakfast cooking as soon as possible," I answered, offering her a plate. "My scrambled eggs may not be as good as yours, but they're still food. Eat up."

She started to say something, but all that came out was a sleepy mumble, then she grabbed the plate and wandered back into the living room. I shot an amused glance at Michael, and opened my mouth to crack a joke, but before I could say anything the sound of a voice raised in alarm interrupted me.

Michael's expression turned to one of concern, mirroring my own feelings. The shouting was coming from the upstairs lobby. If something had figured out a way to get inside, then we were all in danger. I turned and ran out into the living room, with him hot on my heels.

A second later, I burst through the door onto the landing, where I found Tane leaning against the windowsill, staring intently down into the courtyard of our old motel. He glanced back when he heard us, and pointed down into the yard.

"I saw someone down there," he explained quickly. "I didn't get a good enough look to know if it was a survivor or one of the undead, though. I just saw a silhouette moving."

"Let's go find out, then," I answered resolutely. I led the way down the stairs to the lower level. At the bottom of the stairs, I banged on the door until it opened, and Hemi's startled-looking face peeked up at me.

"What's the ruckus, Sandy?" he asked, looking tense and wary.

"There's someone – or something – in the motel," I explained, gently shoving my way past him into the office at the base of the stairs. I grabbed my shotgun from its shelf, and led the way towards the exit. Iorangi was standing guard beside it; he took one look at my face, then hastily unlocked the door and pulled away the blockade to let us out. "Thanks. You two stay here. I don't want anything to sneak in while the door's open."

"Got it covered," Hemi replied. "If you need us, shout."

"Good man. Don't worry, we will." I nodded grimly, and beckoned for Michael and Tane to follow me. I heard their footfalls behind me as I raced down the street towards the corner, and headed for the front door of the old motel. There, I paused and listened for a moment, but I heard nothing.

I felt a soft touch on my shoulder, then Michael leaned past me to point at the sooty ground near the door. A fresh boot-print marred the ash, clear as day, the edges not yet blurred by the breeze or rain. I crouched down and stared at it, then nodded and rose back to my feet. It might have been left by one of the undead, but it was just as likely to have been left by a living person.

Ahead of me, I spotted another boot print on the blackened concrete, then a third and a fourth. They were spaced wide, but an even distance apart. That settled it for me — the infected had an uneven, loping gait, and the prints were too regular for that. Our visitor was a person, and he or she had been running.

I glanced back at the two men following me and touched a finger to my lips for silence. They both nodded in agreement. Lowering my shotgun into a defensive position, I followed the tracks across the soot-stained lobby and out into the courtyard, then followed them up the stairs towards the second level. As quietly as I could, I slipped the safety off my shotgun and brought it up to my shoulder, aiming carefully along the length of the barrel. Without knowing if the new arrival was friend or foe, I chose to err on the side of caution.

The footprints continued along the upper landing, to the door of the room that had been Skylar's. They overlapped one another a bit there, as though the person had paused to look around, then they headed into the room itself. I eased myself down into a crouch-walk as I approached the door, and slid around the corner, ready to fire in a heartbeat.

Then, I lowered my shotgun and stared in shock. "Ryan?"

The befreckled youth almost jumped out of his skin at the sound of my voice. He'd been standing with his back to the door, staring at the blackened remains of Skye's bed, and clearly hadn't heard me come in.

"Sandy!" he exclaimed. "Jesus, what happened here? Is Skye all right?"

I let out a deep sigh of relief, and eased myself back up to my feet. "She's fine. You gave us a hell of a fright, kid. Where have you been?"

"Just... you know, around." He lifted a shoulder in a vague shrug, and stared down at his feet. "I couldn't face it – I couldn't face her – and I had to run away for a while. Clear my head."

"You have a hell of a nerve to come back here," Michael growled over my shoulder; the tone of his voice almost scared *me* out of my skin, because it was one I'd never heard him use before. "You left her when she needed you most. You're the worst kind of coward. How dare you come back here, after what you did?"

Ryan flinched visibly and took a step back away from us. "Look, I-I did what I had to do, you know? I couldn't stay here. I needed to—"

"You ran off and left her!" Michael stepped around me, his face a mask of fury. "She almost died giving birth to your child, and you *left her*! I've half a mind to—"

"Stop it!" I shouted, leaping in to put myself between the two men. I turned to Michael and softened my tone, giving him an appealing look. "Michael, stop. This isn't you. Remember what we talked about? About forgiveness? He's just a kid. Everyone makes mistakes when they're young. Everyone deserves a second chance."

Michael stared down at me, his expression a hostile mask – right up until I lifted my hand, and rested it on his chest, right above the spot where his ring was hidden on its chain around his throat. Then, a flicker of something softer passed through his eyes. He nodded, and looked away.

I breathed a second sigh of relief and returned my attention to Ryan. "We need to get back inside. We're leaving Ohaupo today. Come on."

"If Skye's half as angry at me as I deserve, then I'm probably safer out here," he answered nervously, shifting from one foot to the other as though anxious to flee.

"I have no idea how angry she is." I shrugged and turned away, heading for the door. "She won't talk about it. You're just going to have to find out the hard way."

Behind me, I heard Ryan sigh.

***

By the time we made it back upstairs, breakfast was a charred disaster. I found Skye half way through rescuing as much of it as she could. When I told her who was waiting for her, she dropped her spatula with a clatter, and stared at me in white-faced shock for nearly a minute.

I couldn't blame her. When Ryan had vanished nearly a month before, none of us had really expected him to return.

"He came back?" she whispered. "Why? Why would he come back now?"

"I don't know, but he's waiting out in the lobby if you want to ask him," I answered gently. "You don't have to, though, if you don't want to. I can tell him to go away."

"No, there's no need for that." She shook her head slowly, bit her lip, and looked down at the ground. "I'll go talk to him. Maybe it'll be okay. I mean, maybe."

"Don't let him push you into anything you don't want, okay?" I said, reaching out to my baby sister with a gentleness that I reserved only for her. She nodded and hugged me quickly, then went out to meet her estranged fiancé with a brave face.

Elly and Michael stood nearby, watching the exchange with very different expressions on their faces. Once my sister had left, I gave Elly a long-suffering smile, and Michael a hug. He hugged me back in silence, then detached himself and went off to gather up his belongings.

"There is a lot of tension in this group," Elly observed as she dished up the last of the food for those that hadn't eaten yet. "I hope this will not cause problems later on."

"I have no idea if it will or not," I admitted, accepting the plate that she offered to me. "I guess we'll just have to find out along the road. We can't stay here, so this isn't going to delay our departure."

"Well, eat up, then." Elly smiled at me and gestured towards my plate. "My husband has gone off to fetch the cars that he's repaired for us, and wanted me to tell you that he'll be back soon. Once he returns, we'll need to go."

"Yeah, we will." I stuck a fork into my breakfast and shovelled some into my mouth, trying not to think about how it was going to feel to leave my little home behind. It hadn't been mine for very long, but I had more happy memories in Ohaupo than anywhere else in the last ten years.

As loathe as I was to admit it, I was going to miss that little town. At least this time, I was leaving with a sense of hope in my chest, instead of despair.

***

"All right, here we go. And... up!"

I watched from the side-lines as the men struggled to lift the heavy barrels of fuel up onto the back of one of the new utility vehicles that Zain had managed to scavenge from the outlying farmsteads. The addition of a qualified, experienced mechanic to our team had done a world of good. I would be the first person to admit that I was pretty much just guessing, and had no idea what I was actually doing.

Under Zain's touch, my Hilux was purring like a kitten, and he'd managed to find three more tough, reliable utes to add to our small fleet. Yeah, I was a little jealous of his skills, but I was mostly just relieved. Having cars gave us freedom, and having a real mechanic meant that we could pick and choose rather than going with the ones that I thought I might be able to fix up through trial and error.

Two of the trucks had been relegated for cargo, and the other two for a mixture of cargo and passengers. Now, the women stood guard while the men put their strength to good use, loading everything that we could carry onto the back of the trucks.

"We should be ready to go by mid-morning," I commented, glancing up at the sky. "I don't trust those clouds; I think we'll have rain soon."

"Not much we can do about it," Skye answered, following my gaze up to the darkening heavens. "Let's just hope we find shelter by nightfall."

"We won't – we're sleeping under the stars tonight." I gave her a sideways grin and nudged her in the side. "Good thing we have tarps, right?"

Skye smiled, but didn't say anything. My grin faded away when I realised that she wasn't going to rise to the bait, but I didn't want to call her out on it. She'd been quiet and sullen since Ryan's return, but I didn't really want to push her too hard until she'd had time to recover from the shock. At least she hadn't retreated into herself like when he'd first left, and keeping her active seemed to help her take her mind off it.

"I think that's the last of it," Michael said as he came up to us, dusting off his hands. "Let's go grab your things from upstairs, honey."

"All right," I agreed, leading the way back into our little store. It looked so sad and empty without its layer of trash and junk, familiar objects that I'd gotten used to. For a while, it had been home.

As if sensing my bleak thoughts, I felt Michael's hand fall on my shoulder and I was drawn into a gentle hug. "It's okay, Sandy. We'll find somewhere else. And this time, it really will be ours, won't it?"

"Yeah," I agreed softly. I gave him a weak smile, then went back upstairs to the loft. We had chosen to leave the furniture behind, but we were taking all the blankets and pillows with us, along with the food, cutlery, cookware, and everything else that we had a use for. That had already gone into the trucks, and it left my beloved loft looking strangely barren.

Michael hugged me tight, right at the moment when tears threatened to break through my emotional reserves. With great difficulty, I fought them back and kept myself strong, for myself as much as for him. I knew he wouldn't judge me for crying. The children were already downstairs, waiting safely in one of the new trucks, along with Alfred. Of course, thinking about the dog made me think of my kitten.

"Has anyone seen Tigger this morning?" I asked, suddenly concerned.

"Maddy's got her, don't worry," Michael answered gently, leaning down to press a kiss against my cheek. "When she sat down and put her seatbelt on, Tigger jumped right into her lap, curled up, and went to sleep. I think she's coming whether we like it or not."

"Oh." I took a deep breath, trying to force myself to relax. "That's good, I guess. I mean, I'm sure she'd be fine without us, but... I don't like the idea of abandoning her forever. I'm fond of her."

"I know you are." Michael chuckled softly. He slid his arm around my waist and guided me through the living room, into the bedroom where we'd spent so much of our early relationship getting to know one another. The bed had been stripped, all the medical supplies moved to the trucks, and Anahera had been carried out to the back of the Hilux. The only things left were my personal belongings – my backpack, my salvaged clothing, and the few tiny personal items that I'd collected along the way.

I disentangled myself from Michael's embrace, and went over to finish packing. My backpack was already full, but I had collected a few small suitcases for my spare clothing. No point letting it go to waste. One by one, I emptied the drawers out, and packed the neatly folded garments into the cases waiting for them, then did them up and gave them to Michael to carry downstairs.

Eventually, all that was left was me, my backpack, and my travel items. One by one, I packed my taser, GPS, and medical kit into the pockets of my cargo pants, and put on my backpack. On top of the dresser, a single incongruity stared back at me: the little group of Sylvanian Families bunnies that I'd collected months ago, before I even knew that my sister was still alive.

They were dead weight. Taking them with me would be a waste of space. There had been times when that alone would have been enough for me to leave them behind, but my whole attitude towards life had changed since then. Now, sentiment mattered. It mattered more than anything else in the world. That little family represented my own lost family, and now that I'd found my sister it seemed more important than ever to keep the memory of our parents alive. It took me no time at all to make the decision to bring them along.

Michael had never asked about the bunnies, even though he'd seen them on numerous occasions. He was an intuitive man, so he had probably already guessed what they meant to me. Skylar, on the other hand, shot me a curious glance when I came out the door with the little toys in my hand.

"What are those?" she asked. "I saw them when I was going to the bathroom, but never got around to asking."

"You were probably too young to remember." I smiled at her, then took her hand and put the little family of bunnies in it. "When the plague first arrived in New Zealand, our family travelled through Ohaupo on our way south and we stopped here for a while. You saw these in the old antique store, and begged me to buy them for you. I couldn't, and that made you cry.

"So, consider this my gift to you, baby sis. I couldn't give them to you when you were eight, but I can give them to you now. Hang onto them and keep them safe. One day, one of us will have kids to play with them."

Skylar stared at me with the stunned-mullet expression that she sometimes got when I pulled a real curve ball on her, but I didn't have anything else to say. I just patted her shoulder, and guided her towards her place in the convoy, then went to say my last goodbyes to my store. The door stood open and empty, revealing a room beyond that was dark and shadowy but cleaner than it had ever been before.

"Ah, Benny, if only you could see this place now," I commented to myself. I went through and locked the inner doors one last time, then set the key ring down on the counter. There was no point taking them with me. Unlike when we'd left Hamilton, this time we were leaving nothing behind that we might want to come back for, except our memories. Lots and lots of memories. Thankfully, memories were portable, and they only weighed as much as we let them.

With that thought in mind, I turned my back on my little store, and headed out to the waiting convoy.

Chapter Seven

The rain came around lunchtime. We stopped for a few minutes to shovel down a cold meal, then piled back into the cars, onto the bikes, and resumed travelling. By the time we were on the move again, the rain was pelting down with such force that the fat droplets had our windscreen wipers working overtime.

"Are you sure Hemi and his lads will be all right out there on those little bikes of theirs?" Michael asked suddenly, hunched over the wheel as he struggled to make out the road in front of us. He and I led the convoy in our Hilux, with everyone else strung out behind us along the road south towards Te Awamutu.

"Well, I suggested that they come in until the rain passes, but he said they'd be fine." I shot a glance at him and shrugged. "They know where we are if they change their minds."

"It's going to be a miserable night tonight." He glanced back at me and smiled wryly. "I'm guessing that you plan for us to stop at the same place we spent the night last time?"

"Yeah. It's not dry, but at least it's secure." I returned his smile, and shifted my attention back to trying to fix the radio in my lap. "Like I told Skye, at least we have tarps. We'll rig something up. Gotta be a bit inventive in this day and age, right?"

"True that," Michael agreed dryly. "I think we're about to enter the earthqu—"

Just as he was saying the words, we hit the first break in the tarmac. Years earlier, a terrible earthquake had flattened the city of Te Awamutu, and left the road rippled like a concrete ocean. The jolt took him by surprise, but I'd been watching our position on the GPS so I was braced for it.

I grabbed my walkie-talkie off my belt, and held it up to my lips. "Guys, we're entering Te Awamutu. The ground here is really rough, but your trucks should be able to take it. Go into four wheel drive mode, just in case. Hemi, if you and your boys have any trouble, sing out and we'll put you in one of the trucks."

"We're fine!" Hemi snapped back from somewhere down the line. "It's just a little rollercoaster, like Rainbow's End. We'll – WHOA – we'll be fine!"

"Stubborn, that's what you are," I teased him, then clicked the radio off and looked at Michael. "You wanna take bets on how long it'll be before someone throws up?"

"No bet." He laughed and shook his head. "Honestly, I'm amazed we've made it this far without one of the kids complaining that they need to pee."

"Don't jinx it," I answered dryly.

"What... is that noise?" a voice asked weakly from the back seat. I looked back over my shoulder, and I found Anahera's bewildered face peering back at me. "Sandy? Sandy, is that you?"

"You're awake!" I gasped, surprised and thrilled at the same time. "Thank God. You worried us half to death, Ana. How are you feeling?"

"Terrible," she answered bluntly, slowly lifting a hand to touch her bandaged head. "Where... where am I?"

"You're in a car, heading south with us," I told her. Sympathetic to her discomfort, I grabbed my own water bottle, took the lid off, and held it out to her. "Here, drink this. You've been unconscious for four days."

"Four days?" Her eyes flew wide in surprise. She tried to lean forward, but we'd strapped her in nice and tight to keep her from bouncing around too much while she was unconscious. "Where's Hemi? Where's my son? And Wiremu, Nikora, and Petera? Last I saw them, we were in the pantry, and death was pounding on the door."

"They're all fine," I reassured her. "They're here, in different parts of the convoy. We rescued the four of you from the pantry and brought you home with us, but it was too dangerous to take you back to your camp. Those things are everywhere, so we've all joined together and we're heading south. All of your tribe are with us, except for the ones that... we couldn't get to in time. I'm sorry, Anahera. We saved everyone we could."

"I know," she said softly, sadly. "I know that you would have done everything in your power to save my family. I am grateful that you saved as many as you did." She suddenly seemed to remember the bottle of water I was still holding, and reached out to take it from me. Although her grip was weak, she drank deeply and it seemed to refresh her. When she finished drinking, she handed the bottle back to me, looking a bit more relaxed.

"We did," I agreed. "And we're going to keep doing everything we can to protect your clan, if you agree. I want to combine our groups. If you want to take your men and leave, we'll understand, but—"

"There's no need to explain, Sandy," she interrupted me, a gentle smile touching her lips. "I understand. I was going to suggest the same at our next meeting, anyway. It is a shame that we were not able to gather our things before we left, but our lives are more important than our possessions."

"Yeah." I nodded, screwing the cap back onto my bottle. "There are plenty of things out here for the taking, but we can't replace you, or Hemi, or any of the others. The mutants are spreading, and leaving death in their wake."

"They are." She closed her eyes, her expression turning grim. "I underestimated the threat they posed. Now, I wish we'd taken your warning more seriously."

"Don't blame yourself." I reached back, and rested my hand over top of hers. "We're only just realising what they're capable of. "That's why we're going south. We're going to go as far as we can, and hopefully outrun them."

"What about the others, though?" She opened her eyes, and stared at me intently.

I blinked and stared back at her. "What others?"

"The other survivors," she answered. Suddenly, she grabbed my hand. "There are others out here, though we rarely see them. We must find some way to warn them, or they are lambs to the slaughter. Even the bad ones do not deserve to be eaten."

"I'm all for warning them, but how can we contact them?" I shrugged helplessly. "We had a shortwave radio, but we searched for days and only ever found the folks at the power station, which is where we're heading now."

Anahera went silent for a long moment, then looked me in the eye again. "Avalon. We must go to Avalon."

"...Excuse me?" I stared at her, wondering if she'd been hit on the head a little too hard. Of course, Anahera wasn't one to mince words. She flapped a hand, and quickly clarified what she meant.

"We must go to the suburb of Avalon, in Lower Hutt," she explained. "There, we'll find the Anchorman. He is the only means we have to disseminate information across the entire country."

"The Anchorman? You know where he is?" I asked, genuinely surprised by that news.

"The who?" Michael asked, shooting a confused look at us.

"The Anchorman," I repeated. "The guy who runs the six o'clock news. He's been running it ever since the plague."

"Oh, that guy. Yeah, I think you mentioned him once." His expression turned sheepish. "Sorry, I never watched much television."

"Nothing to apologise for," Anahera said, waving the apology away. She smiled faintly to herself, her eyes drifting out of focus. "He's an old friend. His name is Simon. Simon Wentworth. We knew one another a lifetime ago, back in university, and we used to keep in touch. We haven't spoken recently, but I know that he was working at Avalon Studios around the time when the end came. My bet is that he's still there."

"Okay, so we want to go to Avalon — now there's something I never thought I'd say seriously." I eased myself back into my seat, picked up my GPS, and thumbed in the location. "That's a long, long way south. Almost as far as Wellington."

"It'll get us far away from the mutants, which seems like a very good idea if you ask me," Michael commented dryly.

"No argument here." I chuckled softly, and leaned over to pat his thigh. "We can follow the State Highways south to Lake Taupo, and then try to cut across the Desert

Road from there, but I'm not sure what kind of condition it's in. Last time I was down that way, Mount Tongariro was still erupting."

"Ah, the guilty lovers," Anahera murmured thoughtfully from the back seat. "Yes, let us go visit them. It seems appropriate, though you do not have a husband to betray with your lover."

"I have no idea what you're talking about now," I admitted, glancing over my shoulder at her.

"It is an old legend amongst my people." She smiled at me dreamily, then turned her head and stared off out the window again. "In Maori folklore, different aspects of the natural world are embodied with spirits, just like people. The volcanoes, Ruapehu and Taranaki, were once husband and wife, but while Taranaki was out hunting one day, Ruapehu betrayed him with her fiery lover, Tongariro. Taranaki caught them in the act and fled westwards towards the sea, where he rests to this day, glaring at the traitorous lovers from afar. Ruapehu regrets her infidelity, and sometimes she sighs with longing for him. Tongariro smoulders with jealous anger, for he knows that he can never truly own her heart."

I listened curiously as she told her tale; I knew as much as anyone that the Maori people had legends to explain every aspect of the natural world, but I'd never had the chance to learn that particular one. When she finished the story, I sat quietly for a moment, and then looked at her again. "Were they real people? Ruapehu, Taranaki, and Tongariro? Were the mountains named after them?"

"I don't think so." Anahera laughed and shook her head. "Every tribe has their own variations of the legends. Another one states that there were once seven mountains around Lake Taupo, all male except for the lovely Pihanga. The men fought over her, throwing molten rock high into the air and shaking the ground with their war-dances. In the end, Tongariro won the battle, and with it Pihanga's hand." Suddenly, she grinned. "In that legend, Ruapehu is a male, one of the many vying for Pihanga's love."

"I can't tell if those stories are romantic, or if it's disturbing that no one can agree if Ruapehu is a male or female mountain," I commented, amused. "I mean, surely you could just lift up its skirts and check, right?"

Anahera chuckled at that. "My dear, if you can figure out a way to lift up a mountain's skirt and check its gender, then good luck to you."

***

We reached the campsite overlooking the ruins of Te Awamutu just as the sun was starting to set. The rain was still pelting down, and it drenched me to the bone the moment I hopped out of the Hilux. Ignoring the cold, I raced around to open the gate for Michael. It was the same spot that we'd camped at on our way to Arapuni a couple of weeks earlier, and everything was just as we'd left it. The only difference was that this time, we were leaving for good.

I waited by the gate while each of the trucks drove through, then the outriders on their little motorcycles. Once everyone was safely inside, I heaved the rusty gate closed, and sealed it with a length of heavy chain and an old padlock that we'd brought with us from Ohaupo.

As I wound the chain tight between the bars of the fence, I heard Michael shouting orders. By the time I was done, the trucks had been parked in a ring around our campsite, like a circle of wagons. I paused to admire the simple utility of the action: not only would the trucks serve to protect us from the enemy, but they'd guard us from the wind and rain as well. It amazed me to think about how the tricks used by our ancestors in the early days of colonization had come back into use, hundreds of years later. I didn't have long to think about it, though; there was too much work to be done for me to stand around wool-gathering.

There wasn't enough space in the trucks to bring individual tents for everyone, even if we had enough, which we didn't. Instead, we'd brought along a single huge canvas awning, large enough to shelter us all from the rain. I hurried over to help Michael, who was struggling to lift the heavy pole on his side of the awning. One by one, the other three corners of the awning went up, and we rushed around securing the ground ties to keep it steady.

Michael smiled at me, then leaned down and gave me a quick kiss. "Orders, captain?"

"I thought you were taking command tonight?" I asked, raising a brow.

"Only when you're busy," he answered, a touch of embarrassment flitting across his face. "I prefer to leave it in your capable hands. I never wanted to be in charge. I'd rather be able to focus on just keeping everyone safe."

"Fair enough." I gave him a quick hug, to reassure him that I didn't think any lesser of him for surrendering his leadership position, then I pulled back and did as he asked. "We need a watch for the night. I want four people on guard at all times, one to watch each side. Two rotations, like normal, but give priority to those that won't be driving tomorrow, since they can sleep in the car. Also, I want you to get Priya and that Yousefi boy, what's his name?"

"Matt?" Michael supplied.

"Right." I nodded. "I want Priya and Matt to take a watch. They're old enough to start learning to contribute."

"Good call," Michael agreed. "It'll make them feel more included, too. I'll spare Doc the watch, though — I think he needs his sleep."

"Yeah, spare the wounded." I grinned suddenly and reached up to pat his cheek. "But not me. I'll take a watch. I'm feeling fine."

"If you insist." Michael chuckled, kissed me again, and went off about his business. I allowed myself a moment to savour the taste of his lips, then I went off about mine as well. Thinking about Priya and Matt gave me an idea, another little task to make all the kids feel more included. It seemed odd to put them to work to welcome them, but it was a strange world that we lived in.

I found the two oldest children sitting right where we'd left them on arrival, waiting obediently in the truck with the animals and the younger kids. They looked at me in surprise when I opened the door beside them.

"Hey guys, I need help with something," I told them. "You want a job to do?"

"Yes!" Priya agreed immediately, followed a moment later by Maddy. The Yousefi boys were more reserved; the younger three regarded me silently with large, solemn eyes, but Matt, the eldest, nodded hesitantly.

"Awesome. Now, I'm going to split you into two groups. Matt, Priya, and--" I hesitated for a moment, then looked at the second oldest boy, a scrawny kid of about eleven. "What's your name?"

"Javed," he answered shyly.

I smiled at him and nodded. "Javed. Cool. Okay, Matt, Priya, and Javed, I want the three of you to go over to that old house over there and see if you can find some dry firewood." I turned and pointed past our campsite, at the ruins of the homestead that had once occupied the rear half of the enclosure. "Be careful not to cut yourselves, okay? Bring back whatever you find, and put it somewhere that the rain won't make it wet."

"Okies," Priya agreed happily, practically leaping out of the car. She raced off towards the ruins, leaving the boys staring after her. They exchanged a look, then climbed out and raced after her. Once they were gone, I turned and looked at the three remaining kids.

"You guys are a bit young to go digging around in there, but I have a job for you, too," I explained. Maddy smiled and nodded, but the two younger boys just stared at me. Suddenly, I realised that they were frightened of me – possibly of all of us. It had been a rough few days for all of them, and I was a stranger. "Aw, hey, don't be scared, sweeties. I won't hurt you."

Maddy's smile widened knowingly. "I'm glad you noticed, Miss Sandy. They're very, very, scared."

"I haven't been around kids very much, but I'm learning," I admitted sheepishly. "You hear that? My name is Sandy. That's not a scary name, is it?"

The youngest child just stared blankly, but the older boy was around Maddy's age, old enough to understand what I was trying to say. He shook his head slowly. I smiled at him in return.

"It's not a scary name, because I'm not a scary person." I hesitated for a moment, and decided to channel my inner child a bit. "I'm only scary when the bad monsters come and try to eat you, and then I'm scary to them. I go 'grrr!' and chase the bad monsters away! Remember?"

This time, the boy smiled a little bit and he nodded again. Beside him, Maddy giggled.

"Miss Sandy is very nice, I promise," she added in my defence, then pointed at the boys. "The big one is Barry, and the little one is Ommie. Don't worry, Miss Sandy — they're my friends, so we'll help."

"That's great." Relieved, I reached over and patted the top of the little girl's head. "Thanks, Maddy. What I want you guys to do is start spreading plastic sheets on the ground. No one wants to sleep on the wet ground. The plastic sheets should be in the back of this truck."

"Okay!" Maddy agreed cheerfully. She picked Tigger up out of her lap and set the kitten on the seat beside her, then hopped up and scurried off. Sure enough, the two boys climbed out and followed after her. Once they were gone, I left Tigger to sleep and went off in search of my sister.

I found her few minutes later, sitting on the tailgate of one of the trucks, staring intently at the tip of her left index finger. Curious, I went over to her to see what had her so fascinated. Just as I was getting close, I heard her issue a deep, soulful sigh.

"What's the matter, baby sis?" I asked, suddenly concerned. There hadn't been much time to talk recently, so I had no idea how she was handling the emotional fallout from her painful miscarriage a little over a month before.

"Huh?" She glanced up suddenly, but relaxed when she recognised me. "Oh, hey Sandy. I cut my finger this morning, and it's annoying me. It's not deep or anything, and it's not bleeding, but there's this little flap of skin. It keeps catching on everything, and it's driving me crazy."

I blinked in surprise, then laughed. I just couldn't help it. After everything she'd been through, what made her sound sad was a little flap of skin?

"Gnaw it off," I suggested. "That's what I do. It looks gross, but at least it'll stop catching on stuff."

"You reckon?" She stared at her finger dubiously, then shrugged and lifted her finger to her mouth to do as I suggested. While she was at it, I went over and sat down on the tailgate beside her. It was rare for us to have a moment alone, so I decided it was as good a time as any to check on her well-being.

"How are you doing, Skye?" I asked softly, watching her carefully to gauge her reaction. "With the baby thing, I mean. We've hardly had time to talk at all."

She paused in her nibbling and stared at me for a moment, then shrugged and glanced away. "I'm... coping. It sucks, and it hurts – both physically, and in my heart – but there's no way for us to go back and change the past. At least we learned a lesson from it – listeria poisoning is bad, and now we know how to avoid it. So, when you and Michael have a baby, you won't have to go through that."

"What makes you think that Michael and I are having a baby?" I asked, startled by the notion. We'd talked about it in passing, sure, but mostly just as a joke.

"I've seen the way you look at him, sis," she said with a tender smile. "You love him. You really, really love him. You should have a baby together, because all babies deserve a mother and father that love each other that much."

I stared at her for a moment, then turned away, feeling the heat rising in my cheeks. She wasn't wrong, but that was what made it so difficult to accept. Michael was so ready to be a dad, but I was not ready to be a mother.

"Maybe one day, but not today," I answered. Suddenly, I desperately wanted to change the subject. "So, anyway. I've got the kids finding some firewood. Can I trust you to take care of preparing dinner?"

"Of course," she agreed, rising to her feet. "I'll go see what I can rustle up."

"Thanks, little sis." I gave her a grateful smile. She returned it, and scampered off about her business, leaving me to ponder hard questions on my own.

CHAPTER EIGHT

The night passed more or less uneventfully. Every now and then, one of the watchers called out that they'd spotted something, and once I even thought I heard a growl, but when the sun finally rose there was no sign of danger. If the mutants had followed us, they'd retreated by morning.

We were back on the move as swiftly as possible, following the same road eastwards that we'd used previously. Once we left the earthquake zone, the going was smooth and easy. I napped in the passenger seat of the Hilux for most of the morning, leaving Michael to concentrate on driving. We stopped briefly at the cornfield to bolster our supplies, then we were back on the road again.

Shortly before noon, I felt the Hilux roll to a stop. I dragged myself out of the warm, comfortable embrace of sleep, to find that we'd already reached the point at the base of the hills where the road started to climb up into cliffs and narrow ravines.

"We can't follow the road up there," Michael said, looking at me for guidance. "Remember, there was that break we had to climb around?"

"I remember." I nodded thoughtfully. "We're just going to have to go around the base of the cliff. It's not going to be fun, but at least the rain's cleared up for now."

A few minutes later, I stood with my group spread out around me, enjoying a moment of sunshine while I could.

When the last of them fell into place, I cleared my throat and addressed them.

"All right, guys, we're going off-road for a while," I said. "Unfortunately, there's a bloody great hole in the road up ahead, so we're going to have to take the long way. I need every strong hand that isn't behind the wheel of a car or the handles of a bike out in front, clearing away any obstructions. This is pig country, so everyone stay on high alert. Don't let your guard down. Now, I need two people to ride ahead and scout for the best route. Volunteers?"

The hands of everyone that knew how to ride the bikes – and several who didn't – shot up. I didn't even try to fight my grin. It felt like the bigger our group got, the more people wanted to volunteer to help. They probably just wanted to impress one another, but I didn't mind. It pleased me to see people willing to participate.

"Okay, Skye and Richard," I called, pointing to each of them in turn. "I need you two to find the path of least resistance and guide us to it. Be extra careful, and if you see, hear, or smell anything out of the ordinary, come back. Got it?"

Skylar blinked in obvious surprise. "Really? You want me to go?"

"You put your hand up," I pointed out. "Do you want to go or not?"

"Well, yes, but I didn't actually expect you to pick me," she answered. "You never pick me."

"It's just logistics, sis," I answered, chuckling. "You two are small, agile, and can move quickly, plus I know you can handle yourselves in a fight. Sending you two means I have the stronger lads here to help with the heavy lifting. No offense, Richard."

"None taken," he answered, grinning broadly. Richard was a slender, soft-spoken man, and while he was stronger than he looked, he didn't possess the brute strength of his kinsmen. I smiled back at him, silently acknowledging his understanding.

Skye cocked her head to one side thoughtfully, then suddenly she grinned as well. "Okay, cool! I like this logic. C'mon, Richard. You'll need to show me how to ride."

"Take the quad bikes, they're easier on rough terrain," I called after her.

Once they were off, I turned my attention back to the rest of the group. My group, I realised with a sudden flash of pride. My friends. My family. My... minions? The thought almost made me laugh out loud. Instead, I distracted myself with more logistics.

"Okay!" I clapped my hands and started handing out roles. "Zain, I want you to lead in the Hilux. You know these trucks better than anyone, so sing out if we try to take them somewhere they can't handle. Doc, you're in the second truck with the youngest kids. Ana, are you good to drive?"

"Yes, I should be able to," she answered, nodding.

"Good." I smiled at her, trying to be reassuring. She wasn't quite back to her usual bubbly self yet, but she was definitely on the mend. "Please take the third truck. Elly, bring up the rear. Matt, Priyanka, I want you on watch duty. Do you know what that means?"

"Means we watch," Priya answered immediately, playfully pulling her eyelids back with her fingertips. "We watch for pigs, for bad mens, all bad things. Yes?"

"Perfect." I nodded and grinned at her. "If you see anything bad, or even something you're not sure about, you shout as loud as you can. Okay?"

"Okies!" Priya agreed immediately, nodding. "We watch good. No bads get past us!"

"Very good," I acknowledged, pleased by both her enthusiasm and her quick uptake. I looked at Matt, and gave him a smile as well. "Do you understand what you need to do, too?"

"Yes ma'am," the youth answered quietly. "Watch duty. Anything out of the ordinary, we'll shout."

"Good man," I answered. "Don't hesitate, even if you're not sure. Take Alfie with you. I don't want you two taking any risks, got it?"

Both of the teenagers nodded their understanding. I looked at the rest of the faces in the crowd, and gave them a grin.

"All right, guys," I announced. "Everyone else is with me. Let's get to it!"

***

A few hours later, a cool wind told me that the rain was about to return, and this time it came as a relief. Most of the brush was thin enough for the trucks to just drive through, there were still occasional mounds of deadfall and loose rocks blocking the path. It was hard, heavy labour, and I ended up drenched with sweat in no time at all.

I felt a raindrop land on my shoulder and glanced up at the sky. Dark clouds were rolling in, but they weren't truly threatening. It wasn't a storm, just rain. A few droplets fell on my face, and made me smile.

"What are you grinning at?" Skylar asked.

I jumped at the unexpected sound of her voice, and spun around. "Damn, don't scare me like that. No one told me you were back."

"We just got here," Skye replied. "So, what are you grinning about?"

"Oh, just the rain," I admitted with a shrug. "I like the rain. It's peaceful. Soothing. Washes away all our sins, and leaves the world clean and sparkling."

"It's also wet and cold," Skye said. "Anyway, I need to show you something so we can figure out what to do."

"Okay," I agreed. "Is it far? Should I get a bike?"

"Nah, not far. We can take mine. Richard's back there, talking to Ropata." Skye led the way off into the bush. I grabbed my shotgun and hurried after her. We climbed onto the back of her quad bike, and then we were off.

It only took a few minutes to reach our destination. Skye eased our bike to a stop and pointed ahead of us, but the gesture was unnecessary. I spotted the problem immediately: a shallow stream cut across our path, winding between earthen banks at least a foot high.

"Well, that is a problem," I said, easing myself off the back of the bike so I could take a better look. Skye joined me a few seconds later. "If I remember rightly, we crossed a little to the north on our way home from Arapuni, in the deeper forest. The trucks can't go that way."

"Yeah. We already checked, and this is the only way that isn't blocked by trees," Skye replied, shaking her head. "Unless we want to backtrack for ages, we have to find a way across. Can we build a bridge, do you think?"

"Nah, I don't think we need to," I answered thoughtfully. "We'll just flatten the banks. It'll take a bit of digging, but it shouldn't be too bad." I pulled my walkie-talkie off my belt, and spoke into it. "Michael?"

There was a momentary delay, then his deep voice came on, husky and out of breath. "Yes?"

"Can you please send Richard back this way with shovels?" I asked. "He should be somewhere near you."

"I see him. No problem, I'll pass on the orders. Stay safe."

"Always." I hung up, and put my radio back on my belt. When I glanced back at Skylar, I caught her trying very hard not to laugh. I raised a brow, and gave her a look. "What are you giggling at, little sis?"

"Oh, just you and Michael," she answered dryly. "You're so formal when you know people are watching, but as soon as you think no one's looking, the lovebirds come out."

"Gah, this again?" I threw my hands up in mock irritation. "You're such a gossip fiend."

"Totally am," Skye agreed cheerfully. "What can I say? You're an easy target."

"Don't make me kick your butt, you cheeky miss," I told her, but she must have seen on my face that I was only joking. She just laughed.

"As if!" She planted her hands on her hips, and rolled her eyes dramatically. "I'm your baby sister. You couldn't hurt me if you tried."

"True." I paused, studying her thoughtfully. "Speaking of which, how are you dealing with Ryan being back?"

"I dunno," she admitted with a shrug. "We've... talked, but it's not like it used to be. I'm not sure it'll ever be like it used to be. He's changed so much that I'm not sure he's still the same person I was engaged to."

"Did he tell you where he went while he was away?" I asked, genuinely curious to hear the answer. To my surprise, Skye hesitated.

"He..." She glanced down at the ground, and her expression changed to something I'd never seen before. "He tried to kill himself, Sandy."

"What?" I exclaimed, stunned. "Seriously?"

"Seriously," she said softly, nodding. "Have you noticed that he's always wearing long sleeved shirts now, even though it's not that cold? It's to hide the bandages. He didn't want me to know, but I made him show me. He tried to cut his wrists." Suddenly, there were tears in her eyes, and she was struggling to keep them under control. "He couldn't find a knife, so he tried to use a saw blade. A saw blade!"

"Oh, my God," I whispered, my hands flying up to cover my mouth without any conscious thought on my part. "But he survived?"

Skylar nodded miserably, wiping tears from her eyes. "He said that he passed out in a puddle of his own blood, expecting to never wake up. But he did. He said that he didn't cut deep enough, and he was too scared of the pain to try again."

"Jesus. I think I saw his blood." I plopped down to sit on a fallen log, the strength draining right out of me. "Michael and I did. Just before we left for the power station. We couldn't figure out what happened, so we just... left it. It was a couple of weeks old, so we figured whatever left the blood was long gone."

"It was, sort of," Skye said, wiping away the last tear. "He said he went to one of the farthest outlying farms for a while, and just stayed there. He saw Zain come by when he was out looking for our new trucks, but he stayed out of sight until they left. When he realised that Zain was going back to Ohaupo, he got worried and came to check on us." Skye heaved a long, deep sigh that was painful just to listen to. "I kind of wish he'd stayed gone, but it's hard to stay mad because I understand how he felt."

"Aw, sis," I whispered, shoving myself back to my feet. I went over and put my arms around her, drawing her into a tight hug. "I wish I could make this better for you."

"You can't," she said softly, snuggling up against me. "No one can. I miss Kylie so much, I just... I want to take care of someone's baby, even if it's not mine." She pushed herself back and looked up at me. "Are you sure you won't have a baby with Michael? I'll look after her for you, if that's what you're worried about."

"I can't, honey," I answered, gently stroking her hair back away from her forehead. "Not yet, anyway. Not until it's safe. This journey could take us a couple of months, and I'm pretty sure it would suck to be travelling while pregnant. Right?"

"Yeah," she agreed reluctantly. "But once we find a place to call home, will you consider it?"

"I... I don't know," I admitted. "I'm kind of scared of the idea. I don't know if I could be the kind of mother that you'd be. I mean, I'm pretty crazy, right?"

"You are not crazy!" she yelled suddenly, then she shoved herself back away from me and slapped me hard on the shoulder. "Don't talk about yourself like that. Don't you *dare* talk about yourself like that!"

"Whoa!" Startled, I jumped back away from her, rubbing my bruised arm. "What the hell, sis?"

"That is not you talking," she hissed, stalking up to me to wag a finger in my face like a disapproving school ma'am. "That is Lee talking, and he is dead. You are not allowed to let him control you anymore. Do you understand me?"

"No, I really don't," I admitted. "What are you talking about?"

"This is not you, sis," she repeated, suddenly turning gentle, yet somehow stern at the same time. "The Sandrine McDermott that I remember was a beautiful, confident, intelligent, friendly girl. I remember her. I looked up to her. Maybe I don't know everything that happened to you over the years, but every time you open your mouth and something self-deprecating falls out, it's like I'm hearing someone else's voice coming out of you."

I felt myself flush and glanced away, helplessly trying to derail the conversation with dry humour. "Self-deprecating, huh? That's a big word. You been reading the dictionary?"

"Shut up," Skye told me in no uncertain terms. Suddenly, she grabbed me and shook me hard. The action stunned me so much that I didn't even think about fighting back. "You did this for me once, so now it's my turn to do it for you. Stop trying to sabotage yourself, Sandy. You don't even realise that you're doing it.

"Every time you say something like that, something that puts you down, you're letting someone else's opinion take control of you. Those words are his words, and the way that he controlled you when you were his. You're not his anymore. You beat him. You are your own woman again. You need to learn to stop letting him control how you feel about yourself."

I started to say something, but whatever I was thinking of saying just sort of died in my throat. I wanted to deny it, I wanted to tell her that my words were always my own, but some part of me knew that wasn't true. Suddenly, I realised that the voice of self-doubt that I'd been warring with for so long, it wasn't my voice at all. It was his. It had been his for a long time.

Before I quite knew what was happening to me, I felt my emotional dam breaking down, and the screaming, thrashing, irrational, uncontrollable pain that had been building up behind it broke free. Skylar caught me a moment before I would have collapsed, and held me in her arms while I wept.

Chapter Nine

My fit passed by the time the others joined us, leaving me feeling wrung-out but strangely refreshed. They found us sitting side by side on a log, both of us soaking wet; thankfully, the rain hid the fact that I'd been crying. Michael would no doubt have known at a glance, but he wasn't with them, so I had a brief respite in which to recover.

Richard brought his quad bike to a stop a couple of meters away from us, with Ryan and Nikora close behind him. I shot a glance at my sister to gauge her reaction, but her face was an expressionless mask. She just nodded for me to go ahead, so I rose to my feet and went to meet them.

"Hey, guys," I said by way of greeting. "We need to flatten these banks out so that the trucks can get over them. Skye, Richard, you two keep watch; we can take care of this. When the convoy reaches us, we'll stop for lunch."

"Sounds good," Skye agreed, nodding. She and Richard took up their weapons and went to watch the perimeter, while I took my crew and got to work. I've never been one to dither about when there was something that needed to be done, so I grabbed the nearest shovel and hopped down into the stream. It was only a shallow thing, a slender trickle of water no deeper than my boots. I bent down to examine the banks for a few seconds, then I gestured to Ryan and Nikora.

"Let's shift the dirt over there," I said, pointing a few meters beyond the stream. Ryan nodded silently, but Nikora hesitated.

"Why don't we just fill in the stream?" he asked, shooting me a peculiar look. "Wouldn't that be easier?"

"Easier, yes, but it would damage the ecosystem," I explained. "I'd rather not do that, just to save us a couple of minutes. My ancestors did enough damage to this beautiful land; I want to do whatever I can to preserve her. Don't you?"

The young man looked like he was going to protest for a second, but he stopped before the words left his mouth. He paused and thought about it, nodding slowly.

"True," he admitted quietly. "But it's not just your ancestors to blame. Mine are, too. I think all of us are."

"Exactly." I smiled at him, gesturing broadly towards the natural world around us. "It's down to us now. You, me, and the rest of our tribe. Our choices are the only ones left that can scar Mother Nature's beauty. We have the choice of whether to act responsibly, or irresponsibly."

"Too right." Nikora grinned suddenly, and picked up his shovel. "You're good at this, chica. No wonder they put you in charge."

"I'm only in charge because no one else wants to be," I answered. "I guess Mother Nature is just lucky that I care enough to think about that kind of thing. Come on, let's get started; the convoy will reach us soon."

The two men nodded, and hopped down to join me in the stream. Soon, we were hard at work demolishing the bank, but the rain washed away the sweat as fast as it formed. Every so often, I heard the crackle of the radio on my belt when someone called in to report something, but there was nothing out of the ordinary.

In due time, the convoy reached us just as we'd planned. Skylar shouted a greeting and waved. I stood up straight, running the back of my hand over my forehead to clear the rain from my eyes, and watched as the convoy moved in to park. They had everything under control without me, which left me and my small team to finish up our task in peace.

Soon, the others were settled in and the smell of cooking food tickled my nose. I heard footsteps behind me, and glanced up just in time to catch Michael's sweet smile. He grabbed me around the waist and kissed me quickly, then shoved me back with a good-natured laugh.

"You're wet, muddy, and sweaty, but still somehow manage to be gorgeous," he teased. "I don't know how you do it."

"Thanks for that, honey. You sure know how to make a girl feel pretty," I responded with my usual dry sense of humour, then I leaned up on tiptoes to give him a kiss in return. I caught Ryan looking at us oddly, but he turned away as soon as our eyes met.

"Kissie, kissie, kissie!" Priya's voice rang out, drawing my attention away from Ryan. She flung her arms around us both, and hugged us fiercely. "Kissie for me?"

"Always." I laughed, leaning down to plant a kiss on the top of her head, then I hugged her tight.

Priya giggled and wriggled within my embrace, then she pulled back and looked up at me. "Can I help, Mama?"

"We're pretty much done here," I answered. "You go find Matt, stay on guard duty. You keep the big bads away from the little kids, okay?"

"Okies!" Priya agreed happily. She disentangled herself from us and scampered off just as suddenly as she'd arrived. I looked up at Michael, and found him looking perplexed.

"What?" I asked, raising a brow.

"Mama?" he echoed. "When did that happen?"

"I have no idea," I admitted with a shrug. "Apparently, she just decided. I'm her mama now, and you're her papa. I didn't want to discourage her from bonding with people, so I figured I'd just roll with it."

"Well, that's sweet," he said quietly, a slow smile creeping across his face. "That kid is so far beyond being merely 'resilient' that we need to make up a whole new word just to describe her."

"Let's just stick with 'special', and not in the sarcastic sense of the word." I grinned at him, and gave his arm a playful punch. "Or how about 'inspiring'?"

"Oh, I like that," he agreed. "Let's go with inspiring. That makes her a perfect foster daughter for you, after all."

"If you keep talking like that, you're going to make me throw up." I laughed, shoving him playfully back towards the convoy. "Shoo, Officer Sexy. Go help with lunch. We'll be with you in a minute."

"You got it, boss!" He flailed a dramatic salute and jogged away, leaving me chuckling in his wake. I went to resume the last of the work needed to cross the stream, only to find Nikora watching me with open amusement.

"Hey, now. Don't you look at me in that tone of voice!" I planted my hands on my hips and fixed him with a mock glare. He laughed and started to say something, but his words died on his tongue as a shout rang out from the column. A moment later, the terrible sound of a weapon being discharged shattered the forest's tranquillity.

I leapt out of the stream and was off at a run before my conscious mind even fully realised that there was a threat.

There was a scream and the sound of people shouting, followed by more gunfire. Then, there was a squeal. A blood-curdling squeal. A squeal that I knew very well.

"Pig!" I yelled at the top of my lungs. "Grab your weapons, and find cover! They need space to charge, and they can't climb. If you can get on top of the trucks or up a tree, then do it!"

"Sandy!" Elly screamed my name. Suddenly, she leapt out and grabbed my arm, her expression one of total panic. "It grabbed Ommie!"

"What?" I gasped, frantically searching for the beast; I could still hear it, but I couldn't see it. "Where is it?"

"It went that way!" she cried, pointing past the trucks towards the far end of the convoy. "Please, you have to help him!"

"Stay back, leave this to me," I told her, fighting down the bile that rose in the back of my throat. The thought of what an infected boar could do to a little child... I couldn't bear to think about it. I left her, and ran as hard as I could towards the back of the convoy, following the squeals. The gunfire had stopped now, but the pig's noises were interspersed with heavy thunks and human grunts.

Then, I heard something I never thought I'd have to hear: a young girl's voice raised in anger. "Dumb pig! Look at me!"

Just at that moment, I rounded the last truck in the convoy, and came face to face with a scene right out of my worst nightmares. A few meters in front of me, Ommie's bloody little body lay crumpled in the dirt. Maddy was crouched beside him, tense and alert, her attention fully focused on the battle. A dozen meters further away, Priya and Matt were locked in battle with a large, angry sow.

"No, I said look at me!" Priya demanded, rushing in to strike the beast as hard as she could with a branch. She raced away when it turned towards her, nimbly dodging its bloody teeth. Then Matt leapt forward, struck it from behind, and shouted something to draw its attention back to him. They weren't doing much damage, but they'd managed to lure the beast away from Ommie.

Elly cried out inarticulately and rushed past me, dropping to her knees beside Maddy. I froze for a second, my brain unable to process all the information at once. Then, Priya spotted me. She called out to me, and that made the decision for me. I couldn't do much good for Ommie, but I could still help Priya and Matt.

I left Elly to care for her fallen child and raced past her. The teenagers were doing exactly what they should be doing, but they were just kids. They wouldn't be able to keep it up forever. I crashed through a patch of ferns and leapt over a tangle of fallen branches, all while clutching the shovel in my hands. My shotgun was strapped across my back, but I didn't want to waste the precious seconds required to arm it.

Four more steps, and then I was there. The pig's back was to me. It didn't see me coming. I might not have been as strong as Michael or one of the other men, but I was well-practiced at making my blows felt; my shovel came crashing down on the back of the pig's neck, hard enough to make it stumble and drop to its knees.

Before it could recover, I lifted the shovel high above my head, and brought it down again with every ounce of strength in my body. It struck edge-on, channelling the force into a narrow area, and it had the desired effect. I felt bone crunch and break. I didn't stop, though. I kept hitting it, again and again, until it finally stopped moving.

"Someone go get the accelerant. We have to be certain." I heard a voice behind me, and turned to see Michael coming up to my side, his gun trained on the fallen pig. He gestured to the men standing beside him, and jerked his head towards the nearest vehicle. "I put some lighter fluid in the glove compartment of each car."

I jerked my shovel out of the pig's flesh and stepped back, letting Michael take command of the situation. Priya and Matt came to stand beside me. We watched in silence until the pig was ablaze; only then did I finally remember the important thing I'd forgotten in the adrenaline rush.

"Oh God – Ommie," I whispered, then I turned and raced back to the convoy. There, I found a group of people standing clustered together, whispering amongst themselves. I shoved my way through the wall of bodies, anxiety twisting a knot in my gut. "Please, please tell me that he's still alive."

"He is," Doc answered. "It looks bad, but it's mostly flesh wounds. I'll put in a few stitches and give him a shot to protect him from infections. He should be right as rain in a couple of days."

He glanced up at me, then looked back down at the little boy, who was nestled in his mother's arms. Suddenly, Zain shoved his way through the crowd and dropped to his knees beside her; he wrapped his arms around his wife and child, and hugged them both fiercely. His eyes shone with tears of relief, and I felt a knot of emotion gathering in my own throat in response. When I looked around, I saw that I wasn't the only one affected by the sight.

"Thank Allah." Elly sighed heavily, hugging her child's battered body. "Someone truly is watching over us this day."

The little boy stirred in her arms. His eyes fluttered open and looked up at her. "Mama? Papa?"

"We're here, Omid," Elly said, with the kind of tenderness that only a parent could have. "It's all right, my baby. You're safe."

"Is he okies?" Priya whispered to me. I just nodded and put my arm around her.

"Yeah, he's okay," I answered. "Thanks to you, Priya. You and Matt."

"No," Priya said quietly. I glanced at her, and saw a strange expression on her face, one that I didn't recognise. "Thanks to Maddy."

"What do you mean?" I asked, equal parts curious and surprised.

"Maddy knew," Priya said, turning to look up at me with huge eyes. "Maddy *knew*. She said to me last night that a pig was going to come, and we had to save Ommie or he would die. She told me what we had to do. She made me practice with her, and told me which stick to pick up and keep with me. I thought she was just... strange, but she knew, Mama. How? How she knew?"

"I don't know, honey, but I'm glad she knew." I tightened my grip around her shoulders, pulling her into a hug. "You did the right thing by listening to her."

"The little girl is a prophet?" Suddenly, Zain's voice interjected. I glanced at him, and found him and Elly watching us with wide eyes. "Madeline?"

"I don't know," I admitted, searching for her in the crowd, but now she was nowhere to be seen. I gave up and looked back at Zain. "Maddy has a gift. We don't know exactly what kind of gift, but whatever it is, it's saving lives."

"It's given us much more than that," Elly said, her tone carrying equal quantities of determination and awe. "That child has given us a miracle. You were the one that said to us that we must find our own hope, to save the children. If Madeline is a prophet, then she is the one that can lead us to a new future."

Suddenly, I heard a child laugh. Maddy squeezed through the wall of people and plopped down on the ground beside them, with her hand resting on Elly's arm.

"That's not my job, Missus Yousefi," Madeline told her. She smiled broadly, an expression that made her little face seem almost angelic. "That's Miss Sandy's job. She's going to save the children — *all* of the children, even me." Suddenly, she turned and looked at me, her eyes twinkling. "Isn't that right, Miss Sandy?"

Madeline had a way about her that never failed to take me by surprise. It took me a second to recover, but once I did, I simply nodded my agreement. Maddy beamed for a moment, then her expression turned serious.

"We need to go now," she told us all. "There are more pigs. If we wait too long, then they'll come here as well."

"I don't know about you lot, but that's enough warning for me." I straightened up, and gestured broadly to the people gathered around me. "Sorry, guys. Lunch is going to have to wait. Let's clear the forest, and see where we stand after that."

A chorus of wordless grunts met my instructions, and the crowd dispersed back to their assigned tasks. I waited until Ommie had been transferred to one of the trucks, then returned to the vanguard where I belonged.

CHAPTER TEN

We made it to the edge of the forest safely. A shout from the scouts greeted me as I stepped out of the foliage and back onto solid tarmac. I waved to Skylar, then plucked my radio off my belt and relayed the news back to the rest of the convoy.

Within a few minutes, all the vehicles were lined back up and waiting to go. I did a quick headcount to make sure that no one got left behind, including the animals. Once I was sure that everyone was where they were supposed to be, I climbed back into the passenger seat of the Hilux and we were off. Michael was back behind the wheel again, but this time the only company we had was Alfred in the back. I shot a glance at Michael, and studied the contours of his face in the midday sun.

"You're staring at me," he pointed out without looking at me. "What's up?"

"Nothing," I answered. "I'm just thinking about Ryan and Skylar. Or more specifically, Ryan and Hemi. When Ryan figures out how Hemi feels about Skylar, it's going to be trouble. I can feel it in my bones."

"Ah." Michael nodded thoughtfully, then shot me a quick glance and gave me a smile. "There isn't much we can do about it, so try not to worry. Their relationships aren't our problem."

"It's not them I'm concerned about, it's the structural integrity of the group," I replied, sitting back in my seat and folding my arms across my chest. "Still, like you said, there isn't much we can do about it now. I'm going to try and take a nap. Wake me if you need me."

"Of course." Michael turned his attention back towards the road and fell silent. I shifted around in my seat until I was as comfortable as I could be, then closed my eyes and relaxed. At first, my mind was too busy for me to sleep, but eventually the sound of the rain, the hum of the engine, and the boredom of the road lulled me off to sleep.

***

I snapped awake suddenly, instantly alert but uncertain what had woken me.

"What is it?" I demanded. "What's going on, what's wrong?"

"Nothing at all," Michael answered. I glanced at him, and found him peering at me curiously. "Everything is absolutely fine. We just passed Pukeatua, and we should reach Arapuni in another hour."

"Oh." I paused for thought, suddenly feeling a little bit stupid. "That's good. Sorry, it seems like whenever I sleep in the car, I wake up to bad things happening."

"You do have some particularly bad luck in that regard," he agreed, an amused smile dancing across his lips. "But, not this time. Everything's fine. Let me guess: you were having the shoe dream again, weren't you? You always wake up stressed out after the shoe dream."

"Argh, I never should have told you about that," I groaned, covering my face with my hand. "Yes, I was having the shoe dream again."

"It's okay, honey," he said, his tone deep and soothing. "Tell me about it. What was it this time?"

"Well, I guess there's no point trying to hide it." I sighed heavily, and shot him a long, sideways glance. "Sparkly purple pumps. They were awful and magnificent at the same time, but I didn't have enough money to buy them."

"So, what did you do?" Michael asked. His expression was one of eternal patience, even in the face of my stupid recurring dreams.

"Same thing I always do," I admitted. "I stole them. I ran out of the shop wearing these stupid purple stilettos, but then they turned into roller skates. I was skating down the street, wearing sparkly purple pumps. And then the police were chasing me, and—" I stopped mid-sentence and stared at him, suddenly embarrassed.

"—and I was the police officer, wasn't I?" Michael finished for me.

"Yes, but after you arrested me, you started taking your clothes off." I looked away, feigning interest in the foliage on the side of the road. "And you can guess where it went from there."

"Your recurring shoe nightmare turned into a sex dream?" Michael asked incredulously. "You really are a worry, Sandy."

"I know!" I groaned and covered my eyes again. "I don't even know what it is. I'm not obsessed with shoes or anything. I mean, they're all over the place! They're right there for the taking. If I wanted sparkly purple pumps, I could grab some out of any store, and no one would care. So, why does my subconscious turn me into some kind of kleptomaniac shoe fiend all the time?"

"I suspect it has something to do with issues of possession," Michael answered, his voice turning serious. "You mentioned your philosophy, about everything you possess having to be carried on your back from place to place. I think some part of you hates that, and desperately wants to own something pretty and completely frivolous. That's not such a bad thing, Sandy. In fact, once we find a place to settle, I'm going to bring you lots of pretty, frivolous things. I bet that will put an end to your nightmares."

"You think?" I looked at him, far more curious than I had any right to be. "I mean, I don't need any of that stuff. It's not practical. In fact, it's the opposite of practical. We probably shouldn't waste any time on it."

"Just because we live in a post-apocalyptic world doesn't mean that you can't have nice things, honey," he told me firmly, reaching over to take my hand. He gave it a squeeze and smiled at me. "You want to take a turn driving, to distract yourself?"

"Sure," I agreed. "Let's change over all the drivers for the rest of the way. I'm sure the morning drivers could use a rest."

"No kidding," he commented dryly. "Watching you nap was putting me to sleep."

"Well, that doesn't sound very safe at all." I laughed; somehow, Michael always knew just the right things to say to cheer me up when I was feeling down, no matter what the reason was. He just gave me that dopey grin I loved so much, and eased the Hilux over to the side of the road. By the time I'd conveyed the order to switch drivers, he had already climbed out, and come around to open the passenger door for me.

I felt strong arms around me before I even realised that he was there. He undid my seatbelt, guided me out, and wrapped me up in a hug. It was just a brief hug, but it was enough to make my heart race.

"How is it that you always make me feel like a teenager again?" I asked. "In the good way, I mean. Not the grumpy, hormonal, puberty-is-kicking-my-ass way."

He just laughed, of course. "Are you blaming me because you feel good? Again?"

"No!" I exclaimed, shoving myself out of his grip. I planted a quick kiss on his cheek, and raced around to the driver's side. "It is your fault, though."

"I am more than happy to accept the blame for that," he said cheerfully. While I was buckling up and getting myself ready, he reached over and picked up my radio. "Everyone ready to go again?"

"We've been ready for a while, but you were too busy groping our illustrious leader to notice." Skylar's voice crackled through the radio, laced with a heavy dose of sarcasm. My automatic response was to turn red as a beetroot, but thankfully no one was there to see it.

Well, no one except Michael. And he loved it, because it really was entirely his fault.

***

As it turned out, Michael hadn't been kidding about his desire to indulge in a nap. Within a couple of minutes, he nodded off to sleep with his head resting against the glass. I shot a quick glance at him and smiled to myself, then returned my attention back to the not-so-arduous task of driving.

The roads east of Pukeatua were in decent enough condition, compared to some of the other ground we'd covered. We were still in pig country, though, so I kept myself alert for trouble in all its forms. Of course, thinking about pigs turned my mood sour. To lighten it, I distracted myself by trying to think up ways to improve my group's overall chances of success. Eventually, an idea began to form in the back of my head. I picked up the radio and spoke into it.

"Doc, you there?"

A few seconds later, Doctor Cross' voice came on the line. "I'm here. What can I do for you, Ms McDermott?"

"I want to discuss something," I replied. "First, though – how's Ommie?"

"Young Master Omid is doing very well, thank you," the doctor replied. His voice was even and calm, and immediately relaxed my nerves.

"Oh, good." I sighed heavily, and made no attempt to conceal my relief. "Is he awake?"

"Very much so," Doc answered. "In fact, he seems to be more loquacious than he was before the accident. The children were trying to play I Spy earlier, but it somewhat failed due to the fact that Omid isn't terribly good at spelling yet. So, Madeline has taken it upon herself to improve his reading, and she's teaching Priyanka as well. At this rate, I won't even need to hold lessons myself anymore."

I couldn't help but laugh at that. "That's great news. I don't suppose you've had a chance to assess the other Yousefi kids yet? "

"I have, actually," he said. "Mrs Yousefi tells me that she's been teaching them as much as she can along the road, and she's done an excellent job of it. All four of them are fluent in both English and Farsi, and they have a grasp of mathematics and science well beyond their years. She's quite the teacher, if I do say so myself."

"And I have told you to call me 'Elly', Doctor," a third voice intervened, crackling through the radio in my hand. "But, I thank you for the compliment nevertheless."

"Hey, Elly," I greeted. "I thought you were with the kids?"

"There wasn't enough room," she answered. "I opted to let the good doctor ride with the children, since he can take better care of Ommie at the moment. Besides, it has given me an opportunity to get to know your friend Anahera."

"Ahhh." I nodded my understanding, even though none of them could see it. "I bet you two are getting along like a house on fire. You're cut from the same cloth."

"I like to think that we are, yes," Elly answered.

"Good." I paused for a moment, then took a deep breath and continued. "Speaking of Anahera, is she there?"

There was a moment of silence, then the voice changed to Anahera's. "Yes, Sandrine; I'm here. How can I help?"

"I've got a project for you and Doc," I replied. "We need to start thinking about ways to improve the survivability of our group, and I think the best way we can do that is through education. I don't just mean the kids, either – I want you to go through the entire group, and work out who has skills they're willing to teach. Pair them up with people that want to learn."

"You mean the way you've been picking Zain's brain when you think no one's watching?" Doc asked dryly, his voice carrying a note of deadpan humour.

"We had been trying to avoid making a big deal out of it, but yes, exactly like that," I agreed just as dryly, more amused than annoyed that he'd let the cat out of the bag. Why shouldn't I be the first to do what I was asking the others to? "Talk to people, see what they're interested in. I want everyone to have important basic skills like self-defence, cooking, first aid, driving, and how to start a fire, but we also need to start planning for the long-term survivability of more complex skills. I mean, what would we do if we lost you tomorrow, Doc?"

"To use your own terminology, you'd be pretty much screwed," he replied dryly. "I'm happy to help, of course."

"As am I," Anahera added. "We'll take care of it, don't worry. But, while we're speaking, there is something urgent we need to discuss. I feel it's critically important that we find some way to warn the other people in the Waikato as soon as possible."

"Isn't that why we're going to Avalon Studios?" I asked, uncertain what her point was.

"Well, yes," she answered dryly, "but it'll take us weeks to get there, perhaps even months, and by that stage the entire population of the Waikato may very well have been wiped out. We can't allow that."

"All right," I acknowledged, nodding thoughtfully. "You have a fair point. What's your suggestion?"

"At this stage, I don't know." There was a long sigh on the other end. "But we need to do something. It is our duty to try and save as many as we can, even if all we do is warn them to be away as soon as possible."

"Okay, so we keep our eye out," I said. "If anyone has any ideas or sees anything useful, sing out. Otherwise, we're going to have to keep going and hope for the best. We're almost at Arapuni. Once we get there, I want to find us somewhere secure to bed down for the night. If I remember right, there's a big, empty warehouse somewhere in the north of the town. We should be able to get all the trucks in there and lock the door."

"But we still have a few hours of daylight left," Michael spoke up suddenly in the seat beside me.

I shot a startled glance at him. Everyone else had heard the comment while I was speaking, so I answered them all. "Yes, but we're going to try and convince Rebecca and Jim to join us. If they agree, then they'll need time to get ready. I want you guys to spend the time foraging. Look for clothing and footwear, specifically. We need to get some stuff for Anahera and her blokes, otherwise they're going to be stuck wearing the same thing until their body odour leads the mutants right to us."

A chorus of guffaws and chuckles punctuated my joke. I grinned to myself and put the radio down, then I shot a glance at Michael. "I thought you were sleeping?"

"And I thought you were driving," he countered, grinning right back at me. "I slept for a bit, but you woke me up. My little social butterfly."

"Oh God, that again?" I groaned and rolled my eyes heavenwards. "If I have to be the boss, then I have to act like the boss, and that includes pretending that I know what I'm doing."

"Well, you certainly do a good job of it." Michael leaned over, and pressed a kiss against the curve of my neck, which sent a shiver all the way down my spine. "Have I told you how sexy it is when you get all commanding?"

"No, and I'm not sure that you should right now," I answered, shooting him an alarmed look. "Do you really want to distract me while I'm driving?"

"Maybe not," he answered with a chuckle, easing himself back into his own personal space. "Sorry. We haven't been getting much private time lately, and ever since you freed the genie..."

"That's what we're calling it now?" I teased, giving him a wicked grin. "That does seem kind of appropriate, considering what happens if I rub it just right."

Michael froze, staring at me, then he burst out laughing so hard that he couldn't speak for several minutes. By the time he got himself back under control, we'd crossed the top of Arapuni dam, and turned north towards the power station, and the township.

"Phew," he gasped when he finally started to sober up. "Thanks, I needed that."

"You're more than welcome," I answered brightly. "Now, if you're done, I need you to do something."

"Anything," he agreed immediately.

"Good." I gave him an appreciative smile, then focused back on the road. "I want you to take Hemi, and go bring Rebecca and Jim to talk to us."

"Oh, so you give us the dangerous mission, while you guys slack off scavenging?" He made an indignant sound, but when I glanced at him, I could see on his face that he was only kidding.

"Hah! You're not getting out of scavenging duty that easily, mister," I told him dryly. "I just think it's best if you two go since you're familiar, and I don't want to cross that damn bridge again."

"Fair enough." He laughed and nodded his agreement. "Of course, honey. Wish me luck."

"Good luck," I replied with a knowing grin. "You're gonna need it."

Michael just sighed dramatically, and rolled his eyes heavenwards.

Chapter Eleven

It took us less than an hour to find what we were looking for. My mental encyclopaedia was not infallible, but it was generally pretty good. Once our vehicles were safely stowed inside the warehouse, Michael and Hemi departed and I gathered the remaining people around me to hand out duty assignments.

"Okay, guys," I called, vaulting up to stand on the Hilux's bonnet again, so that everyone could see me. "Doc, Anahera, I'd like you on babysitting detail, please. The rest of you, I want you to break up into pairs and head out into the town. We need clothing, footwear, petrol, and any toiletries you can find. Also keep an eye out for fishing gear. If you can find any, that'll help us supplement our food supply as we travel. Skye, can you think of anything else we need?"

"We could use a couple more sharp knives, and another can opener or two," she called back. "And more propane to power the stoves." She paused and glanced at Doc. "Oh, what was it you asked me about the other day?"

"Citrus," Doc supplied, adjusting his spectacles. "Any kind of citrus. I'm slightly concerned about everyone's vitamin C levels with winter coming on, and want to make sure we're getting enough in our diets. Lemons, oranges, grapefruit, anything you can find."

"Speaking of winter," I added once he was done. "Keep an eye out for clean blankets, sleeping bags, and tents. It's not going to be fun being out in the weather without a few conveniences. If you find something and aren't sure if we need it, bring it back anyway. Better safe than sorry. Everyone good?" A chorus of agreement met the question. I smiled and nodded. "Right, let's get to it, then!"

A spontaneous cheer went up from the crowd, for reasons that I couldn't define. It pleased me, though, knowing that people were more or less content with my leadership. One by one, my companions paired off, picked up their weapons, and headed out into the streets of Arapuni. Soon, the only people left were me, Skylar, and the folks that were staying with the youngest kids.

I shot a glance at Anahera and Doc, and gave them a reassuring grin. "I hope you two don't mind being left behind."

"Not at all," Doc answered dryly. "My back is too old to go out there lugging goodness-knows-what around, anyway. I'm more than happy to leave that for you young folk."

Anahera chuckled softly and nodded her agreement. "While I would be more than happy to help, I appreciate that you must consider me as one of the walking wounded today. I shall turn my efforts towards taming these little monsters instead. The good doctor and I can begin training them in the vitals."

Madeline laughed merrily, and the Yousefi boys gave us grins so naughty that the rest of us laughed as well.

"Come on, Skye," I clapped my sister on the shoulder when the levity subsided. "Let's go see what we can find."

Just as I was turning away, a young voice cried out to me. "Wait!"

I turned back, to find Javed rushing after us.

"I want to come," he told me, his face a mixture of anxiety and excitement. "Please?"

"Oh? We're just going foraging." I raised my brows, genuinely curious. It was the first time that any of the boys had shown an interest in the activity around them, including Matt. While the eldest Yousefi boy did as he was told, he never looked pleased about it.

"I know." Javed took a deep breath, and puffed out his chest; it took all of my willpower not to melt into laughter at the sight. "But I'm almost an adult! I want to help. May I please help?"

My barely-hidden amusement vanished in the face of his earnestness. "Well, of course you can, if you want to. Stay close to us, though. Don't go out of our sight, okay? If you see something you want to investigate, tell us."

He grinned, and nodded in agreement. "Yes, ma'am!"

"Well, all righty then." I laughed and led the way out the door and back into the muted sunlight. Heavy clouds still obscured the sky, but the rain had passed for the moment. I glanced back, and watched as Anahera slid the door closed behind us, locking herself and the others safely inside.

"I saw a house back that way that looked pretty much intact," Skylar suggested, pointing deeper into town. "Shall we go check it out?"

"Sounds good." I unslung my shotgun, and moved it around to rest in the crook of my arm. "Lead on, little sis."

Just as he'd promised, Javed stuck to me like glue the entire way. When we reached the front door, he watched with interest as I picked the lock. I beckoned him closer so that I could show him what I was doing. He was a quick study; within a matter of minutes, the door swung open to let us into the dusty interior.

"Why was the door still locked?" Skye asked, coughing and waving her hand in front of her face to chase away the dust. "Surely those two down at the power station scouted this place."

"They have an entire town to themselves," I answered with a shrug. "I guess they just never needed to. Or maybe they did, but locked it up when they left. Check the pantry, we'll know soon enough."

Skye nodded and passed through a doorway into a dusty dining room. I headed towards the back of the house, to check out the other rooms. I felt Javed close behind me as I made my way across the faded carpet, but neither of us said anything. Ever-cautious, I eased myself into a defensive crouch and slowly opened the first door that I came across.

Nothing leapt out at me, except for a few ancient dust bunnies. I waved them away and took a quick look around the room. It wasn't much, just an old storage room, with a bunch of boxes along one wall, and a few pieces of furniture beneath drop-cloths that had long since become obsolete. I heaved a sigh and eased myself back up straight.

"Javed, can you please take a look through those boxes and see if there's anything useful?" I asked, gesturing towards the crates under the window. The boy nodded and hurried off, leaving me to investigate the rest of the house on my own.

At the far end of the hall, I found three closed doors. The first opened into a linen cupboard, and the second into a small bathroom. By the time I reached the third door, my nerves were on edge. Something wasn't right. It wasn't something I could see, though. It was something I could smell. I smelt the pungent odour of decaying meat.

I took a deep breath and braced myself, one hand on the door handle and the other on my gun. Instinct and experience told me that whatever I found wasn't going to be pretty. Still, better I see it than Javed or Skye. I silently counted to three, and then I swung the door open.

The wall of stench that hit me almost made me retch. In retrospect, I was glad that we hadn't taken the time to stop for lunch, so there was no chance of me losing it all over the floor.

"Jesus, what is that?" Skye demanded. I jumped, and shot a startled look over my shoulder.

"Just... stay out of here," I ordered. "I mean it. Please?"

"Yeah, I'm not fighting you on this one." She wrinkled up her nose and vanished into the bathroom instead. I sighed softly and turned back to the opened doorway, staring into the gloom within.

It wouldn't be the first time that either of us had seen a dead body, and it wouldn't be the last. Still, it didn't feel right to subject my little sister to yet another dose of horror when she'd already been through so much, and I definitely wanted to protect Javed. As much as I loathed what I had to do, I put my feelings aside and stepped into the room.

The lights flickered when I touched the greasy switch, but after a moment they steadied. I almost wished they hadn't, as if that could protect me from the sight of two corpses snuggled in bed together, their flesh almost entirely rotted away. Shrivelled eyeballs stared at me blankly from beneath eyelids that had pulled back due to the natural mummification of age.

I wanted to take another deep breath, but that would only make the stench of putrefaction worse. I pulled my faithful cloth out of my pocket, and tied it over my mouth and nose. The perfume had begun to fade away, but it was enough to at least keep the stench at bay for a couple of minutes while I searched the room.

A few strands of grey hair lay on the pillows, which told me that the couple had been elderly when they died. I stepped around the bed with as much respect as I could, and went over to rifle through their drawers and the wardrobe in the corner. All I came away with was a couple of woollen jerseys that were in fairly decent condition, and a dozen pairs of socks. Everything else was beyond salvaging.

"Sorry," I whispered to the couple as I made my way back to the door, then closed it up tight behind me. Sure, I could have searched more thoroughly and maybe come away with something else, but... it felt wrong. I wanted to leave the elderly couple to their eternal slumber in peace. Still, some part of me thought that they'd like to know that their belongings would help to prolong the human race well beyond their own expiration date.

I found Skylar in the bathroom, digging through a medicine cabinet and tossing assorted jars, bottles, and boxes into the sink beneath it. She glanced up at me, and jerked her head towards a small stack waiting on the floor by the door.

"I've got a few bars of soap, and a tube of toothpaste that's still sealed, plus some assorted medicine for Doc to look through," she told me. "Nothing much in the kitchen besides a few cans of spaghetti. What did you find?"

"Just a couple of jumpers, a few pairs of socks, and some dead people," I answered, tossing my findings down on top of hers. I unslung my backpack and set it down at my feet, then began folding things and stuffing them into the bottom for easy carrying.

"Oh." Skye paused and stared at me, then she shuddered. "Yeah, okay. No wonder you didn't want me going in there."

"Sorry. I know you hate being treated like a baby, but there are some things that I don't want to subject anyone to if I can avoid it." I heaved a long, long sigh, and tried to distract myself with packing the toiletries into my bag. But when I picked up the toothpaste, I paused for a second to look at the label. "Uh, Skye? This isn't toothpaste. It's haemorrhoid cream."

"What?" Skye turned and stared at me, her expression one of total bewilderment. "What's haemorrhoid cream? And how do you spell that?"

"I have no idea how you spell it," I admitted, "but it's supposed to help when your butt starts bleeding."

"Oh!" she exclaimed. "I had that when I was pregnant. It sucks. I didn't know there was a treatment for it."

"It's probably long past its use-by date, but we'll take it back to Doc anyway." I tossed the box into my backpack, and carried it over to her. "Here, put whatever you want to take back in here. I'm going to go check on Javed."

"Sure," she agreed cheerfully. I patted her on the shoulder and left the room.

I found Javed exactly where I'd left him, except now it looked like a small tornado had gone through the storage room. The boxes had been torn open, and their contents lay scattered across the floor. In the middle of the room, Javed sat cross-legged, staring fixated at something on the ground in front of him.

I stepped over a mound of old photographs, and came up behind him. "Hey, kiddo. What have you got there?"

The youth jumped, and shot a startled look back over his shoulder. Once he recognised me, he relaxed and held something up for my inspection. "I don't know. What is this?"

"It's a train," I answered, kneeling down beside him to get a better look at it. "Not a real one, of course. It's a toy train. I bet it used to belong to a little boy just like you, back before the plague."

"A toy?" he asked softly. "My brother uses that word sometimes. What does it mean?"

My heart just about broke at the look on his face. I eased myself down to sit beside him, and reached out to take the train from him. "A toy is a plaything for kids. Sometimes they're for learning, but mostly they're just for fun. This one is a model train. You see this word here? That's the stamp of the people that made it."

Javed took the train back, and turned it over to inspect the undercarriage. He wrinkled his face up, and slowly read the letters out loud. "Märklin Trains... where's Märklin?"

"It's not a where, it's a what," I explained. "That's the name of the people that made this train, and probably the rest of the train set, too. It's from a place called Germany, which is a country a very, very long way away." I paused, and glanced down at the carriages scattered on the floor. "My dad used to collect these, back when he was still alive."

"Oh." Javed went quiet for a moment, then he gave me a long, thoughtful look. "I'm sorry your dad is dead."

"It's not your fault," I said, reaching out to squeeze his shoulder. "I still have my sister. Just make sure that you take care of your mum and dad while you can, okay?"

"Yeah," he agreed softly. He frowned to himself, then looked at me again. "Some people say it's our fault the plague came. My mum said they were lying, but I don't know. Is it our fault?"

"No," I told him firmly, shaking my head. "It's not your fault. It's not anyone's fault. The plague would have come here one way or another, that's the nature of a plague. You and your family are innocent."

"But then why are my mum and dad alive, and yours are dead?" the little boy asked, looking so crestfallen that for a second I thought he was going to cry. "Maddy told me that her parents died, and Priyanka's, and everyone's, but mine are still alive. Why? Why do I get a family, but no one else does? It's not fair."

"Hey, hey, it's okay." I reached out and put my arms around him, to draw him into a hug. He resisted at first, but once the tears finally broke through he slumped against me. "It's *not* your fault, Javed. It's just pure chance. Some people have this immunity, and some people don't. You were just lucky enough to have two parents who are immune, which is why you guys are immune."

"Then why did my sister die?" the boy demanded, rubbing his cheeks as though to banish the tears, but they were insistent. "God punished us for bringing the plague."

"Your sister?" I froze, staring at him. "You had a sister?"

"Yeah—well, sort of." He sighed deeply and shrugged. "When Mum had Ommie, there were two babies inside her – twins, I think it's called. One boy and one girl. Ommie came out first, but when our sister came, she... she wasn't right. She didn't cry. Mum and Dad told me that she was born dead, but she wasn't. I saw her. She was alive, but there was something wrong with her. Mum cried for days and days, then she made us pack up and move on. When we left, she didn't bring our sister with us."

"Oh, God," I breathed, shocked by the story. "So it's true... Oh, my God, it's true..."

"What's true?" he asked innocently, looking up at me.

"Nothing." I took a deep breath to steady myself, and wiped my eyes with the back of my hand. "God isn't punishing you, Javed. It's not your fault that this happened. Promise. I'll tell you what, I'll make you the same deal that I made Priya. If you want, you can bring the train with us, but if we end up walking, then you'll have to either carry it yourself or leave it behind. How does that sound?"

"I can have it?" He stared at me wide-eyed, all thoughts of dead families forgotten. "This train? I'm allowed to have a toy?"

"I don't see why not." I summoned a smile for him, doing my best to shove aside the disturbing topic as well. "I do have to put in a clause for your mother's sake, though. You have to share it with your brothers, okay?"

"Okay!" Javed's expression lit up. Suddenly, he leapt to his feet and rushed around gathering up the pieces of the train set so that he could shove them back into the box they'd come from. I smiled as I watched him, right up until I heard Skylar whoop in delight from the back of the house. Her words were some of my favourite words ever, words that would never lose their potency even after a decade of living in the ruins of our old world.

"Yes! Yes! I found toilet paper!"

"Woohoo!" I cheered, throwing my hands up in the air. Javed shot a bewildered glance at me, but didn't seem to care either way. "Well, I guess that's a girl thing, then."

"What is?" Skye asked, trundling into the room with my backpack over her shoulder, and the sealed package of toilet paper under her arm. It was so old that the plastic wrapping had faded to clear, but the paper itself looked fine.

"The toilet paper thing," I explained, gesturing at Javed. "Kid's more interested in his train set."

"Oh!" She laughed merrily. "Yeah, definitely a girl thing. Boys can be so gross sometimes."

"They sure can." I chuckled as well, and gave her a quizzical look. "Are we all done here, then?"

"I think so." She shrugged off my backpack and handed it to me, and I put it on my shoulders. By the time we were done, Javed had joined us, watching expectantly with the faded train set clutched against his chest.

"Let's head off, then," I suggested. I took point and led the way down the hall, out of the front door, and across the overgrown lawn towards the street. Along the way, I paused to check the mailbox; I'd found more than a few little treasures in them over the years. Sure, it was mostly just stacks of old bills and irrelevant junk mail, but every now and then you struck gold. As it turned out, today it was the latter.

"Hey, what have you got?" Skye asked curiously as I pulled the package out of the mailbox.

"Not sure, but it can't hurt to look," I answered. I turned the package over, and examined the label to try and work out who the sender was, but it was illegible. Skye and Javed came up behind me to watch as I tore open the package.

"Honey?" Skylar shot a bewildered glance at me. "Why would someone have mailed these people honey?"

"It was a thing, back in the day," I answered, excitement rising in my breast to replace the darker thoughts. "Mail-order honey. That means this'll be the good quality stuff. Oh man, Doc's going to be thrilled."

"It'll be nasty after all this time, won't it?" Skye asked, looking at me with interest. "The stuff's just like... sugar and bee spit."

"Actually, honey is one of the few foods that never expire," I explained. As I spoke, I crouched down and set the box at my feet, so I could examine the contents without the risk of dropping it. Inside, four sealed jars of perfect, translucent sweetness sparkled up at me. It was a sight that made me smile. "A few years after the plague hit, I met this guy down south. Up until then, I'd been surviving on trial and error, but that guy was ex-military and a survivalist. He knew a bunch of stuff. He taught me about honey."

"Oh, yeah?" Skye grinned and wiggled her eyebrows. "He taught you about honey, huh?"

I shot her a dark look. "It wasn't like that. We were just friends. He was a lot older than me, and treated me like a daughter, or at least a sister. Anyway, honey lasts forever if it's stored in an air-tight container without any impurities. There are a couple of other foods with an indefinite shelf-life, but honey is the only one that you can eat without cooking. It's a godsend when you're starving and desperate. It's also one of the most powerful all-purpose medicines that the natural world has to offer, so this stuff is going straight into Doc's medicinal stores."

"Oh." Skye stood back, watching as I closed the box and picked it up, then she and Javed both followed as I resumed our trek back to our bunker. She was silent for a few minutes, then she shot me a curious look. "So, what happened to him? You made it sound like you've been entirely alone for the last ten years. You haven't mentioned any friends before."

"There have been a few times when I had companions for a while," I admitted. "But it never ended well. I've been alone for the vast majority of the time. I spent about six weeks with him, but one day he just vanished. There were some gangs starting to develop in the area at that time, so it was getting dangerous for us. He'd taught me that if he didn't come home, I was to go to ground. So, that's what I did. I never saw him again."

"Well, that sucks." Skylar sighed heavily, folding her arms across her chest. "Sorry. Didn't mean to stir up bad memories."

"It's okay." I glanced over at her, and gave her a smile. "He's not a bad memory. In fact, he's one of the few good memories I have from that period. At the time we met, I was having trouble finding enough to eat. He taught me a lot of little things that have helped me to survive over the years, and now I get to teach them to the kids. Right, Javed?"

"Yup!" the boy agreed, even though it was clear he wasn't paying the least bit of attention to either of us. Skye and I laughed.

"Mama!" A voice in the distance called out. I paused and turned to look. A few seconds later, the voice called out again. "Mama, I heared you. Where are you?"

"Over here, Priya," I called back.

There was a rustling sound, then Priyanka appeared on the other side of a tangle of overgrown shrubs, with Matt right behind her. "Mama, we found the stinky stuff that's food for the cars! You come see, please?"

"Sure, sweetie," I agreed. I turned to Skylar, and offered her the box of honey. "Make sure this gets to Doc safely?"

"'Course." She took the jar and tucked it under her arm. "I can take your backpack, too."

"Thanks." I slipped the pack off, and handed it to her with a smile. "I'll see you guys soon."

"Stay safe," she said by way of farewell, then with a wave, she and Javed were off. It wasn't far back to the warehouse and Skye had her gun with her, so there was no valid reason to worry about them. I hurried over to meet up with Priyanka and Matt.

As soon as I found a way around the jungle that had once been someone's hedge, Priya threw her arms around my waist and hugged me. Then, she grabbed my hand and dragged me off without a word. We passed down a street and ducked through an alleyway that terminated beside an old gas station.

At some point in the past, someone had cracked open the underground tanks and started to syphon out the contents, but they'd stopped half way through the task. A large barrel, half-filled, sat on the forecourt with a length of hose still leading back to the tanks, but now both were gathering cobwebs. I detached myself from Priya and went over to inspect the barrel, but before I got within a few meters I knew that the petrol was unusable.

"Sorry, Priya. This stuff is stagnant," I told her gently. Taking the opportunity to educate them both, I lifted a finger to touch the tip of her nose. "Do you smell that?"

"Yeah. Smells like bads." She glanced over at the tanks. "Car food is bads?"

"Unfortunately." I sighed and put my arm around her. "Petrol – the stuff that the cars eat – can last for years and years if it's stored in underground tanks, or in metal containers, but if even a little bit of water gets in then it'll... it'll go bad. Just like how people can't eat bad food, if we try to make the cars eat bad petrol it'll make them sick."

"Oh." Priya's expression sagged, but she didn't have time to mope. A second later, Matt drew a sharp breath.

"Someone's coming," he whispered, taking a nervous step back. I turned to look, just as the shouting started.

"Oi!" Jim yelled, already red in the face and angry. "Just because we asked you buggers for help one time doesn't give you the right to come traipsing all over our land whenever you feel like it!"

"Hold up, mate." I raised my hands in a placating gesture. "We're here for a good reason. Just hear us out, okay?"

"Jim, stop being an ass." Rebecca emerged from between two buildings, followed by Michael and Hemi.

"Shut up, woman!" Jim snapped irritably. "You're not my mother."

"Maybe not, but I know where you sleep," she answered sweetly, coming up behind her 'husband' to place a hand on his arm. Unlike his, her expression was friendly, and she smiled at me. "Hello, Sandy. Nice to see you again."

"You too," I greeted her, lowering my hands. "I'm sorry to show up unannounced. There have been a few changes in our group, and our radio is out of order."

"I assumed as much." Rebecca glanced past me, at the open petrol tank. "That was us. We tried to salvage the fuel a few years ago, but water got into the underground tanks. We have another reservoir up the road, but this one's useless."

"I gathered as much from the smell." I shot another look at the worthless fuel and shrugged. "Not much we can do about it now. Anyway, we came here to talk to you two. We're all leaving the Waikato, and we wanted to invite you to come along with us."

"What?" Rebecca reared back, her eyes wide. "Why are you leaving? I thought you were happy in Ohaupo."

"We were, but... something's changed." I glanced up at Michael, and he gave me an encouraging smile. I returned it and looked back at Rebecca and Jim. "Guys, you remember the things in Hamilton, right? The killer mutant zombies?"

"Hard to forget about those," she answered, her expression turning grim. "Why?"

"They've come south," I answered bluntly. Her eyes flew wide, but I continued before she could say anything. "They attacked us at Ohaupo. We managed to escape without any casualties, but Anahera's tribe wasn't so lucky. While we were busy cleaning up at Ohaupo, they swung around to the west and attacked the hill fort at Lake Ruatuna. There were only four survivors."

"Oh, my God!" Rebecca clamped her hands over her mouth. Jim muttered a few curses under his breath, and put his one good arm around her shoulders.

"So, you think they're coming here next?" he demanded, his voice an odd mixture of anger and resignation. "If they do, it's because you led them here. You know that, right?"

"I know," I admitted. "But we had no radio. If we just went straight south, we might have led them away from you, but maybe not. They might have found you anyway, and they'd have taken you by surprise. You wouldn't have stood a chance." I took a deep breath, and let it out slowly. "Guys, I don't think you realise how much we appreciate what you've done over the years. By keeping the station going, you've helped us to keep in touch with our own humanity, and our link to civilization. Plus, hot showers. I can never thank you enough for the hot showers.

"But it's over now. It's time to move on. All of us. We've gathered up all the people that we know, and we're heading south. We're going to Wellington, and we're going to try something new there: we're going to build a city."

"A city?" Rebecca asked, her expression flickering through a variety of emotions all at once. "You're going to build a city? Seriously?"

"Yep." I smiled at her and nodded. "First, we're going to Avalon, a suburb in Lower Hutt, to find the Anchorman. Then, we're going to find the perfect site to build a new city. It's time. The mutant attacks were the catalyst, but this had to happen eventually. We can't keep just surviving, gnawing away at the bones of a dead civilization forever. We need to create our own civilization."

I shifted my gaze to Jim, and smiled at him as well. "It's going to be a place where everyone is welcome, so long as they're willing to contribute. We don't care about your race, creed, origin story, or sexuality, so long as you can share in our vision. Civilization has fallen, but it's fallen before. Humanity has survived before. We can rebuild. We can begin again.

"These people with me, they're the settlers that are going to found this new civilization, the bones on which the world is going to be rebuilt. There are twenty-two of us at the moment, but if you agree to join us, then there will be twenty-four. Our odds of success would be that little bit better. We need you, Jim, Rebecca. We also want you, as our friends.

"Please come with us, if not for our sake, then for yours."

There was a long silence in the wake of my impromptu speech. Rebecca and Jim just stood there, staring at me. Over their heads, I saw Michael and Hemi watching with interest. Eventually, Jim heaved a sigh and looked at his wife. "Up to you, woman."

Rebecca just smiled. "Well, with an invitation like that, how could we possibly refuse?"

Chapter Twelve

There was perhaps an hour of sunlight left by the time we made it back to the warehouse where we planned to bunk down for the night. Rebecca strode along beside me, content to chatter away about nothing of any real importance, but I could feel Jim's silent thunder at my back the entire way. Although he'd agreed to join us, there was always something off about his attitude that never failed to put me on edge.

A shout of greeting met us as we rounded a corner into the street outside the warehouse. I glanced up, and spotted a couple of the kids waving to us from a window on the second floor. I smiled and waved back, then turned my attention back to Rebecca.

"So, what should we bring?" Rebecca asked. Despite how sudden the proposal had been, she seemed excited by the prospect of going out in search of a new home. Her enthusiasm was infectious, and the only one not affected was her gloomy spouse.

"We'll have to travel light," I answered. "There are twenty-four of us now, and we've only got four cars. In terms of clothing and personal effects, I'd ask you to limit it to what you can carry on your person. So, try to keep it to one bag or backpack. Wear your favourite outfit, and bring your second favourite as a change of clothes, plus as many socks and undies as you can fit in your bag. We need to keep as much room as we can for vitals."

"We have a car," she piped up. "Would that help?"

"Maybe," I said. "What kind of car?"

"My little ladybug." She turned around and looked at Jim. "What's the proper name, dear?"

"Sports utility vehicle," he supplied for her.

"That's it!" She smiled, turning back to me. "I bought a brand new SUV just before the plague hit. Jim's been keeping her in running order for me. Her name is Sophie, and she's lipstick red. Can't miss her."

"Sophie?" I froze in my tracks, and shot a startled glance back at Michael. His expression mutated in an instant, from a genuine smile to one that was very much forced.

Rebecca looked back and forth between us, clearly sensing that something was going on. "What's wrong?"

"I had a niece named Sophie," he said, his expression unreadable.

I reached out and touched his arm, drawing his attention to me. "That just means that it's fated, right? Meant to be?"

Michael stared at me for a long moment, then finally his expression softened. He nodded and gave me a faint smile. "I guess so."

I let out a breath that I hadn't quite realised I was holding until that moment, and put my arm around him. He hugged me in return. Somehow, through some sixth sense that I'd established purely for the purpose of reading my lover's mercurial moods, I could tell that he was okay once the shock had worn off.

"So, anyway," I cut in, directing the topic back to safe territory. "Yes, it would be great if you could bring your car along. You have plenty of food, right?"

"Oh yeah." Rebecca nodded and laughed. "We have more food than we can eat right now. I'm not sure how much of it is still good, but I'll do an inventory when we get home, and then we can work out what's best to bring."

"Sounds good," I agreed. "You also mentioned at one stage that you have a generator. Is it transportable?"

"No, the solar generator is tied into the power station, like the radio," she said, shaking her head. "But I think we have a portable propane generator in storage. You want me to bring that?"

"Yes, and any gas you have as well," I answered. "We have a couple of propane camp stoves, and it's handy to have them since we're going into unknown territory. Do you want me to lend you a couple of the boys for the night, to help with the heavy lifting?"

"That would be appreciated," Rebecca said. She jerked a thumb at Jim and rolled her eyes. "His arm isn't healed yet, and I don't want to give him an excuse to strain it trying to show how manly he is."

Jim shot her a black look, but said nothing.

"It's all good." I smiled at her, amused by the playful banter. "You two head off whenever you're ready. I'll send the boys to meet you when I find them."

"Yes, ma'am!" Rebecca gave me a mock salute and grinned at the folks standing around me. "You know, I think I like having this lady in charge. She knows how to get things done."

I just laughed and shook my head. "I'm only in charge because no one else wants to do it."

Michael let out an indignant snort. "She's just trying to be modest. She's in charge because she's damn good at leading, and she actually has a vision, which is more than I can say for the rest of us."

It was my turn to shoot Michael a dark look as my cheeks started to burn. "I'm sure everyone would be just fine without me."

"Lass, don't put yourself down." To my surprise, it was Jim that spoke up in my defence. "You've managed to get together twenty-four very different people, and give them hope that there's something better out there for all of us. That's no small feat." Suddenly looking embarrassed, he issued an inarticulate grunt and walked away from the group.

Rebecca stared after him until he was out of sight, then laughed and shrugged. "Well, I guess that's that, then. I better catch up before he gets himself killed. Do me a favour, and send those sexy Maori brothers, huh?"

"I'll think about it." I laughed, and made a shooing gesture. "Go on. It's not safe to be out alone at the moment."

"You got it, boss-lady!" Rebecca saluted again, and rushed off. I watched until she was out of sight, then turned to look at my companions. Matt and Priyanka had already vanished, bored by the grown-up chatter, but Michael and Hemi stood watching me with open amusement.

"Are you actually going to send Tane and Iorangi?" Michael asked, fighting to keep a grin off his face.

"No," I answered, feigning a haughty tone. "I'm going to send Iorangi and Richard."

"Eh?" Michael raised a brow, his expression shifting to one of genuine curiosity. "Iorangi I get, but why Richard?"

Suddenly, realisation dawned in Hemi's eyes, and he burst out laughing. "She's playing match-maker! Very clever, Sandy. Very clever."

I grinned at him and nodded. Michael stared at us blankly, looking bewildered. "Matchmaker? Between who?"

"Richard and Jim, of course," I answered.

Michael's eyes widened in shock. "Richard's gay?"

"He's either gay or bisexual," I replied, nodding firmly. "It took me a while to figure it out why he always looks so out of place. He's so quiet and shy, my bet is that he wouldn't know what to say. Jim is the complete opposite. He's discreet, but not shy. If he figures Richard out and there's any kind of spark there, then I'm pretty sure Jim will take the lead. I feel like Richard needs that." I glanced at Michael, and gave him a smile. "Someone strong, to help him feel stronger, himself."

Michael looked surprised but not scandalised, and that pleased me. He'd never struck me as the kind of person that would be homophobic, and my instinct proved to be correct. "Wow, I had no idea. You're right, he does always look sort of lonely and uncomfortable. Let's hope your scheme works, honey."

"It will if it's meant to," I answered with a shrug. "You can't force love where there isn't a spark, and I wouldn't dream of trying. I just hope that there is a spark. Everyone deserves some happiness, right?"

Hemi cleared his throat, and shot an uncomfortable glance at me. "Actually, while we're on the subject... Sandy, could I speak to you alone for a second?"

"Of course." I smiled at him, then looked at Michael. "Can you go check on the foraging teams, please? If anyone's found fishing gear, send them down to the docks to see if they can catch us some dinner. I want them back here before dark, though."

"Sure," Michael agreed immediately. He kissed me quickly, then vanished into the warehouse.

I turned back to Hemi, and gestured for him to follow me. Side by side, we wandered far enough away to give us a little bit of privacy. "Okay. What's up, bud?"

"Aw, mate, it's your sister," Hemi admitted, shooting a helpless look at me. Suddenly, he seemed to fall apart on the inside, like a house of cards. "I think she likes me, but I don't know, I can't tell. I like her, though. I mean, I *really* like her. As more than a friend, you know? I thought I stood a chance, but now that Ryan guy is back... I just don't know any more. What do I do, Sandy?"

"You tell her," I answered, fighting the urge to laugh. I stopped walking and turned to face him fully. "You know as well as I do that the only person who makes decisions for Skylar is herself. I don't know if she likes you as more than a friend, but I know she respects people that tell her the truth. I'm not exactly the best person to give you romantic advice, but I'd say the best thing you can do is be honest with her."

"Honest... right." He nodded slowly, processing the information – then, suddenly, his expression changed to one of open panic. "But what if she says no? What if she isn't interested? What if she laughs at me?"

"I'm pretty sure she won't laugh at you." I gave him my gentlest smile, and reached out to rest my hands reassuringly on his shoulders. "But if she says no, so be it. You're still friends, and that's the most important thing, right? I know it feels terrifying, but even if she says no it's not the end of the world. Just relax and tell her how you feel. You won't know for sure until you do."

"True." Hemi took a long, deep breath, and let it out slowly. "Yeah. Yeah. Too right. Okay. I'm going to go do it right now, just get it out the way, and we'll see how it goes. Yeah! Thanks, Sandy!"

"Any time, kiddo." I released my grip on his shoulders and stood back. Hemi scampered past me and raced back to the warehouse, leaving me alone in his wake.

I loitered for a couple of minutes, just enjoying the sound of birdsong, and the clean smell of the breeze. Unlike many of the bigger cities, Arapuni wasn't full of the stench of decay. I suspected that Rebecca had spent some time cleaning up the bodies, with the exception of the two that she'd missed. She seemed a lot like me, in that regard.

Once I judged that enough time had passed, I headed back to the warehouse. I rapped on the door with my knuckles, and waited until I heard the rusted bolt slide back. The door opened, and the doctor waved me inside.

"Hey, Doc," I greeted. "What's our status?"

Doctor Cross closed the door behind me, and bolted it firmly. "Everyone's reported in to drop off various things, then the good constable came and took most of them down to the docks to fish for supper. The children are upstairs with Anahera and Skylar having a cooking lesson, and I'm working on an updated inventory."

"Great." I smiled at him and nodded my approval. "I'm going to go look in on them, then I'll be off to help the fishers."

"Understood." The doctor adjusted his spectacles, and pointed to the stairs. "Up there, second door on the left."

"Thanks." I nodded in acknowledgement and headed off. Before I could get more than a dozen steps, he called out to stop me.

"Oh, Ms McDermott?" I paused and looked back at him. To my surprise, our perpetually-grumpy doctor was actually smiling. "Excellent find with the honey. Well done."

"No problem at all, Doc," I answered with a grin. "I'm going to teach everyone to keep an eye out for it. It's nature's super-food, after all."

"That it is." He chuckled quietly, and waved me away. I left him in peace and headed up the stairs to the second floor of the building. The noise of the children would have led me right to them, even if he hadn't given me directions; the sound of Maddy's delighted squeals made me smile. I opened the door, and peeked inside.

What I saw was a scene right out of a holiday postcard. Anahera stood at the stove, stirring something in a pot and speaking patiently to the children gathered around her. Even little Ommie was there, swathed in bandages but wide-awake and alert. They glanced up when I entered the room, and I found myself the recipient of many smiles and waves.

"Well, what's going on here, then?" I asked curiously.

"We're learning how to make flour out of white rice, aren't we children?" Anahera looked down at her young charges and gave them one of those smiles that made my stomach do backflips. I was obviously not the only one drawn in by her natural charisma; the kids all nodded happily and shouted excited nonsense.

"Well, that sounds great!" I answered, as cheerfully as possible. "Are you guys having a good time?"

"Yes!" Maddy shouted at the top of her lungs. The volume made me cringe, but it was a good kind of cringe. There was nothing quite like the happy noise of children at play, and they were definitely happy.

"Good." I grinned and looked back at Anahera, my eyebrows raised in silent inquiry. She looked at me knowingly, winked, and pointed in a general 'down-the-hall' sort of way. I nodded, and withdrew. Somehow, she knew that I was hoping to check on my sister, and had supplied the information I needed without words.

I crept down the hallway on stealthy feet, carefully checking each room for any sign of life. There was nothing to be seen in most of them: just a lot of dust, old furniture, and faded paperwork. But then, I reached the door at the end of the hall, which stood ever-so-slightly ajar. With as much subtlety as I could, I snuck up to the door and peeked through.

Inside, Hemi and Skylar were wrapped up in a kiss of such intensity that neither of them noticed me snooping. I just grinned to myself and withdrew, leaving them in peace. My little sister was more than okay, and that meant my interest in the matter was at an end. She was quite capable of handling her own blossoming relationship.

I jogged back down the stairs, just in time to catch Michael coming inside with an armload of fabric, Alfred bounding along hot on his heels.

"Just put it over there, boy," Doctor Cross instructed with a long-suffering sigh, then he vanished through a doorway, back to whatever he had been doing before the interruption.

I fixed Michael with a disapproving look. "Aren't you supposed to be fishing with the others? And while we're on the subject, where's your forage buddy, Constable Chan? You know you're not supposed to go out alone."

"There weren't enough rods for me to help out, so I decided to find something else to do. Don't worry, I had Alfred with me." Michael grinned cheekily. He went over and dumped his armload of clothing where Doc had instructed, then came back to give me a kiss of greeting. "I take it everything is okay with Hemi?"

"It's fine," I answered, shoving my worry back down. Michael was anything but stupid, and he knew that I'd kill him if he put himself at risk. "He just needed a bit of advice, is all."

"Ah." Michael nodded and gave me a curious look. "Did he tell her, then?"

"Apparently." I grinned brightly and gave him a wink in return. "You know, I feel like I'm all up in everyone's business today. I'm not sure how to react to that."

"Well, so long as you're not interfering where it's not wanted, I imagine that it's fine." Michael shrugged, sliding his arm around my waist. "Part of it is your newfound sense of responsibility, I think. You want everyone to be happy."

"You reckon?" I leaned up against him, studying the contours of his face in the artificial light. "I'm not just being a busybody, then?"

"Maybe a little bit, but you mean well," he answered dryly. Sliding his finger up beneath my chin, he tilted my face up and planted a quick, tender kiss on my lips. Then, he drew back and smiled at me. "If we want our species to survive, then the children have to come from somewhere, right?"

"I suppose, if you ignore the fact that I'm trying to set up two gay guys," I pointed out dryly.

"It doesn't matter," he said, shrugging. "Love is love. They're just as entitled to find love as straight people are. Just because their love can't produce offspring doesn't mean they're any different to you or I."

"That's how I see it," I agreed, leaning up against his broad chest. His touch relaxed me, as it always did. I closed my eyes, and relished in his warmth and tenderness.

He seemed to sense my need, as he often did, and held me quietly for a couple of minutes. Eventually, he drew back and looked down at me. "I got you a present."

"Oh?" I looked up at him, curious. His dark eyes were twinkling, and there was a mischievous smile dancing across his lips. "Oh dear. I know that look. What have you done?"

"Why do you always assume I've done something wrong?" Michael exclaimed, his brows knitting together. "I just found something, and I want to give it to you. Is that a bad thing, Miss Negativity?"

"And I was just teasing you, Mister Takes-Everything-Literally," I answered, playfully nudging him in the ribs.

"Oh!" He laughed, his expression immediately brightening. "Sorry. You're so deadpan that I can't always tell when you're kidding. "

"I know." I grinned at him and gave him a wink. "So, what'd you find?"

"Hold that thought two seconds," he ordered, holding up a finger to stay my curiosity. He disentangled himself from my embrace and hurried back over to the mound of clothing he'd brought in a few minutes earlier. He grabbed something black and glossy from the bottom of the pile, and held it up for me to see. "Tada!"

"Whoa, is that leather?" I enquired, closing the gap between us to get a better look at the trench coat.

"Yep!" he answered. "Genuine leather, treated to be waterproof according to the label. I went back to the hunting and fishing store the guys found to see if there was anything else of use to us. If there were any guns in there then they're long gone, but I found a few of these up the back. This one looks just about your size, and it'll last you a lifetime." He turned the trench around so that I could slide it on, if I wanted to.

I hesitated, though. He was right, it would last me a lifetime. And with winter coming, I was going to need it.

But... could I accept something like that knowing that there were other people in need? Reluctantly, I shook my head and took a step back.

"Honey, I appreciate the thought, but I can't take that," I said quietly. "Give it to Priya, or one of the other kids. They need it more than I do."

Michael's expression darkened. Without warning, he reached out and grabbed my arm, though his grip wasn't hard enough to hurt.

"Oh no you don't," he scolded. "I found this, Sandy. Scavenger's law says that I have first right of control over where it goes, and who gets it. You taught me that, and I brought this coat back for *you*, not anyone else."

"But—" I started to protest, but he interrupted me.

"No way. I'm not letting you do this to yourself." Michael heaved a long sigh, and released his grip on my arm. "Just take it, Sandy. Winter is coming, and you're going to need this to keep you warm and dry. Knowing you, you're going to be out in the thick of it all the way south, and the last thing we need is for our leader to freeze to death. The only thing resembling cold weather gear you have is that little army surplus jacket of yours, and that's summer weight."

My automatic response was to keep protesting until I got my way, but something about his expression silenced me. He was so determined, so intensely focused on winning this one particular battle that I couldn't turn it down in good conscience. I looked down at my feet and nodded once.

"Okay. Okay, I'll take it," I agreed reluctantly. "But you better have found something for the kids in there. You know they come first to me."

"I know they do." Michael's expression softened into a smile. He reached out and put the coat around my shoulders, using it to draw me into a warm, leather-scented hug. "But that's exactly why someone has to put you first. You're not immune to the 'flu, you know. What good are you to anyone if you catch a sniffle?"

"Oh, thanks. Much appreciated." I shoved him back and feigned a dirty look. "Some boyfriend you are."

"Fiancé," he corrected, returning my look with a playful grin. "And don't you forget it."

"I'm pretty sure I couldn't, even if I wanted to," I answered teasingly. On a sudden, overwhelming impulse, I leaned up and planted a kiss on his lips. When we separated, I smiled at him. "Thank you. Now, we really should get back to work."

"Yeah," he agreed. "Sounds like the others are coming back from fishing, anyway."

Right on cue, someone banged on the door beside us, making me jump. I laughed and nodded to him. Without me even having to ask, Michael went off to sort out the night's watch, while I went to organise the group going to help at the power station.

Then Skylar appeared, manifesting out of the chaos like a goddess come to tame the throngs, and soon everything was under control.

Chapter Thirteen

"Looks like we pissed off the weather gods," I commented thoughtfully to myself.

The night had passed uneventfully, but when the sun rose it revealed a day that was dark and dreary. The rain had already settled in, and it clearly had no intention of letting up any time soon. I stood in the doorway, watching the weather and absently fingering my radio, waiting for the call from Rebecca that would let us know it was time to leave.

"Indeed. Tāwhirimātea has sent his children to hinder us once again," a voice said softly behind me. I glanced back, and found Anahera standing there, watching the rain over my shoulder. She handed me a bowl of leftover fish stew from the night before. I accepted it silently, and eased to one side so that she could join me in the doorway.

I ate quietly for a couple of minutes, enjoying a moment of peace while I could get it. I'd spent most of the night brooding on what Javed had told me the day before, and my mood was almost as bleak as the clouds outside. Eventually, the silence started to bother me a little. I glanced at Anahera, and asked simply, "Tell me about him?"

"About who?" She looked back at me, surprised.

"About Tāwhiri—what was it?"

"Tāwhirimātea," she supplied, a smile growing on her face. "You're interested in my people's legends?"

"Of course I am," I answered with a shrug. "There's no one else left to keep the tales alive, except for us."

"No, I suppose there isn't," she agreed. Her dark eyes flicked away from me, back to the rain. "How much do you know about our tales regarding the creation of the world?"

"I know a little bit," I replied. "They taught us in school about how the Earth Mother and Sky Father used to be joined together, until their children forced them apart. I also know the origin story of New Zealand. Māui, the demi-god, went fishing and caught a giant stingray which became the North Island. His canoe became the South."

"Ah, yes, an old favourite!" Anahera laughed merrily and shook her head. "Tāwhirimātea, or Tāwhiri for short, was one of the sons of Ranginui, the Sky Father, and Papatūānuku, the Earth Mother. When his brothers were trying to separate them, Tāwhiri fought to keep them together. He argued that they were happy together, so why drive them apart?

"In the end, Tāwhiri lost and his parents were driven apart. He was so angry that he sent his children – the winds, the rain, the snow, and the storms – to attack his brothers endlessly. Unfortunately, we frail mortals are trapped in the middle of that never-ending war."

"Wow," I murmured thoughtfully to myself, staring out at the dark clouds. A few splatters of rain made it past the overhang of the roof and struck me in the chest and stomach, but my new coat reached all the way to my knees, and kept me well and truly dry. "I can't help but wonder if any of it's real. Do you think it is?"

"Yes and no," Anahera admitted with a shrug. "Who are we to say what lives beyond this world that we see?

Who knows whether my gods are real, or yours, or Elira's, or anyone else's. We won't know until we die, and even then I'm not entirely convinced that we'll ever be sure."

"I don't have a god," I said, shooting her a curious look. "You assumed I'm Christian?"

"No judgement was intended." Anahera smiled back at me, reaching out to touch my arm. "I just took a guess. If I was wrong, please don't take offense."

"It's okay. I'm not offended." I shrugged and returned my gaze to the pelting rain. "I guess I just don't know what I believe. Part of me feels like no kind god would ever force us to go through this kind of pain, but another part of me wonders if it's not for the best in the long term."

"Oh?" Even without seeing her face, I could hear the curiosity in her voice. "What do you mean?"

"Well, you remember what it was like," I said, gesturing at the world around us. "We took everything for granted. It was just assumed that you'd grow up, go to school, get married, have a family. We were so busy following the steps that society laid out for us that we never stopped to appreciate the tiny, every-day miracles of the world. I don't know about you, but I notice it now. I hold my breath and marvel at the way the rising sun creeps across the ground every morning. I close my eyes and listen to the sound of the rain on the roof. I marvel at the tiny miracle that can turn a seed into a plant that bears us food. We've all seen so much death, but we're alive." I paused and looked at her. "Life is a gift. I can see that now. I don't think I would have before."

"You are very philosophical for someone awake so early in the morning," Anahera answered dryly. Her dark eyes studied me thoughtfully in the gloom. "What's wrong?"

I shrugged and glanced away, focusing on the falling rain. "It's something Javed said to me yesterday. Do you remember when we first met, we asked you if any members of your tribe had given birth since the plague?"

"Of course," she replied. "You were concerned about whether or not the immunity would be passed from mother to child."

"It turns out that we were right to worry," I said quietly, hugging myself against a chill that came from the inside more than the out. "Javed told me that Ommie had a twin sister, but when she was born she didn't cry. That she was alive, but... wrong. From birth." I glanced at her just in time to see the understanding dawning in her eyes. "You know what that means."

"The child was born infected?" Anahera whispered, a horrified look crossing her face, the kind of look that mirrored the way I'd been feeling since Javed told me. "But the other children..."

"Exactly. Javed was born just before the plague, but Barry, Ommie, and Maddy were born afterwards." I swallowed hard, and closed my eyes. "I don't know what to do, Ana. This changes everything."

"No, it doesn't." Her voice turned firm, and I felt her hand land on my shoulder. I opened my eyes, and saw a look of determination on her face. "We still have to have children, or our species is guaranteed to die out. At least now we know the risk is real, so we can plan for it. If it happens, it will be terrible but it won't be a surprise. It's better to know there is a risk and face it bravely than to have it come without warning and devastate us all."

I had no answer. Nothing seemed adequate. Anahera took the empty bowl from my hand, then she turned away from me. "I must go help Elly and Skylar with the children. Try not to spend too much time brooding on it. We'll find a way to get through this together."

I just nodded silently. Once she was gone, I turned my attention back to watching the wild weather and pondering this cruel new twist of fate.

***

I stayed on watch as the sun slowly climbed higher in the sky. Every so often, someone came over to check in with me and let me know the progress of our preparations to leave, but they had things well under control. Hearing Skylar shouting like a drill sergeant never failed to make me smile, despite my dark mood. It was nearly an hour after sunrise before the walkie-talkie in my hand finally crackled to life, and Rebecca's familiar voice cut through my reverie.

"Testing... testing... hello? Is this working?"

"It is," I answered. "Good morning, sleepy head. I was starting to think I was going to have to come over and wake you myself."

"We weren't sleeping," she snapped indignantly. "It takes time to pack up your entire life, you know!"

"I know, Rebecca," I replied, adjusting my tone appropriately. "I was just teasing you."

"Teasing? Oh. Oh!" The radio crackled for a moment, which I could only presume was the result of her taking a deep breath and letting it out across the microphone without realising what she was doing. "Sorry. It's been a long time since I've been teased. I guess I forgot."

"Don't worry, I've totally been there," I answered, smiling to myself. I understood better than most. "You'll get used to it. Just give it time. Anyway, how's everything going?"

"We're just about ready, but we had a question." There was a long pause, then she asked, "Sandy, what do we do about the power station?"

"What do you mean?" I asked, confused.

"I mean... do we shut it down? Do we leave it running?" She went silent for a few seconds, then Jim's voice came over the radio. "Theoretically, the power station could run itself... well, indefinitely. Most of it is automated. It's only when the unexpected happens that it needs human intervention – like the tree."

"Oh, I'm with you." I paused to think about it, processing the pluses and minuses of each scenario out loud. "If we leave the station running, there is a chance that something could damage it. But we have no intention of coming back, and if we leave it running then that would potentially give us the ability to access its power as we travel south, which could save our precious resources. I think we should leave it running. What do you guys think?"

"I think you're right," Rebecca said. "We haven't really had to do much to keep it running all this time. We just clean out the pipes occasionally, and keep an eye on the warning lights."

"Okay, leave it running," I decided, nodding thoughtfully to myself. "How much longer do you guys need before you're ready to go?"

"Give us half an hour to finish up down here," she answered. "We'll meet you at the warehouse when we're ready to go."

"Good." I straightened up, absently adjusting the unfamiliar folds of my coat around me. "We're pretty much ready to move out now, so we're just waiting on you. Let us know if you need extra help."

"Thanks, but I think we're good," she replied. "We'll see you soon."

The radio went dead in my hand. I tucked it back into its pocket in the lining of my coat, then buttoned it back up over my midsection. My stomach felt a little upset and it bothered me, but I was used to nausea. I had experienced it on a regular basis as a result of my odd, irregular diet.

"Sandy?"

As if reading my mind, I suddenly heard Anahera calling my name. She paused and looked me up and down, tilting her head to one side.

"Are you all right, dear?" she asked. "You look pale. Well, paler than usual."

"Oh, it's the fish," I answered with a strained chuckle. "I'm not used to having fish for breakfast. I'll be fine."

"Oh!" A smile lit up her face, one that was so friendly and understanding that it immediately made me feel better. "I'm sorry, I didn't think about that. I suppose your folks aren't used to having fish for every meal."

"I'm not used to having fish at all, to be honest. I'm terrible at fishing," I admitted sheepishly. "We'll get used to it. Anyway, was there something you wanted?"

"Yes, actually." Anahera sighed heavily and came over towards me. She sat down on the edge of a nearby table, and shot a thoughtful look at me. "I want to go through Tokoroa."

I froze for a second, staring back at her. "Tokoroa was gang territory, last time I checked. I was planning to go around it. Why do you want to go there?"

"There's a radio station there," she said quietly, watching my face as though trying to divine my thoughts. "Like we discussed, the other people in this region deserve some kind of warning. I did a bit of research last night, and found out that Tokoroa's station is the nearest one that we're likely to pass before we leave the Waikato."

I swore softly beneath my breath and turned away from her, staring out the door at the driving rain. She said nothing, just sat watching me and giving me the time I needed to think over the decision. I knew there was really only one choice that I could make, but I didn't like it.

Unfortunately, she was right. Even the gangs included women and children, and not all of the men were terrible people. They certainly didn't deserve to die a bloody, brutal, painful death.

"Fine," I agreed grudgingly. "We'll go through Tokoroa."

***

Even with all the delays, we were back on the road before the sun had climbed high enough to peek over the trees. Michael and I led in the Hilux, with him behind the wheel and me hunched over our maps, plotting our route south.

"We'll need to swing east at the next junction," I told him, tracing the line of the road on the map. "Turn left."

"Okay," he replied simply.

While he was busy watching the road through the deluge, I pulled out my radio and called back to the convoy. "Rebecca and Jim, I need you for a second."

"We're here," Rebecca's voice answered within a few seconds. "What's up, boss?"

"Oh lord, don't start with that again," I protested with a dramatic groan. "I just need to know what we can expect on the roads today. How far east of Arapuni have you travelled?"

"Not far," she admitted. "A few kilometres at most. We really had no reason to go that way."

"Damn," I grumbled. "I don't suppose there's any chance you guys went down Old Taupo Road, is there?"

"No," she replied. "Not since before the plague. Sorry."

"It's all good," I said. "We're just going to have to chance it, and hope for the best."

"Well, if it helps, the roads we saw were in pretty decent condition," she supplied, along with the verbal equivalent of a shrug. "Beyond that... I dunno, sorry."

"Thanks anyway. We'll let you know if we see any problems." I clicked off the radio and set it down on the dashboard in front of me, within easy reach should I need it. "Well, at least it doesn't seem to be a quake zone."

Michael grunted wordless agreement. The rain was coming down thick and fast, making it hard for him to see, so I fell silent and let him concentrate. Rebecca was certainly right about the condition of the roads for the first few kilometres; they were in practically perfect condition. We passed by a few old farmsteads, set amidst overgrown pastures and small patches of native bush.

A few minutes later, we reached a large intersection, with branches pointing out like the spokes of a wheel. Michael slowed down and glanced at me for directions.

"Right," I told him. "Turn right, and keep following that road until I say otherwise."

He nodded, and guided us around the corner, while I picked up my radio to convey the instructions to the rest of the convoy in case they were unable to see us through the gloom. I could barely see a dozen feet in front of the windshield, so I rolled down my window a crack... then I burst out laughing.

"What are you laughing at?" Michael asked.

"Corn," I answered, amused. "More corn. Always corn."

"Food is food," Michael answered. "Think we should stop and top up our supplies?"

"Nah, we're good for the moment." I shook my head, and planted my elbow on the window sill to watch the passing corn fields for any sign of danger. Or anything else, really, but there was nothing to be seen. The corn went on forever, or so it felt. Suddenly, a flash of white plastic interrupted the monotony, but it was only old bales of sodden hay, wrapped in tattered plastic sheets. Nothing of any interest to us. Then, more corn.

I heaved a monumental sigh, and gave Michael a look. "I spy with my little eye, something beginning with..."

"Is it corn?" Michael asked dryly, clearly sensing my mood was drifting into the silly.

"No way!" I feigned surprise. "How did you guess so fast?"

"I'm just lucky like that," he said with a grin. "Man, it's starting to feel like one day the entire Waikato is going to be conquered by an army of cornfields."

"Better cornfields than mutants and zombie pigs," I replied. "At least we can eat corn."

"Well, there's no logical reason to assume that we can't eat zombie pigs," he commented. "I mean, have you ever tried?"

"No!" I exclaimed, horrified by the mere suggestion. "You would have to be a special kind of crazy to actually consider doing that. They're all... rotten and stuff. Gross."

"Yes," he said slowly, as though talking to a child. "I didn't say they were appetizing. I was just suggesting that it's entirely possible that they're edible. Appetizing and edible are two different things."

I opened my mouth to argue, but at the same moment it suddenly clicked that he was trying to bait me. "Hang on just one corn-picking minute... are you just trying to get out of ever being put on kitchen duty again?"

"Of course not!" He made a dismissive gesture with one hand, but it was just a little bit too dramatic to be real. "I'm just saying, don't knock it 'til you've tried it, right? Like Brussels sprouts."

"That's it, now you're doing the dishes every night for the rest of forever," I teased right back, folding my arms across my chest.

"You have no sense of humour at all." He started to say something else, but something out in the rain caught his attention. His eyes flew wide and he slammed on the brakes so suddenly that I was jerked half out of my seat. If we hadn't been travelling at a snail's pace because of the rain, it could have done serious damage. Luckily for me, it just ruffled my feathers.

"What?" I exclaimed, shoving myself back into my seat. "What is it?"

"There's someone out there," he answered, his voice barely above a whisper. "Or something. I can't tell."

"Stop the convoy," I told him, my irritation at the sudden halt vanishing in the blink of an eye. "I'll check it out."

"Sandy, no," Michael protested, grabbing my hand. "Not by yourself."

"I have my gun right beside me, and I'm already dressed for the rain." I gently extracted my hand from his, and pulled the hood of my coat up over my head. "I won't leave your line of sight. Join me as soon as the convoy is safe."

He might have had a few more words to say, but I didn't hear them. In a single, well-practiced motion, I was out the door and in a fighter's crouch, with my shotgun aimed into the mists. I wondered briefly whether the weapon was safe to use in the rain, but there wasn't time to ask. If it was an enemy up ahead, I had to be sure.

The rain was so heavy that it had me drenched in a few seconds flat, but the leather kept my skin mostly dry. As silently as I could, I crept around to the driver's side of the Hilux, and stared at the road in front of us. There was something there, something moving with slow, jerky motions, but the details were obscured by the haze.

Suddenly, the door beside me opened and Michael leapt out, wrapped in a newly-salvaged leather jacket of his own. His lacked a hood, though, which forced him to squint to keep the water out of his eyes.

"What is it?" he asked, so quietly that his voice was almost a whisper.

"I don't know," I admitted softly. I lifted a hand and gestured for him to accompany me, but I didn't wait to see if he followed me. I didn't have to. If there was one person I knew, it was Michael. He'd always be at my side when I needed him, and that was why I trusted him.

I sensed him half a step behind me as we crept forward, weapons at the ready. Slowly but surely, a humanoid figure started to resolve out of the haze. It was moving southwards in a slow, halting gait. I knew without having to see its face that it was probably one of the infected, but I always erred on the side of caution. There was no undo button if you chose to shoot first and ask questions later.

I held up my hand and made a gesture instructing Michael to hold position, and then I crept forward and began to circle the creature. For a few seconds I walked beside it, following a parallel course while keeping myself well out of its reach. Eventually, I drew out in front of it, turning as I moved until I was very nearly walking backwards.

Suddenly, it turned and looked at me. Its mouth gaped, and it let out a terrible, blood-curdling, familiar screech. I jumped back, my finger on the trigger, fully expecting it to leap at me the way the mutants usually did.

Nothing happened. It just stared at me, completely expressionless, and kept on shuffling southwards. I glanced at Michael, but he didn't have an answer any more than I did. Once the creature passed me, it seemed to lose interest in me completely.

Curious, I took a few steps backwards, to bring myself back into its field of vision. Again, it looked at me, issued one of those horrid, skin-crawling screeches, then kept on walking as though nothing had happened.

"What the hell is that?" A breathless voice asked behind me. I glanced back, and saw that Skylar had joined us, along with most of the fighters of the group. "It sounds like a mutant."

"It sounds like one, but it isn't attacking," I answered, just as confused as she sounded. "I don't understand."

"How can it shriek like a mutant but not be one?" Michael asked what we were all thinking. "Why isn't it attacking us? Where's it going?"

"Maybe it's going south for the winter?" I suggested, trying to squeeze a little bit of humour out of a situation that wasn't funny at all.

"It's a proto-mutant," Skylar said suddenly. I glanced at her, and saw her staring back at me with wide eyes. "Like, something halfway between the mutants we know and the normal infected. It's turning into a mutant." She paused and stared at it for a second, then looked back at me. "What's it wearing? Is that a uniform?"

"I think so, yeah," I answered. I hurried back over, and slowly stepped back into the creature's line of sight. Again, it shrieked at me, but made no attempt to attack me, which gave me the time I needed to get a good look at it. "Looks like a nurse, or maybe a cleaner, I'm not sure. I think I see an ID tag. I'm going to try and grab it. Cover me."

A series of grunts, and the sound of bodies moving and guns being cocked was the reply to my request. I nodded once, then I leapt forward and tried to grab the tag hanging around the thing's neck. My first attempt failed, but it didn't even seem to care. I made a second grab, and this time my fingers closed around the cold, wet plastic. The safety clasp holding the lanyard in place popped open when I gave it a good, hard tug, and with that the prize was mine.

"It's so faded, I can barely read it," I said as I returned to my group. "That logo is familiar, though. Do you guys recognise it?"

"Yes," Michael answered, shading his eyes to keep the rain out of them as he studied the tag in my hand. "It's the logo of the hospital where we met. That thing is from Hamilton. How the hell did it get this far south?"

"It seems pretty determined to go wherever it's going," I commented, watching the thing shuffling away from us. Suddenly, realisation dawned on me. "Oh, God. It's not just a proto-mutant. It's a plague-bearer."

"What?" Skye exclaimed, turning to stare at me. "You think it's going south to spread the mutated virus? Can that happen? That the infected be re-infected?"

"I don't know, and I sure as hell don't want to find out." I spun around and pointed at her. "Go back to the convoy and get as much accelerant as we need to get this thing burning. We have to destroy it right now!"

Skylar nodded and ran off, leaving Michael and the others staring at me.

"Sandy, what are you thinking?" Michael asked, running his hand back through his wet hair to smooth it away from his face.

"I'm thinking..." I paused, turning the idea over in my head. The more I thought about it, the worse it got. "Michael, how many people worked at that hospital before the plague? And how many patients were there?"

"I don't know," he said. "Hundreds, at least. Probably thousands. I mean, where do people go when they get sick? They go to a hospital. It felt like half the city was there towards the end."

"So, where did all those people go?" I asked rhetorically, turning to look him square in the eye. He stared back at me, not quite seeming to understand. "Okay, think about it. Let's assume that there were at least a thousand people there. We know that sometimes the virus burns fast and devours everything, but we also know that sometimes it burns slower and takes longer to totally destroy the infected, right?"

"Right..." he echoed.

"So," I continued, "if we presume that half those poor folks have burned out by now, that leaves five hundred people that should have been in that hospital when we met. How many did we see?"

"Only four or five," he said, his eyes slowly widening. "My God... where did all those people go?"

"Out into the countryside," I answered morbidly. "Spreading the mutated infection between them and the regular undead that are still on their feet. If I remember my high school biology right, a virus breeds by consuming a host's cells, which in turn kills the cells and makes them unsuitable for the virus to keep breeding in. The visible decay that we see happens because of that cell death. So, if Ebola X is still living and breeding in these infected after so long, it must have figured out a way to keep reproducing inside dead cells, without destroying them completely."

"Right..." he repeated again, though I could see on his face that I was starting to lose him.

"Michael, this is it," I said, grabbing his arm. "This is why the mutants are happening. Somehow — I don't know how — the virus has been breeding inside dead cells to save itself from dying out. That means it can keep breeding indefinitely inside the same host. It's been doing that for ten years. If we estimate that a single virus produces a million offspring every few hours, what happens when we multiply that by a decade? What happens over the course of thousands and thousands of generations?"

Suddenly, the light bulb seemed to go on behind his eyes. "Evolution."

"Evolution," I agreed, my expression grim. "I think I get it now. I think I finally understand. There isn't just one strain of the virus, not like we thought. There are hundreds of ever-so-slightly different strains, because of the population evolution happening inside each host. We can group them into three primary categories, though — the fast-burning virus, the slow-burning virus, and the new mutation." I counted them off on my fingers, my brow furrowed in thought. "At first, we only had the two strains, fast-burning and slow-burning. Natural selection has most likely killed off the fast-burning strain by now. But, the slow-burning strain survived, because it evolved a way to breed without destroying its host. And then the slow-burning strain kept breeding over and over again, until it started to turn into the new mutation.

"With Ebola X being airborne, when the new strain emerged it could easily spread amongst the available hosts. So, we can assume it evolved in the hospital, where there was – or should have been – that big concentration of people. The infected would have no real immunity, so if the new mutation was dominant then it would spread like wildfire..."

"...and infect all of those docile infected with the new mutation?" Michael summarised for me, a look of horror spreading across his face. "So, if this plague-bearer finds another population of infected..."

"...then it's going to spread the new virus to them, and they'll turn into mutated infected as well," I answered softly.

"We have to destroy that thing. Right now!" His voice rose to a shout, and he raced past me with his weapon at the ready.

"No!" I cried, dashing after him. "Don't waste ammunition! We have precious little as it is, and for all we know the same thing may have happened in Wellington or Palmerston North or anywhere else that there's a dense concentration of infected."

Michael froze with his gun already raised halfway to the firing position. He looked at me, then looked back at the infected. "You want to use your Taser on that thing?"

"Why not?" I shrugged, reaching up to rest my arm on his bicep. "It's reusable, and it works. We need to use renewable energy sources whenever we can, or we're going to end up with nothing left but a sense of regret and an empty chamber."

"Well, that seems a bit dramatic," he said dryly. With a heavy sigh, he lowered his weapon and nodded to me. "Do you want me to do it?"

"No, I've got this," I answered. Just as I was handing him my shotgun, Skylar came running back with a flask in her hands. She watched me pull out my Taser and flick it on, her eyes widening.

"Is that safe to use in this rain?" she asked nervously. "I thought water was conductive?"

"These were made to be safe in all kinds of weather." I made a reassuring gesture with my free hand, and gave everyone a quick smile before I turned to deal with the unpleasant duty at hand. The infected was totally oblivious to me as I crept up behind it, trying to get close enough to use my Taser as a stun gun. Sure, I could have used the shot, but I only had one cartridge and I couldn't exactly run to the store and grab another one.

I drew a deep breath as I closed the last few feet, and reached out to press the Taser to the base of the creature's neck. It stumbled, but righted itself and kept on walking. A second blast of current brought it down, twitching. Before I could say a word, Michael was past me with the accelerant and a lighter.

With the rain pelting down and the wind howling around us, it took all of our combined efforts to get the creature burning to our satisfaction. When the fire was finally hot enough that it wasn't likely to go out on its own, we stood back and watched intently. No one complained about the cold or the wet. None of us wanted to leave until we were sure that plague-bearer was well and truly destroyed.

Chapter Fourteen

The morning encounter left us wary and on edge for the rest of the day. I found myself feeling far too anxious to simply sit passively, so I hauled myself halfway out the window to watch the endless cornfields with a degree of alertness that bordered on paranoia. The cold made my teeth rattle and my butt went numb, but at least I felt better for doing something useful.

Eventually, a line of dark trees started to grow along the edge of the horizon, getting closer and closer with each passing second. I watched it warily, but to my relief our turn-off arrived before we plunged into darkness.

"Turn left in a hundred metres," I called down through the open window. With the rain pounding down on me, I barely heard Michael's grunt of acknowledgement. We reached the corner and turned onto another overgrown strip of roadway, almost identical to the last. A few minutes later, the cornfields ended abruptly, only to be replaced by waist-high grass dotted with dark specks in the distance. I lifted my hand to shade my eyes and stared intently at them, trying to work out what the specks were.

"Sandy," Michael said suddenly. I glanced at him, and realised that he was holding out his binoculars to me. I took them with a sheepish smile, and looked at the specks again. A second later, I relaxed.

"Just cows," I told him. Some things hadn't changed since the fall of mankind, and cows were one of them. They were still the same placid, even-tempered beasts they'd always been. The only difference now was that they were free-range animals, and the entire country was their ranch.

"Good." I heard Michael let out a deep breath, and when I looked at him again I saw that he was smiling. "You should probably come in, though."

"Why?" I asked curiously, lifting the binoculars so that I could scan the rest of the horizon for danger.

"I saw a flash of lightning when you were looking the other way," he answered. "It's still pretty far away, but I don't want my favourite girl getting electrocuted."

"Your favourite girl, huh?" I echoed in my most playful voice. I eased myself back down into the cab, and grabbed a towel out of the back seat to dry myself off.

"You say that like you didn't already know it," he answered dryly, shooting one of his silly grins in my direction.

I laughed and shook my head. "Oh, I know it. I just can't quite believe it."

"Well, believe it." He reached over and took my hand with his free one. "This is happening, Sandy. What we have, it's real and it's special. I've never felt like this about anyone before." He sighed, returning his hand to the steering wheel. "You know, there's something I've never told you."

"Oh?" I raised a brow, instantly cautious. "Are you secretly a serial killer? A failed superhero? A mime stripper?"

"No!" he exclaimed, laughing merrily. "Wait... a mime stripper? That's not even a thing!"

"Well, you better tell me what it is, then," I answered, folding my arms across my chest. "I've had a lot of time to think about this, you know."

"It's nothing like that, I swear," he said, struggling to get his laughter back under control. "I just... I didn't want to say anything until I was sure, you know?"

"You've already told me that you want to marry me and have babies with me," I pointed out. "What else could there possibly be that you were afraid to say to me?"

"Well, it's... a bit strange," he admitted, his expression suddenly turning serious. "Maddy told me I was going to meet you. A year ago."

"What?" I froze, startled. Of all the things he could have said, that was the last thing I had expected to hear.

"Yeah." He sighed softly and shrugged. "I didn't believe her at the time... let me start from the beginning. Maddy's special, you and I both know that. She wasn't always like that. I mean, she's always been a bit odd, but she started developing that strange intuitiveness the summer before last. At first I just assumed that it was because she's a kid. Sophie said strange things at her age, so I thought it was normal. But some of the things that she started saying were... not normal. For any little kid."

"What happened?" I prompted gently, watching his face to try and judge his thoughts from his expression. He hesitated, and then he shot me a look of such sadness and longing that my heart dropped right to my knees.

"I was so lonely, Sandy," he said quietly. "I mean, we talked about it when we first met, but there's no way for me to verbally express it. Even with Sophie, and the others... it wasn't the same. I was so lonely that it hurt. It physically ached inside me. Did you ever feel like that?"

"Yes," I admitted, lowering my gaze. "In the first couple of years, before the... the bad stuff happened. I cried myself to sleep more than once."

"Me too," he replied. I felt his big hand land on mine again, and his fingertips gently rubbed my skin. The touch reassured me; I took his hand in both of mine, and held it while he spoke. "I'm man enough to admit that I've cried over it more than once. We were so young when all this happened. I had never even considered that I'd lose my opportunity to have a family. I just sort of assumed that it'd happen naturally, you know? I figured I'd focus on my career for a while, then when the time was right, I'd meet the perfect woman. She'd be smart, beautiful, funny, and she'd love me as much as I loved her. I had the same vague dreams as everyone else: we'd travel the world together, then one day settle down and start a family.

"One day, I'm in my apartment daydreaming about the future. A week later, almost everyone I've ever known is dead, and my chance for a family is gone forever."

He paused and took a deep breath; I squeezed his hand, feeling the intensity of his emotion through his palm. Suddenly, he looked at me and I could see the terrible pain in his eyes. A moment later, he returned his gaze to the road, and he resumed speaking.

"I never got over that," he admitted. "I accepted the situation for what it was, but I could never get past the pain. It just got worse and worse every day, but I learned to hide it and focused on nurturing Sophie. She was all I had. And don't get me wrong, I loved her more than life itself and put my everything into raising her — but it was never the same as the life I'd dreamed of."

"I know," I whispered, leaning up against him to comfort him in some small way. Even though I was damp and smelt like wet leather, Michael smiled at the contact.

"I wish you could have met her, Sandy," he murmured. His eyes were focused on the road, but his expression said that his thoughts were a million miles away. "She would have loved you, and I think you would have loved her, too. She was a brilliant kid. Obsessed with books, and always smiling and laughing. I think she kept all of us sane, until..."

"I know," I repeated gently, hugging him as best I could without disrupting his driving. "I know that I would have loved her. From the sound of it, she's just like her uncle."

Michael glanced at me, and gave me one of his quirky, lopsided smiles. "I suppose she was, in a way. The laughter kept us going." He sighed, looking back out the windscreen at the pouring rain. "But not always. You know how I am. Sometimes I drop."

"You're a Pisces, sweetie." I leaned up and planted a kiss on his cheek. "Pisces are always moody and mercurial."

This time, the glance he gave me was of amusement. "Oh, are we just? And how do you know that, missy?"

"Sophie wasn't the only one who had a lot of time to read," I answered dryly. "I am a stubborn Capricorn, which is clearly why I'm the boss of you. So there."

"Oh, I see." Michael gave me a dubious, but amused look. "Well, then. I won't contest that. I like it when you're the boss of me."

"I know you do," I teased, playfully running my fingers along the top of his thigh. "Anyway, what were you saying about Maddy?"

"Huh?" He glanced down, momentarily distracted by my touch. "Oh, right, Maddy. Yeah, I was in my room in a dark mood, just lying in bed, staring at the ceiling. Moping, basically. Out of the blue, Maddy came marching into my room with a purpose. She sat down on the edge of my bed, looked me right in the eye, and said, 'Don't worry, Mister Michael. You won't have to be lonely for much longer.'"

"Really?" I sat up straight and looked at him. "She said that? A year ago?"

"And that's not all," he said. "When I asked her what she meant, she just smiled mysteriously, and said 'Your wife is waiting for you. She just doesn't know it yet.'"

"You're kidding me!" I exclaimed, startled. "You have to be making that up."

"I'm not, I swear. Cross my heart." He grinned and glanced at me again. "At the time, I figured she was just talking nonsense, so I forgot all about it. And then this crazy blonde walks into my life, punches me in the face, and suddenly I'm head-over-heels in love. I wasn't a hundred percent sure until you put that ring around your neck, but now I am. You're the one that Maddy saw in her vision. My future wife."

"Well, that's sweet, bewildering, and a little concerning all at the same time," I said, fighting a wave of conflicting emotions. "I mean, if we're, I don't know... fated to be together... well, what about free will? Don't I get any say in the matter? "

"No, and neither do I." Suddenly, he smiled at me. "Either one of us could walk away from this any time we wanted. Do you want to walk away?"

"No," I answered without hesitation. "Do you?"

"Not a chance," he answered just as swiftly. "And that's why we're destined to be together. Because we *want* to be together."

"Oh." I paused to consider his point, and as I considered it I felt myself relaxing. My automatic fight-or-flight instinct switched off, and was replaced by human logic. "Okay. I think I'm good with that."

"Good, because I'd be really upset if you changed your mind now," he said with a laugh. There was a pause, then the subjected changed as swiftly as it had begun. "Hey, I see houses up ahead. Should we stop to look for supplies?"

"No," I said, shaking my head firmly. "This land is claimed. We don't scavenge here, and we don't stop for anything unless we have to. We need to find that radio tower and get out of here before we're noticed. I'm hoping this weather will work in our favour, and we can be far enough south by nightfall to relax."

"I think we may be out of luck in that regard," Michael said softly. I looked where he was pointing, just in time to catch sight of a human figure disappearing behind a house.

I swore under my breath, and picked up my walkie-talkie. "Guys, we've been spotted. I want you to move in close together, and lock the doors if you're inside one of the cars. Don't stop for anything unless we stop, or I tell you to."

Michael waited until I finished relaying the instructions to the rest of the convoy, then he gave me a worried look. "Are these people really that dangerous?"

"I don't know," I admitted, "which means we should presume they're dangerous until we find out otherwise. Gangs are... well, they are gangs. Every one of them is different, depending on the nature of the members and the leader. Also remember that to them, we're a rival gang travelling through their territory, which means that we're automatically a danger to them. They may shoot first and ask questions later."

"If they have weapons," Michael pointed out. "I mean, this is still New Zealand. Guns are rare, and ones that still work are rarer still."

"True," I agreed quietly. "Let's just hope that works in our favour. For now, keep following this street."

Michael just nodded and fell silent, apparently sensing that I was in no mood to be reassured. He was right. My run-ins with gangs over the years had been frequent and mostly unpleasant, and I didn't really want to have another one. Suddenly, I realised that I was clutching my shotgun with a death-grip, and my knuckles were turning white. I forced myself to take a deep breath, and relaxed my grip.

At least this time I had some control over the outcome of what felt like an inevitable conflict. I had people to watch my back. Not just one person, either. Now, I had twenty-three people, one feline, and an elderly sheepdog on my side. I couldn't exactly rely on the kids or animals in a fight, but I trusted most of the adults. The thought made me smile; how far I'd come, that I could use the t-word so freely.

"Something up ahead," Michael said. "I see a car."

I stuck my head out the window, and looked through the binoculars. There was an intersection coming up, where a car waited patiently at the stop sign. After a few seconds, I shook my head. "That car isn't going anywhere. No driver. You're getting as paranoid as me, honey."

"Better safe than sorry," he said sheepishly. We drove past the abandoned car and continued deeper into the city. Well, town. It was certainly bigger than Ohaupo and Arapuni, but not by much.

The trees on the roadside began to get thicker, interspersed with an odd mixture of vegetation. Shrubs and flower beds that had once been well-loved and tame had gone wild without the gardeners to care for them. Now, they encroached on the road and were engaged in a brutal, silent battle with the larger trees for dominance and sunlight.

Every few meters, there was a gap in the foliage and a flash of colour beyond that told me that we'd entered suburbia. Faded weatherboards, broken fences, and the odd piece of discarded refuse paid testament to the people that had once called this place home. They were gone now – or were they? A brief movement caught my eye, but by the time I focused on it, it had vanished.

"We're being watched," I concluded, trying to keep from sounding too morose; the last thing we needed was for me to make everyone else nervous. Nervous people made mistakes. Luckily for me, Michael wasn't the kind of man that disturbed easily. He just nodded silently, and accepted my warning for what it was.

A few minutes later, the roads began to widen and the foliage thinned out, letting me finally get a clear look at the buildings. Most of them were in fairly decent condition, but there was one thing that immediately leapt to my attention.

"Is that graffiti over there?" Michael asked suddenly.

"Stop reading my mind," I scolded, though there was no genuine irritation in it. "Yes, that's gang sign. Like cats pissing on the furniture to mark their territory."

"That's a lovely thought," he answered dryly. "Should we start worrying about your cat doing that?"

"Of course no," I said, putting on a mock-haughty tone. "I'll have you know that Tigger is a lady. She'd never do such an improper thing."

"Oh, I see!" Michael responded by putting on a haughty tone of his own. "Very good, then. Carry on." He returned to his normal tone of voice to ask a question. "Do you know what they mean?"

I lifted the binoculars to my eyes and studied the markings for a moment before it started to make sense to me. "'Aua le sau i totonu'. Looks like the Samoans. That sign looks pretty old, though. The paint is chipped and faded." I studied the various words painted on the buildings nearby for a few minutes, then lowered the binoculars and looked back at him. "If the Samoans are still here, that's potentially good for us. I've had dealings with them before. While they don't trust outsiders, they're unlikely to attack us unless we provoke them."

"I'm sensing a 'but' coming on," Michael commented, his brow furrowing in concern. I nodded grimly and set the binoculars down in my lap.

"But the sign is really old, and I'm not seeing any fresh tags," I replied. "The Samoans are usually quite diligent about keeping their territory markers up-to-date. It's unlikely that they'd let their tags fade that much."

"Unless they've been displaced," Michael said, finishing the thought for me.

"Or wiped out." I shook my head and shrugged helplessly, then I grabbed my GPS off the dashboard and checked our position against it. "Take this right, and keep following the road. We should be coming up to a level crossing in a minute."

"Follow the road? That may be easier said than done," Michael commented dryly.

I glanced up, and promptly swore beneath my breath. I heaved a long-suffering sigh, grabbed my walkie-talkie, and spoke into it, "So, I know you guys are just dying for some exercise. Who feels like wrestling a train?"

An assortment of groans and complaints came across the connection. I waited until the noise died down, then continued, "Yeah, yeah, whine all you want, but it's the fastest way to get where we want to go. Little kids and animals stay in the car with the doors locked. Teenagers and walking wounded, you're on guard duty. Watch the rear and sides. I want every able-bodied adult up at the front of the convoy. It's time to get wet. Sorry."

There were more groans, but I ignored them. Michael and I exchanged a smile as we climbed out and locked the doors behind us. I put my shotgun over my shoulder on its carry strap, and made my way over to examine the train.

"How on earth are we supposed to move that?" Michael asked, his voice raised to carry over the sound of the rain. "That thing has to weigh tons, and the wheels are rusted solid."

"We don't have to move the locomotive," I replied. "If we uncouple the last carriage, then that should give us enough space to get through. Cover me for a second while I take a closer look."

"Okay," Michael agreed, though I could tell from his voice that he was dubious about the integrity of my plan. I heard his footsteps behind me as I headed up to the train, and squeezed myself into the narrow gap between the last two carriages.

The coupling looked like a road map written in a foreign language. Still, I was pretty much used to working out all things mechanical based on pure logic. After a minute or so, I figured out which lever would raise the pin that was keeping the carriages together. I grabbed the lever and pulled, but it was rusted firmly into place. A glance back over my shoulder told me that the others had gathered behind me, waiting patiently for instructions.

"Hemi, can you please go find Skylar?" I asked. "I need a can of CRC, a hammer and chisel, and a crowbar. She should know where the tools are."

"Got it!" Hemi sketched a salute and raced off. I turned to look at the others.

"Okay, the plan here is that we're just going to get the last car loose," I explained. "Then, we muscle it about three meters down the rails. We should be able to squeeze through, no problem. I'm going to need a couple of you strong blokes over here to open this lever. Volunteers?"

Just about everyone stepped forward to volunteer, much to my amusement. I just grinned and beckoned Tane and Iorangi to my side. Just as they joined me, Hemi reappeared with the tools we needed. It took a few minutes of coaxing and a few teeth-grating shrieks, but eventually the lever began to move.

"That's it, we've got it!" I cried victoriously, waving the crowbar to the waiting group. "Okay, everyone. Pick a side, and find something to grab."

Eager to follow my own instructions, I raced up to the far end of the carriage and braced my shoulder against an ancient hand railing. I felt a warm body join me, and looked back to see Michael right behind me, his strong hands flexing on the railing above my head. He glanced down at me, smiled, and nodded his encouragement.

"On the count of three," I cried, loudly enough for everyone to hear me. "One, two, three – push!"

On command, I threw my weight against the train carriage's bulk. My feet slipped in the gravel for a second, then one of them struck a sleeper, giving me something to brace against. Michael growled deep in his throat, a noise of determination more than frustration. I felt him straining along with me, using every ounce of his strength to move the stubborn cab.

For ten long years, it had stayed in exactly the same place, waiting for an engineer that would never return. For ten years, it had endured the elements, exposed, slowly turning to rust. That much rusted metal didn't move easily – but, eventually, it did move.

At first, it was only a centimetre. Then another. Then five centimetres. Ten. Twenty.

"We're doing it!" I cried. "How far are we?"

"About half way!" someone called back; I wasn't sure who.

"Keep going," I gasped, throwing my weight against the railing with renewed enthusiasm. "We can do this. It's coming a little easier."

And it was. The farther we managed to move it, the more those rusted wheels began to loosen up on the railings. Stars began to dance around the edge of my vision but I ignored them. I was intensely focused on the task, and oblivious to everything except that one more millimetre. Just a tiny, tiny bit more...

"That's it!" the voice cried from the end of the line. "That's enough, we can get through."

A collective cheer went up from the people around me. Overwhelmed by a sense of team victory, I shoved myself upright again – then promptly stumbled and fell against Michael's side.

He caught me before I could hit the ground, and turned a worried look on me. "Honey? You all right?"

"Yeah, I'm fine," I lied, waving away his concern. "Just over-extended myself, that's all."

"Okay..." he said softly, but his expression said that he didn't believe me. He gently helped me back to my feet and released me. I smiled at him and went to take a step back towards the others, except that my body didn't want to obey. Before I quite realised what had happened to me, my feet had once more gone out from under me and I was on my way down.

Michael caught me again, but this time he didn't let me go. Despite my protests, he scooped me up and carried me back towards the convoy, past a row of faces that turned to watch with concern.

"Put me down!" I demanded, thumping a fist ineffectively against his broad shoulder. "I just need to sit down for a second, I'm totally fine."

"You have a broad definition of 'fine' and we both know it," he answered, his voice deep, firm, and commanding. It was a tone that I rarely heard from him since I'd taken command, but it was one that brooked no nonsense. Before I could even think about forming a counter-argument, he'd carried me back to the car where Doctor Cross was standing guard over the children.

"What did she do this time?" the doctor asked. Without waiting for an explanation, Doc shoved his gun back into its makeshift holster, and stomped over to examine me.

"Hey, I don't injure myself that often," I complained, but I didn't even bother trying to fend off the examination. Doc was stronger than he looked, and I knew better than to resist his ministrations. "I just got a little light-headed after we finished moving the train. I keep telling him I'll be fine, but you know how much he worries about me."

"And with good reason." Doc stood back and gave me a sharp look, one that instantly made me feel like a naughty child caught with her hand in the cookie jar. "Ms McDermott, need I remind you *yet again* that you suffered a concussion not even a week ago? You are one of the walking wounded, and you know that you're not supposed to be exerting yourself."

"I needed to," I answered sharply; it always made me a little bit cross when he used that tone with me, and now was no different. "It was all hands on deck. We needed everyone."

"Did you let them try without you first? Are you sure that they needed you?" he countered, his eyes narrowed to slivers behind the scratched lenses of his glasses.

"Well, no," I admitted, then swiftly rose to defend myself, "but I didn't want to. A leader should always be willing to do anything that she asks her followers to do. It wouldn't be right for me to ask them to muck in, and not do it myself."

"And yet you were perfectly happy to assign the other walking wounded, myself included, to guard duty," he pointed out. His voice softened suddenly, and his expression turned almost fatherly. "Ms McDermott – Sandy – the most important thing about being a leader is learning your own limitations, and knowing how to follow your own rules. I know that you want to contribute so that the others don't think that you're using your position to slack off, and I understand that. I really do. But, it simply isn't necessary."

I started to protest, but he cut me off with a wave of his hand.

"You're human just like the rest of us, and your unique set of circumstances make you particularly vulnerable. Accept it. You're not invulnerable." He adjusted his glass, and gave me a stern frown. "She's fine, just give her a few minutes to sit down."

Then, before I could say anything else, he marched away to tend to whatever other business was demanding his attention. I blinked in surprise, and looked at Michael.

"What is it with everyone giving me lectures lately?" I asked dryly, both amused and a little annoyed by it. "Skylar, Anahera, Doc, you... it seems like everyone wants to tell me how to do my job."

"You're still learning," Michael said gently, slipping his arms beneath me to lift me up in his arms, as easily as a father lifting a child. "Everyone is, I think. But you're the one that has to learn the most in the shortest period of time, because people are relying on you. Don't worry, they're not lecturing you because of any kind of failure. They're lecturing you because they see so much potential in you."

"Oh." I paused to consider that as he carried me back towards the car. The explanation assuaged most of my annoyance, and left me thoughtful. "Well, that does make some sense."

"I should hope so," he answered, shooting a look at me. When we reached the car, he gently set me back on my feet and braced me against the Hilux's side panel with his body. "Do you notice the commonalities amongst the people that have been trying to educate you?"

"You lost me with the big words," I answered teasingly.

The joke earned a smile from him, and encouraged him to finish his thought. "They're either leaders themselves, or people of uncommon ability or experience. I hate blowing my own trumpet like that, but it's true. Anahera and I both led our groups for a long time, so we have experience with what you're learning now. Doc has the most life experience of any of us, and he's also the student of human nature. He's been studying people like us longer than we've been alive. And as for your sister, well – she has a deeper insight into your nature than any of us, even me. She's been studying, emulating, and loving you her entire life. That makes her an expert in... well, you."

"So, what you're saying," I summarized, "is that I shouldn't think about it like a kid getting a spanking, but more like university lectures?"

Michael laughed and nodded. "Yes, but you're definitely getting a spanking later on. In private."

"Oh my," I intoned dryly, wiggling a brow at him in a playfully suggestive manner. He grinned and gave me a kiss, then reached past me to open the passenger's door.

"In you go walking wounded," he ordered, guiding me back into my seat. For once in my life, I did as I was told. He even went so far as to buckle me in, then kissed my forehead. "You stay here and guard the car while I make sure everyone's safely loaded."

"Okay," I agreed reluctantly. Just as he was walking away, a flash of anxiety twisted my gut. "Make sure you do a headcount! Don't leave Tigger behind!"

"We won't," he replied, waving over his shoulder.

Relieved, I sat back and indulged myself in a long, deep sigh. If there was one thing I could rely on in life, it was Michael taking care of the people I loved. I tilted my head back and closed my eyes, forcing myself to relax. The sound of the rain was always something that brought me comfort, even when I was soaking wet and cold. During the bleak years I'd spent living in the back of that shipping container in Te Awamutu, the rain had always eased my terrors, chased away the demons, and lulled me to sleep.

The vertigo slowly began to fade, leaving me feeling better. I opened my eyes and blinked slowly – then I froze, staring at a distant junkyard. Through the haze, I thought I could see human figures watching us. I fumbled for Michael's binoculars, but by the time I found them, the figures were gone.

The driver's door opened, and Michael climbed in. He was soaked to the bone, rivulets of water oozing off his leather jacket, and his short hair was plastered to his head. Despite that, he still had a smile for me. In the back seat, Alfred lifted his head and yelped a greeting to his master, tail wagging frantically.

"All heads are accounted for and firmly attached to their necks," Michael told me playfully, reaching back to rub Alfred's ears.

I took the opportunity to steal a quick kiss, then I pointed towards the shipping yard a few hundred meters beyond our current position. "I think there are people over there, but I couldn't tell how many. Let's be careful."

"We could go a different way," Michael suggested, turning back to face front. He slammed his door, pulled his seatbelt on, and started the car, but waited while I pondered the suggestion.

"No," I decided, shaking my head. "It's not worth the extra risk. At least we've seen the lay of the land here, so we know more or less what to expect."

Michael nodded, put the truck in drive, and took his foot off the brake, letting us roll forward slowly until we felt the tyres bump across the train tracks. On the other side, a wide, open space yawned in front of us, flanked on one side by thick trees, and the other by warehouses and shipping yards. I picked up the binoculars again and studied the yards carefully, but if anyone lurked there I couldn't see them.

Michael kept our pace slow and cautious as we advanced. I heard the faint growl of an engine, and caught sight of a quad bike rider in my side mirror. A second later, another rider appeared on Michael's side, flanking us. I recognised the riders as ours, but they were so bundled up against the weather that I couldn't tell exactly who they were. One of them glanced at me and waved, but he looked away before I could reciprocate.

"Eight eyes are better than four," Michael explained. "I asked them to ride with us and help us keep watch for trouble. The others are spread out along the column, doing the same."

"Good call," I agreed softly, my natural caution slowly bubbling away beneath the surface and making me uncomfortable. It was only mid-afternoon, but it was darker than it should have been because of the weather. The treeline beside me was full of dancing shadows, which made it hard to determine if there were enemies about.

"Intersection," Michael said. "Direction?"

"Keep going," I replied. "We should start seeing more warehouses and stuff soon."

"Is that... a cannon over there?" Michael asked, sounding both excited and bewildered.

"Yes," I answered, laughing. "The map says that's the old Returned Services Association's hall. Pity that won't help us deal with our mutant problem, right?"

"Yeah, no kidding," he agreed with his usual playful grin. A moment later, he chuckled and pointed at one of the shop fronts up ahead of us. Three ride-on lawnmowers sat nestled amongst a grass verge so overgrown that we could barely make them out. "That strikes me as kind of ironic. Need a mower?"

"Nah, I'm good," I answered dryly. "Besides, good luck getting them to start after they've been sitting out in the rain for ten years. We should be coming up to a roundabout soon. Go straight through it."

"You mean that thing?" Michael asked, pointing to an enormous green dome that sprang up in the middle of the road, verdant with wildflowers and bushes. "It looks like a big green mushroom."

I couldn't help but laugh at the comparison. "It really does. I don't much like the look of those trees on the other side, though."

"They're just trees," he said, his tone turning gentle and reassuring. "Don't worry, it'll be fine."

A few seconds later, our convoy plunged into semi-darkness beneath the thick boughs. What had once been a row of shade trees planted in a neat median strip had become a jungle, just like the rest of the human world. Just as suddenly as it had begun, the trees parted into an area that had been a shopping centre. The glass fronts of the buildings had been shattered and broken away, and gang sign painted over every flat surface.

"Left," I instructed. "We're almost there. Just keep going straight through the next few intersections."

Michael nodded silently and obeyed. With careful determination, he guided the truck around a few cars that partially blocked the road. We found what we were looking for just a few minutes later: a low, glass-fronted building with an assortment of broadcast aerials on the roof. The windows were just as cracked and broken as everything else, but there was no sign of current occupation.

I grabbed my radio, and thumbed the receiver. "We're here. Form a circle in front of the building, bikes in the middle. Get some people up on top of the trucks to stand watch. Skye, Zane, Jim, and anyone else who knows anything about mechanical stuff or radios, you're with me."

As soon as Michael had brought the Hilux to a stop, I hopped out with my shotgun at the ready and scanned the surroundings for any signs of danger. I saw and heard nothing, just the occasional warble of birdsong and the pounding of the rain on the roof of the truck beside me.

"Stay out here and organise the watch," I instructed when Michael joined me. He nodded and went off to direct traffic, while I inspected the building that had brought us all that way. The moody weather meant that it was dark inside, too dark for me to be able to make out much beyond the ragged glass around the window frames. I reached inside my jacket and grabbed my torch, tucking it inside my sleeve to keep it from getting wet.

The golden beam probed the darkness and drove back the shadows, revealing a small room that had once been a lobby. Debris of a hundred different sorts littered the floor and gathered in the corners; I stepped over the window frame and made my way deeper, my feet crunching across a mixture of leaf litter and trash blown in over the course of a thousand windy days. Tiny, sparkling gems of broken safety glass glittered when my torchlight brushed past them, giving everything a strange, otherworldly feeling.

I heard quiet footfalls behind me, then Skylar's voice whispered, "We're here. Where do we go?"

"Cover me while I check the building is safe," I answered quietly. The response was a chorus of metallic clicks as my companions slipped the safeties off their weapons. I did the same, and led the way down the corridor towards the back of the building.

On either side of the hallway, doors hung open like shadowy, gaping maws. I checked each one, and found a couple of offices, a couple of sound studios, a small lunchroom, and a pair of single-stall lavatories beside an exit that let out into an empty car park.

"I guess the folks that worked here all went home to die," I commented, closing the door to the car park and locking it from the inside.

"Well, aren't you morbid today?" Skye answered, her voice dry and sarcastic. I grunted inarticulately in response, focusing on a more important question: was the power working in Tokoroa?

A light switch caught the beam of my torch. I gently slid past my sister and friends, and pressed it with my thumb. Light flared up, but it was dull and flickering, barely enough to see. I ran my gaze across the ceiling, and discovered that most of the bulbs had been shattered: only two were still intact. Whether that was deliberate or not was a mystery that I couldn't solve.

"Well, at least we've got power," I said, trying to make myself sound cheerful for the sake of my companions. I glanced at them to check who I had with me, and found

Jim, Zane, and Ropata following me, in addition to my sister. I nodded and smiled at them. "I saw two sound studios. Let's split up and examine them, see if we can get one of them working."

They nodded obediently. Zane and Ropata headed off towards the studio on the right, leaving me, Jim, and Skye to look at the other one. I found a light switch just inside the door, and this one yielded better results than the one out in the lobby. Unfortunately, what it lit up was a bank of buttons, switches, and dials that looked about as complex as the control panel of a battleship to my inexperienced eye.

"Wow, I have no idea what to do here," I admitted, then I shot a look of appeal at the other two. "Help?"

"Don't worry, I know exactly what to do," Skye answered cheerfully.

Surprised, I lifted my brows and looked at her. "Yeah?"

"Yep!" She grinned suddenly and gave me a playful wink. "We find the manual. Then, we read it."

"Damn, I was hoping to be way out of town by sunset," I said, shaking my head. "Oh well. Nothing we can do about it. Anahera will never let me hear the end of it if we don't at least try."

"It's the right thing to do," Skye reassured me.

To my surprise, Jim also grunted and nodded his agreement. "We may not have liked having to leave our homes, but at least your warning gave us the option to choose. Better that than die unprepared."

"True." The thought cheered me up enough that the smile I gave them wasn't entirely forced. "All right, let's find this manual. You guys look in here, and I'll go check those offices we saw. Let's hope they kept a printed copy on hand, because we can't exactly Google it anymore."

Skye laughed and nodded. "I'll call if we find anything."

I gave her a thumbs-up sign and left the room. Before I made it halfway to my destination, a shout from outside caught my attention. Startled, I raced back to the front of the building and dove out into the rain, just in time to see Michael standing at the head of a nearby alleyway, waving and yelling at someone I couldn't see. Beside him, Alfred was barking and wagging his tail, apparently oblivious to his master's distress.

"Hey! Come back!" he yelled, then shot a frantic look around. I could tell at a glance that he wanted to run after whoever had gone down that alleyway, and was straining to hold himself back.

I was at his side before he even realised I was coming. "What happened?"

Poor Michael almost jumped out of his skin, but as soon as he recognised me he grabbed my arm with a panic-stricken look on his face. "It's Priyanka!"

"What about her?" I demanded, my stomach dropping to my knees. "Is she okay?"

"She just ran off," he explained, out of breath from shouting. "I have no idea why. She just shouted something and then ran down that alley like all the hounds of hell were after her."

I swore under my breath. "We have to go find her. Come on!"

I heard his footsteps behind me as I raced down the alleyway. Alfred let out a happy yelp and bounded along after us. The old dog clearly presumed it was a game and was more than happy to play along. The alley swung sharply to the left, and emptied out into a vast parking lot that ran behind the shopping centre. On the far side, I could see

Priya sprinting away from us as fast as she could go, her little pink running shoes splashing through the puddles.

"Priya!" I yelled as I ran after her. When that didn't reach her, I drew an even deeper breath, and screamed her name as loud as I possibly could. "*Priya!*"

The girl skidded to a halt, and shot a quizzical look back over her shoulder. As soon as she realised that we were following her, her entire face seemed to light up.

"Mama!" she called back, pointing at the row of houses on the other side of the car park. "Mama, there's a girl! I saw her!"

I didn't bother to waste the breath on answering her until we'd closed the gap between us. When we finally got close enough to speak normally, I slowed down to a walk, and then a stop.

"Honey, you can't run off like that," I scolded her gently. "Do you know how much you scared us?"

"Scared?" She blinked up at me, her big, expressive eyes full of confusion. "Why scared?"

I took a deep breath to calm my racing heart. "It's dangerous here. We have to go back, where it's safe."

"No!" Priya stomped her foot with sudden, unexpected vehemence and planted her hands on her hips; she'd never declined any instruction before, so the gesture took me completely by surprise. "I want to find the girl. I want to help her, like you helped me."

"She's probably not alone out here," I explained, gently placing my hands on her shoulders. "There might be bad people, people that want to hurt you."

"Then they'll hurt her, too," she answered stubbornly. "I want to find her and make sure she no hurt. Is dangerous, Mama. You said so."

"I..." I started to try and answer her, but then I realised exactly what she was doing. She was mimicking us, and copying our behaviour. While it was dangerous for all of us, what she wanted to do was ethically right. I sighed heavily and nodded. "Okay, we'll look for a couple of minutes. But we're going to be very careful, okay? Do you have your gun?"

"Yes!" She nodded and patted her pocket. "I have, like Baba taught me."

"Okay." I shot a quizzical look at Michael. "How good is Alfred at tracking?"

"Pretty good," he answered. "I think he was a working dog, back in the day." Michael knelt down, and ruffled the dog's ears. "Alfie? Alfie, fetch! Go fetch!"

The dog let out a delighted yelp, and sprinted off in the direction Michael pointed. The three of us took off after him a second later, and followed when he jumped over a low fence and into an overgrown yard. There, the old sheepdog paused to sniff the ground thoroughly, then he lifted his head and barked. In response to his bark, we heard a child's voice cry out in fear.

"Here!" Priyanka shouted, pointing at an old porch. She dropped to her knees in the mud without regard for her clothing, and peered into the darkness beneath it. "Girl! Come out, girl. Come out. We help you. We nice."

"Go away!" the girl cried back, her words choked by a sob. "I don't want your help. Leave me alone!"

"Whoa, Priya. Back off," I instructed gently. "You're scaring her. Come over here, so we can talk to her without frightening her."

"Me not scary," Priya answered indignantly. "Me nice!"

"You mean 'I'm not scary'. But, just trust me and come here." I smiled at her, and beckoned her over. "Come on."

Priya seemed on the verge of protesting, but she paused to think about it. Then she let out a huffing sound, and pushed herself back to her feet. "Yes, Mama."

"Mama?" the little voice under the porch echoed the word. Suddenly, I found myself being watched by a pair of large, delicately-slanted eyes, through a tangle of wild black hair. The girl froze, staring at us with a look of terror on her face, clearly torn between warring emotions.

"Yes, that's me." I reached up and put my hood back to reveal my face. The rain plastered my hair down against the sides of my head and oozed down the back of my neck, but I considered it a worthwhile sacrifice. "Hi there, sweetie. What's your name?"

The girl inched back a bit, hiding within the shadows under the porch. A quick glance around told me that there was only one way in or out, so she was stuck there unless she wanted to risk running past us to get away. To try and show her that I wasn't a danger to her, I put my shotgun back over my shoulder, and held my empty hands up for her to see.

"It's okay," I said softly. "We're not going to hurt you. My name is Sandy. Do you have a name?"

"Of course, I have a name!" This time, it was her turn to sound indignant. In spite of the tension of the situation, I laughed.

"Sorry. That was a dumb question, I guess," I admitted. "What I meant is, will you tell me your name?"

There was a moment of silence, then the girl let out a long sigh. "Fine. My name is Jasmine. Will you go away now?"

"Not just yet. Maybe later," I said dryly, impressed by the girl's spunk. "It's nice to meet you, Jasmine. How old are you?"

"I'm twelve," she snapped, though her voice trembled in such a way that it gave away her fear, even if she didn't want it to. "I'm old enough to fight you! If you think I'm going to let you take me away, then you're crazy!"

"Take you away?" I shot a glance at Michael, and found him looking as alarmed as I felt. "No one's going to take you away. We're just passing through on our way south, and stopped to see if we could make the radio work. Priya saw you, and wanted to make sure that you were okay." I slowly lowered myself down to crouch, so that I could see her huddled under the porch and she could see me. "Are you all alone?"

"No!" she snapped, inching back further into the shadows. "I have friends. Lots of friends. Big friends! They'll fight you if you try to take me to him! I don't want to get married!"

"Married?" My jaw dropped in surprise, and it took me a second to piece my wits back together. Then, understanding struck and a dark cloud of anger began to descend across my mind. "Jasmine, is someone around here hurting your friends?"

There was silence again, and this time it dragged out even longer. Then, I heard a soft, tell-tale sniffing sound that told me the girl was crying. My heart dropped to my knees.

"Jasmine?" I asked again, as gently as I could. "Honey, who did they take?"

"My sister," the girl whispered, barely loud enough for me to hear her voice. "Lily. We were just playing, like we always do, and he surprised us. He grabbed her, and said that she was a pretty little flower, just ready to be plucked, and that she was his wife now. Then he threw her in his truck and drove away."

I took a deep breath to try and calm myself, but it didn't do much good. Rage seethed within my chest, driven by my own experiences combined with outrage that anyone would do such a thing to a child. "When did that happen?"

"This morning," Jasmine said miserably. "One of my friends went to go look for her, but he hasn't come back."

"Did you know the man?" I asked. "Do you have any idea where he lives?"

"We've seen him sometimes," she answered. "He comes to town and takes things, but he looks scary so we stay away. We call him 'the farmer', because he always smells like dirt. He comes from outside of town. From that direction." She pointed towards the south.

I nodded and eased myself back to my feet. One look at Michael's face told me that he felt the same way I did. Jasmine took the opportunity to scramble out from under the porch and run away, but none of us made any attempt to stop her. There was no point, and no need. She had the choice to be free, and she made it. Her sister didn't have the same option.

"Well, I don't think we have any choice in this matter," I said. "We have to go save that girl."

Michael just nodded solemnly.

Chapter Fifteen

The others were in a state of near-panic by the time we made it back to the radio station. The second that we stepped out of the alley, a cry went up and we were enveloped in a friendly mob. Once the initial excitement passed, I gathered everyone in around me and quickly explained the situation to them.

"I need two people to come with us to rescue the girl," I said, my voice raised enough to be heard over the general noise of rain and upset people. "Tane, Iorangi, you game?"

The brothers nodded vigorously and shouted their agreement; I could see the outrage etched on their faces even from afar.

"Good." I nodded, and looked at the others. "Everyone else, stay here and focus on getting the radio going. I suspect we're going to have to stay the night whether we want to or not, so scout out the local buildings and find one that we can secure. We also need to get some food into people before too long."

"We'll take care of it," Anahera said. Beside her, Skylar and Elly nodded silent agreement. "You just go. Save that little girl, before it's too late."

I gave them an appreciative smile, but wasted no more time on words. With a gesture to my companions, I raced over to where the bikes were waiting for us, and leapt onto one. Michael was a heartbeat behind me, and the brothers just behind him. There was a collective roar as we all started up our bikes, and then we were off.

I led the way towards the main road south, since I was the only one that had studied the map in great detail. Within minutes, we were bouncing along the uneven tarmac through a small shopping district that swiftly devolved into suburbia and even more swiftly transformed into farmland. Young native bush sprang up on either side of the road, fern fronds waving in the stiffening breeze.

Suddenly, a flash of lightning illuminated the world, followed by a deep-throated roar of thunder. A moment later the rain redoubled, as if someone had overturned a bucket in the sky. The full force of the storm had taken its time reaching us, but now it had arrived, it was vicious. The noise was so deafening that I barely heard one of my companions shouting an alert.

I carefully eased my bike to a halt, and looked back at the others strung out behind me. At the rear, Tane was yelling and pointing frantically into the bush, but he was too far away for me to make out what he was saying. Michael looked at me and tilted his head towards him; I simply nodded my understanding. Together, we wheeled our bikes around and drove back to the brothers.

"I think there's a pathway through there," Tane called as soon as we were close enough, pointing into the dense bush on the side of the road.

"I think you're right," I yelled back, shielding my eyes from the stinging rain. "I see tyre tracks in the mud, and the branches have been cut back recently. Come on!"

We should have dismounted and travelled on foot, but my gut told me that time was of the essence. There was no time for caution. I opened the throttle all the way, and guided my bike into the gloom. All of our bikes had headlights, but the bouncing, uneven light made me feel even more reckless. Still, what choice did we have? At least the boughs of the trees kept the rain more or less at bay.

The path swung around a particularly large tree, and I followed it. It wasn't until I was fully committed to the manoeuvre that I spotted the human figure hiding in the brush beside the path. I slammed on the brakes so hard that my bike went into a spin, and came to rest facing back the direction we'd come. The beam of my headlights cut through the gloom, and illuminated the crouched figure; before the others even realised what was happening, I had my shotgun out and trained on the bushes.

"I see you!" I shouted; even under the trees, the storm was loud. "Come out with your hands above your head."

"Don't shoot!" The voice that responded was male, deep and hoarse. He stood up slowly, one hand raised and the other shielding his face from the glare of my headlights. "I don't want any trouble. I just want the little girl back. She's part of my group."

I lowered my shotgun, and took a deep breath. "You're Jasmine's friend, then?"

"Jasmine?" The man sounded startled. I squinted to try and make out the details of his face while he was speaking, but I couldn't see them. "Yes, Jasmine is her sister. Please, I just want Lily back. We don't have a lot, but we'll give you anything you want."

Suddenly, it struck me that he thought we were a gang, and somehow responsible for what had happened. I shoved my shotgun back over my shoulder, and shook my head.

"We have nothing to do with the guy that grabbed Lily," I explained, deliberately softening my tone. "We were coming through town from the north-west, and caught Jasmine spying on us. She told us what happened. We're here to free Lily, too."

"Free her?" Now, he sounded bewildered. "Why would you want to do that?"

"Because she's a person, and every person has the right to choose her own destiny," I answered firmly and resolutely. "I'm not going to let someone force a young girl into marriage. Hell, I'm not going to let someone force anyone into marriage."

"Amen to that," he agreed, slowly lowering his hands to his sides. "I'm not armed. I was going to negotiate to get her back. What's your plan?"

"First, we find her," I said. "Then, we figure it out from there."

"Leave those bikes here and follow me, then," the stranger said. "It took me all day to find them, but I think this is the right place."

"Show us," I said. I switched off the bike, dismounted, and pocketed the keys. Around me, the others did the same. As soon as they were ready, the stranger beckoned for us to follow him and led the way through the damp, shadowy bush towards the east.

As we travelled, I realised that there was something familiar about him, but without seeing his face I couldn't put my finger on it. There was something about the set of his shoulders, his voice, or perhaps the way he walked. He had a pronounced limp, but I couldn't recall anyone that I'd known who had the same. Then we rounded a corner, the house came into view, and all considerations were forgotten except for Lily's welfare.

"Stop," I whispered, my voice barely audible over the storm. "Stay here for a minute while I scout around."

I only just saw their nods of agreement in the semi-darkness, but it was enough. Leaving my friends behind, I slid out of the bush and across the worn driveway towards the homestead in a military-style crouch-walk.

The house was nothing special, just another one of the basic, prefabricated boxes that had been popular in the late seventies. The weatherboards were faded and dirty, and the driveway pocked with potholes. I had to step carefully to avoid breaking an ankle, but there was just enough light for me to keep myself safe.

I crept down the right side of the building, and found myself in a narrow alleyway between the house and a vegetable garden framed by old-fashioned wooden fences. I paused beneath a window where the curtains didn't quite meet properly, and eased myself up to take a peek inside. What I saw made my belly curdle with rage.

A young girl lay on a filthy mattress, her hands bound cruelly behind her back. Although her hair covered part of her face, it only took me a second to realise that she wasn't just Jasmine's sister – she was Jasmine's twin.

A twelve-year-old-girl. That man planned to force a twelve-year-old-girl to marry him. Not on my watch.

I took a deep breath to cool my surging temper, and reached up to carefully test the window. It was firmly latched from the inside. Lily appeared to be either sleeping or unconscious, and didn't respond when I tapped softly on the window pane. I would have to find another way in.

Easing myself back down into my comfortable crouch-walk, I stepped softly up to the corner of the building and peeked around it. A beat-up old truck sat under a carport nearby, and farther away I could see an open barn. There were no people around, as far as I could tell. A few chickens clucked in a henhouse nearby, but nothing else stirred.

I paused to consider the evidence around me. It seemed unlikely that the farm could support more than one or two people at the most without extensive scavenging, and there was only a single pair of dirty gumboots by the back door. I saw nothing that indicated anyone else lived there, which meant we most likely only had one enemy to worry about. My hopes soared for a moment, but I fought them back down to avoid letting them colour my reasoning.

I resumed scouting, checking each window and door that I could reach. They were all locked from the inside, but the back door was so flimsy that I felt sure we could break the latch without any trouble. Then, through a side window, I finally spotted the villain himself. It wasn't much to see: just a fat old man with a balding pate, slouched in an armchair in front of a TV playing a rerun of an old sitcom off DVD. The man had a beer in one hand and the remote in the other, but his eyes were closed and his chin was resting on his flabby chest. As far as I could tell, he was asleep.

I slipped back down and continued scouting, but I saw no sign of anyone else on the property. Once I was satisfied I had the lay of the land, I crept back to the bushes where my friends were waiting for me. As soon as they saw me approaching, I heard the stranger's voice.

"Is she okay?" he asked urgently, his voice trembling. It didn't take a psychologist to tell that he was nervous.

"It's hard to be sure, but she seems uninjured," I answered. "She's sleeping in a back bedroom... and she's still dressed. That's a good sign."

"Thank God," he whispered, his shoulders slumping. "I'm not sure I could bear to lose another one."

Sympathy blossomed in my chest. I couldn't see his face, but I knew that tone. It was the same tone that Michael used when he was talking about Sophie, the little girl he'd loved like a daughter.

"Don't worry, mate," I said, reaching out to squeeze his shoulder. "We'll get her back. I have a plan."

The man nodded silently in the dark, and gestured for me to continue. I turned, and pointed towards the house as I outlined my plan for the others.

"The house is just your basic prefab – rectangular, one door in the front, one door in the back. The back door leads right into the living room. The farmer is sleeping on the couch. Michael, Tane, Iorangi – I want you to go in the back. Give us sixty seconds to get in place, then storm that door. It's old and thin, you should have no trouble busting it open. Don't kill him, though. Just make sure he doesn't run or grab a weapon. While you're covering him, we'll sneak in the front door and grab Lily."

"Geez, you should have been on the Armed Offenders Squad," Michael commented dryly from behind me.

I laughed and shook my head. "Get out of here, you three. Remember, don't kill him. That's not who we are."

He nodded and then the three of them were off, mimicking the stealth I'd used earlier to the best of their ability. I beckoned the stranger to follow me, and led him towards the front door instead. A bolt of lightning lit up the sky, illuminating the world for a moment, and then the roll of thunder masked our footfalls in its wake.

I knelt at the front door and pulled out my lockpicks. The lock was as old as the house; it took me barely a minute to open it, even working by touch. Just as the last tumbler was sliding into place, I heard the sound of wood shattering, followed by deep-throated male shouts.

I threw open the door and hurried inside, ducking down the corridor that I guessed had to lead to the girl's room. The door at the end of the hall was locked, but it was so flimsy that this time I didn't even bother to pick it. I just threw my shoulder against it with all of my might. A second later, I felt the stranger's mass hit it beside me. The door buckled. One more good, co-ordinated charge from both of us was enough to shatter the lock. The door burst open, and we tumbled into the room.

I fell and landed on something soft: the mattress. I leapt up as though I'd touched a red-hot element, feeling a twisted kind of horror that I couldn't name. Beside me, I saw the stranger roll up to his feet as well, but he obviously felt no such disgust. His entire focus was on the girl. He grabbed her gently and rolled her over, struggling to untie her hands.

"Lily!" he demanded urgently. "Lily, wake up!"

I spotted a light switch on the wall beside me and flicked it on, then immediately wished I hadn't. In the semi-darkness, it had looked like the dark shadows on the bed were just mud, but under proper lighting I realised that it was a mixture of dirt and blood. The girl's cheeks were a mass of bruises, and her hair was matted. Fresh blood shone against her porcelain-pale skin, and made her look like a broken doll.

I heard the stranger swearing at the sight, but I was too stunned and angry to say anything at all. A cold, dark sense of purpose twisted my gut, and drove me out of the room, following the sound of voices raised in anger. My companions had the florid-faced farmer cornered, but even confronted by three men with guns he was still shouting.

As soon as he saw me, the farmer turned his wrath in my direction. "Oi! Are you the leader of these ruffians? Get out of my house! How dare you come storming in here like you own the place? I'm a taxpayer, and I—"

His words were cut off abruptly, when my fist connected with his jaw. The farmer stumbled backwards, knocking his television off its stand and sending both of them tumbling across the floor. By the time he recovered enough to realise what had happened, I had my shotgun off my back and aimed right at his face.

"Let me make one thing clear," I told him, my voice soft but cold as ice. "The thing that makes us human is our ability to make choices, and you have made a very, very bad one. If you ever take away someone else's right to choose again, then I will have you held accountable before a tribunal of law. We don't have jails anymore, so you better believe that our justice will not be gentle – but it will be just. You're lucky that we don't have time to deal with you right now, so consider this your lucky night – but if you *ever* touch anyone else without their permission again, then I will personally bring so much wrath down on your sorry head that you'll wish you'd died in the plague. Do you understand?"

The man just stared at me, open-mouthed, blood leaking from his split lip. I narrowed my eyes and tightened my grip on the shotgun, but I didn't have to use it. The gesture alone was enough for him. He nodded frantically, shoving himself as far back away from me as he could, terror written across his face.

I nodded once and left the room without another word. This time, no shouting followed me. No sounds. Nothing but silence, and the distant sound of begging.

"Lily? Please, honey, come on, wake up... It's okay, *Onīsan* is here..."

I re-entered the bedroom to find our hooded stranger kneeling on the mattress, cradling Lily's battered body in his arms. He'd managed to free her hands and feet, but the girl was still unconscious. It took all of my willpower to work up the courage to kneel down beside him on that awful mattress, which brought back so many painful memories. As soon as I did, the stink of alcohol struck me. I hadn't smelt it before, so I knew it wasn't coming from the man; it had to be coming from the girl. Then, I spotted something even worse, lying on the mattress beside her.

"He's drugged her," I surmised, picking up the little white prescription vial. "Sleeping pills, and alcohol by the smell of it. Our best bet is to try and get as much of it out of her system as possible. It's not going to be pretty, but we need to make her vomit."

The man just nodded. With surprising confidence, he turned the young girl onto her belly and stuck his finger down her throat. Her entire body convulsed. The man held her until she finally threw up the entire contents of her stomach all over the floor. The stench of it was terrible, a combination of far too much alcohol, and half-digested sleeping tablets. As soon as she stopped convulsing, the girl curled up in a ball and started sobbing piteously.

The man just sat beside her, gently holding her through it all. "It's okay, honey. You're safe. I'm here."

"Onīsan?" she sobbed, her voice slurred. "I want to go home."

"I know, Lil. I know." The man looked up at me suddenly, and the light finally hit his features. "Thank you so much. These kids mean everything to me."

I had no response. He'd gained a lot of scars and one of his eyes was milky and blind, but I would have recognised his face anywhere.

"...Gavin?"

Chapter Sixteen

The man blinked his one good eye in obvious surprise. "You know me?"

I didn't have any words to express how I felt. I just reached up and folded my hood back, revealing my own face for the first time. It took a few seconds before recognition dawned, and his mouth fell open.

"Sandy!" he cried. Before I quite knew what had hit me, I felt a strong arm clamp around my shoulders and I was pulled into a hug. "I thought you were dead, kid."

"I thought you were dead, too," I admitted, my shock finally passing enough for me to figure out how to use my words again. I shoved myself back out of his embrace, and gave him a long look. "You've seen better days, old man. We'll have plenty of time to catch up later, but for now let's focus on getting Lily home."

Gavin nodded his agreement, and looked back down at the battered young body nestled in the crook of his arm. "How about it, little sister? You ready to go home?"

The girl nodded weakly and gave him a smile. I took one look out the window at the driving rain, and then I shrugged off my coat and held it out to him.

"Here," I said. "Wrap her up in this. It won't keep her entirely dry, but at least it'll keep her warm."

Gavin hesitated, but Lily's needs outweighed any concerns either of us might have had about me. He took the garment and gently wound it around her frail body, pulling the hood forward to protect her face. I took a deep breath, and used the moment to broach the subject of what to do with the farmer.

"Gavin," I said quietly, resting my hand on his shoulder. "The man who did this to her, he's still alive. You probably heard that we don't kill indiscriminately. However, we do have a code of justice. I've already put the fear of God into him on your behalf, but if you want to, we can bring him back with us and have him put to trial before a judicator--"

"No," Gavin answered sharply, shaking his head. "I don't want to put Lily through that. Right now, the only thing that matters is getting her home safely."

I nodded silently and rose to my feet. Gavin picked up the child's leather-wrapped form, and followed me back to the front door. We found Michael and the others waiting for us there.

"Where's the farmer?" I asked, shooting a wary look back towards the living room.

"Curled up in the foetal position, crying like a baby," Michael answered dryly. "I think you scared him, honey."

"Honey?" Gavin shot a startled look at me, his brows raised. "You have changed."

"I had to," I answered with a shrug. "Gavin, this is Michael, my fiancé. The bloke with the dreads is Tane, and the one with the tattoos is Iorangi. Guys, this is Gavin. He's... an old friend."

"Oh?" This time, it was Michael giving me the surprised look. "I wasn't aware that you had any old friends."

"Neither was I, until about five minutes ago," I admitted sheepishly. "Looks like reports of his demise have been greatly exaggerated."

"I wouldn't say 'greatly'," Gavin said. "It was pretty close for a while."

I gave him a curious look, but it wasn't really the time or place to ask. Instead, I pushed my curiosity aside and turned my attention back to what mattered.

"We need to get Lily back to Doctor Cross," I said. "I don't think she's been... violated, but she's been beaten and drugged. I want him to make sure she's going to be okay. Michael, she's not entirely conscious so I want you to ride double with her. Gavin, you can ride with me."

"Much appreciated," Gavin replied dryly. "It's a long walk back."

"In this storm, it's going to be a long drive, too." I shook my head and gave him a wry smile. "Come on. If we leave now, we should make it back before sunset."

All four men nodded their agreement. Michael started to unzip his jacket with obvious intentions of giving it to me, but I didn't give him a chance. I'd already made up my mind about getting wet, so I wasn't about to let him take on that particular burden this time. Out into the driving rain I went, leading the way across the compacted gravel towards the edge of the bush beyond.

The rain hit me like a waterfall, soaking me to the bone within seconds, but I refused to let it bother me. Some days, it felt like I was never going to be dry again. By the time I made it to the shelter of the trees, I was absolutely drenched. I paused to wait for the others, hugging the thin fabric of my old army surplus jacket close around my shoulders to preserve what little warmth I had. Michael was on me a second later, with a dark look on his face.

"You didn't have to get wet," he protested, annoyed with my stubbornness. "I would have given you my jacket."

"I'm already wet," I said with a shrug. "No point both of us getting drowned."

"Sometimes I really don't know what I'm going to do with you," he answered, sounding exasperated. I just grinned at him, and reached out to touch his hand in the cavernous gloom. Before either of us could say anything else, the others caught up with us and our brief moment of privacy was gone.

We arrived back at our bikes a few minutes later, wet and muddy but intact. Gavin and I helped Lily up in front of Michael, so that he could catch her if she started to slip. The girl was only half-conscious and trembling convulsively; even though he was a stranger, she huddled into Michael for warmth, her eyes glazed and distant.

I put my hand on Gavin's shoulder in some small attempt to reassure him. He just nodded faintly, and gestured for me to lead the way. I did, and soon we were on our way back to Tokoroa, bouncing along, with me in the lead, and Gavin's arms around my waist.

Once we burst back out onto the road, I found myself having to contend with stinging rain; I made a mental note to find some goggles for our riders to wear in bad weather, and squinted at the road in an effort to see where we were going.

Maybe helmets, too. Suddenly, helmets seemed like a very good idea. The last thing I wanted was to lose one of the last remnants of my species to a farm bike accident.

The wind howled around us, wailing like the mournful ghosts of the billions of souls lost to the plague. Lightning illuminated the sky in a blinding flash. The sun had begun to go down by the time we made it back to town, and it was so dark that I barely saw our turnoff in time. At the very last moment, I spotted a light glowing out of the corner of my eye, and that turned out to be the beam of a torch.

I hurled the bike around the corner with such reckless disregard that Gavin shouted in alarm, but we made it intact. Some part of my brain warned me against that kind of behaviour, but my conscious mind didn't care. I only had one concern, and that was the little girl nestled in my lover's embrace. Another stray. Another child, a forgotten throw-away left behind when civilization abandoned her. At least this one wasn't entirely alone, like my poor little Priyanka had been.

By the time I brought the bike to a stop in front of the radio station, there was a crowd of people waiting for us. They shouted greetings and questions, waving frantically at us from beneath their makeshift rain-gear. Behind me, I heard Gavin's sharp intake of breath.

"There are so many people," he said softly, just loud enough for me to hear. "Sandy, did you join a gang?"

"I did at one stage, but that's another story," I replied. "This isn't a gang. The group you see before you are going to be the founding members of the first city our country has seen in far too long. We just need to make it far enough south to lay the foundations."

"Good God," he murmured, easing himself off the back of the bike so that I could get up as well. "Sounds like we're going to have a lot to talk about."

"And you're going to have a lot of names to try and remember," I teased. I killed the bike's engine, and went over to meet my friends. It was just at that moment that I realised something was missing. "Guys, where are the cars?"

"We moved them around the corner," Skylar explained. She rushed over and threw her arms around me, hugging me close. Then she shoved me back roughly and gave me a disgusted look. "Ugh, you're sopping wet!"

"And now you are, too," I replied with a playful grin. "You're welcome."

She snorted in mock annoyance, but then she suddenly seemed to remember why we'd gone away to begin with. "Did you find her?"

"Yes," I said, looking back over my shoulder at the other riders, who were just coming to a stop beside my bike. Gavin rushed over to help with his young charge, his discomfort apparently forgotten for the moment. I looked back at Skye, and gave her a sad smile. "She's in bad shape, though. Where's Doc?"

"He's around the corner, too," she answered, jerking a thumb over her shoulder. "There's a big, abandoned office building behind the radio station. It's not much, but it has a kitchen and toilets, and it's dry. I left him, Anahera, and the kids setting up beds, but they should be about done by now."

"Can you take us to him?" I asked. She nodded and beckoned for me to follow her. I passed the gesture along to Michael and Gavin, and soon the four of us were hurrying through the driving rain, leaving the bikes to be tended to by the rest of the group.

Skylar ducked through a wild garden that had probably once been a courtyard, and down a pathway between two buildings. We came out next to a glass door that was, miraculously, still intact. Skye rapped her knuckles on the metal frame, and we waited.

A minute later, we saw Doc's face appear on the other side of the glass, ghostly pale in the dim light. He nodded, unlocked the door, and let us in. Everything seemed fine, right up until the moment that he saw Gavin, and realised that he was a stranger. He took a step backwards, blocking the hallway leading deeper into the building.

"And who is this?" he demanded warily, jerking his chin at Gavin.

"This is Gavin. He's an old friend of mine," I replied, glancing back over my shoulder at him. "Gavin, this is our doctor, Stewart Cross."

The doctor's brows knitted, and Skylar turned to look at me in surprise. Her eyes widened so suddenly that I realised she hadn't figured out that Gavin wasn't one of our own until that moment. With his hood up and the rain in her eyes, it wasn't all that surprising.

"Please elaborate, Ms McDermott," the doctor demanded, his brows knitting into a frown. "Do we know him well enough to let him near the children?"

"Don't worry, it's fine," I replied. "Gavin's good people. He helped me a lot when the plague first hit – I probably wouldn't have survived without him. I think it's fair to say I know him well enough to vouch for him."

"Wait, is this the honey guy?" Skye asked, curiosity flickering across her face. "I thought you said he was dead?"

"I thought he was dead, but he wasn't," I admitted with a shrug. "Just like I thought you were dead, but you weren't. Apparently, I'm just really bad at keeping track of the people I care about." I made an abrupt gesture with one hand to derail the conversation, and directed it towards the more urgent topic. "Anyway – Doc, we need you. Lily's hurt."

My words seemed to touch just the right nerve. Doc dropped his gaze to the leather-wrapped bundle in Gavin's arms. He glanced briefly at me, then looked at the girl again. Whatever else he might have been feeling, his healer's instincts clearly took precedence; he nodded once, and gestured for us to follow him.

"We found a cache of mattresses stashed away upstairs," he explained as he led us through the hallways. "There's some old food and clothing, too. Looks like someone used to live here, but they're long gone."

I glanced at Gavin, and he nodded. "There used to be a gang here, so it was probably theirs. As far as I can tell, someone came in and wiped them all out. One of the kids survived but he won't talk about it. Won't talk about much of anything, to be frank."

"How many people do you have with you?" I asked him as we climbed the stairs up to the second floor.

"Four," he replied, with just the faintest of smiles. "All kids. I've got the twins, Solomon — that's the kid who survived from the gangs — and another girl named Melody." He heaved a long sigh, his one good eye focused on the stairs at his feet. "After I lost you, I felt so guilty that I made it my duty to protect the kids. All of the kids. Whether they like it or not."

I couldn't help but laugh at that. "Sounds like they didn't want to be protected."

"No, not at all," he admitted. "They hate it, but they've accepted me hanging around because I'm good at finding them food. Melody and the twins were together for a long time, possibly since the beginning. When I first found them, they were like a pack of wild cats."

"Put her down on the mattress there," the doctor instructed, interrupting our discussion. Gavin did as he was told, then we went into the next room with the others, to let the doctor work in peace. The room turned out to be a kitchen, and Anahera was in there stirring something in a giant cooking pot. I took a moment to introduce both her and Skylar to Gavin formally.

"Go sit down," Anahera ordered once introductions were finished. "I'll bring you some dinner. You must be freezing."

"Yeah." I nodded my agreement, and went over to a nearby table with my dripping companions. Once we were comfortable, I gave Gavin a curious look. "You were saying the girls were like wild cats?"

"Yeah. It was so over the top that in retrospect, it's pretty funny," Gavin said, shaking his head slowly. "If Melody lets you meet her, then you'll get it."

"If she *lets* me meet her?" I echoed, amused. "Oh dear, now you have to tell me. What happened?"

Gavin laughed and nodded. "Yeah, all right. I was travelling through... I don't remember where, one of the towns on the east coast. You know how cautious I am, but I'm not as capable as I used to be before I lost my eye. These three little hellcats managed to ambush me. This would have been about three years ago, mind."

"Wait. Let me get this straight." I paused and did some quick maths. "You were ambushed by a pair of nine-year-olds, and — how old was Melody at the time?"

"About fifteen," he supplied, a mixture of amusement and embarrassment written on his scarred face. "Yes, I was ambushed by a fifteen-year-old girl and a couple of nine-year-olds. And they won."

"They won?" I echoed, surprised. "Are you serious?"

"I'm ashamed to admit it, but yes." Gavin shrugged and glanced down. "I'm not the man I used to be, Sandy. The reason I vanished was because I was grabbed by a bunch of gang-bangers, led by this big bloke with a bald head and the evilest eyes I've ever seen on another human being. They accused me of hunting in their territory."

"Oh, God," I whispered, my good mood suddenly vanishing. "So they're the ones that… did that? To your eye, I mean?"

"Yeah." He sighed heavily and nodded. "They broke both my legs, cut me up like a side of meat. The only thing that spared me was luck. One of their scouts spotted something that was apparently more interesting than me, and called them off. I managed to drag myself away and hide, but they didn't come back." Suddenly, he reached out and grabbed my hand, a look of absolute panic crossing his face. "I was so afraid that they'd spotted you. I looked for you for weeks, once I could walk again, but I never found you – or the gang."

Sympathy welled up in my breast. I reached out to place my hand over his, trying in some small way to reassure him. "I was fine. Well… I was fine at the time. I was captured by a gang later on, but that was years later. As you can see, I escaped.

"But not without scars," he said softly, reaching up to touch the pink mark on my cheek that had been left by Lee's knife, a few weeks earlier. "Though, this one here looks fresh. What have you been up to, girl?"

"It's a long story," I admitted. "But it actually sounds a little bit familiar. Tell me, the man with the evil eyes – was he a big guy, with a beer gut and tattoos all over his face?"

"Yes," Gavin said, surprise flickering across his face. "A real big bastard, with a full facial *tā moko*." He paused and shot a sheepish glance at Anahera, who also wore the Maori tattoos he was describing upon her chin. "No offense intended, ma'am."

She smiled and nodded. "None taken."

Gavin glanced back at me, and gave me a quizzical look. "Why do you ask? Have you seen him?"

"You could say that." I glanced over at Skylar, and held her gaze for a second, then I looked back at him. "I'd rather not talk about what he did to me, so let's just stick with the good news. He's dead. Skye killed him."

Gavin's expression flickered through an assortment of emotions in rapid succession, which eventually settled at relief. He nodded once, and looked down at his hands. "I'm glad. I looked for them when I was trying to find you, but all I found were... bodies. Mostly the bodies of girls."

"That's why we're doing what we're doing," I answered, gently squeezing his hand. "I've got a lot more scars that you can't see right now, but I survived them. I consider it my duty to help protect other young girls, so that they don't have to go through the same pain."

"Me too," he agreed. "After I lost you, I wasn't sure if I could forgive myself. I've spent all these years seeking redemption by helping other kids." Suddenly, his one good eye flicked to Michael, and his grip on my hand tightened. "You better take good care of her or else I'll have to kick your ass."

Michael blinked in surprise, then he laughed. "If I don't take good care of her, then I'll *let* you kick my ass."

"Good man." Gavin nodded firmly, and gave Michael a faint, lopsided smile. His gaze returned to me, and he turned the conversation back towards more pleasant things. "So, I was telling you about meeting Melody, wasn't I?"

"Yeah, you were saying something about getting kicked around by three little girls," I said, giving him a teasing grin. "How did that happen?"

"They came in from my blind spot, the clever little minxes." Gavin sighed and sat back in his seat, finally releasing my hand. "I should also mention that my hearing's been screwed up in that ear since the attack, so I didn't even hear them coming. One second, I thought I was alone. The next, I was flat on my back, with these three wild-eyed, filthy kids holding knives to my throat.

"They tried to rob me, as you can probably expect. I didn't have much for them to take, but I did have a few things that I'd made before I left my roost the night before. Particularly, honey rice cakes. I knew from looking at them that those kids had been on their own for a while, so I just gave them the cakes. You should have seen their eyes bug out. They inhaled them, and then demanded more. I told them I didn't have any, but that if they wanted I could show them how to make them. They've been following me around ever since."

"Ah, the way to a kid's heart is through her stomach." I laughed, and everyone else laughed right along with me.

"Speaking of which," Anahera cut in, setting a bowl of hot soup down in front of me.

I took it gratefully, and smiled at her. "Thank you."

"Of course, dear." She just smiled back, and set bowls down in front of the others. Once spoons were handed out, the conversation halted while we all tucked in. I hadn't eaten since that morning, so even plain fare was better than going hungry.

Just as I was wolfing down the last mouthful, Doctor Cross appeared in the doorway, holding my coat in his hands. I set my spoon down, and looked at him expectantly.

"Well, I have good news and I have bad news," he told us, absently handing the coat back to me. "The good news is that she'll live, and she wasn't sexually abused. The bad news is that she's going to be very sick for a while, until her body recovers from the beating he gave her. She has some internal injuries, but nothing that requires surgery. I would like to keep an eye on her for a few days, if we can."

Gavin looked at me, frowning. "Can you stay for a few days?"

I paused to think about it, and shook my head. "We shouldn't. It's not safe. The reason we're on the road is because there's a mutation of the virus spreading south, and it's turning the human infected into... well, it's making them like pigs. We've already lost way too many people. I can't risk losing any more." I paused, and looked at him. "You and the kids are welcome to come with us, though."

"I don't know how they'll feel about that," he admitted. "I'd be lying if I said I was in control of them. We just travel together, nothing more. I suppose I could ask them if they want to go."

"I'd appreciate it," I said, nodding. "They don't have to stay with us forever, just until Lily's feeling better."

Gavin nodded and slowly rose from his chair. "I'll go find them. Jasmine's going to be panicking about her sister, anyway. I should try to put her mind at ease."

I shot a glance at the others, then looked back at Gavin. "Can I send an escort with you? I'd hate for something to happen to you."

"No, I'll be fine," he said, shaking his head. "It's not far back to the place we're currently staying at. If they want to come and see Lily, then we'll be in a group. If not, I'll come back in the morning."

"Okay." I took a deep breath, and let it out as a long sigh. "If you're sure. Just be careful, okay? It's not safe out there."

"I'm always careful," he replied. "You just watch out for yourself, and keep an eye on Lily for me."

"Of course," I agreed. He nodded, patted my shoulder, and then he was gone. The doctor followed him out, presumably to go back to tending his young patient. I turned and looked at the others. "Well, that was unexpected."

"The mysterious honey-man reappears, bringing with him a pack of wild kids," Skylar joked. "Sounds like trouble just waiting to happen."

"Oh, probably." I shrugged and gave her a smile. "Still, at least Lily's okay, and I'm pretty sure that guy on the farm won't try anything like that again any time soon."

"Did you kill him, then?" Skye asked curiously.

"No," I answered, shaking my head. "We're trying to avoid doing that, remember? I just scared the hell out of him, and made him realise that there are still rules in place."

"Oh." Skye actually sounded a little bit disappointed. She shrugged and stood up. "Oh well, not our problem. I'm going to go check on the kids. Don't go anywhere."

"Yes, boss," I agreed, giving her a smile. I watched until she left the room, then glanced at the others. To my surprise, I found Anahera watching her as well, her eyes narrowed. Once Skylar was out of earshot, she came over and sat down at the table near Michael and me.

"There is something I should probably tell you," she said, her voice low and discreet.

"What, about Skye?" I asked, uncertain how to interpret her expression. "Has she done something?"

"I don't know," Anahera said thoughtfully. "I have no idea what the implications are. I just want to make you aware of it. After you were attacked by Lee at our camp, I sent my boys out to catch the two men that grabbed Skylar. Do you remember that?"

"I remember enough, yes," I answered with a nod. "I mean, I was in pretty bad shape, but I know you sent people out to capture them. I never found out what happened after that."

"No, I never had an opportunity to tell you privately, until now." Anahera sighed, sitting back in her chair. "My men found them dead. Both of their throats had been slit."

"What?" Startled, I looked over at Michael and saw that he was just as surprised as I was.

"She said that she hit them with your taser, then ran back to find me so that we could save you," Michael said. "You think that she killed them?"

"I suspect so, yes," Anahera said, nodding. "My men said that the bodies did show odd burn marks that I presume are the kind left by a taser, but their throats had been cut afterwards. My men estimate that they were unconscious at the time, lying face down."

"Wow," I murmured, unsure what to make of the revelation. My baby sister just didn't seem like the kind that would cut a man's throat in cold blood, even when her life was on the line. But then, how well did I really know her? We hadn't seen each other in ten years. A person can change a lot between the ages of eight and eighteen, particularly in a world as brutal and unforgiving as ours.

I glanced at Michael, and saw the same kind of uncertainty reflected on his face. He'd known her longer than I, but only by a few months. I wasn't sure what to say, and he certainly didn't seem any more confident. I felt a hand touch my shoulder, and glanced over to find Anahera watching me with sympathy.

"I told you because I wanted you to know, not because I expect you to do anything about it," she said gently. "These are unpleasant times, and sometimes we must do unpleasant things in the name of the greater good. If your friend's story is true, then it is likely those men have done things just as terrible as Lee had. I would have done the same thing, in her situation."

I let out a long breath that I hadn't realised I'd been holding, and nodded slowly. "Yeah. You're right. It's just... I don't know how to feel about it."

"I understand." She smiled at us, and gently squeezed my shoulder. "Don't worry, Sandy. Just take your time to think over it, and your feelings will sort themselves out."

I nodded and gave her a grateful smile. Just at that moment, Skylar came rushing back into the room, forestalling any further discussion about her.

"Hey, guys?" she called, her tone urgent. "Have any of you seen Priya?"

"Not since before we left," I answered, shaking my head.

"Well, we have a slight problem, then." Skye glanced back over her shoulder, then looked at me. "She's gone."

Chapter Seventeen

"What do you mean, she's gone?" I demanded, leaping up to my feet. "Where did she go?"

"I have no idea," Skye said with a shrug. "I put her to bed with the other kids about an hour ago, but she's not there anymore. I checked all the bathrooms in the building, but I can't find her anywhere."

I muttered a few choice words beneath my breath, and slammed my fist down on the table in an attempt to vent my distress physically. "She must have gone off looking for those kids again. I'm going to kill her."

"Calm down, honey," Michael said, in his most soothing voice. He put his hands on my shoulders, and turned me to face him. "She took care of herself for ten years before we found her. She can take care of herself for an hour or two."

"But what if she doesn't come back?" I asked, my gut twisting itself into all kinds of unpleasant shapes. "What if she decides to go with them instead of us?"

Michael just smiled, and drew me into a hug. "I doubt that she will. She loves you. She knows where we are; when she's ready to come home, she will."

"This is what it feels like to be a parent, Sandy," Anahera said sympathetically. "Every time your child leaves your sight, you worry that they won't come home. Usually, they do. Sometimes, they don't."

"I don't like this feeling," I admitted. "I'm torn between losing my marbles and bawling until she comes home, or storming off in search of her. Someone decide for me."

All of them laughed at that. Suddenly, I found myself in the middle of a group hug, with both Anahera and Skylar adding their arms to Michael's.

"How about we take the first watch?" Michael suggested. "That way, you can keep an eye out for her. I know you have trouble sleeping when you're worried."

"Good plan," I agreed immediately, relieved to have the decision taken away from me for a change. Although I was usually perfectly comfortable with being in command, there were some moments when I wanted the choice removed so that I couldn't blame myself if it was the wrong decision. I sighed heavily, and extracted myself from the web of arms. "We should start shutting up shop. Who's been fed so far?"

"Just you lot and the children," Anahera replied. She went over to stir her cook pot, which still simmered on the stove. "Dinner's ready, though. Time to feed the rest of the monsters. Someone needs to go call them in."

"Michael and I will go," I volunteered, then I glanced at Skye. "See if you can get some food down Lily? I imagine she's probably starving, but her stomach will be a bit sensitive."

Skye nodded her agreement. "I'll try her on some broth, and if that doesn't work then I'll figure something else out."

"Thank you." I smiled and touched my sister's arm. "Be gentle, though. That kid's had a rough time."

"Of course." Skye put her hand over mine, and squeezed it gently. "Don't worry, I'll take good care of her. Besides, if I don't then I'm pretty sure honey-guy will kick my butt."

"Actually..." I paused for a moment, turning her words over in my head. "Get a bit of that honey off Doc, and mix it in with some warm water. That'll give her some vital calories, and she's probably more likely to drink it. It should also help her immune system, and hopefully help with the pain."

"Okies!" Skye agreed brightly, then she punched my arm lightly. It took me a second to realise that she was mimicking Priya's favourite phrase, just to tease me. I laughed in response, and gave her a playful shove. Skye took it as a running start, and dashed out of the room giggling like a schoolgirl.

Once she was gone, I glanced at the others and shrugged. "Sometimes, I worry about her. But, you were right, Ana. She's tougher than I ever gave her credit for."

"Of course I'm right," she answered dryly. "I'm Mum, remember? Mum is always right."

"Not always," I said. "But mums do tend to have more life experience than their kids give them credit for." I sighed heavily, and looked at Michael. Suddenly aching for a moment of closeness, I reached out and threaded my fingers through his. "Come on. Let's go herd the monsters."

Michael just smiled and nodded, apparently sensing my needs the way he so often did. I gave him a shy smile in return, then waved goodbye to Anahera and led him out of the kitchen. Happy with silent companionship, we made our way back to the door we'd come in through. There, I spotted a group of wet, bedraggled folks standing on the other side of the glass, hugging themselves and bouncing from foot to foot to keep the cold at bay.

"Why are they standing out there?" I asked, confused.

Suddenly, Michael laughed. "Gavin locked the door on the way out, didn't he?"

"Oh." I paused for a second, then burst out laughing as well. "Oh! Of course!"

I raced over to the door and undid the latch that locked it from the inside. The group turned around, and I immediately recognised them as Hemi, Ryan, and a bunch of the other blokes. As soon as I pulled open the door, they all bundled inside.

"Aw mate, am I glad to see you," Hemi greeted us; I could almost hear his teeth chattering. "We knocked and knocked, but no one heard us."

"Sorry," I apologised, feeling more than a little bit guilty. "We didn't hear you. You go on up and talk to your mum; she's got some nice, hot soup to warm you up."

"Brilliant." The young man grinned, showing the straight, white teeth that he'd inherited from his mother. He turned to leave, then suddenly seemed to remember something and turned back to us. "Oh, Mike. Your dog's still sitting in the truck. We tried to get him to come in, but he just wanted to sit there."

"We'll go get him," Michael replied. He took the car keys from Hemi's outstretched hand, and tilted his head in my direction. "What about Sandy's kitten?"

"She went inside with Maddy, I think." Hemi shrugged, glancing at the others. They all looked just as uncertain.

"It's all good, I'll find her later." I smiled and waved them off. "Go on, before you catch a cold."

"Speaking of which – put your coat on before you go out there," Hemi told me. "There's a southerly rolling in, and it started getting cold as soon as the sun went down."

"Thanks." I nodded and did just that, unfolding my coat from over my arm and pulling it around my shoulders. I was still sopping wet, but at least the coat would keep the wind at bay. By the time I finished doing up the buttons, they were gone and I was alone with Michael again. I gave him a long, sideways look, followed by a playful grin. "I thought you hated being called 'Mike'?"

"I do," he said with a shrug. "But, you know me. I'm a fish. I just go with the flow."

I laughed and nodded. He put his arm around me, a gesture that was so simple and natural that it made both of us smile — but the second that the wind hit us, I was really, really glad it was there.

"Cripes, he wasn't kidding!" I gasped, snuggling in against Michael's side. What had been a dreary day had turned into a truly miserable night, and the driving rain had a bite to it that chilled me to the core. "Brrr! Let's go get everyone in before this gets much worse. Where'd they park the truck?"

"They said around the corner, so I'm guessing..." Michael trailed off, peering around in the gloom. Suddenly, his expression brightened. "Oh, it's right over there!"

"Convenient." I put my arm around his waist so that I could tuck my hand in the pocket of his coat, and guided him off towards the truck. Alfie saw us coming before either of us noticed him, and let out a happy yelp of greeting.

"Hey, buddy," Michael greeted his canine friend, juggling the keys with his free hand until he managed to get the door unlocked. As soon as it was open, Alfie jumped out and bounded around him, barking happily. Michael laughed, and reached down to ruffle the dog's ears. "That's a good boy. You didn't poop in the Hilux, did you?"

Alfie let out a high-pitched yelp that sounded for all the world like a vehement denial. We both laughed and looked at one another.

"Well, that's one monster," I said, tugging my hood down to protect my eyes from the stinging rain. "Who else are we missing?"

"It's getting hard to keep track, isn't it?" Michael paused to think about it, then rattled off a list of names. "Just the Yousefis, the Merrits, and Richard, I think."

"They're probably still working on the radio," I surmised. Michael nodded his agreement, and we set off together.

We found the back door to the radio station still locked, so we ducked through the overgrown courtyard to the street front. Sure enough, there was light glowing through the remains of the front window. As soon as we crossed the threshold, we found ourselves face-to-face with two very alert guards: Elly and Rebecca, both armed, both rational and calm. As soon as they recognised us, they smiled and lowered their weapons.

"Time to call it a night?" Elly asked, slipping her gun back into its holster. "I hope Anahera and Skye do not mind that I was not there to help with dinner. I worry about leaving Zane alone."

"I'm sure she understands," I replied. "Yes, it's time to turn in. Ana's got some hot soup waiting. Grab the blokes and head inside; we'll be back tomorrow to work on this."

"Good." Elly paused, and glanced back over her shoulder. "I fear that success is coming slowly. None of them really know what they're doing."

Suddenly, a new voice entered the conversation, from the gloom behind us. "Then count yourselves lucky that I'm around."

I almost jumped out of my skin, and had my weapon halfway to the firing position before I recognised the voice. "Damn, Gavin. You scared me half to death."

"Sorry." He stepped into the light, though his hood was pulled so far forward that I could barely see his face. "Old habits, you know?"

"Better than most." I smiled, then turned back to introduce him to the others. "Gavin, this is Elly and Rebecca. That's Zane just coming out of the office up the back – oh, and there's Richard and Jim. Guys, this is Gavin. He's an old friend. Please don't shoot him."

"She's kidding, Jazz," Gavin said, glancing back at the shadows behind him. "No one's shooting anyone."

I followed his line of sight, and could just barely make out a human outline hiding amongst the bushes. If I hadn't known where to look, I never would have seen her.

"Hello again, Jasmine," I said gently, making my voice as soft as possible. "We found your sister. She's a bit beaten up, but she's okay. Would you like me to take you to her?"

I heard a faint rustling sound, but beyond that there was no answer. Gavin heaved a sigh and looked at me. "That was a yes. She's feeling a bit non-verbal at the moment."

"So I noticed," I answered dryly, but I gave the girl another smile anyway. "I can't say I blame her. There are a lot of bad things out there that want to hurt girls like us, aren't there Jasmine?"

This time, I heard a faint reply from her dark hiding spot, a single word of agreement: "Yeah."

"It's okay, I get it." I pushed my gun as far back over my shoulder as it would go, and held my hands up to show her that they were empty. "I have no intention of hurting you, and I won't let anyone else lay a finger on you, either."

"These folks are okay, Jazzy," Gavin added, holding his arms out to the girl. "Come on. They've got a doctor looking after her right now, and I'll make sure you're safe."

There was a long minute of silence, then the girl dashed out of the bushes, and fled into Gavin's arms. She hid her face against his chest and peeked warily at me over his arm. Gavin just hugged her, and made gentle, paternal sounds of comfort.

To my surprise, I found tears gathering in my eyes. I glanced at Michael, and realised that he was no less affected by the sight. He glanced at me, and his hand silently tightened around mine. I knew in some guttural, instinctive way that he longed to have that kind of bond with a child again. What we had together was one thing, but the love between father and child was a whole other experience. He'd had it with Sophie, and we had something similar growing with Priyanka, but would it ever be the same as having a child that was truly ours?

Suddenly, I realised that everyone was watching me. I took a deep breath and brushed away the tears that threatened to bring my emotional dam crashing down. Now was not the time for that, so I pushed my feelings down and focused on the present.

"Okay, let's head back," I said, gesturing to the members of my group. "You guys go first. We'll bring Jasmine and Gavin up once you're settled in. We don't want to scare her."

The others nodded and filed out past us, heading back to the office block. We waited while they filed away, and in the meantime I looked at Gavin.

"I don't suppose you've seen my foster daughter, have you?" I asked, cuddling in against Michael's side for warmth. "She's an Indian girl, a little older than the twins."

"Wearing bright pink, with a buzz cut?" he asked. I nodded. "Yeah, she somehow managed to follow me home. She stayed behind with Melody and Solomon. Melody seems to have taken a shine to her, so don't worry about anything bad happening to her. Anyone that messes with Melody is just asking for trouble."

"You know, I actually can't wait to meet this girl." I grinned and beckoned for them to follow me. "Come on. The others should have cleared off by now, so let's get out of the cold. I'm sure Lily wants to see Jazz, too."

Gavin nodded his agreement. He released Jasmine from his embrace and made as though to follow me, but Jasmine didn't. She straightened up, threw her shoulders back, and gave me a dark look. "You're not allowed to call me that."

I lifted an eyebrow, a little surprised by her vehemence. Somehow, I sensed that my response to her defiance would count for a lot more than it would in any normal conversation. It was something I understood, though. Names were power, and they could also bring pain if used incorrectly.

I just nodded to her simply, accepting her choice without protest. "Well, I'll just have to try and earn the privilege, won't I?"

The girl jerked back a little, surprise written across her young face. I just gave her a smile, then I turned and walked away, with Michael at my side. A few seconds later, I heard footsteps following me, but I didn't look back until we reached the door to the office building. There, I found Skylar waiting for us, looking anxious.

"Jasmine," I said pointedly, glancing back at the girl. "This is my sister, Skylar. She's been looking after your sister since we got her back."

"About that," Skylar interrupted, hugging her cardigan

around her to combat the wind. "There's another problem."

"Oh, God." I heaved a long-suffering sigh. "What is it this time?"

"Well, Lily's awake," Skye answered, backing up a few paces so that I could herd my group inside. Michael and Gavin went willingly, but Jasmine skidded to a halt, glaring at Skylar from beneath her messy tangle of hair. Skye stared back at her, obviously surprised. "Oh, they're twins." She glanced at me and opened her mouth to say something else, but her comment was interrupted by a screech from upstairs, followed by the sound of shattering pottery. Skylar flinched, and gave me a helpless look. "And that's the problem. She's freaking out, but she's still pretty out of it and doesn't seem to understand what we're saying."

I muttered a few choice words beneath my breath and looked at our guests. "Well, guys, it sounds like Lily needs you. This way!"

I hurried past my sister and raced up the stairs, taking them two and three at a time. At the top, I glanced back and found Jasmine just a couple of steps behind me, with Gavin right behind her. As soon as they'd caught up, I rushed off again, hurrying down the maze of passages towards Lily's screams. The sound of them put me on edge, even though I knew instinctively that they were screams of rage and fear, rather than pain. Somehow, that was no better.

I rounded the last corner at full speed, and almost bowled Doctor Cross right off his feet. He shot me a shocked look, and I gave him one in return; his glasses were missing, and a set of vivid red welts tarnished his cheek from where someone had obviously tried to take his eyes out with her fingernails.

"Sandy!" he gasped, in an mix of relief and surprise. "Help me! I'm not sure how long I can keep this door shut."

"Is it the infection?" I asked urgently, suddenly terrified that the worst had happened. Had the virus mutated enough to infect the immune? If so, then we were all screwed.

"No, no, nothing like that," Doc replied. "It's some kind of reaction to the cocktail of drugs and booze that man gave her—" Suddenly, he let out a terribly unmanly shriek. "Look out! She's behind you!"

"Huh?" I jumped and looked back, only to find Jasmine and Gavin skidding to a halt right behind me. "Oh, no. That's Jasmine, her twin sister."

"What's wrong with my sister?" Jasmine demanded, her little hands balled into fists at her side. "Let her out!"

"We're going to, I promise," I said, struggling to keep my voice calm and even. "Jasmine, she needs your help. The man that took her – the farmer – he drugged her. We're trying to help her, but she's angry and afraid. Can you calm her down?"

Jasmine gave me another dark look, and put her hands on her hips. "Open. The door. Now."

I glanced back at Doc and nodded. He swallowed hard, then released the door handle and jumped back with a degree of dexterity that I'd never seen from him before. A second later, the door popped open, and Lily exploded out, shrieking in a language that I didn't understand.

Jasmine leapt on her sister without a moment of hesitation, sending both of them tumbling back into the room. I heard the doctor protesting behind me, but there was nothing that either of us could do. The twins wrestled for a few minutes, until finally Jasmine got on top of her sister and managed to pin her to the ground.

"She doesn't recognise me," Jasmine shouted to us. "Why? What did he do to her?"

"It's the drugs," Doc called back to her. "She's... she's drunk, for lack of a better word. Just hold her for a moment; I'll give her something to make her sleep. And for the love of God, be gentle! The poor child has internal injuries."

Jasmine grunted something that sounded like a wordless agreement, but she was obviously having trouble holding her sister down. Lily thrashed beneath her, kicking and screaming with all her might, and even trying to bite her sister. I watched for a moment, then made a snap decision.

"Gavin, grab her legs," I instructed, and then I dove into the fray. I threw myself to my knees near the youngster's head, and pinned it still to keep her from injuring either herself or her sister. "Hold her, but be gentle! I don't want her to hurt Jasmine."

Jasmine looked up at me, her face just a few inches from mine as we awkwardly pinned her writhing sister to the ground. For the first time, there was something in her gaze besides hatred, something that might have even been respect. She gave me a faint nod, then she focused her attention on keeping Lily down. The doctor rushed up to us a few seconds later, with a syringe in his hand.

"Forgive me, child," he said quietly, though it wasn't clear which of the twins he was talking to. I saw Jasmine stiffen up, but she let him administer the dose of sedative to her sister. Lily screamed at the pinch of the needle and tried to fight even harder, but there was nothing she could do against two grown adults and her own sister.

"It's okay, sweetheart," I whispered soothingly as the sedative started taking effect. Once she stopped fighting us, I released her and gently smoothed her tangled hair back out of her face. "It's okay... no one's going to hurt you anymore. I won't let them. Shhh... you just go to sleep, and when you wake up you'll feel much better. I promise."

Lily stared up at me with eyes so dark and fathomless that it felt like I could fall into them and drown. Her mouth opened and closed a few times, but no words came out. Eventually, her eyes closed and she fell into a deep sleep.

I sighed heavily and sat back. "Are you sure the sedative is safe, Doc? We don't know what drugs are in her system already."

"I have no way to know," he admitted. "I didn't want to use this on her, but she really gave us no choice. I have no intention of leaving her alone until I know that she's going to be all right, though. "

"Good," I agreed, nodding. "If you need someone to assist you, I'll find someo—"

"Why?" Suddenly, Jasmine spoke up and interrupted me, her tone sharp and accusative. "Why are you trying to help us? We didn't ask for your help."

I looked at her, and gave her the faintest of smiles. "You didn't have to ask. Jasmine, I'm going to tell you a story. It's not very nice, but it's the truth and I think it will help you understand why I wanted to save your sister. Come over here, let's get out of the way so that the doctor and Gavin can get her back into bed."

I eased myself to my feet, and offered her a hand to help her up. She ignored my hand, but did as she was told. We moved out of the way, and watched while Lily was tended. I felt an arm slide around my waist from the other side, and knew without looking that Michael and Skye had joined us.

"Two summers ago, I was travelling alone when I was taken by a man kind of like the farmer," I said softly. I felt

Michael's arm tighten around me, and silently appreciated the support. "I was just minding my own business, like you two were, when he saw me and decided that he was going to... make me his wife, to put it kindly."

I looked down at Jasmine and saw her watching me, her expression unreadable. I gave her a sad smile and looked away. "You shouldn't even have to know what that means at your age, but I think you do. I managed to escape, but only because I was very, very lucky. Since then, I've made a vow never to let anyone take away the rights of another human being, even if it costs me my life fighting to save them. I'd help anyone who needed it, but I admit that I have a particular empathy for young women like you, because I know from first-hand experience how hard it is for us to survive in this world. That's why you didn't have to ask for help, Jasmine. I'd give it to you willingly, because it's the right thing to do."

Silence descended on the room when I finished speaking. I closed my eyes, and savoured in the strange feeling of pride that washed over me. I'd made the decision to take up the cause to protect humankind on a whim, but today was the day that I'd finally been able to prove my conviction – not just to those around me, but to myself. It was no longer just words to appeal to the group. Now, it was reality, and I was living it.

Eventually, Jasmine sighed heavily. I looked at her, and found her staring down at her feet with great interest. A few seconds later, she glanced up and gave me a shy smile. "On second thoughts, I think you are allowed to call me 'Jazz' after all."

Chapter Eighteen

It was a long, noisy, and anxious night. Jasmine and Gavin stayed glued to Lily's bedside; eventually, we decided to drag a few extra mattresses in so that they and the doctor could sleep in shifts. One by one, the others came to peek at the newcomers, but Jasmine wouldn't let anyone get close to her sister except for me and Doctor Cross. In the end, we brought them some dinner, then closed the door and let them be.

Before bed, I gathered the members of the group that weren't otherwise occupied in the kitchen, and spread out a couple of big maps on the table so everyone could see them.

"We need to decide on our route south," I told them, pointing to the large lake in the centre of the map. "Lake Taupo is just south of here, but before then we need to pick whether we want to follow the highway along the western shore, or the east."

"What's the difference?" Skylar asked, shooting me a curious look.

"The eastern route will take us through Taupo city, while the western won't," I explained, tracing the two routes with my fingertip. "I haven't been through Taupo since before the plague, but from what I've heard it's a hub of gang activity."

"It is," Anahera confirmed, nodding slowly. "The location is perfect. The lake has several feeder rivers to the south, which provide a constant supply of fresh water, not to mention the fish, ducks, and other game in the area. There's always someone living there. I sent a trading convoy there once, but they never came back."

"What happened to them?" I asked.

Anahera just shrugged.

"We have no way of knowing," she admitted. "They just vanished. It's possible they ran into that pack of racists you met heading to Arapuni, or perhaps they ran afoul of some other gang. Maybe it was a pig. It could have been anything, really."

"But we know that they were heading for Taupo." I stood back and sighed, rubbing my fingers over the bridge of my nose. "That's not good. From what I remember, the western route is just scrubland, with no towns or buildings to speak of, but it's been a while. God knows what kind of condition it's in."

"So, whichever route we pick is a gamble." Anahera looked at me and tilted her head inquisitively. "May I suggest we take the western route, just to be safe?"

"Suggestion noted. All right, let's vote." I straightened up and looked at the others. "All in favour of the eastern route, raise your hand." I paused and waited. No one moved. "Okay, and in favour of the western route?" Hands popped up all over the room. I nodded, and leaned over to fold the maps back up again. "Western route, it is. Head to bed, everyone. We've got another long day ahead of us tomorrow."

Most of the group drifted out to go find their berths for the night, but Ryan lingered behind. I shot a curious look at him, but he averted his eyes and pretended to be very interested in a smudge on the paintwork until the last person had left the room. Only then did he finally glance in my direction, his expression unreadable.

"Can we... talk for a second?" he asked softly, his voice barely audible.

"Of course," I replied, equal parts wary and confused. He'd been quiet since he rejoined the group, so quiet that sometimes I forgot he was there at all. Given what he'd been through, his silence didn't surprise me. What did surprise me is that he'd pick me to chat with.

Ryan drew a deep breath, and slowly lowered himself down to sit in a chair. "Thanks. I don't really have anyone else to talk to. I mean, there's Skye, but it's not the same. And the others..."

"I know," I said, seating myself at the table beside him. Although I had every right to be angry at him, all I felt when I looked at him was pity. "Sometimes it can be really hard to earn forgiveness. You don't need me to lecture you about what you did wrong, though. You already know that, better than anyone. So, what did you want to talk about?"

Ryan fell silent, his gaze focused on a speck of nothing in the middle distance. I'd never seen anyone looking quite so forlorn, not even my sister on the day she had to bury her firstborn. His hands tightened into fists, but I knew on some instinctive level that his tension was not a threat to me.

Suddenly, he looked at me and I saw the full force of his despair reflected in his eyes. "What do I do now?"

I frowned at him, not entirely sure how to interpret his request. "What do you mean?"

"I mean..." he hesitated and glanced away again, his eyes drifting back out of focus. "It's always been her and me. Ryan and Skye. Just the two of us against the world. Then, it was the two of us and the baby. I knew what to do. Now it's all gone. My friends don't want to know me, Skye hates me, and my baby's dead. I don't know what to do anymore."

"She doesn't hate you," I told him gently, reaching out to rest my hand over the back of his fist. He tensed up for a moment, then slowly relaxed when he realised that my intentions were innocent. He glanced at me, and I gave him a faint smile in return. "No one hates you, Ry. They just don't understand. They will, eventually, but they need time. If it makes you feel any better, I understand why you left."

"You do?" His expression changed to one of surprise, then I saw the faintest flicker of hope pass through his eyes. "I thought no one did. I mean, Michael..."

"Yeah, I know what he said." I sighed softly and gave his hand a squeeze. "Sometimes, when you're faced with something so devastating that your conscious mind isn't capable of processing it, your animal instincts kick in. It was fight or flight. You didn't have a choice. There was no one that you could fight, so you chose to flee. It could have happened to anyone."

"He called me a coward," Ryan repeated, darkness falling back across his face like a veil. "He's right. I am a coward. I ran away. He wouldn't run away. If it had been you, then he would have stayed."

"Maybe, but you're not him and you don't have to be," I told him firmly. "You're different people, and you are entitled to react to a tragedy in the way that best helps you to cope with your grief." I paused and glanced down at his wrists, still hidden beneath his long, black sleeves. As gently as I could, I laid my hand over the hidden injuries, and gave him a look of pure sympathy. "No one can know what they would do in the face of that much pain, and no one should have to find out. Skye told me what you tried to do, Ry. I hate to think about you suffering like that all by yourself. I know that at heart, you're a good man. Do you think it would help if we put aside a little time each day, just to hang out and talk?"

The young man fell silent for a few seconds, then he nodded slowly. "I think... I think it might. I don't know, Sandy. But maybe, yeah. Maybe talking would help." He managed a weak smile, and stood up slowly. "I should go. I'm on the late watch, so I have to be up at midnight. Thanks for listening."

"Any time," I answered. I rose to my feet, and pulled him into a quick hug. "You're not in this alone, mate. We'll get through it. Promise."

He didn't seem sure what to do with the hug at first, but eventually he relaxed and hugged me back. When we separated, there was a faint but genuine smile on his face. Suddenly looking embarrassed, he ducked out of the room before I could say another word, leaving me to stare after him thoughtfully.

A few minutes later, Michael stuck his head into the room and called my name inquisitively. "Sandy?"

"Yeah, I'm coming," I replied, shaking off my bout of melancholy to focus on the evening's tasks.

***

Michael and I took the first watch. With all the downstairs doors firmly locked from the inside and Alfred's nose on the task, we felt secure enough to cut the watch down to two at a time. We set up a guard post and barricade at the top of the only staircase up to our area, and watched it with vigilance.

One by one, the others stopped by to say goodnight before they turned in, until the only people left awake were the two of us. Outside, the wind howled and moaned, but inside there was only silence and the occasional sound of snoring. I lingered in the doorway to the main sleeping room for a few moments, enjoying the strange feeling of pride that came with it.

Those people were more than just my friends, now. They were my charges. They looked to me for guidance and protection. They trusted me to watch over them while they slept. It was a good feeling, and I liked it. I withdrew and went off to finish my patrol, then I returned to the barricade where Michael waited.

He glanced up as I sat down beside him and smiled at me. With that gentle strength that I loved so much, he drew me beneath the blanket wrapped around his shoulders, into the warmth. The scent of his body was familiar and comforting, and it stirred something inside me the way no other man ever had. I smiled back and leaned up to give him a kiss, then we settled in to silently watch and wait for midnight.

Eventually, midnight came and our replacements arrived to relieve us. We retreated to one of the beds left warm by their absence, and snuggled down to sleep. Even as I was drifting off, I was acutely aware of one fact: Priya still hadn't come home.

***

I woke late the next morning, lulled into a deeper sleep than usual by the incessant pounding of the rain. When my eyes finally opened, I realised that it was well past sunrise, and that everyone else was already up and about.

Maddy was the only one to notice that I was awake. She waved vigorously, then went right back to what she was doing. She was sitting in a circle with the three younger Yousefi boys, pawing over a couple of grimy children's books.

I tried to sit up, but as soon as I moved I felt a sharp, stabbing pain in my hip. Startled and still muddled with sleep, it took a second for me to realise that the source was Tigger, who was sitting primly on my hip, washing one of her paws. I tried to move again, and she dug her claws in deeper in protest.

"Ow," I complained. "Would you knock it off, please? I need to get up."

Tigger gave me the filthiest look in return, but she stood up and stretched dramatically. Then, she finally jumped off and trotted over to Madeline, her tail held high.

Despite the pain, the sight brought a smile to my face. I eased myself out of bed and indulged in a long, luxurious stretch of my own. Every inch of me was still damp and sticky, but there was nothing I could do about it. The rain was still coming down with force, so I was unlikely to dry off any time soon.

I put on my coat and shoes, and padded down the hallway to the ladies room. On the way back, I stopped in to the doctor's sick room to check on things. Doctor Cross was out like a light, lying fast asleep amid a tangle of blankets. Lily was still unconscious, and Gavin sat on the floor beside her bed with his head lowered, as still as a stone gargoyle.

I cleared my throat softly, to see if he was actually awake. He looked up, and held one finger to his lips to indicate silence. I watched from the doorway as he eased himself quietly to his feet and snuck over to me.

"Where's Jasmine?" I asked in a whisper, tilting my head towards the room. "I thought she wasn't going to leave her sister's side?"

"She wanted to go home and get some things," he replied, absently running his fingertips over the door to muffle the sound as he pulled it closed behind us. "She'll be back in a bit."

"Ah." I nodded my understanding. "What about Lily? How is she?"

"The doctor thinks that she'll be fine." He smiled again, an expression of such open relief that it warmed my heart. "Thank God. Did I ever tell you that I lost my wife and my little girl to the plague?"

"I think you mentioned it once, but you didn't seem to want to talk about it," I replied. On a whim, I reached out to touch the back of his hand and offer him some small iota of comfort from my presence. "I figured it must have been something like that."

"She died on her sixth birthday." He heaved a deep sigh, staring down at my hand as though seeing it for the first time. "She was my life. My wife had a medical condition, and the doctors told us that it was unlikely she'd survive to carry the baby to term. She was so determined to try, even if it might kill her. The day our baby was born, I honestly couldn't tell you which one was more beautiful: her, or my wife."

"I'm so sorry, Gavin," I said sympathetically, squeezing his hand gently. "You don't have to talk about it, if you don't want to. I understand."

"I know." He glanced up and gave me a smile. "But I want you to really, fully understand. I don't want anyone thinking that I'm just some old creep that likes keeping little girls around. It's just... I see these kids, and I see my daughter. I couldn't save her, but maybe if I save enough of them then I'll figure out how to forgive myself."

I let out a long, deep sigh, and pulled him into a hug. "It won't help if I tell you that it wasn't your fault, will it?"

"Of course not." He chuckled faintly and shook his head, but he accepted the hug without protest. "I know that. Intellectually, I know that. Emotionally... that's different."

"Yeah, I know exactly what you mean." I drew back, but left a hand resting on his shoulder. "Maybe this will help. If it weren't for the things you taught me, I probably wouldn't be alive today. You helped to save at least one person."

"True," he said, his expression brightening. "I honestly can't tell you how happy I am to see you, Sandy. I mean, I know I've said it, but the words can't express how overjoyed I am that you survived. I've seen some bloody nasty things done to women and children and been unable to stop it, but... you're right. That does help. Thank you."

"No, thank you," I replied, giving him a light-hearted nudge in the ribs to soften the seriousness of the conversation. "You gave me knowledge that saved my life; I haven't done anything to deserve thanks."

"Careful, those never healed quite right." He grunted, rubbing his ribs. "Yes, you have. You saved Lily, remember? That and what you did for Jasmine more than repays anything I did for you, and puts me firmly in your debt."

"Huh?" Confused, I blinked owlishly at him. "I didn't do anything for Jasmine. I mean, aside from saving her sister, but I would have done that anyway."

"It's way more than that," he replied, shaking his head. "You've given her something that I can't. You've given her a role-model. She's never seen a grown woman that's smart, capable, and a leader before. You impressed her in a way that I never could. I mean, do you know where she is right now?"

"You said she went to go get some things?" I answered, shrugging.

"I did, but to be specific, she's gone to *pack* her things." He grinned suddenly, and grabbed my arm. "She wants us to go with you, Sandy. I've never seen her this excited about something before. She told me that she wants all of us to follow you, so that she can learn to be like you when she grows up." He paused, and gave me a long look. "If you'll have us, that is."

"Well, that's a silly question," I said with a laugh. "I plan to build a city, Gav — I'm going to need as many people as I can get. And if those kids really want to join us, then they're welcome. All that we ask is that they contribute to the group in some way, and... you know, not try to claw Doc's eyes out again."

Gavin joined in laughing, nodding his head. "That wasn't normal! Lily's the shy, gentle one. She would never have done that under normal circumstances."

"Then they're both welcome, and I hope that the other kids will come along as well." I glanced back over my shoulder, in the direction of the makeshift bedroom where our children were busy teaching themselves to read. "Everyone's welcome, so long as they agree to abide by our rules."

"What rules are those?" he asked, looking at me expectantly.

"Simple ones, really." I glanced back at him, and smiled. "Don't kill, hurt, or threaten another member of this group unless it is in self-defence. No one has the right to abuse anyone else, verbally, physically, or sexually. Don't steal from us, or from each other. Treat other people the way you want to be treated. Breaches of the rules will be decided before a quorum chosen from within the group, as will the punishments."

"I see you've put some thought into it," Gavin replied. He went quiet for a moment while he considered what I'd said, then nodded slowly. "Sounds good to me. We should go get your radio message out, so that we can move on before it gets too dangerous here. I, for one, have no desire to meet one of your mutated infected."

"Hey, they're not *my* mutated infected," I protested, only half joking. "They're everyone's problem."

"I know." He gave me a weak smile. "Sorry, that was meant to be a joke. I remember you having quite the sense of humour."

"And you never were any good at telling jokes." I grinned at him in return, and clapped my hand on his shoulders. "All right, then. Do you want to wake up Doc?"

"No, no need," he replied, shaking his head. "Lily's fine. Doctor Cross told me that she passed the danger point in the middle of the night, and now she's just sleeping it off."

"Good. Poor kid doesn't deserve that kind of treatment." I stepped past him, and led the way towards the exit. Along the way, I found Michael sitting on the floor in one of the side rooms with a bunch of assorted weapon pieces spread out on old towels all around him. I stopped and leaned against the door frame, watching him work. Gavin joined me a second later, but neither of us said anything.

It took a few seconds before Michael noticed us. When he did, he glanced up and gave me a smile. "Morning, sunshine. Just cleaning the guns; they don't like being wet for too long. The shotgun's already done, if you want it."

"What, you're not going to tease me for sleeping so late?" I commented dryly, folding my arms across my chest.

Michael laughed and shook his head. "Now, would I do a thing like that?"

"Of course," I replied with some amusement. "That's why I agreed to marry you, isn't it?"

"Oh yeah. How could I forget?" Michael grinned that silly grin of his, and picked up the shotgun resting beside his knee. He held it up to me, and I took it. I quickly checked that it was loaded and the safety was firmly in place, then I put the strap over my shoulder and adjusted it across my back.

"Thank you for cleaning it for me," I said, turning serious again. "I should have remembered to do that myself, but after yesterday's excitement..."

Michael just held up a hand, and shook his head. "You don't have to apologise to me, sweetheart. That's what husbands are for, remember? We're partners. We watch each other's backs. We help each other up if we fall down. We may not be married yet, but that's what I want to be for you: your partner, through the good times and the bad."

I felt a flush of heat rise in my cheeks, and suddenly I was both pleased and embarrassed. I gave him a shy smile, then glanced away and quickly changed the subject. "We're heading down to work on the radio. Do you want to come?"

Michael paused to consider it. I glanced up just in time to see him shake his head. "Nah, I better stay here and finish up. I need to get these back to the troops as soon as possible. It's still pretty nasty out there, so most of them are holed up in one of the rooms downstairs, playing cards."

"Okay," I agreed. "I've got my radio on me. Call if you need anything."

"Will do." Michael sketched a salute, and then he glanced past me at Gavin. "Keep an eye on her, old man. I'll hold you responsible if anything eats her."

His sense of humour might have been a little rusty, but Gavin clearly understood the light-hearted comment for what it was. It was hard not to, when Michael was grinning like a fool. Gavin gave him a mock salute in return. "Sure, I'll keep an eye on her... but only one. I've only got one to spare."

"Okay, that one was actually pretty good," I said with a laugh. "I'm going to have to make you two spend some quality time together, so Michael's sense of humour rubs off on you."

Both of them laughed at that. I grinned and waved to Michael, then led Gavin out of the room. Once we were out of earshot, Gavin glanced at me and smiled. "He's a good man, your fiancé."

"I know," I said. "To be honest, I don't think there's another man alive who could have done what he did. I was a total wreck when we met. I didn't think it was possible for me to fall in love again, but he proved me wrong. I don't know what I'd do without him."

"Let's hope that you never have to find out," Gavin said softly. I just nodded my agreement, and led us onwards. We made our way past the barricade, down the stairs, and into the lobby where I found Nikora and Wiremu on duty beside the door.

"Morning, Nick, Will," I greeted them, using their preferred nicknames. "How's it going?"

"Pretty shite, but it could be worse. At least we're not out in that." Nikora grinned good-naturedly, and jerked his thumb over his shoulder at the door. "You two for in or out?"

"Out, unfortunately," I replied, pulling my hood up over my head. I shoved my hair under the leather as best I could, and peered past them at the gloomy weather. "I guess winter finally caught up with us."

"Well, we were about due for it," Will commented, heaving a long, dramatic sigh. "Ah, well. So the Lord deems it, so it must be. Let's just hope it doesn't start snowing."

"Amen to that," I agreed. Nick unlocked the door and held it open for me. I nodded my thanks and stepped out, only to be hit in the face by a blast of frigid wind. Behind me, I heard Gavin gasp and mutter a curse under his breath, to which I could only grunt wordless agreement. I pulled my collar up and hurried off towards the radio station as fast as I could, ducking from one patch of shelter to the next.

No matter how hard I tried, I still ended up soaked by the time I reached the front door. I hopped over the broken frame, and ducked into the shelter within. Elly was alone on watch this time, huddled up inside a thick woollen blanket for warmth. She nodded to me, but said nothing.

"Morning," I greeted her. "No Rebecca today?"

"No, she has come down with a cold," Elly replied. She sniffed and rubbed her nose, then gave me a pathetic look. "She is not alone, but I would rather be here watching over Zain than anywhere else."

"Aw, no one told me you guys were sick." I frowned at her and put my hands on my hips. "You should have said something. We found a bunch of jars of honey in Arapuni, so the doctor could have mixed you up something to make you feel better."

"I know, but I did not wish to wake him." Elly gave me a pathetic attempt at a smile, and made a shooing gesture. "You stay away. I do not want you to get sick as well."

"Okay, but you're on light duties until you feel better," I instructed gently. "And if anyone has a problem with that, tell them to bring it up with me."

Elly nodded quietly, and huddled under her blanket again. I took her silence to mean that her throat was probably hurting, so I didn't press her to keep talking. I just gave her a sympathetic smile, and headed down the hallway towards the back of the building. Both of the studios were empty, but the sound of voices arguing led me to the old lunchroom where I found my more technically-minded companions sitting around the table, looking frustrated.

"This is ridiculous," Jim complained, pounding his good fist on the table. "I'm not a sound engineer. None of us are. How on earth are we supposed to work this out?"

"He's right." Zain sighed deeply. He was holding a thick book, which he dropped on the table with a heavy thud. "This manual may as well be written in Greek, for all the good it does us."

Suddenly, Anahera appeared from behind the partition that separated the kitchenette from the tables, with mugs of steaming hot black coffee in her hands. She set one mug down in front of each of the men at the table.

"Calmness, my friends. We'll work this out together." She glanced up and gave me a warm smile. "Good morning. Would you care for some coffee? I also have some leftover food back here, if you'd like some."

"I can't tell if that's my stomach rumbling or the thunder, but I'd love some of both, please," I said. She nodded and went back to the kitchenette, while I shifted my attention to my unhappy engineers. "As for the radio... well, it turns out that we have someone right here that can help. Gavin?"

"I was a communications officer in the army for ten years," he explained, right on cue. "Radios were my life blood, until I resigned my commission to start a family. These commercial stations are a little different to the ones I'm used to, but I should have no trouble getting it going. You blokes willing to give me a hand?"

Zain and Jim exchanged startled looks, but Richard and Ropata smiled. All of them rose to their feet and nodded their agreement.

I glanced at Gavin, and raised a brow. "Well, looks like you've got your assistants. Don't you want to wait until after breakfast, though?"

"No, I don't usually eat in the morning, and I'd rather get this sorted." Gavin gestured to his newfound comrades, and then the five of them vanished into the hallway.

A second later, Anahera returned with a steaming cup in one hand, and a plate of scrambled eggs in the other. The eggs were cold, but I took them gratefully anyway. I sat down in one of the recently-vacated seats, and sipped my coffee. Anahera seated herself opposite me, watching me thoughtfully.

"You know, I don't think we've ever had the chance to speak alone," she murmured, trailing her fingers across the hot surface of her own mug.

I paused with a forkful of eggs half way to my mouth, and gave her a curious look. "Well, there was that one time on the docks at your old place."

"Ah, yes. I'd forgotten about that." She sighed and glanced down at her drink, as though seeking to divine something from the dark brew. "It's still hard to believe that I'll never see my home again."

"I know." I put my fork down, and reached across the table to touch her hand sympathetically. "I just wish that we'd thought to warn you earlier. I don't think I've told you how much I regret that."

"You don't have to." She smiled faintly, and placed her free hand over top of mine. "I understand you, Sandrine McDermott. I see much pain in your eyes, yet so much determination. It was a mistake that anyone could have made in a time of such stress. I hold nothing against you."

"Thank you." I smiled back at her, and gently withdrew my hand so that I could resume eating. Cold or not, the moment that I felt that food on my tongue, I was ravenous. I had almost finished before I realised that Anahera was watching me closely. I paused, and looked at her quizzically. "What is it?"

"Nothing, my dear. You just seem to be feeling better this morning, and that pleases me." She gave me one of those enigmatic smiles of hers that always made me feel like she knew something I didn't. "Would you like another helping? I wasn't sure how many we were going to be feeding, so I made more than necessary."

"I won't say no," I replied, setting my fork down on the empty plate. "Doc keeps hounding me to put some more weight on."

"As well he should. You are still much too thin." Anahera took my plate and stood up, her expression one of maternal kindness. "Don't worry about it too much. Now that we're living together I'm sure I'll be able to fatten you up."

"Don't fatten me up too much, or Michael will cancel the wedding," I said with a laugh, even though I knew it wasn't true. Hell, Michael seemed to like me even better when I gained a few more curves.

"Wedding?" Anahera popped back around the partition and stared at me, wide-eyed. "You two are engaged now?"

"Oh." I froze, suddenly realising that she was probably the one person that didn't know. "Oh, yeah. I guess I forgot to tell you. After the talk you gave us, we decided to get tentatively engaged, and just let things progress as they will. We've swapped rings, but it's nothing set in stone."

"Oh, Sandy, that's wonderful news." Before I quite knew what had happened, she'd pulled me out of my chair and swept me up into a hug. "Congratulations! I am thrilled for both of you."

"I thought you might be." Laughing, I hugged her back. "Sorry. I told you about everything else but I guess I forgot about that. It's been a busy few weeks, you know?"

"No, I completely understand." Anahera pushed me back and smiled radiantly at me. Just as suddenly as she'd grabbed me, she let me go. A second later, I found myself back in my chair with another helping of eggs in front of me. "Now, eat up and tell me all about it."

Chapter Nineteen

Anahera and I talked for almost an hour over our coffee. At one stage, I got up to check on the men, but they were deeply engrossed in what they were doing and informed me that another set of hands would just get in the way. We went back to the kitchen and talked some more, until I accidentally disclosed that Elly was feeling ill.

Unsurprisingly, Anahera wasn't about to let her suffer. She hurried off to find the fixings for hot, honeyed tea, leaving me on my own. I washed my dish and mug out of habit, and returned them to the cupboard that they'd been borrowed from, then I went out to check on Elly. She was still awake and alert but miserable, and waved me away when I tried to enquire about her welfare.

With nothing better to do to pass the time, I decided to check out the local shops and see if there was anything left that had survived the riots. I ducked across the road, only to discover that the buildings over there were a perfect cross-section of things that were utterly useless to us now: several banks, a few offices advertising law services or politicians, and a post office. The only place that might be remotely useful was a small optometrist's office on the corner. Thinking of Doc's scratched lenses, I made a mental note to bring him over and check it out before we left town. In the meantime, I headed eastwards along the road, back towards the shopping centre.

My instinct told me that if there was anything useful left here, then that was where I'd find it. Part of me felt guilty for defying my own orders and going off on my own, but I was confident in my ability to defend myself should the need arise. I slipped my shotgun off my shoulder, just in case, and eased the safety off.

I ducked across a silent intersection, picking my way between a half-dozen cars in various states of disrepair, to the footpath on the other side. There, through the twisting vines of an overgrown plant, I spotted the familiar logo of a chain brand pharmacy. As soon as I got close to the door, my heart sank. The pharmacy had been ransacked.

"Since when did you get so spoiled that you care about that?" I muttered to myself, suddenly amused. I lifted my shotgun to my shoulder, and carefully stepped into the carnage within.

As soon as I crossed the threshold, I realised that 'carnage' was not an overstatement. Pieces that had once belonged to other human beings lay scattered across the floor, now reduced to nothing but bones and scraps of flesh. I took a deep breath and swallowed hard, struggling to keep my breakfast down. It wasn't hard to piece together the scene from the way the bodies lay; they'd come in frantically looking for medicine, and never left. I guessed they had been fighting one another for what little was available – not that any of it would help them.

I stepped carefully over the remains of someone's torso, and picked my way towards the back counter. The moment I got there, I realised that the hunt was going to be useless. I could see shattered vials and half-crumbled pills scattered across the floor like a carpet of melting candy. Someone had already been there, and thrown whatever they didn't want into a heap on the floor. Sorting it out would be impossible, even with the doctor's expertise. I withdrew, and focused my attention on searching the shelves instead.

A quick search of the usual places turned up a few packs of cloth bandages that had slipped under a shelf, but little else of value. I tucked the bandages into the inside pocket of my coat, and ducked back out into the rain.

Next door, I found a Salvation Army store that had been covered in graffiti but otherwise left alone. The door was still firmly shut and locked; the butt of my shotgun made quick work of the glass window pane. The noise made me flinch, but nothing stirred either inside or out. I waited for a second, just to be sure that I wasn't going to be ambushed, then I stepped over the broken glass into the store itself.

It took a moment for my eyes to adjust, but once they did I was pleasantly surprised to discover that the store was mostly intact. There were no stinking corpses, and I saw very little in the way of mould. Our world was full of discarded clothing, but I was painfully aware of the fact that the resources available to us were finite. Cloth didn't expire like food, but it did rot, tear, and fall apart with wear and exposure to the elements. Our generation might be able to pick and choose for a while, but the next would not survive so easily.

I paused in front of a rack full of children's clothing. The tiny garments attracted me, in some way that I couldn't quite name. I reached out and trailed my fingers over a baby-sized romper, marvelling at the softness of it. The texture brought back memories of holding Skylar when she was an infant. So soft and fragile, a tiny doll that smelt like baby powder and milk. She'd been so completely helpless, and reliant on us for everything...

Suddenly, I felt nauseated. I barely made it back outside before the heaving began, with such force that it knocked me to my knees on the cold pavement. My entire body convulsed, but to my relief nothing actually came up. Just dry heaves, enough to make me feel miserable without actually wasting any food.

When the heaves finally passed, I lifted my head and wiped my mouth with the back of my hand. It was only then that I realised I was being watched from the bushes across the street. The shotgun trembled in my hands as I lifted it, but I did my best to hide the weakness as much as I could.

"Who's there?" I demanded. My voice was hoarse, but it was still strong and confident. That was what I needed.

There was a long moment of silence, then a familiar voice called a greeting. "Is me, Mama. Priyanka."

"Priya!" I gasped in a mixture of relief and anxiety. "Oh, honey, you worried me so much when you vanished last night. Are you okay?"

"I fine, Mama. No worries about me," she called back. I saw her head pop up, easily visible under its bright pink raincoat, but she didn't immediately come to me. Instead, she looked down into the bushes and seemed to be holding a soft-spoken conversation with someone that I couldn't see.

I swiftly put two and two together. "Is that Melody with you? Or is it Jasmine?"

"Both, Mama, and Solo too," Priya called back. Someone hidden near her protested, but she just gave them a glare and made a curt gesture. This time, she spoke loud enough for me to make out what she was saying. "You shoosh! That is my mama you talking about, you not say like that. I love Mama."

My eyes blurred with tears all of a sudden, and I felt a rush of warmth at her words. Though it took strength that I wasn't entirely sure I had, I levered myself up to my feet and put my shotgun back over my shoulder.

"I love you too, honey," I called back. "Tell your friends that they can take as much time as they need. I understand how they feel. It's hard to trust."

Priya glanced at me, but before she could say anything, a second youngster popped up beside her. It took a few seconds before I realised that it was Jasmine, all wrapped up in a dark green oilskin raincoat. Jasmine said something that I couldn't quite make out, then shoved her way out of the bushes and crossed the road towards me. I just waited, watching her approach without making any sudden moves that might frighten her.

My caution was unwarranted. Jasmine came at me with stalwart determination, and didn't stop until she was standing right in front of me. She crossed her arms over her chest, and regarded me curiously. "Are you okay?"

"Huh?" I blinked in surprise; that wasn't what I expected.

"Are you okay?" she repeated, as if she were speaking to a slow child. "We saw you being sick."

"Oh!" Realisation hit like a sledgehammer, and left me feeling stupid. Of course, they were worried about illness. They'd seen all of their families die of the plague. "Yeah, I'm fine. I had a concussion a few days ago — a hard bump on the head — and sometimes that makes your body do dumb things like want to throw up for no reason."

"Oh. Okay." Jasmine nodded her understanding, then turned and looked at the bushes across the street. "You can come out. It's safe."

"She better not be infectious," a third voice called. There was a momentary argument between the third voice and Priya, but it ended when Priya made a rude noise and stomped out of the bushes. She came over and gave me a hug. I hugged her back, and planted a kiss on the top of her head, to which she responded with a much happier noise.

"I'm not sick," I called back, trying to clarify the situation for them. "I had an injury to my head, and it hasn't healed fully yet. That happens sometimes when you have a bump on the noggin. You're Melody, right? Gavin was telling me about you."

Finally, Melody stood up, along with a slender youth that I presumed must have been Solomon. I couldn't make out many of the details of their features from afar; just like the rest of us, they were wrapped up in raincoats to keep the storm at bay. Melody glanced around warily, then finally she crossed the road towards me. I caught a glimpse of fair skin tanned golden-brown and ash-blonde hair, but that was about it. She stopped a few feet away from me, studying me with an expression that was an odd balance of hostile neutrality.

"So, you're the one that saved Lily?" she demanded, her voice carrying an edge of violence that made me equally wary of her motives.

"I wasn't alone, but yes. I saved Lily." I straightened up to my full height and gave her a long, frosty look. Although I had no intention of acting in a hostile manner towards her, she clearly needed something a bit tougher than my usual mannerisms. Tougher was something that I understood. "Our doctor has taken care of her all night. She's going to be fine."

"Good." Though she was almost a hand span shorter than me, Melody did not look intimidated in the least. She folded her arms and met my eye with unwavering confidence. "As soon as she's well enough to walk, I want you to send her home."

"She's free to go any time she chooses, so long as she's sober enough to make the trek safely." I shrugged, but didn't break eye-contact. I sensed in some instinctive way that there was a contest happening, and the first of us to look away would be the loser. "My people stay with me because they choose to, Melody. Because I offer them protection, and all I ask in return is their best efforts to help the group survive. No one in my company is a prisoner."

The girl's gaze wavered. Finally, she blinked and looked at Jasmine. The two exchanged a few whispered words, then she looked at me with great interest. "Why are you going south?"

"Because there are monsters coming from the ruins of Hamilton," I told her bluntly, making no attempt to sugarcoat the truth. "They've already killed our friends, and members of our group. One of them was a girl, the same age as Jasmine and Lily. The monsters tore out her throat, and she bled to death in her uncle's arms. I have no intention of staying around to let them kill anyone else."

"Monsters?" Jasmine gasped and looked at Melody with wide eyes. Solomon looked back and forth between them nervously, hugging himself. Suddenly, all three of them looked at Priyanka, who just nodded.

"Bad monsters. Bitey. Screamy. Maddy told me." Priya cuddled up against me, and hid her face against my shoulder. "Mama protect us. Take us far away from the bad monsters."

"Have you guys ever seen a pig?" I asked, looking back and forth between the three young faces in front of me. Jasmine and Solomon shook their heads, but Melody nodded hesitantly.

"Only once," she said, her voice dropping to a quiet, almost reverent tone. "It chased me for half a day before I managed to lose it."

"Well, these new monsters, they're like that... except they look like people." I hugged Priya's wet little body against me, stroking the back of her hooded head. "They have arms and legs, and they can run as fast as you or I if they want to. They hunt in packs, and if they catch you they'll rip you to shreds." I glanced up and caught Melody's eye. "I outran a whole pack of them to get back to my family so I could lead them away from danger, and I'd do it again in a heartbeat."

"Is true," Priya echoed, backing up my story. "Mama ran and ran, so far and so fast! And Mama saved me and Baba from the bad mans that wanted to make us dead, too. Mama is very brave." She tilted her head back and looked up at me with those enormous eyes of hers. "Mama teach me to be like her, yes?"

"I don't think I have to teach you anything, little miss." I grinned and gave her a playful squeeze. "Did you tell your friends about the time that *you* fought a pig?"

The three youngsters gasped in surprise. Priya shook her head, looking a little embarrassed. "No... not yet. Too busy."

"Well, why don't you go tell them about it?" I suggested, gently releasing her from my grasp. "I need to go get a few people to come and see what we can retrieve out of this store, before the rain gets in and ruins everything." I shifted my gaze to Melody and the others, and gave them a smile that was a little bit playful and a little bit friendly. "As for you lot... we're leaving town as soon as we're done at the radio station. If you want to join us, then you're welcome to."

None of them said anything, so I turned and walked away. It was a risk, but a calculated one. Michael was right about Priya; she'd survived for ten years without me, and she'd clearly managed to forge some kind of bond with the little pack of ragamuffins. The likelihood that her friends would hurt her was slim, and even if they tried... well, I'd already learned that she could hold her own. It was hard for me to detach myself emotionally, but intellectually I knew it was for the best.

I made it almost twenty metres back towards our base of operations before I heard running footsteps coming up behind me.

"Hey, wait up!"

I turned back, and saw the four teens running after me, their feet splashing wildly through the puddles. A few metres away, they skidded to a halt. The other three looked at Melody, who in turn looked at me.

"We'll help," she said simply.

"With what?" I enquired, lifting an eyebrow.

"With the shop," she replied, gesturing back towards the Salvation Army store. "If we're going to come with you, then we need to contribute somehow. That's how it works, right?"

It took a moment before her meaning sunk in, but once it did I felt a slow smile creeping across my face. I nodded. "Yep, that's right. Are you sure about this, though? Tokoroa is your home."

"It's not our home," Melody said sharply, shaking her head. "Our home is wherever our group is, and my group wants to go with yours." She paused for a second, and gave me the tiniest of smiles. "And I want to go with you. Just for a while, though. I mean, if anything happens and we decide that we don't like it, then we're gone."

"Like I said, any member of my group is free to go at any time." I shrugged and gave her a smile. "While you're with my group, you're going to need to follow my commands. I won't ask you to do anything that I wouldn't do myself, ever. But, I need to know that I can rely on you to do what I tell you to the best of your abilities. Can you do that?"

Melody lowered her head and thought it over for a moment, then she nodded the affirmative. "Yeah. Yeah, we can do that. I can't promise we'll like it, but we'll do it."

"Good." I grinned at her, and beckoned for the group to follow me. "Come on, then! We've got lots of work to do, and not much time to do it in."

***

By midday, we'd cleared out most of the Salvation Army store, and brought anything that was salvageable back to the office block where our own little army waited for us. There would be no salvation for any of us except that which we made ourselves, but we were certainly grateful for the stuff.

Introductions were made between our newcomers and the rest of the group. To my surprise, it was Jasmine that meshed with the rest of the group most swiftly; Melody was wary and standoffish, and Solomon was so quiet that I wondered if he was mute.

It was Priyanka that really came into her own, though. She spent the entire morning darting back and forth between the new members and the old, and I could practically see her carefully weaving a web of understanding between them like an artisan creating a complex tapestry. I was grateful for it, too; I spent most of the morning feeling mildly queasy, and it only started to pass by lunchtime.

Everyone gathered in the little kitchen for lunch. There weren't enough seats, so we stood or sat around chatting while we ate. Priya sat with her new friends in a tight circle, talking softly amongst themselves. I stood by Michael, discreetly watching them and keeping to myself.

"Thank you."

The voice was so sudden and unexpected that it made me jump. I glanced over, and realised that Gavin had snuck up beside us undetected.

"For what?" I asked, surprised by the gratitude.

"For taking us in," he said quietly. His eye swivelled to the children, and he gestured towards them with a tilt of his chin. "For having the patience to take them in. I know it's not easy."

"It's not meant to be easy," I answered, shaking my head. "It's meant to be bloody hard. I knew that when I took this mission on. You don't decide to rebuild a broken world and expect anything to be easy. We are going to have to fight tooth and nail for every little thing, just like we have for the last ten years. But, do you know what the difference is?"

"Yes." He gave me a lopsided smile, and nodded. "Now we get to do it together."

"Exactly." I gestured towards the people all around us. "And every one of these souls is going to fight at our side. With teamwork and effort, we can achieve anything."

"Speaking of which," he said, changing the subject. "The radio station is up and running. We just need to record a message to put on infinite loop. I think you should be the one to record it."

"Oh yeah, that's not terrifying at all. My voice on record for all eternity, broadcasting into the ether." I heaved a dramatic sigh, then put my plate down on the table with the others. "Let's go get this done, then."

He nodded and led the way to the door, with Michael and me following him. For reasons unknown, several of the others decided to join us. By the time we'd reached the radio station and Gavin had helped me get settled into the recording booth, our entire group was crowded around outside the door, jostling one another to make sure they could hear me. Every single one of them. The only person missing was Doctor Cross, who refused to leave Lily's side.

It was an unfamiliar feeling, knowing that there were so many pairs of eyes focused on my every move, and ears hanging on my word. I should have been used to it by now, but I didn't think I ever would be. It was strange and alien, but it was also a powerful feeling. With that thought in mind, I took a deep breath and nodded to Gavin. He patted my shoulder reassuringly, and pressed the button that set the big microphone in front of me recording.

"Survivors of New Zealand, heed my call," I said slowly, clearly, and with as much confidence as I could project. "The virus has mutated. As I speak, there are new infected spreading across the Waikato region. They came from Hamilton, but they are not stopping there.

"I implore you to leave your homes and head south. I repeat, head south. If you are currently north of Hamilton, exercise extreme caution when you're travelling through the Waikato. Assume that you'll never be able to return, and pack accordingly. Bring as much food and water as you can, along with anything that you hold dear.

"The mutants are pack hunters, and are recognisable by their distinctive howl. Carry a weapon at all times. If you are attacked, aim for the legs and cripple it. Then, you must set it alight, otherwise it will keep attacking you. Usual methods are ineffective. Fire is the only sure way to destroy them.

"My name is Sandrine McDermott. I am the leader of a large group. There is safety in numbers, so we will welcome anyone who comes to us in peace. We will be leaving from Tokoroa and heading south along State Highway 32 past the western shore of Lake Taupo, and then we will follow State Highway 1 south from Turangi. If you wish to join us, meet us along this route.

"If you're thinking of ambushing us, then I strongly advise against it. We are well-armed, well-trained, and we will defend ourselves.

"If you are uncertain whether to join us or not, then know this: our group has formed with one purpose, and that is friendship. We have numerous women and children with us, and every member of my group will fight to the death to protect any other member. We have no interest in power or material gain, only in helping our friends to stay happy and healthy.

"This message was set four days after the first full moon of winter, and will play on an indefinite loop. For further updates, please scan the nearby frequencies."

I glanced at Gavin and indicated for him to stop the recording. He did so, then he stood back and gave me a long, thoughtful look. Behind him, I heard faint murmuring from the others, then something happened that I didn't expect. Someone started clapping. I couldn't see who it was, but it spread like wildfire through the group. Before I quite knew what was happening, anything else I might have said was drowned out in a sea of applause.

Chapter Twenty

We left Tokoroa at the crack of dawn the next morning, or what passed for it when the sky was perpetually clouded with rain. Before we moved off, I paused to do a headcount and check everyone's name off against a list that I'd written for myself the night before. There were so many people with us now that it was the only way I could keep track.

Michael and I led the way, to no one's great surprise. At some point during the journey, it had just sort of been assumed that was our position and that we were the trailblazers for the rest of the group. In the back seat, Melody and Solomon sat staring out the windows, leaving Priyanka to natter away happily between them. She'd already adapted to life on the road, but it would take the newcomers time to get used to it.

A few hours into the journey, I caught Michael watching me and shot him a curious look. "What?"

"You're scowling again," he pointed out. "What's on your mind now?"

"Oh." I indulged myself in a long, deep sigh, then I shrugged helplessly. "I'm worried about gas, to be frank. I estimate we've only got eight, maybe nine days of fuel left. We've been incredibly lucky so far in terms of fuel, but I don't think it's going to last. Hell, even with Zain working on the trucks every night, we can't guarantee that they'll last forever, either."

"So if that happens, we get out and walk," he suggested with a shrug.

"Even the little kids? The wounded? Doc?" I replied, staring thoughtfully at the road in front of me as I guided the Hilux forward. "No... we need to start thinking about ways to conserve fuel. Or better yet, alternatives to petrol. It's not so bad up here, but petrol was starting to get scarce last time I was down south."

"Hmm..." Michael sat back, and went silent for a couple of minutes while he thought it over. Suddenly, he glanced at me again. "What about propane?"

"What about it?" I asked, confused.

"Well, propane doesn't expire, right?" he answered, his brow furrowed in thought. "And I remember there being a big conservationist movement before the plague, dedicated to converting cars from petrol and diesel to natural gas. Could we do the same thing?"

This time, it was my turn to stop and think about it. I hadn't even considered the possibility. I picked up my radio with my free hand, and thumbed the receiver. "Zain? Come in Zain?"

A few seconds later, I received a reply. "I'm here. What is it?"

I glanced at Michael, then looked back out at the road in front of us. "Is it possible to convert a car to run on natural gas? Propane?"

"It's theoretically possible to convert a car to run on just about any fuel, with the right tools and parts," he replied. "Why do you ask?"

"Because I want you to start looking for the right tools and parts whenever you can," I answered. "Our supply of petrol is running low, and I'm sure I don't need to tell you how hard it's getting to find more."

There was silence for a few seconds, then his voice came back on the line. "I can't guarantee anything, but I'll try. We'll need to search every workshop and auto parts store that we pass. Alternately, we may want to consider going back to basics."

"What do you mean?" I asked.

"Horses," he replied. "Or even cows, if we can train them to pull a cart. Draft animals."

"Well, what was good enough for our ancestors is good enough for us," I commented, nodding thoughtfully. "All right, let's keep both of these ideas in mind. If anyone else has any suggestions, please bring them to me, even if they're far-fetched."

"We should build a rocket car!" Skylar suggested brightly. I sighed and rolled my eyes heavenwards.

"Not quite that far-fetched," I said dryly. "Put your thinking caps on, guys. We'll talk later."

***

That day passed without incident as we followed the road southwards, and so did the ones after that. For five days, we followed the winding path southwards, through landscape that gradually changed around us with every kilometre. The rolling hills of the Waikato became steeper and less forgiving, but we managed to find a path even when the road was impassable. It wasn't until an hour before sunset on the sixth day that we encountered a real problem. I slammed on the brakes and stared at the road in front of me, uncertain how to react to what I was seeing. Michael glanced up from his book, and uttered a few choice words under his breath.

"How in the world are we going to get through there?" he asked, leaning forward to stare into the dense brush blocking what had once been the road. "Do we need to backtrack?"

"If we backtrack, we'll lose days," I said, shaking my head. "No, let's at least give this a chance. Call the others to a halt and have them start setting up a base camp here. We need to get out and scout the area before it gets dark."

Michael grunted a non-verbal agreement and grabbed the radio to do just that. While he was busy, I put the Hilux in park and pulled up my hood to protect me from the incessant rain.

"What about us?" Melody asked from the back seat, her sharp voice cutting through my thoughts like a hot knife.

I glanced back at her, studying her face in the gloom. "You want to help me scout?"

"Why not?" Melody shrugged, obviously trying to look nonchalant to disguise her tension. "We've been on our own for years without you; I'm pretty sure we can handle ourselves."

"Your age has nothing to do with it." I winked at her, and jerked a thumb towards the window. "I'm just surprised that you'd volunteer to get wet. If you guys want to come along, you're more than welcome."

"Oh." There was a long pause, then she nodded firmly. "Well, we're coming."

"Okay." I glanced at Michael, who had paused in his conversation to look at me. "I'm taking these guys with me; you stay here and help with setting up camp."

"You got it." He leaned over and planted a kiss on my cheek, then resumed his conversation.

I threw open my door and slid out from behind the wheel. The ground beneath me felt moist and squishy; an odd combination of thick mud and spongy leaf-litter layered the old tar seal. I tested it a couple of times with my foot before I committed my full weight to it; it was a bit slippery, but it didn't give out when I stood on it. By the time I was ready, Melody, Solomon, and Priya had bundled themselves up and joined me.

"I don't much care for this weather," I said, pausing to look up at the sky. "It's raining too much. If it doesn't stop soon, then we may have to worry about flooding."

"I think we've still got a bit of leeway," Melody answered, following my gaze up to the clouds. "But, you're right. It smells dangerous."

"Exactly." We both stood silently for a few moments to consider the possibilities, then I sighed and shook my head. "Let's try to find somewhere elevated for them to pitch camp first of all. I'd hate to sleep in this mud."

"That way," Melody said, pointing westwards. "The land slopes up a little. Let's check beyond those bushes."

"Good call." I nodded my approval, then I reached back to grab my shotgun from its resting place and slammed the door behind me. "I'll take the lead. Melody, you watch my left flank. Priya, watch the right. Solomon, you keep an eye on our rear. Got it?"

"Yes, Mama," Priya agreed brightly.

I glanced at her, and saw that she already had her little pistol in hand, and was holding it exactly the way Michael had shown her. After her encounter with the pig, I felt confident that she could handle it. I shifted my gaze to Solomon, who just nodded silently. That was about as much as I was likely to get out of him, so I took it at face value. Shifting my shotgun into the offensive position, I eased myself down into a crouch and led the way into the brush.

Thorns grabbed at my sleeves as I forced my way between the bushes, but the leather kept them from biting my skin. With careful use of my forearm, I pushed my way through, and came out the other side into long, wild grasses. The landscape had begun to change from the Waikato region's lush greenery into the tough, mountainous foliage of the central plateau; I'd seen it a thousand times before, but I could see that the kids were less confident in unfamiliar territory.

"Up here," I said, guiding my charges deeper into the brush. A few pathetic trees clung to the slope, but the grass was tough and demanding, and sucked away what little nutrients they might have been able to find. Past the trees, a small clearing opened up, framed by more bushes and grass but otherwise clear; the ground was firm beneath my feet, and I felt stone under the leaf litter.

"There's a stream over there," Melody said, pointing to our left.

"Good," I replied. "That'll help us keep our water reserves going. Priya, you and Solomon head back to the convoy. Tell Michael to send people up here to cut back the brush, so we can set up camp here."

"Okies!" Priya agreed on behalf of both of them. Without another word, she turned and scampered away, Solomon hot on her heels.

I lowered my shotgun, and looked at Melody. This was the first chance we'd had to be alone together, so it seemed like a good chance to get a feel for exactly how much she knew. "Tell me what you see here."

The girl looked at me, her eyes unreadable. "What?"

"I need to know how much you know," I explained. "So, humour me. Look around, and tell me what you see."

Melody went quiet then, but her expression changed from defensive to thoughtful. When she finally spoke again, her voice was soft and even. "I see a steady supply of fresh water, with a good, solid wall of foliage that should block the wind from most directions. It's an elevated position, so it should be easily defensible. I can hear the birds singing in those trees over there, so there aren't any predators around. If there were, they wouldn't be singing."

"Good." I nodded my approval. "What else?"

Melody paused again, then pointed towards northern edge of the clearing. "Those rocks should also give us some more shelter. They look stable enough to climb on, so if we can get up there we should be able to scout the road ahead."

"Perfect." I smiled at her, and nodded towards the rocks. "Do you want to lead the way?"

She set off without a word, leaving me to follow along behind her. I did so, after taking a moment to return my shotgun to its normal place across my back. The afternoon chorus was loud enough that we'd know long in advance if anything was coming our way.

A few bold fantails danced across the trail as we slipped back into the brush, completely unafraid of our intrusion. The sight of them made me smile; I remembered a time when fantails had been endangered, thanks to humans destroying their habitat. If there was one good thing about the end of mankind, it was the fact that the rest of nature's children had a chance to flourish again.

Melody led me around the outside of the clearing until we reached the rock face. On closer examination, I saw that it was compiled of a single enormous boulder, surrounded by a dozen smaller ones of assorted sizes. She hopped up onto the lowest one, and nimbly climbed from one to the other until she reached the top of biggest. A second later, I joined her. We stood carefully, side by side, and stared towards the south.

"I can barely see the road," Melody admitted. "The bushes have managed to grow on the concrete. We can probably cut them back, I guess..." For the first time, she paused and looked at me uncertainly.

"We can," I said with as much confidence as I could muster. "It's not going to be easy, but we can do it."

"What are you going to do?" Melody asked. The question surprised me, and forced me to stop and think.

"I'm going to put it to the vote tonight," I said at last. "We have two choices. We can either backtrack and head south through Taupo, or we can cut our way through here. It's a decision that's going to affect everyone, so everyone should have their chance to have a say. In the meantime, let's go circle the camp and make sure there's nothing to worry about."

Melody nodded her agreement, and followed me back down to ground level. By the time we'd finished inspecting the surrounding area thoroughly enough to feel safe, Michael and the others had cut a path through the scrub from the road up to our campsite. He already had people standing guard, so Melody and I joined in with the setup instead.

By the time night fell, we had our camp ready. There were a couple of individual tents now, but most of us still slept under the roof of the giant tarpaulin. It wasn't all that comfortable, but it was good enough. I was tired and anxious to get to bed, but too stubborn to take a break when there was work to be done.

Rebecca and Elly were still recovering, so we decided to err on the side of caution. We put them straight to bed in one of the tents, with as many extra blankets as we could spare. With her primary helper out of the running, poor Skye was rushed off her feet trying to get dinner ready. I volunteered my own services to help her, and Melody's as well. She didn't complain. Priya soon joined us, and the extra hands were welcome.

Dinner was simple, but nutritious and filling. Once they'd eaten, we sent the younger kids off to bed, and gathered everyone else around the fire to discuss the matter of the road. I explained what we'd seen, and then put it to the vote. To my surprise, no one wanted to backtrack through Taupo. It turned out that they'd rather put in days of hard labour cutting a path than risk unknown danger.

After that, we sent everyone off about their duties. We were gradually falling into a routine, where every person knew what their task was in the group. Michael, Hemi, and a few of the other Waikato Iwi men organised the watch rotation amongst themselves, while Zain, Ryan, and I went down to check the cars as best we could by torchlight. By the time we got back, everyone was turning in for the night.

As soon as Michael spotted me, he finished his conversation and hurried over to greet me. "Hey there, pretty lady."

"Hey, yourself." I returned the greeting, and gave him a long look. "What are you grinning about?"

"We finally have enough people on the watch roster that we can swap people in and out," he answered, grinning even wider. "That means people can have a full night's sleep when it's their turn to have a night off."

"Oh, yeah?" I raised a brow, amused by his enthusiasm. "That's good, I guess."

"No, it's great!" Suddenly, he laughed and grabbed me by the waist to draw me into a hug. "The other guys insisted that we take the first night off."

This time, both my brows shot up. "Oh? So we get a full night's sleep? Tonight?"

"Damn straight." He planted a kiss on my lips, then pushed me back and grinned at me. "I don't know about you, but it feels like I haven't had a solid night's sleep in forever. Go get ready for bed. Long drop's over there, about five meters past that big rock."

"I feel like I should be concerned that you're so excited about getting me into bed, yet your only interest is sleep," I commented dryly.

Michael laughed and spun me around, pointing me towards the makeshift facilities. "I know! Who would have guessed? Oh well. Go pee, then come and have a cuddle."

"Yes sir, Officer Chan, sir!" I gave a mock salute, and headed off to do just that.

By the time I'd finished doing my business and returned to camp, Michael had already stripped down to his underwear, hung his clothing up to dry overnight, and snuggled down in our communal nest of blankets. I'd gotten used to the lack of privacy, and didn't even think twice about stripping down to my underwear to join him. I hung up my coat and clothes, dried myself off on a towel, and snuggled down beside him.

Michael put his arms around me and drew me in against his warmth. That, combined with Alfred sleeping at our feet like a big, fur-covered space heater, left me quite warm and comfortable despite the weather and the stone beneath the tarp. I closed my eyes, buried my face in the curve of Michael's neck, and was asleep before I had time for any other thoughts.

***

The dawn chorus woke me the next morning, though it was so dark that I could barely even tell that it was daybreak. Michael was sound asleep, and didn't even stir when I carefully extracted myself from his embrace. Alfred lifted his head and whined in greeting, his tail thumping happily against the ground. I held my finger to my lip playfully, as if that would keep the dog quiet. Regardless, he seemed to understand well enough. He put his head back down on Michael's foot, and went right back to sleep.

I indulged myself in a stretch, and looked around the camp. Sleeping bodies surrounded me in the early morning gloom; the only sounds were birdsong, rain, and snores. I smiled to myself as I reached up and plucked my clothing from the lines strung overhead. My pants were still damp around the ankles, but Michael had definitely been right about that coat. It did an admirable job of keeping me mostly dry from the knees up.

I'd just finished pulling on my shirt and trousers when a soft cry split the peace. I jumped and spun around, but there was only silence again. Then, the doctor's tent flicked open, and Stuart looked out. He spotted me, and beckoned me over.

"Lily's awake," he explained quietly once I was close enough to hear him without him having to wake the entire camp. I glanced past him, and saw the twins clinging together inside the tent.

I took a deep breath and nodded. "I'll talk to her."

Doctor Cross absently adjusted his new spectacles, looking relieved. "I'll go find Gavin. I think he'll want to know."

"Good plan," I agreed. I waved him off, and then I slipped into the tent to take his place. There weren't many places to sit, so I just eased myself down to sit cross-legged on the pile of blankets that had probably been Stuart's bed. Both of the girls looked up at me, and I found myself wondering how on earth I was supposed to tell them apart. They were identical in every way, except for their strength of spirit.

Suddenly, I realised that was how I could tell them apart. I could see fear in Lily's eyes, but none in Jasmine's.

"Good morning, Lily," I said softly, keeping my voice as low and unthreatening as possible. "I know you're scared, so you just take as much time as you need, okay? Gavin's coming, and I'm pretty sure Melody will be here soon, too. All your friends are here, and you're safe."

The girl said nothing. Jasmine leaned down and whispered something in her ear in a language I didn't understand, then hugged her tightly. Lily nodded silently, and buried her face in her sister's shoulder. It wasn't hard to guess that she was feeling just the way I had when I'd woken up with Michael's group for the first time, so I didn't push her. I just sat back and waited.

Sure enough, less than a minute later the tent flap opened and Gavin hurried inside, with Melody on his heels. I just sat nearby and watched while the four of them reunited.

Tears were shed, more words were whispered, and I was ignored for quite some time. It was fine, though. I completely understood. Eventually, my patience was rewarded.

"Lil, this is Sandy. She saved your life."

My attention snapped back to the present when I realised that someone was trying to introduce me. I lifted my head, smiled, and waved. It was Gavin, of course. No surprise there. He hugged the three girls one more time, and then he shoved himself back and plopped down on the bedding beside me with a long sigh of relief.

"I told you she'd be okay," I said, trying to reassure him.

"I know, I know." He gave me a lopsided smile, and shrugged sheepishly. "You'll understand once you're a parent. You always worry, even when they're all grown up, no matter how smart and capable they are. I know all of my kids can take care of themselves, but how I feel isn't always rational."

"I think I understand," I replied thoughtfully. "It's like my mum used to say: we were always going to be her babies. It's human nature. The bond between parent and child is nearly unbreakable, even if they're not technically your children."

"Yeah, that's exactly it." He nodded his agreement, watching the three girls talking softly amongst themselves. Melody shot him a dark look, but said nothing. I found myself grinning in spite of everything.

"And that's exactly the same look I used to give my mum when she said that kind of thing," I commented. This time, her glare was directed at me. I held my hands up in self-defence, struggling not to laugh. "Sorry, but it's true. Anyway — Lily, you're with my group. We're all heading south, to find safer territory down near Wellington. I need to go get everyone out of bed. Is there anything I can get you?"

Lily just stared at me with enormous eyes, as if I'd asked her to jump out of an aeroplane. Jasmine sighed and shook her head. "No, thank you. Me and Mel will take care of her."

"All right," I agreed. "I'll leave you guys to it, but if you need anything you can call any one of us, okay?"

The girls just nodded, and turned their attention back to Lily. I took that as my cue to leave. Gavin followed me out of the tent, and trailed after me as I went off to get breakfast cooking. I found Skylar already there, in the process of making rice porridge. I knelt down beside her, and began unpacking our eclectic collection of bowls and cutlery from the plastic packing crate that we carried it in.

"Morning," she said cheerfully. "You two are up early. Did I miss something exciting?"

"Lily's awake," I explained, setting the bowls down on the tarp beside me. I flipped the plastic crate upside down, and then put the bowls back on top of it to use it as a table. "She's a bit freaked out, but she's going to be fine."

"Yeah, just give her time," Skye agreed pleasantly. She grabbed a jar of sugar out of the food stores, and chipped a generous chunk off the solidified granules inside. It went into the pot of porridge, then she looked over at me again. "So, what's the plan now? You do have a plan, right?"

"I always have a plan," I replied, matching her playful tone. "I'm leaving the wounded and ill here with a couple of guards while the rest of us get our hands dirty and try to clear the path. I estimate that we're only about ten kilometres from the next town, so there can't be that much of this. In the meantime, I want you and Anahera to take the kids down to that stream we saw, and see if you can catch any fish. We're probably going to be stuck here for a couple of days, so we may as well make the most of it."

I expected her to protest about being left behind, but for once Skylar just accepted my instructions without question.

"Just promise me that you won't over-exert yourself again," she demanded, fixing me with a dark look. "If I hear about you fainting because you're pushing yourself too hard, I'm going to go up there and drag you back by the ear."

"Yes, ma'am!" I agreed, sketching a salute. Both she and Gavin laughed. I eased myself back to my feet then, and set about the arduous businesses of waking people that really didn't want to have to get out of bed. I couldn't blame them, but that didn't mean I was going to show any mercy. There was a lot of work to be done, and every day we were on the road was a day closer to winter without permanent shelter and a steady supply of food.

Chapter Twenty-One

My estimate, as it turned out, was a bit too generous. It took us eight whole days to clear the road southwards, even with every able-bodied person on the job from dawn 'til dusk. Luckily for us, the surrounding area turned out to be rich with wild game, and we found plenty of fish, eels, and ducks to pad out the supplies we'd brought with us.

Rather than waste fuel driving the trucks forward a couple of kilometres a day and going through all the effort of having to tear our camp down and set it up again, we left our camp set up on the ridge beside the stream. Each morning, the eight people chosen to work on clearing the road climbed on the bikes in pairs, drove out to the end of the road, and spent the day hacking back brush in the incessant rain. The respite gave Elly and Rebecca time to finish recovering from their colds, and also gave everyone a much-needed break from the tedium of travel.

Clearing the road was long, filthy, and unpleasant work, so we drew up a roster to try and give everyone some time off every couple of days. Compared to labouring in the mud, watching the camp or helping to collect food was practically a holiday.

Michael and I were in the road-clearing gang on the ninth day, when we finally broke through to the other side. A shout went up from the pair sent to scout ahead and plan our path, and then a second later Hemi came rushing back with the biggest grin on his face.

"We're through!" he exclaimed, waving his arms. "Just another ten meters or so, and then it's clear sailing from here on out!" He paused to gulp down an excited breath, and then clarified his meaning. "Well, not totally clear sailing. I mean, it's just a mud track, but there's no plant life growing on it. That's an improvement."

"Amen to that," I agreed, standing up straight to stretch my back. "Grab one of the bikes and head back to the campsite. Tell them it's time to go. By the time they finish packing up, we'll be just about finished here, I reckon."

Hemi nodded and raced off, leaving the rest of us to finish clearing the path. It was almost midday by the time the convoy was ready to move, and it took another hour before the trucks caught up to us. Exhausted, sopping wet, and splattered with mud from head to toe, we stripped off our soiled outerwear and tumbled into the seats reserved for us. The people who had been on guard duty back at camp piled out and grabbed the bikes, then we were back on the road again.

Progress was slow, but steady. The mud was so deep that at times we had to get out and push one of the trucks clear. Each time that happened, I worried that we were about to lose one of our precious vehicles, but by some miracle we managed to keep going. By mid-afternoon, we were all cold, filthy, and miserable, and more than one of us was starting to show symptoms of catching the 'flu.

"We're going to need to think about stopping somewhere for a couple of days, to let everyone rest up," I commented to Michael as we huddled in the back seat of the Hilux together, with Priya contentedly napping in the front.

Anahera, in the driver's seat, made a soft sound of agreement. "I think the group is desperate for it. Even you and I are exhausted, though we've both been trying to hide it. Tempers are starting to flare up. Yesterday at lunch, your friend Ryan exchanged heated words with my son. I was genuinely afraid that it was going to come to blows."

I swore softly beneath my breath. "I'll have a word with them when we make camp. We can't have infighting; it'll tear the group apart."

"Don't worry, I already handled it," Anahera replied, a faint, amused smile dancing across her lips. "I don't think they'll be doing that again any time soon. Anyway, I believe that we will reach Tokaanu by nightfall. Tokaanu is a lovely town. It would be a good place to stop and rest for a while."

"You know the area?" I asked, my annoyance melting into curiosity.

"As a matter of fact, yes," she said. "My grandparents lived there. Tokaanu was my home away from home when I was a child. It's a geothermal area, with rich fishing. We should be quite comfortable for a while."

"Geothermal?" I sat up straight, suddenly very interested. "You mean, hot springs?"

"Oh yes," she replied, laughing. "There are many hot springs in the area, along with mud pools, geysers, and some of the most beautiful rainbow trout you'll ever lay eyes on. My people have been going there for centuries to bathe in the springs. I think you'll like it, Sandrine."

"Oh, I know I'll like it," I answered dryly. "We've been half-arsed bathing in an icy stream for the last week and some. A soak in a hot spring sounds like heaven."

"Agreed!" Michael commented playfully. "You're starting to smell like Alfred."

I knew better than to take him seriously, so I just laughed right along with him.

***

We travelled southwards for the rest of the day. The heavy bush on either side of the road made it hard to judge distances. The road wound around overhangs and ledges, up steep hills and down slopes. Every so often, there was a gap in the foliage that revealed a glimpse of rolling green hills in the distance, dotted with flocks of sheep clustered together for protection against the weather.

Then, suddenly, between one glance and the next, the landscape changed. Gone were the rolling hills, replaced by a broad, sparkling expanse of water that could only be Lake Taupo.

"We must be getting close," I commented, as much to myself as to anyone else.

"We are," Anahera agreed. I glanced at her, and saw a troubled look on her face. "I haven't been here since before the plague, but I recognise the lay of the land. There should be a thermal resort along this road a few more kilometres — assuming it's still there."

Sensing her disquiet, I leaned forward to rest my hand on her shoulder. "We can keep driving, if you want. I… understand. I'm not sure I could go back home. Not now."

"No, our people need to rest, and this area is perfect for it." Anahera shook her head, and straightened her shoulders. "My grandparents would have wanted us to take advantage of the hospitality that Aotearoa has to offer us, even if they're not here to join us. This is our land now, and we must not be afraid of where the road takes us."

"Amen to that," I agreed quietly, settling back in my seat. We all fell into silence after that, each of us alone with our thoughts. I felt Michael's hand close over mine, but there was no need for verbal communication. The touch said enough. I leaned against his shoulder, and stared out the window at the bush on the lakeside of the road.

Eventually, the bush vanished and was replaced by a carpet of thick grass along the edge of the lake. As I watched, a flock of birds exploded out of the reeds and flew up high, startled by the noise of our engines. I watched them until I could no longer see them, then I resumed staring at the lake.

"It's beautiful, isn't it?" Michael said softly, his lips right beside my ear. "Sometimes I forget just how lovely our world really is."

"Yeah," I agreed, snuggling up against him. "When you get too focused on the details, you can miss the magnificence of the whole picture."

Michael made a noise of agreement and nodded, but he said nothing.

Priya stirred in the front seat and looked around, rubbing her eyes sleepily. She yawned, then turned and looked at me expectantly. "Mama, why?"

"Huh?" I shot a confused look at her. "Why what, honey?"

"Why the trees?" She wrinkled her nose up, and pointed at a the road ahead of us. "They not be green."

"Oh, those beech trees over there?" I found myself smiling at her inquisitiveness. "The colour is called orange."

She turned back and stared at me with those enormous eyes, the way only she could. "But why?"

"Why what?"

"Why orange!" she exclaimed, making a gesture of frustration. "Trees are green, not orange."

"Oh." I paused, and glanced back at the trees. "It's because they're deciduous, Priya. That means their leaves die in autumn, and then grow again in spring. Haven't you seen that before?"

"Oooo." She nodded slowly, making a long, drawn-out sound of understanding. "Yes, have seen, but I never knew why. I wanted to know."

"That's okay." I smiled at her, trying to reassure her. "You can ask any time you see something you don't understand. Most trees here are evergreen – their leaves don't fall off in winter time. But some are deciduous, like those ones. The leaves will grow back again in spring. If you like, I can ask Doctor Cross to teach you about it in his lesson plan."

"Yes, I want to learn," she agreed, nodding firmly.

"And he should have some time," Anahera spoke up suddenly, distracting us, "because we're here."

"We are?" I sat forward, and looked over her shoulder as she eased the Hilux off the road, into the parking lot of a low, rambling building in surprisingly good condition. Warning bells went off inside my head. "Someone's been living here, Ana. Look – that hole in the roof has been patched up, and the bushes by the front door have been cut back."

"I'm not surprised," she replied. "It's too prime a location to be completely abandoned. Still, we should check."

"I want you to stay here," I told her. "Michael, you're with me."

The pair of us jumped out of the truck with our weapons at the ready. As soon as the rest of the convoy came to a halt behind us, I gestured for Hemi, Tane, and Iorangi to join us. The five of us headed for the front door together.

Before we could get there, the door opened from within. A tiny old woman shuffled out, ancient and withered with skin like carved wood. She took one look at us, then grunted something inarticulate, made a vague gesture, and vanished back inside.

I froze, uncertain how to respond or what the gesture was supposed to mean. A few seconds later, the old woman stuck her head outside again, and bellowed at us. "Come on, then! It's bloody cold out here! Get in and close the door."

Michael and I exchanged glances. There was a slim possibility that it might have been a trap, but it seemed... unlikely, somehow. I shrugged, and decided to just go with it. Shifting my shotgun into a more casual grip, I headed for the front door and followed the old woman inside.

"And about time," she complained. "Well, this is more people than I've seen in one place for a long time – and led by a woman, to boot." She paused and looked me up and down thoughtfully, but spoke again before I could say anything. "You're that McDermott woman, aren't you?"

"I am," I answered, surprised that she recognised me. "You heard our broadcast, I take it?"

"Aye, aye." The woman made another vague gesture, then turned and shuffled over to the reception desk at the back of the lobby. "Gets a wee bit lonely around these parts, so sometimes I like to see if there's anything on the radio. Lo and behold, my favourite talkback show is gone, replaced by your broadcast. How many rooms are you going to need?"

"Rooms?" I asked in genuine confusion.

She stopped and gave me the kind of look usually reserved for particularly slow children. "Aye, rooms! This is my establishment, and I'm presuming you want to stay and ride out the storm, so you'll need some place to sleep."

"Wait, you're actually running this resort?" I glanced around the lobby, and looked back at my friends. None of them had an answer any more than I did.

"Of course." She heaved a long-suffering sigh, and pulled a thick, dusty guest book out from under the counter. "I don't get many visitors these days, but when I do, I try to be courteous. I expect the same in return. Please provide your own food, and if you make a mess, clean it up. Other than that, you can have the run of the place."

My brow furrowed. "Ma'am... no offense intended, but you don't know us at all. You're just inviting us into your home? We could be thieves, murderers – anything."

"Don't call me 'ma'am', young lady." She gave me another dark look. "You may call me Mrs Swanson, Netty, or Nana, but not 'ma'am'. I'm not running a brothel, here."

"Sorry," I apologised automatically, cringing in spite of myself. I couldn't help it. The woman had to be in her late eighties or early nineties, but she carried herself with an air of total confidence. "But my question does still stand."

"I'm too damn old to be afraid of anything these days," Netty answered dryly. "I've been running this place for the better part of thirteen years, and no one's lifted a finger against me yet. I doubt you plan to be the first."

"Well, no," I agreed, shifting uncomfortably under her scrutiny. "But... what about the gangs? Haven't they come after you, if you're here all by yourself?"

"Why would they?" Netty shrugged, picked up a pen, and started slowly writing my name in her guest book with hands that trembled with age and infirmity. "I'm everyone's nana. They know that if they ever hurt me, they'll unleash the wrath of every other person in the area on their stupid heads. Now, it was Sandrine, wasn't it? Spell that for me, dear?"

I did as I was told, and spelled out my first name for her. Once that was done, I took a breath and shook my head slowly. "I can hardly believe that you've been on your own here for this long, without anyone taking a shot at you. But... you're right. Now that I've met you, if anyone tried to hurt you I'd kick their backsides all the way to Australia and back."

"Exactly." Netty gave me an uneven smile, and laid one frail finger beside her nose. "Now, the rules of my establishment are simple. You may use any of the facilities, but I expect you to respect my space. Room 25 is mine, so stay out of it. Please attend to your own linens and cooking – I'm your landlord, not your maid. If you want access to consumables, then you're going to need to trade for them."

"Of course," I agreed immediately. "It's been a hard trip from the north, so we were planning to stay for about a week. We were going to send people out to fish and catch game birds, and I'm happy to give some of our catch to you if you'll let us stay that long... and if we can use the hot pools."

"The hot pools are open to everyone, and the same rules apply," Netty replied. "Except, there's one more: anyone that pees in the pool has to drink from the pool."

"Ew. So noted." I wrinkled my nose up, and shook my head. "Is there anywhere dry that we can store our vehicles in the mean time?"

"Aye, there's a big storage shed in the field next door. I'll find the keys." Netty turned to leave, but I stepped forward to stop her.

"Wait," I said quietly, uncomfortable with what I needed to ask but it felt necessary. "Before we agree to stay, we need to check this place is safe. Please, don't be offended, but... we've all seen some horror stories in our time, and we've got small children with us. I can't do anything that puts them at risk. I hope you understand."

"Oh, fine." Netty heaved a long-suffering sigh, and beckoned for me to follow her. "Come along, then. But, your boys can't come into my room! It wouldn't be proper. They'll have to wait outside."

"Agreed." I gave her a smile, and set off after her with my 'boys' hot on my heels.

Inspecting the entire building took most of the time we had left before sunset, but I felt better for it. I'd seen enough horror movies to know that if someone says to keep out of a particular room, it's usually the first place you want to check in case it's full of bodies. Netty's wasn't; she was just old-fashioned, and uncomfortable with the idea of men other than her husband seeing where she slept.

As we spent time together, I grew to like her more and more. She had a harsh, no-nonsense way about her, but underneath that I sensed a kind spirit. She guided us through the passages, and let me spend as much time as I needed inspecting things to ensure my charges would be safe. Eventually, we found ourselves at the rear of the building, where a heavy, fire-stop door blocked the way.

"Through here is the kitchen," she explained. "My joints don't much care for the weather. Would you mind getting the door, dear?"

"Of course," I agreed immediately, stepping past her to put my shoulder against the door. It groaned with age, but swung open reluctantly to reveal a massive, professional-grade kitchen that was very nearly as clean and tidy as the day the world had ended.

"Wow," Hemi breathed, peering over my shoulder. "Skye's going to have a field day in here."

"Just so long as she cleans up after herself!" Netty snapped, shooting a dark look at him. Then she looked back at me, and her expression immediately softened. "I've managed to keep just about everything here in working order, so feel free to use things. If you're staying for a few days, you may want to catch some extra fish and dehydrate them; the dehydrator is right over there."

"Why did a resort have a dehydrator?" I asked curiously,. "Particularly an industrial-sized one?"

"Oh, that wasn't here originally," she explained, patting my arm in a motherly fashion. "One of the groups passing through brought it to me as a gift. It was their way of thanking me for my hospitality."

"Is that how you've survived all these years by yourself?" I enquired, looking down at her with interest. "I mean, most women I know have only barely made it, usually because they've had groups to protect them."

"Yes." Netty chuckled, slipped her arm through mine, and led me back out of the room. "Gratitude, kindness, and a whole lot of luck. I let people stay here, and they offer me kindness in return. I can see in your eyes that you've already been thinking about what you're going to give me. Everyone looks at me like that."

I stiffened in surprise, but the shock didn't last for long. "You're right," I admitted, laughing. "Well, sort of. I was actually thinking about how I could convince you to leave and come with us when we go."

"Well, it's sweet of you to offer, but I would have to decline. I'm much too old to travel." Netty turned a corner and led me out into a large, open-air courtyard. Around the edge of the room, mature vegetable plants grew in large planter boxes, sheltered from the elements by the walls around them. The centre of the courtyard was dominated by a tiled pool, steaming in the cool, stormy air.

I paused and sniffed, then shot a curious look at the little old lady. "I smell sulphur. Is that a geothermal pool?"

"It is," she replied proudly. "People have been coming here for centuries to bathe in the healing waters. There are less people now, but they still come. Don't spend too long in this pool – it's quite hot, and can make you light-headed. Now, come this way, I'll show you where you can park your vehicles..."

***

Once our inspection was complete, we returned to the vehicles to find everyone waiting anxiously for us to appear. It wasn't until I'd gathered everyone together and explained the situation that they began to relax. Smiles started to appear on people's faces, and I could practically feel the tension lifting away like a palpable weight.

Netty vanished before I could introduce her to everyone, but I couldn't blame her. A crowd of that size must have been intimidating to her. Once the situation had been explained, people drifted off to choose their own rooms, and fetch their things from the convoy. The complex had enough rooms for everyone to have their own space, except for the people that actually wanted to share.

Unsurprisingly, Michael and I were amongst that group. Sometime between posting the lookouts and helping unpack the gear from the convoy, we found ourselves alone together in our room. Michael stuck his head into the attached en suite, then gasped and gave me a wide-eyed look.

"We've got a spa bath in here," he announced, sounding utterly shocked. "And a shower, and our own toilet. This place is like... like..."

"...like a luxury resort?" I finished dryly.

"Yeah!" he exclaimed, as excited as a schoolboy. "No wonder people come here and bribe Netty to let them stay. This place is amazing."

"I know." I sighed, wandering over to lean against his broad back. "It's so warm in here. I read on a pamphlet by the front desk that they've got the pipes running under the building that heat all the rooms naturally. Can you imagine? The room we're standing in right now is heated by water from the heart of a volcano."

Michael stiffened at that comment, then looked back at me with an anxious expression. "Oh, I never thought of it like that. Do you think it's safe?"

"You heard Anahera, and Netty. People have been coming here for centuries, and they're all fine." I grinned at him, and gave him a playful slap on the bottom. "Stop worrying, and go back to thinking about how much fun we're going to have in that spa bath."

His expression instantly brightened. A second later, I found myself swept right off my feet, my startled squeal muffled by enthusiastic kisses.

Chapter Twenty-Two

When we first arrived at Tokaanu, the plan had been to spend a couple of days. Nearly two weeks later, we were still there. Every time we planned to leave, someone came down with a cold, or we decided that the weather was just too foul, or the latest batch of fish wasn't quite finished drying. Although we still set watches every day and night, nothing bad happened at all. Tokaanu became our oasis, a place to stop and rest in the middle of an arduous journey.

On the thirteenth morning, Anahera and Michael found me down by the lake front pretending to fish. I hadn't even baited the hook, but I needed time to think and it seemed like a valid excuse. I didn't realise they were even there until I felt the dock move ever-so-slightly under someone's foot. I glanced up, and found them both watching me with serious expressions on their faces.

"You heard it too, then?" I asked quietly, tugging my hood forward to keep the rain out of my eyes.

"The talk about settling here permanently?" Anahera asked. "Yes, that's why we're here."

"As much as I hate to say it, we need to move on soon," Michael said, easing himself down to sit beside me. "This place is wonderful, but..."

"But we need to keep moving," I finished, turning away from him to stare down into the murky water. "I know. We're still too close to the outbreak. But the question is, do we stay here until spring and then move south, or do we risk it and try to push across the Central Plateau now?"

"We have to go now," Anahera said, her expression dark and serious. "The Plateau gets snow, and if we wait even another day then we may find ourselves trapped here with no way to travel further south. What happens if the mutants reach us while we're trapped here? How would we defend ourselves?"

"We can't." I sighed and rubbed my hand across my forehead. "We need to go south, and try to beat the snow. If we can just make it across the plateau, that'll give us a solid barrier between us and them. How are our supplies looking?"

"Excellent," Anahera replied. "We've caught and preserved enough fish and duck to keep us going for a month if we ration it. Our water reservoirs have been refilled, and Zain managed to find enough parts to convert two of the bikes and one of the trucks to propane. We found a little more usable petrol in a small community down by the lake front, which should keep us going for a while."

"And the guns?" I asked, shifting my gaze to Michael. "Are they still in working order after all this rain?"

"Yes." He nodded and smiled at me. "I've checked them all over, cleaned, and lubricated them, and I'm about ninety percent sure that they shouldn't misfire at inopportune moments."

"That's going to have to do," I decided, starting to rise to my feet. Half way up, something tugged on the line and startled me so much that I ended up falling on my bottom. "Oh damn, I think I caught something!"

"Yes, that will happen when you're fishing." Anahera laughed, leaning past me to help me manage the rod. "Relax for a moment, give him a little slack, then reel him in slowly."

"But I didn't even bait it!" I protested, horrified. Thank goodness no one impressionable was watching, because my response was a wee bit embarrassing: I tried to shove the rod into her hands. "I can't do this, Ana. You do it."

"Oh no you don't," she said firmly, pushing the rod back into my hands. "Even the children can fish, Sandrine. I know how you feel about hurting animals, but you have to learn sometime. Here, I'll help you. Like this."

Despite my protests, Anahera leaned over my shoulder, and guided my hands through the motions of reeling in the fish with the strength and confidence that she applied to everything she did. Her soft, even tone calmed me down from the verge of panic. Together, we hauled in the fish and pulled the poor, thrashing thing out into the light of day.

"Oh, wow, it's so big!" I cried, feeling a strange combination of horror and pride about what I'd done. "I... please don't make me kill it. I can't. I'm not ready."

"All right, all right." Anahera laughed, grabbing my struggling catch by the line above its mouth. With an expert touch, she put it out of its misery and then held it up for me to see. "This is a beautiful fish, though. It's a rainbow trout. He'll make a delicious dinner for your family tonight."

I took a deep breath to calm my rattled nerves, and let it out as a long, drawn-out sigh. "First thing tomorrow morning, we head south. We better go tell the troops."

***

The announcement was met with an odd mixture of disappointed groans, and excitement. For some, the idea of leaving our little home-away-from-home was depressing; for others, it was just another step in an on-going adventure into the unknown. I wasn't quite sure where I stood, but I knew that it had to be done. Like it or not, we had to go south.

Netty took the announcement with silent stoicism, though I could see the sadness in her eyes. By the time I'd finished answering the inevitable onslaught of questions from my groupmates, she'd vanished from the room. As soon as I could do so politely, I extracted myself from the crowd and headed to her room in search of her.

Half way there, I spotted her shuffling along slowly, one hand on the wall and the other clutching something around her throat.

"Netty?" I called, hurrying to catch up with her. She paused and looked back at me, a haunted expression on her face. It gave me pause, and slowed my approach. Suddenly, I felt a lump in my throat the size of a baseball. "Netty, please come with us. Don't make me leave you here all alone."

"I can't, dear. You know that. At my age, the journey would kill me." The old woman gave me the faintest of smiles, then looked away. "Besides, Tokaanu is my home. I've lived here for ninety-three years. I married my husband here, and buried him here. I raised four children and twelve grandchildren here, and then I buried all of them as well. I want to stay with my family."

I started to protest, but before the words even left my mouth I realised that they were fruitless. She'd made up her mind, and even if I did manage to dissuade her, she'd always regret leaving. My shoulders slumped, and my gaze dropped to the floor. "I... I understand. Is there anything we can do to help before we go? Anything that needs fixing, anything we can leave to make you more comfortable?"

"Just one thing, dear. Take this with you." She smiled and took my hand. I felt the sensation of metal against my palm, and when I looked down at it I saw that she'd given me a locket on a chain, still warm from around her neck. I looked up at her quizzically, and her smile widened. "That trinket belonged to my grandmother, who got it from her grandmother. None of my grandchildren made it through the plague, but I would like to see the tradition continue."

"I would be honoured to take on the tradition for you," I answered, blinking back the tears that threatened my vision. "Thank you, Mrs Swanson."

"The honour is mine, Sandrine McDermott," the woman replied. Suddenly, I felt her arms around me, and I was drawn into her embrace. "It makes me happy to know that the future of our kind is in the hands of someone like you."

With those words, she released me and shuffled away. Everything that needed saying had already been said. Suddenly, I found myself facing the overwhelming urge to cry. I managed to keep myself together long enough to find Skylar, but only just.

I came up behind her and touched her arm. "Sis, I need a few minutes. Can you get everyone moving?"

She glanced back at me, but something about my expression must have warned her off asking too many questions. She just nodded and shrugged. "Sure, okay."

I couldn't find the words to thank her. I just nodded once, then I turned and fled back to my room. Michael was already there, folding our things and packing them back into our bags. He took one look at my face, and silently held his arms out to me. I ran to him, buried my face in his chest, and wept for what felt like a very long time.

***

It was unusual for our group to do anything in a subdued fashion, but preparing for our departure from Tokaanu was one of those rare times. Even the children seemed to sense that something was not right; no laughter accompanied their play, and everyone's smiles were tinged with sadness. No one suggested that we force the old woman to come with us, even though we hated the idea of leaving her behind. It was her choice, and we had to respect it.

By nightfall, the trucks were freshly fuelled and ready to go, and the bikes were strapped beneath a tarpaulin on a trailer that we'd scavenged from one of the nearby suburbs. The rain still hadn't let up, so it seemed logical to squeeze everyone into the trucks instead. It was a tight fit, but it could be done. The territory we were approaching was rough and dangerous, and the weather would make it even more treacherous.

We ate a quiet dinner, cleaned up after ourselves, and put ourselves to bed. Crying had left me exhausted; I fell asleep quickly, but my sleep was troubled by dark dreams. I woke up early as a result, feeling wrung out and exhausted, but indulging in a hot shower refreshed me. Michael was still sleeping, so I dressed quietly in the bathroom, crept out into the hallway, and closed the door behind me.

Then, I turned around and almost fell over Doctor Cross. He jumped back and peered at me, a confused, sleepy look on his face. "Oh, Ms McDermott. Have you seen my granddaughter?"

"Not since last night," I replied, glancing down the hall towards their room. "Perhaps she went to the kitchen to get a drink?"

"Oh, maybe..." He yawned broadly, and rubbed his eye. "I should go get my glasses."

"It's okay, you go back to bed," I said reassuringly, patting his shoulder. "I'll find her."

"If you insist," he agreed without complaint. I helped guide him back to the right doorway, then headed off towards the kitchen to check for Maddy.

There was no sign of her, or anyone else. It was well before sunrise, so everyone was still fast asleep except for the lookouts on the roof. A quick call to them on the radio confirmed that the little girl hadn't left the complex overnight. Fighting the rising concern in my gut, I headed out to check the pool, the storage rooms, and anywhere else I could think of, but there was no sign of her.

I was on my way back to raise the alarm and start arranging search parties when a strange sound caught my ear. I stopped and listened intently. Someone was crying. A child was crying. The sound was coming from Room 25. Netty's room.

Fear and concern twisted my gut. I raced to the door and tried the handle, half-expecting it to be locked. It wasn't, though. It popped open effortlessly, and the scene I saw was one that I hadn't expected. Maddy was sitting on the floor beside Netty's bed, clinging to the old woman's hand and sobbing like her little heart was breaking.

At first glance it looked like Netty was just sleeping, until I realised that she was too still. The hair on the back of my neck rose as my instincts came to grip with the fact that there was a dead thing in front of me. No, not just a dead thing. A dead person.

"Netty?" I whispered, frozen with shock. My eyes saw things, but my brain didn't want to understand what they meant. There was a prescription vial on the dressing table beside her bed, and a folded slip of paper, but that just confused me. I couldn't bring myself to understand what I was seeing. "Maddy, what… what happened?"

"She called to me," the little girl sobbed, tears rolling down her cheeks. "She called to me in my sleep. She said that she didn't want to die alone."

"No… no, no, no, she can't be dead." Tears welled up in my eyes all over again, but this time they galvanised me into action. I rushed over to the bedside, and leaned down to touch the old woman's cheek. It was still warm, but not as warm as it should have been. I knew right away that she'd been dead for nearly an hour, but that didn't stop me from crying out to her. "Netty! No, you can't do this. What about your family? W-what about—"

My voice caught in my throat, and came out as a choked sob. Maddy grabbed me while I was close to her, and clung to me as though desperate for contact with the living. I put my arms around her and picked her up, but when I tried to carry her out of the room she wailed in protest.

"No!" she cried, hitting my shoulder with her little fist. "No, no, not yet! I promised I wouldn't leave her alone!"

"You already fulfilled that promise, honey. She's already gone." I struggled to keep hold of her, but she was a growing girl and weighed more than I could comfortably lift. I gave up and set her back on her feet.

She promptly raced back over to Netty's bedside, and threw herself back down beside her. "No, she's still here. I can see her, standing by the door! I promised that I'd stay until she'd left!"

"By the… what?" I turned around, and stared at the door, but I saw nothing. If the hairs on the back of my neck hadn't already been standing up, they would have just about jumped clear off my skin at that point. "There's no one there, Maddy. She's dead. You need to go back to your granddad, I'll take care of her."

"No!" she wailed, with a vehemence that made me flinch. "She's right there, and she's talking to you! Why aren't you listening? Listen to her!"

"I can't hear anything," I cried back, frustrated and scared at the same time. "There's no one there!"

"There is!" Maddy burst into tears all over again, and pointed right past me at the doorway. "She wants you to be careful. She says that you shouldn't tell Mister Michael yet, because it would break his heart if you lost it. She wants you to promise that you're going to be careful. Promise her!"

"I don't understand," I admitted, tears rolling down my own cheeks. I shoved them away anxiously, and looked back at the door. "I just... I don't understand..."

Maddy turned and looked at me, her eyes huge and glistening with tears. "You're pregnant, Miss Sandy. You're going to have a baby."

***

The shock of that pronouncement left me speechless. I managed to whisper some kind of promise about being careful, but that was it. When the others finally came looking for us, they found Maddy and me sitting side by side on the floor, just staring in shock at the body. I faintly heard voices whispering behind us, but I couldn't make out what my friends were saying. Maddy looked at them, then stood up and went over to them.

"I'll show you where she wants to be buried," she said, then I heard footsteps retreating.

I felt a warm body come up behind me and recognised Michael's familiar scent, but I couldn't figure out what was going on. His arms closed around me, but today there was no comfort in them.

Netty was dead, and I was pregnant. How could that even happen? How? I was taking pills to prevent it, but… a baby. Oh God, I was going to have a baby? Was that why I'd been feeling ill over the last few weeks? I'd blamed the nausea on the head injury, or bad food, or car sickness, anything but… that.

And… and Netty… oh God, why?

Suddenly, I remembered the note sitting on her nightstand, beside the bottle of pills that had taken her life. My hands felt stiff and robotic as I reached for it, and I couldn't quite convince them to grip it. I felt Michael reach past me and take the note for me, but he hesitated over whether or not to give it to me.

"Are you sure, Sandy?" he whispered, his voice heavy with emotion. "It won't make it better. It might make it worse."

I just nodded dumbly, and reached for the note again. This time, he surrendered it to me willingly. I unfolded it with trembling fingers, and stared at the elegant, flowing script. The letters were beautiful and careful, with only the slightest indication that her hands had been shaking as much as mine when she wrote it. Netty had obviously laboured over her last words to the world, to make them as perfect as possible. I took a deep breath, and then read the note out loud.

"'To my visitors, and especially to Sandrine McDermott,'" I began, fighting the fresh wave of emotion that came from seeing my name in her handwriting. "'By the time you receive this, I will be dead. I ask one last favour of you at this time:

please bury me beneath the old cherry tree in the back yard. Ten years ago, I lay my husband to rest there, and I would very much like to spend my eternity at his side.'"

Tears obscured my vision, and I heard a muffled sob escape my throat. I felt Michael's hand close around mine, and then his deep, husky voice took over where mine had given out. "'Do not weep for me, my new old friends. I lived a good life, a long life – far longer than an old blasphemer like me had any right to, really. My husband would have scolded me, and told me that suicide is a sin, but I feel that this is my last opportunity to put my fate in the hands of someone that I think I can trust.

"'I'm dying anyway; I can feel it in my bones. This summer would have been my last, and I wouldn't have lived through the winter. Despite that, I want to thank you. You've given me a gift far beyond a little food and companionship. You – all of you – you gave me the chance to remember what it was like to be surrounded by family again. I know I'm a grumpy old chook, but seeing those children running around again has made me happier than I've been in a long, long time.

"'Sandrine, we didn't know each other for very long, but I feel like I understand you. I don't want you to feel guilty. You've given me the chance to do something beautiful one last time, and I know that I can trust you to lay me to rest, and to remember me. I give you permission to take anything you want from my supplies, if it will help you. Take your people south, build your city, and know that I'll be watching over you from beyond.

"'Well, that's it. There's no graceful way to end this note, except to say goodbye. I'm off for an adventure of my own, into the last unknown frontier. It's time to find out whether my husband's faith was right. If it was, then I guess I'll be seeing him again soon. If not, at least I won't care anymore. Goodbye and with love, Netty.'"

"And just like that, another life is snuffed out," I said bitterly, my voice hoarse with tears. "She didn't have to do that. She could have asked us to stay."

"There was no point." I heard the doctor's voice from the doorway. When I looked at him, I found him looking sad. "She... she was suffering, Ms McDermott. Cancer, I think. It's hard to tell without the proper tools, but I know that she was in pain. She had been consulting with me for a while, but... I couldn't cure her. I just wish that she'd said something, so we could have all been here with her."

I looked up at the old man, struggling to make sense of what he was telling me. "Did you... did you give her the pills, Doc?"

"No." He shook his head slowly, his expression as numb and miserable as I felt. "I don't think I could have, even if she had asked."

"Of course." I slumped down, the strength draining out of me. Michael caught me, and hugged me tight against his chest, as if he could inject some of his strength into me through physical contact. Somehow, it seemed to work. I took a deep breath, and hugged him back. "We should bury her, and then we need to go."

"Let me take care of her," Michael said softly. "I know that the two of you were close. Why don't you go find something else to do? I'll call you when everything's ready."

I wanted to protest, but I knew that he was right. I needed some time alone, to think everything over and digest it. Nodding silently, I let him help me to my feet, and once I was steady I extracted myself from his embrace.

There was always too much to do and too little time, but at that moment I really didn't feel like doing anything at all. I went out into the courtyard and plopped down at the end of the pool beneath a shade umbrella, to watch the water and let my mind wander. The sound of the rain striking the water comforted me, but it also struck me as sad. It always seemed to rain on funerals, as if nature wept right along with us.

I was still sitting there staring into space when Michael came to find me. He wrapped me up in my coat and led me out to the freshly-dug grave. I watched like a statue as my friends lay Netty's body in the hole, wrapped in her favourite blanket. One by one, people stepped forward to say goodbye, but when my turn came, I couldn't find the words.

Once it was over, Michael guided me back inside and helped me to change into my travel clothes. He and the others took care of everything – packing my bags, carrying things out to the car, organizing the group, and even the unpleasant task of going through Netty's supplies to see what we could make use of. I hated that we had to, but I was grateful that they did it for me. The thought of picking over that old woman's home like a pack of vultures made me feel even more nauseated than I already did. It was like losing my grandmother all over again, and I wasn't sure how I was going to cope with that kind of pain.

Eventually, we were ready to leave. Michael helped me into the passenger's seat of the Hilux, then he vanished for a few minutes to make sure everything was in order. When he returned, he glanced at me and gave me a weak smile.

"I left everything unlocked but closed up," he said. "With the keys on the front desk, and a note saying that anyone who needed a place to stay was welcome there, so long as they clean up after themselves — and stay out of Room 25. I don't know if anyone will respect it, but... it seems like the least we can do."

I glanced at him and nodded my approval, unable to find the words to thank him. I didn't need to, though. I could see it in his eyes. He reached out to gently squeeze my hand, and from that gesture I knew that he understood my pain, and that I needed time.

When he put the car into gear and finally led our convoy away from the township of Tokaanu, I closed my eyes and let the sound of the rain on the windshield soothe me. I was almost asleep when something sharp stabbed me in the shoulder, taking me by surprise. I flinched, but that just made Tigger dig her claws in deeper. With stalwart determination, the kitten scrambled over me and descended down my shirt front into my lap, where she promptly curled up and went to sleep.

I was stunned by the gesture. Even though I had been the first human to feed her, Madeline had practically adopted the little tabby. Tigger rarely let me pat her, let alone actually cuddle her. Half-expecting to be clawed, I lifted a hand and gently ran it along her back, feeling the softness of her fur.

Tigger didn't claw me, though. She did quite the opposite. She rolled onto her back and stretched out, purring contentedly. The sight of it was beyond adorable, and I found myself smiling in spite of everything.

How was it that the animals always knew?

Chapter Twenty-Three

For three days, we travelled southwards, slowly but surely making our way up onto the central plateau. The region had once been a national park, dominated by three massive volcanic cones, and miles of rocky desert. Nature still stood strong, even after the laws protecting it had vanished.

I wasn't surprised to discover that the road had seen better days; there had been at least one eruption in the last ten years, and numerous earthquakes. Here, the roads had been shattered and torn apart, only to have the cracks filled in by dirt, dust, ash, and weeds. It made for an uncomfortable journey, but that combination was still better than the deep mud on either side of the remains of the highway.

The group was subdued for most of the trip. I couldn't tell whether it was Netty's death bothering them, or if it was having the three volcanoes looming over them. I couldn't even say which one bothered me more. We made it past the two smaller cones without incident, but the sight of the last one – Mount Ruapehu – sent an ominous shiver down my spine.

Her familiar, jagged outline was hidden beneath a thick layer of cloud, but I didn't need to see her crest to recognise her. That mountain had been responsible for more deaths in my country than any other. If she chose to, she could wipe out my tiny party in a single swipe, and with it destroy what little hope my species had left. I kept my mouth shut, and my fears to myself. There was no point in making the others any jumpier than they already were.

By midday on the third day, we were almost clear of the central plateau. The weather had eased over the course of the morning; for the first time in weeks, the sun came out from behind a cloud.

"Let's stop for lunch," Michael suggested from the passenger seat. "Let everyone stretch their legs, and enjoy the weather while it lasts."

"I don't know," I admitted warily, my eye following Ruapehu's outline as the clouds began to lift away from her. "I'd feel better if we pushed on for another hour or two."

"Paranoid again, honey?" he teased, leaning over to playfully pat my thigh.

I gave him a dark look, then sighed and nodded. "Okay, okay. Just for a couple of minutes."

"Ten at the most." He smiled and gave my knee a gentle squeeze. "We won't even unpack anything, promise. If anything happens, we'll be ready to run in a heartbeat."

I cringed internally and cursed myself for a fool. Of course Michael knew what I was thinking. He could read me like a book. I just muttered something inarticulate and made a vague gesture for him to make the arrangements, then I focused on finding somewhere solid to park the truck.

Within a few minutes, everyone was on their feet and lunch was being handed out. Michael took Alfred down to the bushes beside the road to address the call of nature, leaving me alone. I took the opportunity to go find Dr Cross.

I found him sitting on the back bumper of one of the trucks, eating his lunch and absently swatting at the prolific sand flies that infested the region. He glanced up when I neared, adjusting his glasses.

"Ms McDermott?" he enquired. "May I assist with something?"

"I need to talk to you for a second, Doc," I replied, nervously glancing back over my shoulder to make sure that we weren't being observed. "Can we walk for a bit?"

"Of course." He eased himself up off the bumper, and gestured for me to lead on. I did so, and took him down a rocky bank beside the road, so that we were out of sight.

As we walked, I found myself silently brooding again. There was no way to be sure, except to ask my doctor. The problem was, I didn't entirely know how I felt, so I wasn't sure what answer I was hoping to hear. On the one hand, the idea of having to lug a tiny person around inside me for nine months while struggling to lead my group to a new home and found a city was almost too much for me to bear. On the other, I could imagine the look on Michael's face when I told him the news. If I really was pregnant... that would give him a reason to go on. And perhaps, it would give me one as well.

"You seem awfully concerned about privacy, Ms McDermott," Dr Cross pointed out. I looked at him, and found him watching me with the intense frown he got when he was trying to work out a puzzle.

"Well, it's a private matter," I admitted. I took a deep breath, and glanced back over my shoulder to make sure no one had noticed our departure. No one had. I turned my full attention to the doctor. "Doc... you remember when we first met, you gave me a prescription of the contraceptive pill? And you made me promise to take one every day, at the same time, and never miss a day?"

"I issue a lot of prescriptions to a lot of people, but that does sound like something I'd say," he replied in a half-hearted attempt at humour. "What of it? Do you need some more?"

"No, it's not that." I folded my arms across my chest, and stared thoughtfully across the plains at the vast, sprawling flanks of the volcano. "I've been taking them every day, just like you told me. Every day, at the same time, and I haven't missed any days. Is there... is there any chance that the pills could fail?"

"There's always a chance," he answered. "There is with any medication, particularly when we're relying on chemicals that may be well past their use-by date." He paused, then looked at me. "Do you think you're pregnant, Ms McDermott?"

"I don't know, Doc." Suddenly, I found tears welling up in my eyes, no matter how hard I tried to stay strong. "Maddy said I was. She said that Netty knew, and now that I think about it, I have been feeling pretty odd recently. Is there... is there any chance she's right?"

"There's always a chance. No contraceptive is a hundred percent effective," he answered dryly. "How long has it been since you last menstruated?"

"About six, maybe seven weeks," I replied, fighting the urge to panic. "But you said I could expect them to be irregular for a while, so I didn't notice."

"Which is entirely possible," he agreed. "Have you experienced any dizziness or nausea?"

"Yes, both." I hugged myself a little tighter, and closed my eyes to try and steady myself. "But not just in the mornings. I've always gotten travel sickness though, and I did have a concussion. I assumed that was why."

"It very well could have been either of those things. You've also been eating food that you're not used to, which can set off nausea as well," he said. "You may also be particularly sensitive due to hormonal changes in your body, pregnant or not. I believe I have some anti-nausea medication in my kit. Remind me to prescribe you some medication for the travel sickness. Now, have you noticed any tenderness, swelling, or general discomfort in your joints? Unusual fatigue?"

"My back hurts a little," I replied, with a vague shrug. "And I feel tired all the time, but I think we all do right now."

"I can't tell you for sure until we've run the appropriate tests, but it does sound like congratulations may be in order," he said thoughtfully. "Or perhaps, commiserations? I can understand if you're not particularly comfortable with the idea, after what happened to your sister."

"Christ!" The word just exploded out of me, and I buried my face in my hands. "It's not just that, Doc. I've... I've... been pregnant before, after the... the... you know... my body couldn't support it, I was too malnourished, and... God, Doc – I'm scared. I don't know if I want this or not. I don't know how to feel. What if... what if I have it, and it's born infected?"

I felt a sympathetic hand on my back, and heard him make a few reassuring noises. "It's all right, Sandy. If you don't want this, then we can... take care of it. If you are pregnant, then it's still early enough to—"

"What?" I jerked my head up and stared at him. "Are you suggesting..."

He shrugged helplessly, and gave me a weak smile. "Only as an option. No one's going to force you to do anything that you don't want to do. We don't even know for sure that you are pregnant yet. Don't jump to conclusions. Still, if it turns out that you are and you don't want the baby, then you don't have to have it."

"No!" I cried, horrified beyond words by the mere suggestion. "No, God, no — I'm not going to kill Michael's baby! No, no, no—"

"You don't have to." He grabbed my shoulders suddenly, bracing me upright. "Believe me, the last thing I want is for you to take that option but I would be doing you a disservice as your physician if I didn't at least make it available to you. You're in control of your own destiny now. You have the right to choose. No one can make the decision for you. Not Michael, not me, not your sister, not anyone else — only you get to make the choice."

"I-I... I can't do that." I swallowed a lungful of air and squeezed my eyes closed. "I just need time to think, to accept it. Please don't tell Michael, not until I'm sure."

"It's for the best. The first trimester is a dangerous period, particularly when you're still recovering," Dr Cross explained gently. Suddenly, he froze, staring over my shoulder. "Uh... Ms McDermott, perhaps it would be best if we continued this conversation another time?"

"Huh?" I glanced back over my shoulder, and stared at the not-so-distant mountain. "Is that what I think it is?"

From the crater of the mountain, a thin tendril of white smoke swirled up into the blue sky above. It looked so small, so innocent, and yet we both instinctively knew what was about to happen. We exchanged a look, then we turned and ran back towards the convoy.

We almost made it before the first earthquake struck. Almost, but not quite. Just as I tried to scream a warning to my friends and family, the ground jerked sharply and my legs went right out from under me. Panic took over when my strength failed me; the moment that the earthquake died down, I leapt back to my feet and grabbed Doc by the elbow.

"Go! Get to the cars!" I cried, half-dragging and half-guiding him the last few meters towards the nearest truck. Around us, people were screaming. A couple of the children were on the ground not far away, cowering in terror; I grabbed them, and guided them to a vehicle.

"What's going on?" I barely heard Skye's voice over the chaos, but I felt her grab my arm.

"Ruapehu's erupting!" I yelled back, forcing my voice to pierce the noise all around us. It wasn't just human voices trying to drown me out, though; a low, deep rumble echoed through the earth all around us, making it hard to hear, and nearly impossible to think. I looked at Skylar, and then I lifted my voice as high as it could go and screamed an order. "Everyone, in the cars! Go! Don't stop unless you can't drive anymore! Go, go, go!"

I grabbed my sister without another word and shoved her towards a vehicle. She stumbled but managed to keep her feet, and she took the hint. She shouted something that I couldn't quite make out, and then she was shovelling people towards cars as fast as she could. I spun around on the spot, frantically counting heads and trying to make sure that everyone was accounted for. Unfortunately, they weren't. With a devastating twist of my gut, I realised that Michael and Alfred were nowhere to be seen.

"Michael!" I screamed at the top of my lungs. "Michael! Where are you?" There was no answer, or at least no answer that I could hear. I drew a deep lungful of air, trying desperately to project my voice a few inches further, but it did me no good.

I glanced back at the others, torn with indecision. There was no way I could abandon Michael, but the children needed me, too. Skye caught my eye and made a sharp gesture, then pointed towards the rocks leading down from the road. It took me a second to work out that she was trying to tell me where my fiancé had gone.

There was no time to thank her, I just turned and ran. The pebbles crunched and gave way underfoot, just as another tremor tore through the earth. I went down hard on my knees, bruising myself painfully, but I only stayed down until the aftershock faded. As soon as I could stand again, I was up and off down the gully, searching for him.

A footprint in the mud caught my eye, and then another. I followed them deeper into the gully, past boulders the size of small cars and razor-edged desert grasses. I spotted a pile of fresh dog droppings near the path, but no sign of Michael. A quick search revealed more tracks, this time further spaced out. Something had sent Michael running in the wrong direction.

Suddenly, I heard a shout, but I couldn't make out the words.

"Michael?" I yelled again, racing towards the sound of the voice.

"I'm here!" he yelled back. "This... this stupid dog..."

Just at that moment, I rounded another large boulder and found them both on the ground, rolling in the mud; Michael was frantically trying to hold the dog down, while Alfred was just as frantically trying to get away from him.

No, not from him, I realised suddenly. *From the volcano.*

"I can't..." Michael gasped, out of breath and obviously nearing panic. "I sprained my ankle chasing this stupid mutt, and I can't walk and carry him at the same time."

"You focus on walking, I've got Alfred," I instructed, flinging myself into the mud without hesitation. Between the two of us, we managed to hold him down long enough for me to get a solid grip on the old sheepdog. He was heavy, but fear lent me strength from reserves that I didn't know I had. Alfred whined and howled, but once I had him he didn't fight me. He just cowered, and tried to bury his head in my armpit.

"We need to go," Michael said urgently, levering himself up on the boulder. "I smell sulphur. That can't be good."

"It isn't. We need to get out of here before there's a gas cloud, or a lahar, or something equally awful," I answered, hefting the old dog up and bracing him against my chest. "Lean on me if you need to, but we're getting the hell out of here."

Michael tried to answer, but the noise around us was too loud for me to hear him. He didn't try again. I felt his hand on my shoulder, and then we were off. It was slow going, but at least when the next tremor hit I didn't fall again. Thank heavens for small favours; my knees already felt like they were black and blue. The three of us, gasping, stumbling, and struggling to keep our balance, retraced our steps back towards the road.

By the time we reached it, all the cars were gone except for one. I heard a voice call out to us, and then Skylar ran around from the far side. She yanked open the back door, and helped me to bundle Michael and Alfred inside. A few seconds later, she was back behind the wheel again and starting the car. I flung myself into the passenger seat and slammed the door.

"Get us out of here!" I ordered, but even inside the truck it was hard to hear one another. She shouted something back, and the car leapt forward, bouncing and juddering across the uneven ground. I turned to stare out the back window, just in time to spot a wave of something grey and ominous rolling down the side of the mountain.

"Ash!" Michael gasped, his voice still ragged. "Christ, it's coming right for us. We need to cover all the vents: it could be toxic."

"There should be blankets under the seats," I answered, reaching beneath my own in search of one. Sure enough, my fingers connected with something soft. I yanked it out, and grabbed my pocket knife out of my cargo pants. With a frantic haste, I cut the blanket into strips, and handed them out. "Here, tie this over your face!"

"What do I do?" Skye begged, her tone one of absolute panic. I glanced at her, and saw that her knuckles were white on the steering wheel, and her foot on the accelerator was almost to the floor. The truck was rocketing along at entirely too fast a pace for the condition of the road, but we really had no choice.

"Just keep us going in that direction," I cried, pointing towards the distant horizon. "This is a long, straight road. Just keep going. I'm going to tie this over your face, okay?"

"Okay," she agreed, obviously struggling to stay brave. I shot a glance at the incoming ash cloud, then immediately wished I hadn't. I turned away, and focused on getting us ready. We couldn't outrun it, so we had to prepare for the possibility that the ash was poisonous. Once I'd finished tying the cloth over Skye's face, I cut off another strip and did my own.

"It's here!" Michael cried.

His warning was unnecessary. A second later, the wall of ash hit us and our world plunged into darkness. I heard Skylar scream, and had to grab the wheel to keep her from accidentally driving us off the road. I barely had time to brace myself when she slammed on the brakes, and brought us to a sudden halt.

"I can't! I can't do it!" she sobbed, tears in her eyes. "I can't see anything. Oh, God."

"Keep it together, baby sis." I grabbed her hand, and shoved a wadded up ball of cloth into it. "Hold that over those vents there. We have to keep the ash from getting in here. Michael, get the back ones."

"Got it covered." His reply sounded like it was coming from a thousand miles away, barely audible over the roar. I shoved the rest of the torn-up blanket over the vents on my side of the car, then I curled up against my sister and silently prayed for our salvation.

***

After what felt like forever, the roaring finally faded away and the ground stopped shaking. Silence descended in our dark world, aside from the sound of our coughing; we'd managed to keep most of the ash out, but not all of it. I felt my sister trembling and knew instinctively that she was crying, but it was too dark for me to see her face. The ash on the windows was too thick for us to be able to tell whether it was safe to get out or not.

"The engine probably won't start now, even if we could see where we're going." Michael's voice was disembodied in the darkness. He coughed heavily, then added, "The ash is probably made up of crushed rock, volcanic glass, and silica. We'll need to clean the engine out completely before we can start this damn thing."

"So, we're stuck here?" I asked, my voice barely more than a whisper. "I left my radio in the Hilux. Does anyone else have one?"

"No," Skye replied, sounding miserable. "I didn't think I'd need it."

"Me either," Michael replied. "Whose car was this? Maybe there's one in the glove box?"

"I think this was the one Jim was driving," I replied. "I suppose they might have left something. I'll look."

I fumbled for the torch in my pocket, and found it by touch alone. The thin beam barely illuminated the darkness, but it was still enough to make me squint. After a few seconds of searching, I sighed and shook my head. "Nothing in here but someone's afternoon snack. Well, at least we have some food, I guess."

"Pass the torch here? I'll check the back." Michael's hand appeared over my shoulder from the shadows of the back seat. I placed my torch in it, and then both vanished. I heard him moving around for a few minutes, then he heaved a sigh of obvious frustration. "Nothing here, either."

"Shh!" Skye hissed unexpectedly. "I hear something."

We froze, listening intently. A moment later, it came again and this time we all heard it: a faint scraping sound.

"Oh, please don't let that be lava," Skye whispered, clinging to my hand.

"We'd know if it were lava," I replied. "Pretty sure we'd already be dead. Besides, lava doesn't talk." I raised my voice, and shouted at the top of my lungs, "Hey! We're in here!"

There was an alarmed cry outside the vehicle, but I couldn't make out the words. The scraping sound picked up in urgency, then suddenly light penetrated our world. Light, and a familiar face.

"Hemi!" Skylar cried, her relief so palpable that it sent a shiver down my spine. The youth called a greeting back, and thumped on the window until the last of the ash fell away.

I leaned past her, and rolled down the window just a crack so that we could speak. "Boy, am I glad to see you!

We've got Michael and Alfred in the back. Is everyone else accounted for?"

"Yeah." Hemi coughed and tightened the makeshift mask covering his face, similar to our own. "You guys okay? The doc's waiting down at Waiouru, but we can go get him if you need it."

"No, please just get us out of here," I answered, shaking my head. "This truck is a write-off. We need to get the supplies out, and see if we can find another one along the way."

"Okay. Just hang in there, we'll get you out," he agreed.

True to his word, Hemi and his companions had us out of that truck and into the back of theirs within a couple of minutes. It was a squeeze to fit all of us in there along with Alfred and the supplies, but we made it – primarily because I ended up sitting on Michael's lap. Despite his ankle, it was a situation that neither of us minded very much.

I draped my arms around his shoulders and stared out the back window at the shadow of the volcano against the horizon.

"I can barely see her through the haze," I commented. "There's still too much ash hanging in the air."

"She just tried to kill us," Michael answered dryly, slipping his arms around my waist to brace me securely in lieu of a seatbelt. "Do you really want to see her?"

"She didn't *try* to do anything." I shifted back a little bit, just far enough to look into his eyes. "She's a volcano. She's just doing what volcanoes do. I would like to know if she's done, though. Do you think that's it for the eruption?"

"Hard to say." He sighed heavily, nuzzling his face into the curve of my neck. I closed my eyes and relaxed, letting the contact calm my frazzled nerves. "It could be that was the first stage of a larger event, or it could be that she just needed to let off a little steam. Ruapehu isn't the kind of volcano that spits lava a thousand feet into the air, thank goodness. If she were, we'd probably all be dead."

"Next time I decide to take a shortcut through a volcanic field, talk me out of it," I replied. Michael grunted something halfway between a snort and a laugh, but said nothing. I let the conversation trail off and just enjoyed the closeness. Michael was a snuggler by nature and sometimes that bothered me, but not today.

After our brush with death, all I could think was how lucky we were that we'd all made it through. My family was safe. My fiancé was safe.

My fiancé. My mate. Maybe even father of my child. For the first time, that thought brought a smile to my face. I felt a flush of heat run up the back of my neck, and suddenly I wanted nothing more than to find some way to express my feelings in the most romantic way I could think of. I pushed myself back away from him, and looked at him with a smile.

"You know what? Screw it. Let's just do it," I told him in no uncertain terms. "Tonight. No more waiting."

"Huh?" Michael just gave me a bewildered look. "You're doing that thing where you say stuff you've been thinking about as if I'm privy to your thoughts. Use your words, sweetheart."

"Oh, sorry." Embarrassed, I laughed at myself, and then I elaborated for him. "Let's just forget about waiting and get married. Tonight. My gut's been telling me all along that you're the one, but I've been resisting it. I'm just afraid of change and commitment, but I need to stop listening to my head and listen to my heart for a change."

"Oh." Michael went silent for a second. The silence made me worry, but I could see on his face that he was just trying to process my spontaneous change of heart.

Beside us, Skylar laughed gleefully and gave me a nudge. "Well, look at you! When did you grow a set of balls, sis?"

"I'll have you know that balls are soft and squishy, and not really all that tough at all," I replied with playful mock-haughtiness. "I'm quite happy with having a vagina, thank you! They're much tougher than balls, and can put up with a heck of a pounding." Skye stared at me, wide eyed, her mouth hanging open. Suddenly, the reality of what I'd just said struck me, and I started blushing furiously. "That... came out all wrong."

Around me, the car erupted in laughter. I barely heard Michael's reply above the sound of my friends teasing me.

He said one simple word, the one that I wanted to hear more than anything else in the world. He said, "Yes."

Chapter Twenty-Four

News of our spontaneous nuptials spread through the group like wildfire. By the time we'd checked in with the doctor and been given mostly clean bills of health, everyone knew. As soon as I stepped outside, Skylar grabbed my arm and dragged me away from the motor lodge where we planned to stay the night.

"You can't see the bride before the wedding!" she told Michael in no uncertain terms, shoving me in front of her despite my protests. Hemi and his friends appeared as if out of nowhere, and dragged my poor, limping fiancé off without another word. Skye gave me a wicked grin, grabbed my hand, and led me off towards the township of Waiouru proper. "Come on! We need to find you something to wear."

"Why bother?" I groused, though I knew better than to really fight her when she had her mind set on something. "Michael doesn't care what I look like. I mean, he sees me dressed like this every day."

"But this isn't every day," she answered, dancing ahead of me with such enthusiasm that she almost tugged my arm out of its socket. "It's your wedding day, Sandy-pants! For one day, you get to be as much of a princess as you like. And I am going to make you the prettiest princess of them all!"

"And just how do you plan to do that, little sis?" I asked dryly. "This used to be a military town. There isn't exactly a bridal boutique here."

"Maybe not, but I spotted a sign on someone's fence offering tailoring services," she replied. "I'm betting that if anyone has dresses for us, it'll be them!"

"Wait, us?" I tried to stop, only to get almost pulled off my feet. "What us? Is someone else getting married?"

"No, dummy." Skye sighed and rolled her eyes. "For you and your bridal party, of course. I'm going to be your maid of honour, Maddy's the flower girl, and everyone else is... well, they want to look nice, too!"

"Okay, this is getting way too complicated," I admitted, suddenly feeling nervous. "I just want things to be simple."

"Oh, come on, Sandy," Skye stopped suddenly and turned to fix me with an imploring look. "For once in your life, relax and have a little fun. This is supposed to be the happiest day of your life, and I want to enjoy it with you. Besides, if you want to rebuild everything that we lost, then you need to lead by example. I've never been to a wedding before, I've only seen pictures in old magazines. They're supposed to be happy – and more importantly, normal. Don't we all deserve a chance to be normal again?"

I started to protest, but something about the look on her face made me stop and reconsider. Suddenly, I realised that she needed it even more than I did. She needed to see me happy, and to share the moment with the people that she cared about. How long had it been since any of us had been able to enjoy a wedding? For all I knew, this might have been the first one since the plague struck. That thought struck me as poignant, and important somehow. There were going to be a lot of firsts in the days to come, and who was I to stop other people from enjoying them?

"I... I'm sorry. You're right," I admitted quietly. "Sometimes it's hard to remember just how much my life has changed."

"I know." She smiled at me, an expression so vibrant that it felt like it lit up the whole world. "Don't worry, sis. You've got friends now. We're taking care of everything. All you have to do is enjoy yourself."

I took a deep breath to quell the twisting in my gut, then smiled and nodded. "Lead on, then! Let's go get pretty."

Skylar let out a delighted whoop and raced off down the street with me in tow. A few minutes later, we found ourselves jogging up the front steps of an ordinary-looking house, flushed and out of breath from our run.

"This is it," she explained, panting. "Melody and the twins went ahead to look for—"

Just at that moment, the door exploded open, and the three girls raced out to meet us. Their expressions startled me even more than their sudden appearance: all three of them were grinning broadly. They'd been slowly relaxing over the weeks since they'd joined our group, but this was the first time that any of them had looked truly happy. Before I could say anything, I was grabbed and half-dragged, half-ushered into the living room.

"There are so many dresses!" Jasmine told us gleefully. "In all kinds of different sizes!"

"And there's sewing stuff," Melody added, her sun-browned face split in a wide grin. "So we can adjust things to fit, if we have to."

"We found one for Sandy already," Jasmine cut in, her excitement quite obvious. She raced over to the big mound of dresses they'd gathered in the centre of the room, and pulled out a simple, elegant gown made of soft, cornflower-blue satin. It was a tiny bit crinkled, but otherwise perfect.

I was too stunned to say anything, and just stood there with my mouth hanging open while Skye raced over to grab the dress.

"Oh my gosh, yes! This is perfect!" she cried. She rounded on me, clinging to the satin as though it were the most precious thing in her life. "You need to put this on." She paused, her eyes wide. "No, wait! You're all ashy! You need to go have a shower, right now."

"Um, Skye... you're ashy, too," Lily pointed out. She was quieter than her twin, but tended to have more well thought-out comments when she did opt to speak. Now was exactly one of those times.

"Huh?" Skye shot her a wide-eyed look, then looked down at the dress in her hands. Suddenly, she dropped it as though it had burned her. "Oh, no! Is it dirty? Did I get it dirty? I'm sorry!"

Melody knelt to inspect the dress. "No, it's fine. Nothing we can't dust off. You two get cleaned up. There's a bathroom down that hallway, second door on your right."

"You're first, sis," Skye instructed. She grabbed my hand and dragged me down the hallway. The indicated doorway opened into a fairly ordinary-looking bathroom, with a bath, shower, and toilet all in the same room. Skye looked around for a moment, and came back with a comb. "Sit down. Let's brush the ash out of your hair first. I don't know how you deal with that much hair all the time."

"It is kind of a pain," I admitted. "I've been thinking of cutting it off, but I grew it out to honour Mum and... I'd feel weird without it."

"No way!" she gasped, sounding genuinely horrified. "Your hair is gorgeous. I will not let you cut it. Now, sit your ass down in that bathtub, and let me comb it out."

"I can brush my own hair, thanks." Laughing, I tried to grab the comb, but she held it out of my reach.

"No! I want to brush it," she replied playfully. "Like we used to when we were kids. Remember?"

I paused and stared at her. "Wow, I'd almost forgotten about that. How old were you? Three? Four?"

"Four, I think." Grinning, she guided me over to the bathtub and helped me to sit down. With gentle fingers, she undid the elastic holding my hair in its usual thick braid, and gently unwound it. "You must have been, what... fourteen? I was obsessed with your hair for ages. I don't remember why."

Suddenly, the memory came rushing back in force, and it left me laughing so much I could hardly breathe. "I remember! You kept getting nits at kindy, so Mum gave you a pixie cut. You hated it."

"Is that what it was?" Skye burst out laughing as well. "I just remember desperately wanting to have hair like yours, and being ridiculously happy when you let me brush it for you. I was such a weirdo."

"Nah, you were a little kid," I replied. My laughter faded away into thoughtful silence, as I delved back into those happy, innocent memories. "You were the sweetest little thing, Skye. Did I ever tell you how much I missed you when I thought that you were dead? I cried for you so often. I don't think I ever really recovered from the grief."

"I know." I felt her fingers in my hair like a gentle caress, and it sent a shiver all the way down my spine. I sighed and drew my knees up to my chest, letting her touch relax me. After a few minutes of silence, she finally spoke again. "There is one thing I've always wondered, though. When we got separated, why didn't you and Mum come back for us?"

"Grandma insisted," I replied. A surge of grief rose up in my belly all over again, thinking about the family that I'd loved so much and lost. "She decided that it was too much of a risk, with the riots already starting. I think she was afraid that she'd already lost one granddaughter and that if we went looking for you then she might lose everyone else as well. To be honest, none of us were thinking clearly at the time, and when she made the decision we just went along with it because at least it was some kind of decision. People make stupid choices when they're in life-or-death situations." I paused, and looked back over my shoulder at her. "I'm sorry, Skye. I wish it had happened differently."

She just gave me a sad smile, and gently guided my head back around to face front. "It's okay, sis. Like you said, people make dumb choices. We both made it, and that's the most important thing. Now, sit still!"

"Yes, ma'am!" I replied, sketching a salute. Skye giggled, and went back to brushing out my hair.

When she was finally done, she tossed the comb into the sink and offered me a hand up. As soon as I was up, I realised why she'd put me in the bath; a cloud of fine dust had come out of my hair with every stroke, and the bathtub kept it from going everywhere.

"In you go!" she ordered, pointing to the shower stall. "And don't forget to wash your hair."

"But it's cold!" I protested, shooting her a mortified look. "And it'll never dry in time for the ceremony. Do you want me to get married looking like a drowned rat?"

"God, you're such a drama queen," Skye complained, rolling her eyes. "We'll make it dry in time, okay? Just wash your damn hair. Today is a special day, and requires special effort."

"But--" I started to say something else, but she cut me off mid-sentence.

"No buts! Just do it, little miss!" She planted her hands on her hips, and gave me a look that resembled our mother's scolding face so closely that I burst out laughing.

"Okay, okay!" I held up my hands in mock self-defence. "I'm washing, I'm washing. Jesus. You're so demanding."

"And that's why you love me," she answered brightly.

She hopped into the bath and started combing out her own hair, while I stripped down without modesty, and stepped into the shower stall. The water was as cold as ice, but my body was a mess of bruises and grazes again and the cold helped to numb the discomfort. The soap was so old that it was shrunken and crusty, but there was a clean washcloth sitting on a little shelf beside the door. I made do with that, and it was good enough.

By the time I finished scrubbing my hair with lavender-scented shampoo and had let it soak under conditioner for a few minutes, I was shivering convulsively. Skye was waiting with a big, soft towel when I finally stepped out. I didn't bother to ask where she'd found it, I just took it gratefully and wrapped myself up in it. I was about to get dressed again, when I realised that my clothing was gone.

"Hey!" I complained. "Where are my pants, Skye?"

"We took them back to the convoy," she replied cheerfully. "You're not going to need them tonight. Melody! She's ready!"

Melody appeared in the doorway with a wicked smile on her face. She grabbed me by the shoulders, and steered me back out to the living room dressed in nothing but that towel. I spluttered in protest, but nobody seemed to care. When I got there, I found the twins holding a small mountain of towels, and soon I was being dried off from every angle by enthusiastic helping hands.

When they finished, the twins vanished for a second and then returned holding a set of very fancy lingerie.

"What is that?" I demanded, confused and a little horrified. "Guys, you don't expect me to wear that, surely. It's... it's..."

"It's pretty," Melody supplied. "And yes, you are going to wear it. Put it on, or we'll put it on for you."

"Okay, fine, geez. Give it here," I grumbled. The twins grinned in perfect unison, and handed the frilly garments over to me. Careful not to drop the towel and flash anyone more than necessary, I pulled on the knickers and fastened the bra over my chest. "Wow, this is... almost a perfect fit. Where did you guys find this?"

"There's a whole storage room full of them off the garage," Jasmine replied. "I don't know why, but they're all pretty like that. Nothing plain or practical at all."

"Whoever owned this place was probably buying it in bulk, to supply the ladies living in town," I said, staring down at myself to consider the fit of the garments. They were pretty, and very, very feminine – something I was not used to being. "I feel a bit silly, guys. Are you sure about this?"

"It doesn't look silly," Lily said, shaking her head. She came over to me holding the dress. I stepped into it, and then three sets of hands helped me to pull it up and zipped it at the small of my back. Once it was on, Lily reached into her pocket and pulled out the tiny, antique locket that Netty had given me. "We took your clothing and your ring back to the motel, but I thought you might like to wear this."

"Oh! Yes, thank you," I said, reaching out to take the locket from her outstretched hand. I fastened it around my neck, and then straightened up and looked at the girls. "Well? How do I look?"

The three of them stood back and stared at me consideringly, their expressions ranging from pleased to uncertain.

"Should we do something about the scars?" Jasmine asked suddenly. "We could try to hide them."

"No." Melody shook her head firmly. "The scars are part of who she is, and she looks lovely despite them. He's marrying all of her, not just the parts that are still in mint condition. If he doesn't realise that, then he doesn't deserve her."

I felt myself flush at the compliment, and gave her a smile. "That was well-put. Yeah, Michael's marrying all of me, and he's already seen the scars. He doesn't care. Hell, we've both taken scars defending one another in the past, and we'd do it again in a heartbeat. That's why we're getting married."

"See?" Melody looked at the twins, and gave them a stern frown. "Real life isn't like those stupid romance novels you two insist on reading. Nobody's perfect, but the whole point of love is that the feeling is perfect, even if the people are not."

Jasmine blew a raspberry at her, and all of us laughed. By the time the levity cleared, Skye was back. The twins vanished to make use of the shower, leaving the two of us alone with Melody.

I glanced between them, then looked at the door. "Someone is on watch, right?"

"Yeah, Solomon is," Skye replied. She came over to study me, and nodded her approval. "This looks good. I think we should keep it simple. Right, Mel?"

"Right," she agreed. "This is our world now, and we can do whatever we like. I think she looks beautiful just like this. Nothing fancy, nothing over the top. Just beauty the way nature intended it."

"Good grief, when did you two become philosophers?" I asked, amused. "You're starting to sound like me."

"I'll take that as a compliment," Skye said with a grin. "Okay, what are we wearing, Mel?"

"Well, we want her to stand out, so we should wear dark colours," she replied decisively. "Blue, or as close to blue as we can find, so that our dresses compliment hers."

"Sounds good to me." Skye glanced at me, and made a shooing gesture. "You go sit down, we've got this covered."

"Yes, ma'am," I agreed dryly. I found a seat on a nearby couch, and settled in for an hour of doing nothing while the other girls played dress-up. It was something that I hadn't seen in so long that for once in my life I didn't mind the inactivity at all.

***

The gap in the weather held off for most of the day, though the stench of sulphur permeated everything. By the time my little wedding party was ready, the sun was starting to set and cast the world around us in long, elegant shadows.

I held my skirt up to keep it out of the dirty streets as we walked back, for fear of damaging the satin. It had survived the years unscathed because the girls had found it hanging in a dress bag; now it was mine and I felt both confused and beautiful while I was wearing it. The girls had dried my hair thoroughly and brushed it until it shone like silk. They'd found a few pretty hair pins to sweep it back behind my ears, but other than that it was all natural.

I was so focused on watching where my feet were going that I didn't notice the figures lurking in the shadows until we were almost on top of them. Suddenly, someone stepped out into our line-of-sight, and the girls shouted in alarm. I jerked my head up and stared at the person, wide-eyed in shock. She stared back, her eyes narrowed, the hands holding her rifle steady and confident.

The two of us just stared at one another for the longest time. She was straight-backed and proud, dressed in the uniform of the army. Chevrons adorned her breast, but I didn't know the ranks well enough to understand them. She was substantially older than me, but there was something in her eyes that I understood on an instinctive level. A longing, a desire to protect, and a wariness of the unexpected.

Suddenly, I realised that she was waiting for me to explain our presence in her territory. Her stance was cautious but not threatening, and her expression was one of careful neutrality. It was like looking in a mirror at the person that I had become since I met Michael and found my sister again. My shock vanished, and I found the words I needed right on the tip of my tongue.

"Sorry, we weren't expecting anyone in this area," I admitted, raising my hands slowly to show that I was unarmed. That meant dropping my skirt in the process, but the stretch of pavement I was standing on at the time seemed clean enough. "We've just stopped for the night to celebrate my wedding, and we'll move on in the morning.

My name is Sandrine McDermott, and these are members of my group." I quickly introduced Skye and the others, then looked back at the soldier. "I apologise for the intrusion. We had no idea this land was claimed, Lieutenant...?"

A smile cracked the woman's neutral visage. "Sergeant, actually. Sergeant Erica Bryce, Royal New Zealand Army." She lowered her rifle, and looked me up and down with some interest. "I heard your broadcast. We've been watching the roads for days for your group, but you took so long to get here that we were starting to think you'd been wiped out. Good to see that you weren't."

"The road has been much wilder than we expected," I replied, lowering my hands. "The weather hasn't exactly been very accommodating, either."

The Sergeant barked a sharp laugh, and nodded her agreement. "That it hasn't. You seem like a smart leader, so I presume there must have been good reason to move your people at this time of year. You said something about a mutation of the virus."

"Yeah. We had no choice," I replied with a shrug. "The mutants attacked us in our old home territory up near Hamilton. We lost so many people that it was worth risking the weather to head south." I paused, and shot her a long, thoughtful look. "We're heading for Avalon, in Lower Hutt. We're going to build a new city. You and your men are welcome to come, so long as we can trust you to obey the laws."

"Perhaps," she answered noncommittally. "We're quite comfortable here for now, but we'll think it over. I would be willing to consider letting you use our radio tower to update your broadcast, if you like."

"Oh?" I stood up a little straighter, surprised and pleased by the generosity. "You have the equipment up and running?"

"Of course." She shrugged and smiled wryly. "We just don't have anything to say most of the time. Sometimes, it's safer to just stay here and protect our own resources."

"I understand." I smiled back at her, and pointed towards the motor inn where my companions waited. "Why don't you and your men come to my wedding? My groupmates kind of took over when I told them I wanted to formalize my engagement, but I'm sure there will be food – and there will definitely be good company. We can talk a bit more, and get to know one another."

Sergeant Bryce paused then, and for the first time I saw a look of some uncertainty on her face. After a few long moments, she shrugged. "We'll... we'll think about it. Maybe. We know where you are, so if we decide to come we'll let you know."

"It's fine. I completely understand." I made a broad, welcoming gesture, and then I saluted her. "You're welcome if you want to, but if not then that's your choice. I know how it feels to suddenly be confronted with a large amount of people. Take all the time you need, Sergeant."

She returned the salute and nodded. "Well, we'll let you go. I'll definitely be in touch regarding the radio, whether we come or not." She paused, then gave me a shy smile. "Congratulations on your nuptials."

"Thank you," I said with a grin. Then, suddenly, the reality of it hit me in the face like a sack full of doorknobs. "Oh my God, I'm getting married."

Behind me, Skylar and the others laughed. "You wanted this, sis. Too late to back out now."

"Are you sure?" I asked, feeling a wave of terror unlike anything I'd ever felt before. "I mean, Michael would forgive me if I ran like a coward, right?"

"No, I'm pretty sure he wouldn't." Skye grabbed me by the shoulders, and started pushing me off towards the motor inn. "Besides, you wanted this. You made the call. This is all you, sis. Now, own it!"

"Yeah... yeah, you're right." I took a deep breath to steady myself, then gave them all a sheepish look. "So that's what they mean by cold feet."

Everyone laughed at that, even the Sergeant and her soldiers. They let us leave without complaint, and made no attempt to follow us as we returned home. There, I found the entire group waiting for us. One of the look-outs shouted and pointed, and then a cheer went up from the entire group.

Skye stopped pushing me, and took my hand instead. She guided me in through the front gate, past my cheering friends, and into the courtyard of the inn. I skidded to a halt, shocked by the transformation. The courtyard had been decorated with ribbons, streamers, and more flowers than I'd seen in one place for a very long time. An assortment of folding chairs had been arranged in two groups, with a short aisle down the middle. At the far end, Anahera stood resplendent in a long, black gown, and in front of her was my fiancé.

Michael glanced at me, and I saw his eyes widen — whether it was shock or delight, I couldn't tell. He was freshly-scrubbed, and dressed in his full police uniform, right down to the hat. He looked so handsome that I could hardly believe my eyes.

"Come on, big sis," Skye whispered in my ear. "It's your time to shine."

She led me forward by the hand, and suddenly I found myself excited all over again. Butterflies danced in my stomach and left me feeling light-headed and a little ill, but it was all in a good way.

Getting married. I was getting married. To Michael.

Suddenly, tears blurred my vision, and I was fighting the urge to cry. Thankfully, Skylar understood my moment of weakness, and she was there to keep me steady. She squeezed my hand and guided me down the aisle to stand opposite my beloved, and then she and my other bridesmaids went off to find their seats in the front row.

I could feel the presence of all my friends gathering, and hear the sound of chairs scraping on concrete as they settled down to watch. There were whispers and chuckles, but they were all friendly and kind – and throughout it all, I only had eyes for Michael, and he for me.

"You look beautiful," he said softly. I felt him reach out to take my hands, and the touch sent a thrill right through me.

"T-thank you," I stumbled, my wits half-gone. I tried to say a few things, but none of them quite came out right. It didn't matter, though. Michael understood. He always understood. He just smiled, and squeezed my hands.

"Dearly beloved, we are gathered here today to witness the union of our friends, Sandy and Michael." Anahera's voice rose as crisp and clear as a cool breeze on a hot summer's afternoon. A hush went over the crowd. We all looked at her. She looked back, smiled, and then continued. "Marriage has been so many things over the centuries of human evolution, but now it falls to us to set its definition.

These two before us have become instrumental in guiding us to the new destiny for all humankind, so it seems fitting that their wedding be the one that sets the standard for our new culture.

"It is time for the concept of marriage to evolve once again. The two of you are warriors who would fight back to back to the bitter end to protect one another, and trailblazers who share a vision for a new world for all of us. You have faced so many trials together already, and there will probably be many more in your future, but this marriage symbolizes your desire to face them together. You will always have one another's backs, and always be there to help if one of you falls.

"Michael Chan, do you pledge yourself in love and loyalty to Sandrine for the rest of your days? Do you swear to guide her, help her, and protect her for as long as you both shall live?"

"I do," he answered without hesitation, his gaze shifting back to me. I looked up at him, wide-eyed, frozen, uncertain. And then, I heard Anahera speaking to me.

"Sandrine McDermott, do you pledge yourself in love and loyalty to Michael for the rest of your days? Do you swear to guide him, help him, and protect him for as long as you both shall live?"

"I do." The words came out of my mouth even though my brain was a chaotic jumble of conflicting emotions, but the moment that they were out I felt like a huge burden had been lifted off of me. Skye was right. I did want this, more than anything else in the world. The possibility of having a baby had nothing to do with it; I wanted this for me, and not for anyone else. After all the pain I'd been through, I had finally found the one person that I knew I could trust beyond anyone else, and now… he was going to be part of my family. It just made so much sense.

"Madeline, the rings?" Anahera called. Maddy rushed forward, dressed like a tiny, raven-haired doll in a fluffy party dress. She handed the rings to Anahera, and then rushed back to her seat. Anahera held the rings out to us, one in each hand, and we took them.

Michael's strong, gentle hands took hold of mine, and guided the ring onto my finger with a tenderness that delighted me. I watched, and then I looked up at him again and saw a smile of such happiness on his face that I almost burst into tears right on the spot. My fingers trembled as I reached for his hand, but he understood. He gently guided my hands through the motions, and then he leaned down and kissed me.

Our friends burst into wild applause all around us, cheering so loudly that I could barely make out Anahera pronouncing the marriage complete. It didn't matter, though. None of it mattered. All that mattered was Michael. My friend, my lover, and now my husband. I wrapped my arms around his neck, and kissed him back with every ounce of emotion in my body.

Eventually, our lips parted and he pulled back just a little. He started to say something to me, but the cheering, dancing mob overwhelmed us before he could. Suddenly, we were both swept up into the crowd, and carried away with the tide. After that, everything became a blur of voices and friendly, smiling faces.

"You're not going to believe what Zain managed to pull off," Skye commented gleefully, from right behind my ear. I tried to turn and look at her, but she was gone before I could locate her. Then, something happened that distracted me completely: for the first time in ten years, I heard the strains of music floating above the sea of voices.

"No way!" I gasped, stunned. Music hadn't been a part of my existence for so long, and the sound of it made me want to weep with joy. Before I could give in to my emotions, though, Michael caught me around the waist and swept me away onto the makeshift dance floor that our friends had created in our honour.

Another cheer went up from the crowd, but it was promptly hushed by other members of the crowd that wanted to savour the precious notes. The song wasn't familiar to me, but it didn't matter; I remembered the feeling, the way the music could make my imagination soar, and the way it could manipulate my emotions with such skill and subtlety that I didn't realise it was doing it.

"You're crying, Sandy," Michael whispered to me, his arms protectively tight around my waist as he guided me through the unfamiliar steps of a waltz, his footing careful due to the bandaged sprain he'd managed to hide under his uniform. Neither of us really knew how to dance anymore, but that didn't matter, either — the point was being together, and we were. Nothing could separate us now.

"I'm... happy," I whispered back, my voice husky with tears. "I... I forgot how to feel like this. I forgot so much. I j-just wish that my mother and father could be here..."

"I know." He drew me in closer with a gentle hand on the small of my back, and ran his free hand through my hair. "I wish mine could be here, too. But we have to make the best of the hand that life's dealt us, and we are." There was a moment of silence, and then he gave me a thoughtful smile. "I think that you should keep your maiden name, though. Like Anahera said, this is our world now, our choices, our traditions. I don't want the McDermott name to die out when the last two women bearing the name marry. You two are the only ones to keep the name alive, and it deserves to be remembered."

I listened as he spoke, nodding slowly. When he was done, I took a deep breath and nodded again, a bit more firmly this time. "I agree. I was thinking, we could make it a tradition that when we have kids, any daughters we have take the McDermott family name, while any sons we have take the Chan family name. Or, when they're old enough, we let them pick which last name they want to have. That way, both our names have a chance to continue into the next generation."

Michael shot me a curious look. "Oh? You've been thinking about us having kids? I thought you hated the idea?"

"I don't hate it," I said softly, breaking eye-contact. I couldn't lie to him, but it was still too early to tell him everything. "I'm afraid of it. There's a difference. But sometimes, you have to confront your fears in the name of the greater good, right?"

"Very true." Michael smiled at me, and slipped his free arm around my shoulders to draw me fully into his embrace. I snuggled up against him and rested my face on his chest. I felt other bodies around us as more people piled onto the dance floor, but I ignored them. Michael's warmth and scent enveloped me, and for a few minutes my life felt perfect.

Suddenly, a shout from one of the lookouts interrupted our peace, and Wiremu came running in from the courtyard in a panic.

"Riders!" he shouted above the sound of the music. "We have three riders coming this way on horseback!"

"Three?" I lifted my head and looked at him. He nodded. "Okay, I think I know who that might be. Don't panic, guys. I invited them."

"Who are they?" Michael asked, a look of worry crossing his face.

I shook my head and smiled at him. "There are some locals in the area that we met while we were out dress-shopping. I think they're all that's left of the army. I'm pretty sure that there were three of them. Let's go out and see."

I took Michael's hand, and helped him to limp through the crowd to where Wiremu waited in the doorway. The three of us went out onto the street front, just in time to watch the riders coming to a halt not far away. It was hard to tell in the shadows of dusk, but I was fairly certain that the lead rider was familiar.

"Sergeant Bryce?" I called, cautious but not overly concerned.

The lead rider dismounted from her horse in a single, graceful movement, then turned and saluted me. As she did so, the fractured light from the courtyard struck her face, and I recognised her. She was not a pretty woman, but she was distinctive: short and stocky, with sun-browned skin and eyes that shone with intelligence.

"Ms McDermott," she greeted me. "Or is it Mrs now?"

"I guess so, but I don't really care. I'm keeping my name, so I'll probably stick with 'Ms'," I answered with a smile. "This is my husband. Michael, meet Sergeant Erica Bryce. Sergeant, this is Michael Chan."

"A constable, I see?" Erica smiled and offered Michael her hand. "Nice to meet a fellow public servant."

"Likewise." Michael took her hand and shook it. "Would you like to come and enjoy the party?"

"We would, actually," she answered. "My men and I decided that there aren't exactly many opportunities to enjoy ourselves anymore, so we may as well make the most of it. We even brought a couple of bottles of liquor out of our stores."

"Well, that'll make Jim happy," I said with a laugh, then I beckoned for all three of them to follow me. "Come on inside. There are a lot of people that I'd like you to meet."

***

A few hours later, we'd all danced until our feet hurt, laughed more than we had in years, and eaten until our bellies wanted to pop. After dinner, Doctor Cross rounded up the little kids and took them off to bed, leaving the older ones to do what they pleased. Michael and I had both opted out of the alcohol, but we still enjoyed ourselves watching the antics of our friends, particularly when they were starting to get a little tipsy.

We found ourselves a corner of the couch that was cleaner than the rest, and sat down side by side to cuddle, talk, and watch the others from afar. Michael slid his arm around my waist, encouraging me to snuggle in against him, which I was more than happy to do. We sat together like that for ages, just talking quietly, sipping water, and enjoy our first hours of married life together.

Eventually, Gavin wandered over to visit us. He plopped down on the other end of the couch with a glass of whiskey in his hand, and heaved a long, drawn out sigh. Then, he flicked his one good eye over to us, and lifted a brow. "You two look cosy. Getting tired already?"

"A little bit," I admitted. "I'm not used to late nights anymore. Besides, I forgot how much fun people-watching is." Michael laughed, and Gavin grinned.

"True that," he said thoughtfully, sipping his drink. He was silent for almost a minute, then he shot another glance at us again. "I've been meaning to say, thank you. Not just for inviting us along, but for... doing this. All of this. Moving south. Welcoming people in. Helping us to open up and remember what it was like before fear turned us into a bunch of self-interested tortoises with our heads crammed so far up our own arses that we forgot how to have fun at all."

This time, it was my turn to laugh, but it faded into seriousness after a few seconds. I glanced out across the room at all of my companions, studying them from afar.

"I don't think I really had a choice, Gav," I answered. "Look at them. Every single one of them is a refugee from a life that none of them chose. They were okay on their own, sure, but look at the joy that bringing them together has brought. These people don't just need me – they need each other. They need friends. They need a family. They need a tribe."

"They need a name," he said thoughtfully. "An identity to attach themselves to, along with this ideal that you've been crafting." He took a long sip of his drink, then smiled at us. "*Nga Tama o te Tumanako.* The Children of Hope." Suddenly, he stood up and headed back towards the festivities, leaving Michael and me to think over what he'd said.

"It's a good name," Michael said softly, his eyes distant. "We could call our city that. Tumanako. Hope."

"And we're the children of Hope." I smiled to myself, absently running my hand over my belly, my thoughts drifting to the tiny baby growing within. "We're all children of hope in a way, aren't we?"

"We are." I felt Michael's fingers on my cheek, and let him tilt my face up until our eyes met. "And that's what you've been saying all along, isn't it? The children are our future, and our hope for a chance to start over."

"Yes." I sighed and lay my head down on his shoulder. "We can do it, Michael. Together, we can save them all, and give all of our people the hope that they deserve."

***

To be continued, in The Survivors Book IV: Spring.

AFTERWORD

Thank you for taking the time to finish *The Survivors Book III: Winter*. If you enjoyed this book as much as I enjoyed bringing it to you, please consider leaving a review on Amazon. Reviews are the life-blood of all independent authors, and are vital to our success. Plus, I love hearing that people enjoyed my story!

I love to hear from my readers, so please feel free to contact me via any of the following with your questions, comments, or feedback:

Email: info@vldreyer.com
Amazon: http://amazon.com/author/vldreyer
Facebook: http://www.facebook.com/VictoriaLDreyer
Twitter: @VL_Dreyer
Patreon: http://www.patreon.com/vldreyer

Acknowledgements

This book would never have been finished without the loyalty and dedication of my family. Without your eternal faith in me, Sandy's adventure would have forever remained untold.

To all of my fans from my early days as a graphic novelist, thank you as well. Your love and endless stream of inquisitive questions gave me the strength to carry on in the darkest hours, and opened my mind to all kinds of new possibilities.

To Holly, my editor, for her incredible patience and high degree of tolerance to my idiosyncrasies.

To the following supporters of my fundraiser: Adrienne Smith, Clare Stones, Dennis Swanson, Donna Gray, Hazel Godwin, Rachael Babbington, Rebecca Rakes, Rebekah Andrews, Sarah Hayward, Sonia Rudolph and of course, the anonymous donators who requested not to be named. Thank you for helping me bring this tale to light.

And most of all, to Alyssa, for being my Skylar. Where would I be without you? You pick me up when I'm feeling down, smack me down when my ego gets too big, and call me out on my grammar at every turn.

Thank you.

The Cast

THE NARRATOR
Sandrine "Sandy" McDermott

THE OHAUPO GROUP
Michael Chan
Doctor Stewart Cross
Madeline "Maddy" Cross
Ryan Knowles
Skylar "Skye" McDermott
Priyanka
Tigger the Kitten
Alfred the Sheepdog

THE PARATA TRIBE OF LAKE RUATUNA
Anahera Parata
Hemi Parata
Ropata Parata
Iorangi Parata
Tane Parata
Richard Parata
Petera "Peter" Parata
Wiremu "Will" Parata
Nikora "Nick" Parata

THE ARAPUNI GROUP:
Jim Merrit
Rebecca Merrit

THE YOUSEFI FAMILY:
Zain Yousefi
Elira "Elly" Yousefi
Mathias "Matt" Yousefi
Javed Yousefi
Baraz "Barry" Yousefi
Omid "Ommie" Yousefi

THE TOKOROA GROUP:
Gavin Church
Lily & Jasmine
Melody
Solomon

MISCELLANEOUS:
Erica Bryce
Simon Wentworth

DECEASED:
Sophie Chan, niece of Michael.
Everyone else in the whole world.
May they rest in peace.

Kiwiana Language Guide

Aotearoa	Maori, New Zealand. Literally "The Land Of The Long White Cloud".
Arapuni	Location; a town in the central Waikato, home to the Arapuni Power Station.
Bush	Specifically, "native bush". This term refers to an area of native forest, which is characterised by a particularly thick shrub layer dominated by indigenous ferns and bushes – hence the colloquialism. Native bush is often very thick and dark, and can be very difficult to travel through as a result.
Cark It	Colloquial, to die. *Example: "We were half-way to Tauranga when the car carked it."*
Central Plateau	Colloquial, the Tongariro National Park. It is an area of major cultural significance to the various peoples of New Zealand, and contains numerous Maori sacred sites. Above ground, it is a massive rock desert that covers approximately 795.98 kilometres and is home to the volcanic cones Tongariro, Ruapehu, and Ngauruhoe. Below ground, it is the centre of a massive geothermal field that spreads across most of the North Island. It is one of the few areas in the North Island that regularly sees snowfall.
G'day	Colloquial version of "Good day".

Hangi	Maori culture, an underground oven used to cook food.
Hongi	Maori culture, the pressing together of the nose and forehead in a greeting. Used in a similar fashion to the handshake in Western culture. Symbolises the mixing of the breath of life integral to Maori folklore.
Kai	Maori, "Food".
Kia Ora	Maori, "Hello".
Kumara	Maori, a sweet potato.
Maori	Relating to the original peoples of New Zealand. May be used to refer to their cultural traits (*e.g. "she tried to live by the traditional Maori ways."*), language (*e.g. "he spoke Maori."*) or ethnicity (*e.g. "my grandmother was Maori"*). The Maori culture evolved from Polynesian migrants that arrived in New Zealand around 1,000 years ago.
Mate	A contextually sensitive word that is usually used in place of the word "friend". Can be used sarcastically or in threat just as readily as being used in a friendly fashion, *e.g. "You're going to regret that, mate."*
Ngauruhoe	Geography; the central volcano in Tongariro National Park. Ngauruhoe is an active stratovolcano.
Pā	Maori, can refer to a village or settlement, but usually describes a hill fort.
Ohaupo	Location; a small town in the Waikato region, approximately 17 kilometres south of Hamilton.
Onīsan	Japanese, "Big Brother".

Rēwena	Maori, literally "ferment/rise". In terms of bread, it refers to a traditional Maori potato bread.
Ruapehu	Geography; the southernmost volcano in Tongariro National Park. Ruapehu is one of the most active stratovolcanoes in the world.
Tā Moko	Maori Culture; traditional Maori face and body tattoos.
Taupo, Lake	Geography; the largest lake in New Zealand, and second largest freshwater lake in Oceania. Lake Taupo fills the caldera of an ancient supervolcano. Some scientists believe this volcano was responsible for the largest eruption to take place on Earth in the last 70,000 years, which may have triggered the last ice age. It is considered dormant rather than extinct due to frequent geothermal activity in the region.
Taupo, Town.	Location; a large township on the north-eastern shores of Lake Taupo.
Te Awamutu	Location; a medium-sized township in the central Waikato. In the *Survivors* world, this town was razed by a large earthquake several years after the plague.
Tokaanu	Location; a small township on the southern shore of Lake Taupo.
Tokoroa	Location; a medium-sized town located in the central Waikato, half way between Hamilton and Taupo.
Tongariro	Geography; northernmost volcano in Tongariro National Park. Tongariro is an active compound volcano.
Waiouru	Location; a small town in the Manawatu-Wanganui region, located approximately 25 kilometres south of Mount Ruapehu. It is home to the Waiouru Army Camp and Airfield.

About The Author

V. L. Dreyer is an international best-selling author from the wild back country of New Zealand. She is best known for her post-apocalyptic series, *The Survivors*, as well as the *Immortelle* series under her pen name, Abigail Hawk. Her earlier works include an assortment of graphic novels, short stories, blogs, and works of art, and her preferred genres are science fiction, post-apocalyptic survival, and romance – and sometimes all three at once.

Ms. Dreyer is the unlikely miracle offspring of a science fiction geek who dreamed of teaching, and a biker computer technician. She penned her first novel at the age of 14, and started her first business at the age of twenty. From 2003 to 2011, she ran the publishing house Blue Scar Productions, then went on to produce numerous literary and artistic works under her personal brand, Cheeky Kea Creations. In October 2017, Ms. Dreyer expanded the publishing division of her brand, Cheeky Kea Printworks, into a full hybrid publishing house, to help others see their ideas take flight.

Ms Dreyer suffers from an advanced form of Meniere's Disease, which has left her with a hearing impairment. In her free time, she is an avid gamer, reader, and enjoys learning new and sometimes completely random things.

www.vldreyer.com

About The Publisher

Cheeky Kea Printworks began as the personal publishing house of author V. L. Dreyer, and later became the brand under which she freelanced as a publishing assistant for other authors. In 2017, CK Printworks took the final step to becoming a publishing house in its own right, by securing the contracts to translate and publish several Polish manuscripts into English.

CK Printworks specializes in science fiction, fantasy, urban fantasy, romance/erotica, and anything else that helps the imagination take flight.

To learn more about CK Printworks and the authors represents, please visit:

www.ckprintworks.com

To receive an alert when new books are released, subscribe to the CK Printworks Mailing List:

www.ckprintworks.com/subscribe